THE THIRD HEAVEN CONSPIRACY

Giulio Leoni is a professor of Italian literature and
history. He lives in Rome with his family.

GIULIO LEONI

The Third
Heaven
Conspiracy

TRANSLATED FROM THE ITALIAN BY
Anne Milano Appel

VINTAGE BOOKS
London

Published by Vintage 2007

2 4 6 8 10 9 7 5 3 1

Copyright © Giulio Leoni 2004

English translation copyright © Anne Milano Appel 2006

Giulio Leoni has asserted his right under the
Copyright, Designs and Patents Act 1988 to be
identified as the author of this work

First published with the title *I Delitti del Mosaico*
by Arnoldo Mondadori Editore S.P.A., Milan, 2004

First published in Great Britain in 2007 by
Harvill Secker
Random House, 20 Vauxhall Bridge Road,
London SW1V 2SA

www.vintage-books.co.uk

Addresses for companies within The Random House
Group Limited can be found at:
www.randomhouse.co.uk/offices.htm

The Random House Group Limited Reg. No. 954009

A CIP catalogue record for this book
is available from the British Library

ISBN 9780099492764

The Random House Group Limited makes every
effort to ensure that the papers used in its books are
made from trees that have been legally sourced from
well-managed and credibly certified forests. Our
paper procurement policy can be found at:
www.randomhouse.co.uk/paper.htm

Printed and bound in Great Britain by
CPI Cox & Wyman Ltd, Reading, RG1 8EX

FOR ANNA

Cast of Characters

DANTE ALIGHIERI—poet and prior of Florence in June 1300. His full name was Durante degli Alighieri.

The Third Heaven

ANTONIO DA PERETOLA—jurist and notary, scholar of civil and canon law

AUGUSTINO DI MENICO—natural philosopher, master of alchemy and ancient languages

BRUNO AMMANNATI—Franciscan, theologian

CECCO D'ASCOLI—astronomer

IACOPO TORRITI—architect, surveyor, and mathematician

TEOFILO SPROVIERI—physician and apothecary

VENIERO MARIN—seaman, former captain in the Venetian navy

Other Characters, Living and Dead

ANTILIA—dancer of obscure origin

AMBROGIO—master mosaicist and a member of the Comacine guild

BALDO THE CRUSADER—keeper of a tavern on the outskirts of Florence

POPE BONIFACE VIII—born Benedetto Gaetano (sometimes referred to in the novel as Caetani) in 1235, he served as pope of the Catholic Church from 1294 to 1303

CECCO ANGIOLIERI—poet, acquaintance of Dante's

GIANNETTO—a beggar

GUIDO CAVALCANTI—poet, friend and mentor to Dante (born circa 1255, exiled from Florence in June of 1300, dies in August of that year)

CARDINAL MATTEO D'ACQUASPARTA—supporter of Pope Boniface VIII, ambassador to Lombardy, Romagna, and Florence

NOFFO DEI—Dominican friar, inquisitor, member of Boniface's faction

The Third Heaven Conspiracy

PROLOGUE

St. John of Acre, dawn, May 28, 1291

IT CAME with a hiss that pierced the air as if all the snakes of the desert had raised their heads from the sand. At the peak of its trajectory it hung, motionless and glittering, in a sky brightened by the first light of dawn, then plunged to its goal, striking the gate tower with a crash. Fragments of brick and stone exploded in every direction; the tower's foundations shook; the outer shell, split to its base, listed slowly and began to slide to the ground, dragging with it the beams of the upper floors. Above the roar of collapsing masonry briefly resounded the screams of terrified men as they pitched forward into nothingness, and then the entire upper story gave way, toppling onto the defensive wall and opening a breach alongside the gate. An immense dust cloud arose, obscuring the rubble. A fresh projectile, hurtling down with its malign hiss, vanished in the grayish pall.

This time there was no crash, only a muffled rumble as the second massive boulder sank into a mound of debris. But on the other side of the gate, several yards away, an observation post swayed ominously. "They've used their devil's engine again, brother," said the younger of the two men who were watching, rising painfully from the floor and hastening to view the extent of the disaster from his peephole. "The wall will not hold much longer."

His comrade, who had withstood the jolt by clinging to the heavy oak table at which he was busy writing, brushed plaster dust from his garments and glanced up at a crack in the wall, then bent once more to the papers spread out before him. He rubbed his eyes, trying to fend off the exhaustion of a sleepless night, and jotted down a few more words. Then he looked up again, his eyes clouded with despair.

"The report is finished. But it is useless if it does not reach his hands," he said. "We are done for."

"No!" his companion shouted, grabbing him by the shoulders and shaking him. He stopped suddenly, as if regretting his action. "We are done for, but there is hope for them," he went on excitedly. "Down at the port there is a ship. If the Hospitallers can hold the wharf for one hour, until the tide rises . . ."

"Fortune was not written in our stars, brother. But perhaps you are right. Let us try our luck once more," the man at the table replied, and gestured toward a small chest, banded with iron, that lay open on the floor. Quickly, with the help of his companion, he placed his papers in this box and secured it with a strong leather strap.

A long sword with a cross-shaped hilt lay on the table, encased in its sheath. He picked it up and was about to affix it to his side, then changed his mind and hurried toward the door. His companion followed, the chest held tightly under his arm.

They stepped out onto the parapet and were struck by the battle's furious din, the thunder of enemy drums as the Saracens stormed the fortress of Acre, the last Christian stronghold in the Holy Land. Cautiously, they began moving along the narrow walkway built into the crenellated wall. Below, in the desert valley, the besiegers were rearming two gigantic catapults, tall as the towers they assailed. Dozens of men, lashed forward by the eunuchs of the Sultan's personal guard, struggled to push the deadly contraptions toward a new firing line.

The older man paused, observing the scene closely. "They mean to strike the port. We must hurry."

From behind the ramparts came a bedlam of shouts, orders, and imprecations, as knots of haggard soldiers rushed to defend the breached wall, while men, women, and children surged panic-stricken in the opposite direction, clutching bundles of household and other goods, vainly seeking an escape.

The two comrades descended the wall, turned their backs on the doomed fortress, and dove into the maze of narrow passageways that cut through the center of town. They advanced rapidly, pushing their way through the terrified throngs that fought to reach the landing. As they neared the inner harbor, still protected by a standing wall, they saw the ship: a black galley, tilted to starboard, its keel resting on a shoal exposed by the low tide. On the white sail wrapped around the mast, a glimpse of red could be seen: the cross of the Knights of Saint John. On the black flag that fluttered from the stern, a skull and bones flashed white. The entire crew stood armed on the deck, wielding their oars to beat back the hordes of refugees frantically trying to hoist themselves aboard.

Both men plunged into the shallow water, forcing their way among the crowd, trampling the bodies of those who had already slid to the muddy bottom, laboring until they reached the side of the ship, just below the figurehead. The tip of a crewman's spear came dangerously close to their heads; they heard threatening shouts.

"We do not wish to get on board. Just take this, for the love of God!" the older man cried, as his comrade heaved the chest above his head with the strength of desperation.

In a corner of the fo'c'sle stood a small group of passengers, clad in the garments of the nobility, who stared dazedly at the horrifying scene.

One of these, who held a woman tightly in his arms, hearing the desperate plea, released his companion and approached the side of the ship. Leaning down, he managed to take the chest from the younger man's hands. "What should I do with it?" he asked.

"The Temple. It must get there," the man replied, pointing at the flag in the stern.

"What is it?" The nobleman seemed about to say something else, but his voice was drowned out by the creaking of the hull as the vessel shifted, borne upward by a mounting swell. As it sank back, a snakish hiss was heard, then a roar as an enormous column of mud and water spurted up a few yards from the galley's broadside.

The surge dislodged the ship's keel from the muck and submerged dozens of shrieking refugees.

The younger man surfaced, gasping for breath.

Desperately, he looked around for his friend, but saw no trace of him among the sea of floundering bodies.

"What is it?" the man from the galley shouted again. The sailors had begun to use their oars as levers, pushing against the seabed to propel the ship into open water.

"The truth!" the young man whispered, as a final hissing pierced the air.

I

Florence, June 15, 1300, toward midnight

HE HAD filled several sheets of paper with his fine script, and now the candle on the table burned low. Several hours must have passed since he had started writing his account. He broke off to read over what he had set down.

He felt drained. A migraine pounded in his temples, and sleep was still a long way off.

"Of course, this is how it is. The opposite theory defies reason and the facts," he muttered, passing a hand across his forehead.

On the table stood a pitcher and two goblets. He poured water from the pitcher into one of the goblets until it overflowed, spilling to the ground, where it formed a puddle and then a little stream that trickled along the irregular bricks until it seeped into a crack and disappeared from view.

"It flows downward. It must flow downward," he said aloud. And the ghost that stood before him nodded in agreement.

OUTSIDE, something broke the perfect silence of the night. Heavy steps approached his door, accompanied by a metallic din like the rattling of tin plates—or naked swords. His hand flew to the dagger that he always carried with him, in a pocket concealed inside his garment.

Armed men at his door, at that hour of night. How much time had passed since the curfew bell had sounded?

His eyes sought a sign, any sign that would restore his sense of time, but the dark sky beyond the narrow window showed no trace of dawn. He rose and extinguished the candle, then crouched beside the doorjamb, holding his breath.

Outside, the clanking continued, a sound like soldiers milling about. His hand tightened around the handle of his weapon. He heard two dull thumps at the door, and then a harsh voice calling his name.

"Messer Durante?"

Dante Alighieri, poet of Italy and now prior of Florence, bit his lip, uncertain what to do next. San Piero should be under the watch of the priory guards, especially at night. The ceremony in which he had been formally invested had just taken place two days ago. Were those scoundrels betraying him already?

"Messer Durante, are you in there? Open the door."

He must not hesitate. Perhaps his powers were required for the public good. He hastened to don the stiff square biretta cap with its long veil, and put the gold signet ring engraved with lilies on his index finger. Then, after carefully arranging the folds of his garment to resemble a Roman toga, such as he had seen on the statues in Santa Croce, he lifted the latch.

A short, thickset man stood before him, dressed in chain mail that fell to below his knees. Over it, instead of the usual tabard with its emblazoned lily, he wore a coat of armor made of metal plates joined by leather thongs. His head was encased in a cylindrical helmet, like those worn by crusaders. A sword was strapped to his shoulder, and two daggers made a fine display on his girdle.

"What do you want, you rogue?" Dante spoke harshly. "It is forbidden to go about the city at this hour. Only brigands and pickpockets dare to violate the curfew, and they pay for that on the gallows," the poet went on in a threatening tone. The man at the door was dumbstruck. Despite his martial appearance, he did not seem like a dangerous sort. Even so, Dante kept his eyes fixed on the man's hands: one held up an oil lamp; the other hung unarmed at his side. He would be easy to attack, Dante thought. An inch-wide gap between his helmet and the collar of his chain mail exposed his neck. His open visor, though harder to reach, offered passage for a mortal thrust.

"I am the Bargello," the man finally said. "I am here because of my official function. And because of yours, given that they have appointed you prior and that we will all be dependent on you for two months." His voice was plaintive, though he pulled himself up to his full modest height.

Dante leaned toward him, trying to read the features obscured by the helmet. Through the cross-shaped visor he glimpsed a prominent nose and small, close-set eyes, beady like a rat's. Now he recognized him: it really was the Bargello, Captain of the Guard for the Commune. A thief in charge of other thieves.

He released his grip on the hilt of his dagger. "And what sorcery might bring our official functions together?"

"A crime has been committed in the church of Saint Jude, at the new walls." The man hesitated, unsure of himself in the presence of the prior. "A crime that . . . perhaps requires the presence of the Commune's authority," he added nervously.

The Bargello, with difficulty, loosened the straps of his helmet and wrenched the heavy armor from his head, which emerged damp with sweat.

"We do not know anything yet," he said. "But it would be best if you came to see with your own eyes."

"Tell me first what happened."

"Well, something . . . strange, unnatural . . ."

Dante began to lose patience. "Let me be the judge of what is or is not strange. *Omne ignotum pro magnifico,* as our elders used to say. Everything surprises us, if we lack knowledge of it." He clapped him on the shoulder. "You are certainly not the man best suited to judge whether something has occurred in accordance with nature or against it. Only attentive study and full awareness of what is, together with a knowledge of what is not, entitle the learned scholar to draw the line between the ordinary and the marvelous. There is a passage in Lucan, in that regard, which you should ponder."

"Yes . . . I understand," the man said doubtfully.

"So then, tell me what *is,* not how it appears to you."

The Bargello wiped the sweat from his face. "A man. Dead. At Saint Jude. Inside the church. Killed, I think."

"And why do you want to involve the Commune, the highest authority, in such a matter? Is finding and arresting criminals not your job?"

"Yes, of course . . . but. . . . Well, I would prefer that you come see with your own eyes. I beg you."

This last request seemed to have cost him a lot. Dante looked him straight in the face.

"One does not see with one's eyes, Bargello, but with one's mind. It is my mind that you require. You as well as all the other blind men. But you did well to turn to me. And thank Saint John the Baptist, the protector of us all, who willed that I become prior, if the circumstances are as grave as you represent."

"Will you come, then?" the man repeated anxiously. "There is water on the ground here," he added, pointing at the floor.

Dante did not answer. He turned his gaze to the slice of sky beyond the window opening, staring at the stars, reading their patterns in the celestial vault. A strange way to begin his charge as helmsman of the Commune. These ill omens were making him uneasy.

He roused himself, abruptly raised his head and picked up the gilt cane he had set down on the chest. "Come with me," he ordered, preceding the Bargello out the door.

They crossed the portico that led past the doors of the convent's other cells. Dante thought about his five fellow priors, who must certainly be sunk in the turbid sleep of weak minds, populated by the specters conjured by lust and gluttony. Then he stopped, arresting the Bargello with his hand. "Why did you come looking for me?"

The other cleared his throat. He seemed embarrassed. "Because they tell me that you know letters better than anyone. You are a poet, are you not? You have written a book."

"And in what special way could I, a poet, be of help to you?"

"There is something odd about this death."

Dante decided not to take offense. What could he possibly say to this idiot?

"They say that of all the priors you are the most suited to . . ." The Bargello hesitated.

"Suited to what?"

"To . . . to look into secret matters." The captain of the guard spoke those words in a particular tone, one of both admiration and suspicion. To his simple mind, secrets must seem the antechamber of crime, the poet thought. Perhaps the man considered Dante himself a potential criminal. When his term of office was over he would have to watch out for this Bargello. But for now he seemed sincere in his desire for a learned man's help. He nervously wrung his hands, rhythmically shifting his weight from one foot to the other.

Dante started walking again and the Bargello followed him in silence.

THEY CROSSED a large earthen square illuminated by a radiant full moon. The ground was still strewn with the remains of the houses of the Uberti, destroyed after the Ghibellines' defeat at Benevento. For more than thirty years these ruins had served as a stone quarry to build the city's new structures. Ahead of them, in shadow barely relieved by the glimmer of oil lamps burning over toward Ponte Vecchio, rose the lateral buttress of the tower that had been the stronghold of Farinata, head of the Uberti lineage.

The ruins stuck out of the earth like a giant's broken teeth. That ravaged plain was now to become the center of the city, according to the designs of the planning superintendent. In the distance the dark mass of the new Priors' Palazzo could be glimpsed, in the final stages of construction. Its ostentatious tower seemed a sleeping Titan, roused by one of Jove's thunderbolts, arm outstretched to smite the heavens. Who knew how many stones stained with Ghibelline blood had been incorporated into its walls?

Had the same pride not erected the tower of Babylon? The entire city seemed gripped by a frenzy to destroy and to rebuild. To bring down whoever might rise up and then surpass him in arrogance: envy lurked in the Florentine heart like a serpent.

Dante turned to the Bargello. "The abbey of Saint Jude, you said . . . but that church is not within the first circle of walls, but far outside them." If memory did not deceive him, well beyond the gate, on the road to Rome. "Many years ago it was the seat of a community of Augustinian cenobites. They spoke of it at Santa Croce, in the lectures given by the Franciscans . . ." For a moment the pleasures of those days came back to mind. "I thought it was abandoned," he said.

"That's true, it was. The monks abandoned it many years ago, and it fell into disrepair. But a new congregation has decided to restore it. I have heard that it will become the seat of a Florentine studio."

"You mean a studium?"

"Yes . . . that's it."

"But there is no university in Florence," the poet replied in surprise.

The Bargello shrugged. "Nevertheless, that is what they want to put there. Come, we will go in my cart."

At the corner of Via dei Tintori stood a sturdy four-wheeled wagon. The two men climbed up to the coachman's box, covered in hemp, while their retinue settled in the back. Beneath the canopy the heat was excruciating, but at least the poet was not forced to ride side by side with the bargellini.

The cart bumped noisily over the flagstones. The horse liked this nocturnal run no better than his masters and shied at every jolt and shadow.

Dante's migraine continued to worsen. Through a side slit in the canopy he glimpsed the old, rugged ashlar walls, then the cart swerved toward the Arno, and the ramp that led onto the Ponte alle Grazie. Here they were stopped by the district guard. The Bargello identified himself and ordered the guard to remove the chain that barred the bridge.

On the other side of the Arno the air grew denser as they moved away from the city center. The paving came to an abrupt end, and their wheels whooshed along on packed earth. Masonry structures gave way to the clusters of wooden shanties that flanked the road to Rome like knots of tattered beggars. Only from time to time was the monotony of the landscape broken by the more solid shadow of a chapel or by the open spaces of fields and vineyards. The lights of Ponte Vecchio were no more than a memory now. The most intense darkness reigned over the entire district, relieved only by the moon's dim reflection.

As they pushed on through the darkness, Dante became aware of a presence at their side. A perfidious thing, heavy as the blanket of yellowish mist that rose from the meadows, it seemed to glide alongside the cart, becoming more palpable as they penetrated this remote area. It was Evil. The Evil that had come from outside, had thickened around the city, and was now suffocating Florence in its grip.

"Who is the dead man?" he asked suddenly. Only then did he remember that the Bargello had never answered this question. Could a man descend thus into the void, his name unknown, without one compassionate word said in his memory? Without letting anyone see, he touched the cart's wooden side.

"We don't . . . we don't know. Wait. You will see with your own eyes."

Dante shrugged and fell silent. When all was said and done it was better that way. If he was to formulate an explanation of what had happened, he would prefer to rely on his own observations rather than on the uncertain perceptions of others. His thoughts returned to his cell in San Piero, to the writing that had been interrupted. He surrendered himself to the rhythm of the wheels, now smooth, trying to relax his weary body.

THE CHURCH came into view roughly a mile south of the river, in an area of open countryside within the third circle of walls. Originally it must have been a parish church on the road to Rome. Construction materials, tools, and planks were piled up beside it.

A part of the apse had been incorporated into the wall of the new bastion, and the old bell tower had been reinforced at the base by a buttress and made into an observation tower. The building bore signs of numerous other transformations, changes made over the centuries, resulting in a strange complex at once religious and military. The facade, a pointed portal connected by two narrow, cross-shaped window openings, was typical of a more ancient style. Dante had heard similar structures described by pilgrims returning from overseas.

Sometime in the past someone had tried to bar access to the church with a fence, but since then most of the posts had been uprooted or knocked down. The door was open, and they could see the flickering gleam of moving torches within.

"Inside, there, is where the body was found," the Bargello said. His nostrils were dilated like those of an animal scenting danger.

Dante had seen a similar expression on beasts on their way to slaughter. Yet he knew that this man was no coward. In the battle of Campaldino, eleven years earlier, he had seen him stand firm when the Arezzo cavalry had hurled itself against the disorderly ranks of Florence. Why was he frightened now, in front of a church door?

The pain in his temples exploded violently again. He fought back a wave of nausea and impatiently pushed aside the Bargello, who still hung back. He wanted to attend to the matter quickly, and return to the peace of his cell. He proceeded through the nave, which was plunged in shadow, toward the torchlight that gleamed in the back.

"Prior . . . wait! Stop!"

The Bargello's voice behind him, strained by anxiety, seemed to come from an immense distance. The pain in his head must be altering his perceptions. A mind fortified by virtue and knowledge cannot always overcome the fragility of the wretched body, he thought. He had taken perhaps another twenty steps when the voice called out to him again.

"Wait, stop!" This time the sound was different, reverberant, as if an echo had been added to it.

He took another step or two then swayed, overcome by a fit of dizziness. He became aware of another presence, the same he had sensed a few hours earlier back in his cell. A hand grabbed his arm.

"Stop, for your life!"

The hand that grasped him belonged to a young soldier, who seemed to have materialized out of thin air. Long fair hair stuck out from under his helmet. He was holding a torch, source of the light that had enveloped them. Keeping a tight grip on the poet's arm, he lowered the torch. Dante glimpsed the blue reflection of his eyes, then looked downward and was horror-struck.

They were standing on the edge of an abyss. The nave was split from one side to the other. A chasm yawned in the middle of the floor as if an enormous weight had dropped from above, shattering the great stone slabs before plummeting to the bowels of the earth. Lucifer cast down from the heavens. Only two walkways scarcely a yard wide remained along the side walls.

One more step and he would have fallen to his death. He wiped a hand across his forehead, and then bent over his knees trying to recover. It was at least a minute before he felt his strength return. The migraine had disappeared. He turned toward his savior, but the young man had vanished. Then he cautiously approached the edge of the pit, trying to estimate its depth. There must have been a crypt there, once. Or else the church had been built atop an earlier structure, perhaps the cistern of a Roman villa.

He looked up again beyond the chasm, toward the apse. Beside him he heard the gasping breath of the Bargello, who had caught up with him at last. "Messer Durante . . . fortunate that you stopped in time."

Dante thought he caught a false note in his expression of concern. He pushed him away with a brusque gesture and approached the wall, moving cautiously across the narrow walkway alongside the pit.

Now he could clearly distinguish the small group of armed guards leaning against the wall of the apse, torches raised, in front of a structure of supports that disappeared into the darkness above. Their torches were trained on a figure in front of them: a tall man, who seemed oblivious to the commotion around him. He stood straight and completely immobile, his hands behind his back. His head was turned toward the nave, as if he were searching the shadows, awaiting someone's arrival.

A shroud seemed to cover his features, making them indistinct.

Dante quickly covered the last steps. He snatched a torch from the hands of one of the bargellini, and brought it close to the body.

The dead man was propped against one of the support posts of the scaffolding, his hands tied behind his back. He was dressed in grayish, threadbare garments. His feet were wide apart, his knees slightly bent as if he were about to bolt. His head and neck were covered by a layer of quicklime that roughly reproduced their physiognomy.

The effect was stupefying. Dante read his own incredulity on the faces of the bargellini crowding around. This figure seemed to be at once the victim and mute witness to the crime.

The Bargello moved closer to him, like a dog terrified by thunder.

Dante had to suppress an impulse to revive the upright body: impossible that there could be even a single vital spark left in it. It must be the bound hands and mortar mantle that held him erect, tilted slightly forward, like a macabre figurehead on a ship. *Charon, who ferries the shades, could use him as an ornament on his boat,* he thought.

"Now you understand why it is fitting that the Commune's highest authority attend to this. We should . . . we must summon the Holy Inquisition. The devil is in this desecrated church . . ." the Bargello stammered.

How many times have I questioned human perfidy? the poet thought. *Now I find myself facing it in its most despicable form.* "You acted wisely, bringing me here," he said aloud. "As for the Inquisition, leave them out of it for now. There will be plenty of time to summon them, if I conclude that it is appropriate and necessary."

He moved closer to the cadaver. Alive, the man must have been more or less as tall as Dante himself. Behind his mask he seemed to be observing the poet. What kept his deadweight upright? Dante asked one of the soldiers for a dagger and with a few clean strokes cut the cords that bound the rigid hands.

The man's arms fell slowly forward, a movement as deliberate as if their owner were alive. Yet the body remained erect, to the horror of the soldiers, who exclaimed and crossed themselves.

Dante touched the mask lightly with his hand. The mortar was hard as a rock. It did not seem like the ordinary mixture used for masonry, as if the killer's hand had added something more tenacious. Using the hilt of the dagger, Dante began tapping the hard casing along the nape of the neck, producing a series of small cracks, as he had once seen done in a kiln for making bells. The still glowing metal had emerged little by little as the bellsmith's hammer struck away its earthen prison.

Now, like the bell, the head began to appear, and with it, something the mortar had concealed: a cord passed under the dead man's chin, binding his throat to the post. This was what kept him upright. The Bargello let out a sigh of relief.

Dante chipped away at the casing, starting in back where the layer was thinnest, revealing tufts of grayish hair. But in front the plaster held firm, as if a demon's claw gripped the dead man's face to keep him in the realm of shadows.

The people believed that the death of the soul did not occur until two hours after the death of the senses, and that between the first death and the second the deceased might be called back to life with necromantic rites. Perhaps the killer had wanted to make sure that not even a sorcerer could undo his work, the poet thought.

By this time the back of the man's neck was almost completely exposed. Dante delivered one more sharp blow and felt movement beneath his fingers as the casque of mortar began to loosen. Suddenly the mask fell away, and the torches shone on the dead man's face.

A horrified murmur arose from those who had gathered to watch what he was doing. He heard them take a step back. The Bargello groaned and crossed himself.

Only Dante remained motionless, staring into those unseeing eyes, clutching the plaster shell that had concealed that horror. He was tempted to put it back in place, to expunge what everyone had seen, and had to fight the impulse to leap back himself.

A leper seemed to be inviting him to dance in his arms.

Behind him there was chaos. Abandoning discipline, the bargellini were fleeing toward the pit, in danger of being swallowed up in their headlong rush to get around it. Their commander nearly followed them; then, recovering his sense of dignity, he stopped just in front of the opening. Dante now also stepped back, but only to pick up one of the torches that the guards had dropped. Holding the veil of his biretta over his nose and mouth to protect them from the noxious exhalations, he studied the corpse under the light.

As he did so, his heart stopped pounding. The caustic lime had gouged those lesions, streaking the skin with scarlet, and when the casing was removed, shreds of flesh had been torn from the face, ravaging the features so that they resembled those of a diseased man. The hands and neck were clean, without sores of any kind. Summoning his courage, he pulled back the sleeves of the man's tunic, exposing his arms. They showed not a trace of contagion.

The lime had been poured over the man's living face, scalding him, and had solidified as his death throes advanced. Dante let the veil drop from his mouth. The Bargello took this as a reassuring sign and cautiously approached again.

"He is not . . ."

"No, you are safe. He is not a leper. On the contrary, judging from the look of his muscles, he must have been in good health at the time he died."

The Bargello had overcome his fear and now stared boldly at the corpse. "But of course!" he exclaimed suddenly. "I recognize him!"

"You know who he is?"

"Now I do . . . it is Ambrogio, the Comacine master."

"A *magister cum machinis*?"

Dante looked around. The project to restore the church must have been ambitious indeed, if they had thought to call upon a member of the Comacine, the most important builder's guild in northern Italy. He frowned. The fact was totally unforeseen, and came at the worst possible time. What would happen when this powerful society learned of their colleague's hideous death?

He must prepare for the worst. He shuddered, as if an icy wind had suddenly swept through the suffocating air inside the church. "A master builder . . ." he murmured.

"Yes, an architect," the Bargello explained. "And a great mosaicist as well. He was commissioned to oversee reconstruction of the church. . . . How do you think he was killed?"

Dante did not reply at once. Better to ask *why* such a man had been killed, he thought. Still, the Bargello's question was not unreasonable. Did not the manner in which a deed was done often provide a clue to its motive? He showed the Bargello a laceration on the back of the victim's neck. "Perhaps he was attacked from behind and knocked senseless, then suffocated."

"With that cord?"

"No, he was not strangled," the poet said, testing the hemp that held the body in that unnatural position. It had never been pulled tight enough to stop the man's breath; the mark it had left on the neck was too faint. "The assassin tied his hands and bound him to the post while he was unconscious. Maybe the murderer meant to extort a secret, a confession when he woke. Or vengeance. Some time later he poured the lime over him, which caused the man's death—and became his funeral mask. Look!" He turned the grimy shapeless shell, and from its interior leaped the imprint of a contorted human face, lips curled back and teeth clenched together in a grin of agony. A mirror image of the dead man's head, turned to stone by the terrible gaze of a Gorgon.

Dante averted his eyes from that horrific sight. As he did so, a flicker of torchlight illuminated the wall and he noticed for the first time a huge mosaic looming over the dead man.

Curious, he raised the torch and took a few steps backward, to get a better sense of the composition. The picture was dominated by the majestic figure of an elderly man with powerful musculature, more than twenty feet tall. His gaze was turned to something on his right, his legs were slightly bent, as if he were about to set out toward it. His right arm was outstretched, as if held in readiness. The artist's skill had found in rigid tiles a pliancy that gave this work life and feeling.

At first Dante thought the giant was dressed in a multicolored garment, such as those worn by allegorical figures in sacred representations, then he realized that the body itself was composed of tiles of various materials. The head was formed with tesserae of fine gold, cleverly painted to give depth to the eyes and texture to the hair, and to animate the painful grimace that marked the bearded face. The chest and arms were silver, and the torso as far as the groin was hammered copper; the left leg, supporting the body's weight but poised as if about to move off, was composed of iron fragments. The right leg, slightly flexed to suggest a step, was not metal at all, but a reddish material, probably terra-cotta.

At various places throughout the composition there were patches of bare stone, where groups of tiles had evidently been removed as if the artist had changed his mind.

"So this was what Master Ambrogio was working on while death was breathing down his neck," Dante said pensively. "But why . . ."

"What does it mean?" the Bargello broke in. He, too, was looking up transfixed, as if the enormity of this figure had obliterated the presence of the dead man beneath it.

Dante glanced at him, for once indulgently. "It represents a passage from sacred history, an episode concerning the pagan king Nebuchadnezzar and a statue that appeared to him in a dream. The statue symbolizes humanity in its decline from the golden age to the present: the noblest of metals degenerated into base earth, the clay we use for common pitchers. And this, the world of choices that lies around him."

At either side of the colossus, the artist had outlined in stone two groups of towers, walls, and temples, and the giant seemed to be on the point of leaving the city on his left for the grander one that lay to his right. Dante approached the latter to illuminate it better, attracted by a detail he had noticed among the forest of towers and cupolas sticking up from the encircling, crenellated wall. It was indeed an image of the huge fortress that he had seen during a sojourn in the Christian capital: Castel Sant'Angelo, built on the massive ruins of Hadrian's tomb. Its profile, though barely suggested, was unmistakable.

So it was the vault of Rome toward which the steps of that great mosaic figure were directed. A doleful humanity, corrupted by sin, on a pilgrimage to the Holy See, perhaps to obtain pardon on the occasion of the *Centesimus,* the grand Jubilee year proclaimed by Boniface VIII to celebrate the new century.

He lowered his torch and the light fell on a handful of multicolored tiles that had fallen at the base of the scaffolding. On the wall directly above were traces of the lime mortar. The artist had been killed with the material of his art. He looked once more at the dead artist, who was standing in front of his creation as if wanting to claim it proudly for all eternity. There had to be some connection between the figure portrayed on the wall and the horror of that crime. "It is no accident that you were killed right under the mosaic," the poet whispered in the Comacine master's ear, as the Bargello, forgotten, tried vainly to catch those softly spoken words.

It was even possible that the motive for the crime did not lie in the work that was evident, but in the unfinished part, a vision in the mind of the deceased. Around the colossus, an ample tract of wall had been prepared for the continuation of the scene. The mosaic was to have been much more extensive, once it was completed. Dante glanced quickly around the perimeter of the apse. He saw nothing of interest, only a few piled-up boards. "Look all around," he ordered the bargellini. "Canvases, sheets of paper with drawings . . . the cartoons for the mosaic must be here someplace."

The men walked around with their torches raised, led by the Bargello, who was glad to put some distance between himself and that living man who spoke to the dead. Meanwhile the poet had resumed studying the cities outlined in the mosaic. The small one on the left resembled one of the turreted towns depicted in the landscapes that adorned all the churches in Italy, now that frescoes had become the mode. Unlike the city on the right, it had no detail that he recognized. The only feature of interest was a door at the center of the city wall, with four lion heads crowning its lintel.

There were several marks just at that point, directly behind the body of the dead mosaicist, scratched onto the surface of the plaster. He bent down to observe them more closely. Meanwhile the Bargello had returned from his reconnoitering.

"There is nothing, Prior. Only debris and abandoned tools. No papers, no drawings."

Annoyed, Dante turned around abruptly and handed him the torch. Let the idiot make himself useful.

The Bargello took it with a wounded air. But his curiosity was stronger than his pride. "You said the master was alive when he was tied to the post. How long do you think he lasted after that?"

Dante pointed out the scratches on the wall. "Long enough to write something here, while his hands were bound behind his back."

The Bargello brought the torch closer to the wall. There, barely legible amidst a muddle of reddish smears, were marks that resembled the letters IIICOE.

Dante leaned over and studied them. The strokes were shallow, scratched there, perhaps with the edge of a tile.

The Bargello followed the prior's movements attentively, bending down in turn to observe the marks. Then he stood up again. "I see, yes. . . . And what do they mean, Messer Alighieri?"

"Nothing. Perhaps IIIC is the number ninety-seven, followed

by a word that the master lacked the strength to complete. But I am not certain."

His idea that these marks had been made at the time of the murder was merely a supposition. They could have been made days earlier, and been simply a note on the work in progress. He must clear his thoughts, or they would founder in a sea of hypotheses. "Who discovered the body?" he asked after a moment's reflection.

"A passing shepherd. He claimed he was seeking a lost sheep. Maybe he really came in to steal something. But he sounded the alarm. He was terrified."

Absorbed in thought, Dante gazed at the scene once more. His headache had returned and there was a shooting pain behind his eyes. Even his dizziness had come back to torment him. He needed air and rest. There was nothing more to be done in the church, he told himself.

"Order your men to have the body removed and transported secretly to Misericordia hospital. Use the wagon in which we came. I will walk back. Leave instructions at the gate for me to be admitted."

"But it is not advisable at night."

"Matins already chimed some time ago. In a little while it will be daylight. I need to get a breath of air. To think."

HE MADE his way out of the church carefully, retracing his path around the open pit. As he passed the abyss, he had another fit of dizziness and nearly fell. There was no helping hand to support him, this time.

They say that a just man is known by his unhesitating step. They also say that there are only a few just men in every city, and that nobody heeds them.

He recalled the young soldier who had come to his rescue. He would have liked to thank him, but had not recognized him among the weary, fearful men he saw around him.

At the doorstep he bid the Bargello a curt goodnight and left him nonplussed. Had the idiot perhaps expected him to point out the perpetrator right on the spot? The man's disappointed look made the poet think that was exactly what he had expected. He felt a sudden prickle of pride. In the end, that miserable rogue was not far wrong. If his head had been clearer, he told himself, clasping his aching temples, surely he would have made sense of what he had seen, have been able to give those pieces of the truth a final, coherent form.

But a voice inside him whispered that it would take much more than an hour to arrive at the truth. *Tomorrow. We shall take it up again tomorrow. We all need some rest—and daylight,* he told himself.

He stepped outside into the first diffused glow of dawn. The austere lines of the church now seemed perfectly ordinary. Yet within those walls there was something perverse, as if the hundreds of hands that had shaped and reshaped the structure over the course of centuries had each left its own trace of human iniquity branded on the stones. *Destiny leaves its mark on places, just as it does on men's lives,* he thought. And like lives, stones could be shaped to evil ends.

He needed to be alone, to breathe freely the fresh, healing morning air. He thought of the small supply of aconite that he kept in his cell—there wasn't enough left to ease his pain. And at that hour of the morning no apothecary would be open.

He remembered one of his public acts, written when he was a member of the Council of the One Hundred. He had always been proud of his memory—even at that moment, distracted and ill, he could have recited entire books of the *Aeneid*. He could see that act as clearly as if it were still before his eyes. "By license of the prior of the guild . . . the right to open a shop . . . is granted to Master Teofilo Sprovieri, physician and apothecary, born in St. John of Acre, and having come from there . . ."

Sprovieri's shop was on Via Lunga, near Porta Romana. He would drag him out of bed. When all was said and done, that man owed him something. Besides, he was a prior, and he could violate the curfew. He could do anything. Then, too, he was himself a member of the apothecaries' guild. A colleague ought to greet him with open arms.

Some medicine . . . some medicine and a bit of fresh air, and he would rout the pain.

THE WALK to Porta Romana did not do him as much good as he had hoped. By this time all the humors of his body seemed to have curdled. He was exhausted; his hair and beard were soaked with sweat. He'd gotten himself lost in the maze of alleys that radiated like a spider's web from the church of Santo Spirito, just after the gate.

As he turned into a side street he ran into a potbellied cleric hobbling in the opposite direction. The fellow was out of breath, huffing and puffing; he had the sickly look of one who is often forced to resort to physic. His expression was shifty; Dante caught a flicker of fear in his eyes as he hastened past. He stepped forward and barred the way, fixing the cleric with bloodshot eyes.

"There's an apothecary around here. Where?" he asked sharply.

The clergyman blanched. He took in the poet's robe of office, then his distressed face. Dante adjusted his cap and straightened the folds of his clothing before repeating his question.

"There . . . to the left. Just behind the Fontana della Morte . . ." the man stammered, indicating the direction with a trembling hand.

Dante started off, pleased with the effect the marks of his authority had on his fellow townsmen. He turned again to look at the cleric, who was scurrying away, relieved to have escaped from a madman dressed as a prior.

The poet walked on, stumbling over the cobblestones. By now the pain in his temples was obscuring his vision, transforming the irregular pavement into a sparkling haze. Somehow, he reached the Fontana della Morte. The gray blocks of "the fountain of Death" were topped by the remains of a Roman statue. Over the centuries the woman's marble face, once beautiful, had corroded, so that it now resembled a grotesque mask. He bent down to take a sip of the icy water at her feet.

Then he sat on the fountain's edge a moment, trying to catch his breath. Here, too, death loomed over him, he thought, its blind gaze like a malign caress.

What a bizarre idea, a pharmacist's shop in a place with such a name. Or had the apothecary's choice been a wise one? Restoration and Death, as inseparable as two sides of the same coin in the geography of Florence, as well as in that of life.

HE CONTINUED down an alley off the side of the piazza, and from afar he saw a door whose jambs were carved with the insignia of the guild. He covered the final stretch almost in a dream.

Despite the early hour the shop was open. A fitful light seeped from the door, as if someone inside were moving about, carrying a lamp.

Inside, the place was arranged almost like a library. Tall shelves lined the walls; instead of books, they were filled with neatly arranged jars and pots made of glass and colored ceramic. On a large central counter covered by a marble slab stood mortars of various sizes, in stone, bronze, and wood, along with a row of burners on which small pans and copper vessels were boiling, giving off a subtle aromatic vapor. In the back, he glimpsed the faint reddish gleam of a furnace.

The man behind the counter was about the same age as Dante, slender in build, with raven hair and dark, slightly oblong eyes. He was busy pounding dried herbs in a mortar, while he watched the poet curiously. His eyes were lively and intelligent, and there was something feline in the way they moved, and in the phosphorescence of their pupils in the lantern light.

"How can I help you, sir?" he asked, inclining his head politely, revealing a dense web of wrinkles on his forehead.

Before replying, Dante looked around. There was an agreeable sense of linearity and order in that setting, a balance of shapes and a logic in the use of space. He felt reassured. He had not fallen into the den of some trickster. The light of intellect shone inside that place, and the wisdom of the new science. The surroundings truly seemed to be a symbol of the times, reflecting clarity of thought upheld by reason, in accordance with the Parisian school. The place was . . . yes, modern.

"Aconite root and powdered hawthorn. And an infusion of thyme, peppercorns, and fresh willow bark," he said at last.

The apothecary studied him as he continued pounding the mixture in his mortar. He seemed to be mulling over the significance of that request. "What you are asking for is a strange combination. As if you wanted to both contract and relax your viscera. And you appear to underestimate the danger of aconite. Who prescribed this potion for you?" There was a shadow of suspicion in his voice, which nonetheless sounded kind.

"I am Dante Alighieri, a prior of the city," the poet replied brusquely. He thought he would die as the pain flared up again. "And I am a master apothecary experienced in medical arts. I know very well that aconite can cause death . . ." As he spoke he approached the counter and picked up one of the bronze pestles. "I have no intention of destroying myself. I only want the medicine to facilitate the release of bile from overfull veins, so that it may dissipate through natural means, along with its effects. So give me those damned herbs, before I grab you by the throat!" He immediately regretted the outburst, and hastened to lower his upraised hand.

The apothecary had followed that breathless argument with close attention. He did not seem offended by the poet's arrogant manner. On the contrary, he seemed pleased. "Dante Alighieri?" he said, opening his arms. "What pleasure your unexpected visit brings me! You, the master of the poetic word, here in my shop! Do you remember me? I am Teofilo Sprovieri. We met as students, years ago, in Bologna . . . do you recall?" he repeated, observing Dante's puzzlement with a trace of disappointment.

Though he remembered signing Sprovieri's license, Dante did not remember this. Then a memory stirred in his pain-fogged mind. Years ago, when he was composing love poems for Beatrice, during his brief period of study at the university. "Yes . . . now I do. Forgive me. The pain I am experiencing clouds my vision."

He hoped those words would be sufficient. But the pharmacist, instead of turning toward the shelves of medicines, came closer to him. "What is the nature of the illness that is consuming you?" he asked, staring at him as though trying to diagnose his suffering with his eyes alone.

"Black bile, an excess in the veins. It is scalding my forehead like fiery lava."

Sprovieri's eyes flashed. "Perhaps I have something . . . a new drug," he said. He seemed delighted to have the chance to be of help to such an esteemed man and at the same time to shine as a master of the medical guild. "Trust me, Messer Alighieri, and allow my modest science to add a small grain to your much vaster knowledge."

In the corner of the shop stood a large chest of solid wood, its edges reinforced with metal bands and its lid secured with a double padlock, like those of the cash boxes of the leading money-lenders of Florence. The apothecary took two iron keys out of a cabinet and inserted one into the upper keyhole.

Though almost blinded by spasms of pain, Dante observed this masterpiece of mechanical art admiringly. The lock was in-geniously constructed so that it was necessary to alternate the keys in a secret pattern in order to open it. Sprovieri turned the first key once, then slid the other into the lower keyhole and turned it in the opposite direction for a seemingly interminable number of times.

Finally, with a click, the hidden talon of the lock released the steel shackle, and the apothecary threw open the heavy lid.

From where he stood, the poet could not see clearly what the chest contained. He sensed that Sprovieri was deliberately block-ing his view. Dante was just able to glimpse a roll of papers tied with a string, on the bottom, and, on a sort of ledge, a vessel the size of a wine beaker, filled with a greenish liquid and sealed with a metal stopper.

"This is the drug I was telling you about," Teofilo said. "A remedy against any distress that might afflict the frail human body. Even the suffering of the spirit is vanquished by this nepenthe."

He set the vessel down on the counter with extreme care. Dante thought he knew what it might be. Even in Florence there had been talk about an herb brought to Europe by crusaders re-turning from overseas. The herb was said to belong to the Assas-sins, the villainous followers of the terrible Old Man of the Mountain. It had the power to soothe the senses and quiet the emotions, to wipe away memories and certainties. The ancient Greeks had written of it, calling it lotus. He knew it was in use even in his city.

"I believe I already know of your remedy, Messer Teofilo, but I do not think that lotus extract is the most appropriate treatment to redress an imbalance of humors."

"Oh, no, master, this drug is not derived from the herbs of Libya," the apothecary replied in an enigmatic tone. For a moment he seemed not to want to say anything more, then he continued. "Its place of origin is much more distant. It does not come to us from the arid deserts of the Moors, but from the luxuriant shores of a land unknown even to Alexander. Two years ago, in Aleppo, in Syria, a traveler gave me the small quantity that you see here. He had silks and precious stones with him, but this was his most precious possession. He told me that it was called *chandu* in the language of those who first discovered it."

"What does it contain?"

Sprovieri did not reply at once; he seemed to be pondering something.

"You say that the mixture is not lotus, that it comes from distant lands," Dante persisted. An intuition had dawned in his mind. "Is it perhaps . . . meconic?"

"Meconic?" the apothecary repeated slowly.

"The substance that is extracted from the poppy of the Orient, the *opion* of which Pliny the Elder writes. The drug used by the great emperor Marcus Aurelius to assuage his worries and soothe the cares of governing."

The pharmacist's expression was unreadable. "I see that your knowledge is equal to your renown, Messer Alighieri," he said. "It is my most precious possession. And the most secret. I would be honored if you chose to benefit from it."

He took a slender glass tube from a drawer, and drew from the bottle enough to fill a small vial. The greenish liquid shimmered as it slid from glass to glass, and a bitter odor hung in the air.

The poet reached for the vial. His head was pounding; he would do anything to vanquish the pain. But Teofilo held the ampoule back.

"Observe these doses," he said. "Their precise regimen derives from those who carefully and yet sometimes fatally experimented with its effects on the human body. Ten drops induce stupor and allay the most intense pain, such as that which sometimes flares up in the teeth, in the ear canals, or, as in your case, the folds of the brain. Twenty drops and the mind rushes headlong into a delirium peopled with violent images. The veil that God has lowered over our most secret shames is torn and the rational intellect penetrates the realm of the soul. The mind acquires the blasphemous gift of a prophetic power inspired not by God, but by an envious demon. The excitement at this stage is so intense that the body can be hacked to pieces by surgical instruments or an assassin's blade and the pain would not distract the dreamer from his visions."

As the man spoke, the name of the mixture resounded in the poet's head.

"If I were not fearful of incurring the wrath of our Holy Church, I would say that the primogenitors of the human race had plucked this *chandu* from the branches of the Tree of Knowledge," the apothecary continued. "Go back to your quarters now and use it according to my instructions. By nine o'clock your pain will be gone."

"And more than twenty drops?" Dante asked. He already knew the answer.

"Do not try it. Ever. More than twenty drops and the gates of Paradise may open, but no one has ever visited Paradise alive."

CALLING UPON his last ounce of strength, Dante traversed the stretch of road to the convent. At San Piero there was no one at the door or on the stairs. Even the guard seemed to have vanished, after that infernal night. He hurried to his cell, and immediately dissolved ten drops of the preparation in a cup of water. Then he added another five drops, drank, and fell fully clothed across the large, tall chest that served him as a bed. He hoped that Teofilo's words were true.

At first he was not aware of any particular sensation. The light of early dawn brightened the window. But the noises from the street seemed muffled, as if a felt carpet had been spread over the stone pavement. Incomprehensible voices reached his ears; an indistinct murmuring as if all of the city's wayfarers had decided to congregate down there in the street. Certainly the news had already spread through the city that Dante Alighieri, the Florentine prior and poet, was living there.

He felt a sudden urge to lean out the window of his cell to thank them, but was overcome by weakness. His limbs refused to obey him. His body seemed to have disappeared, leaving only his mind, an island in a churning sea of oblivion, a small reef on a course deserted by ships, where no sirens sang.

He could not have said how long that silence lasted before it was broken by the dull whistling of blood in his temples. Soon he could hear all of his humors surging inside him. He was poised on the edge of an immense torrent that was crashing down into the bowels of the earth. He was deafened by the uproar of his own body.

Gradually he became aware of a faint shuffling behind the

closed door. People crowding around, trying not to be heard, muffling their voices with their hands so as not to disturb him. But the hour was growing late, and the cardinals who had come to announce the time of the election were awaiting him outside. Were they perhaps scheming behind his back? Why had he not been summoned to the conclave? And yet it would be he who decided who was to be Boniface's successor. Better yet, it would be he who would be offered the pastoral staff, illuminated by the Grace . . .

"Come in, then!" he cried toward the shuddering door. Glittering lights came filtering through its cracks. Between those wooden planks six fiery letters were materializing, letters of death: IIICOE.

Light was seeping in through every chink. Suddenly the door turned on its hinges and radiance exploded like a bolt of lightning. The mouth of a volcano, or of hell itself, yawned in his room. A dark figure silhouetted against the glare slowly approached the bed on which Dante lay outstretched.

It was a woman, loosely draped in a tunic of white, green, and scarlet silk, her seductive figure visible beneath veils through which shone a dazzling light. She drew nearer and nearer, until her legs brushed the bed. The poet became aware of the heat of her body as she leaned over him, unfastened her robe, and shoved her belly toward his face.

Then her abdomen revealed its gaping wound, a foul, bloody gash. A living forest rose up around her face, and a tangle of hissing snakes, striking at Dante. He tried to draw back, straightening up and sitting against the head of the bed, as if he could sink into the wall behind him to escape the infernal pursuer.

Medusa's eyelids, disfigured by leprosy, slowly began to open, as a terrible scream tore through the silence, striking his head like a hammer blow.

2

June 16, toward nine o'clock in the morning

DANTE AWOKE in a pool of cold sweat. The echo of his own scream still resounded within the walls of his cell. The dream's dazzling light had given way to the glare of the sun, now high in the sky.

He got up, staggering, his mind confused. He put his head in his hands, trying to rouse himself. He felt as if he had just emerged from the depths of a sea populated with monsters. Still, the searing agony in his temples was gone. An extraordinary sense of well-being pervaded him, and the last trace of pain had melted away.

His mental sharpness had been restored and his faculties re-invigorated. The events of the night were as clear in his memory as if he had just returned from the church that that murder had stained. The tormented face of the mosaicist was once again before his eyes and seemed to be urging him to action, as if Dante were his kinsman, bound to a blood feud.

Surely his conscience was goading him: as a prior of Florence, was he not in fact a father to his fellow townsmen? Was not their blood his blood? He must act without delay and, without regard for anyone, proceed as his reason and conscience advised him.

He went to the loggia and signaled to the guard watching over the row of cells. "Is the priory secretary here? Summon him at once," he ordered.

Instead of hurrying off to obey, the man stared and smirked. "Earlier a certain Manetto came by. While you were sleeping. And you sleep like a log, prior."

"Ser Manetto? What did he want?"

"He was looking for you. A sour character, bitter as a lemon. He mentioned some bills. He says he will go to your brother if you don't pay him."

Dante was outraged. That accursed moneylender. To come and look for him at the priory! And that dog of a guard, staring at him contemptuously.

"Do what I told you, at once," he ordered sharply.

Vexed, he watched the man move unhurriedly toward the stairs, then returned to his cell and sat down at the desk to wait. His gaze fell upon a stack of papers that he had been working on the night before he had entered the shadowy realm of mystery.

His dissertation: the one he wanted to submit to the senate of the university of Padua, once his mandate was completed. He read the title: *Quaestio de aqua et terra.* Over and above his laurels for poetry, that slim work would bestow upon him eternal glory among the sages.

He had written it to refute the impious and illogical affirmation that water rose above the land in a certain part of the globe and that there was something other than ocean in the southern hemisphere.

Those theories were folly, and yet more than one man defended them, citing mountain springs as evidence. To credit such arguments would be tantamount to declaring that water might flow upward.

The pitcher and goblets that he had filled during the night were still on the table. He was tempted to repeat the experiment, but the pitcher was empty. No one seemed to trouble about service at the priory, he thought with some irritation. But in the end it was a waste of time. The authority of Aristotle was enough to refute such foolishness, an unequivocal sign of the decline of learning.

THE SECRETARY was a middle-aged man, completely bald. He appeared at the door with a hefty book under his arm. Its pages were securely bound between two wooden tablets decorated with images of saints.

"You wanted to see me, Messer Alighieri? I imagine you want a report on the City's finances. I have brought with me . . ."

"Thank you, Messer Duccio," Dante interrupted. "There will be time enough for that. Do you keep records of the work that is being done on the new walls?"

"Yes, of course. Although another account book would be needed to . . ."

"Who is restoring Saint Jude? And why?"

The secretary searched his well-organized memory for a moment. Then he recited, as if reading from an invisible archive, "That church and the buildings adjacent to it once belonged to the Augustinians. But the order abandoned them. They remained unoccupied for more than fifty years, until they were transferred to the City's holdings as *res nullius,* unowned property. Last year a request came from Rome to endow the buildings for use as the seat of a *studium generale.*"

"From Rome?"

"Yes, through a legate of the Urbe's senate. The monks of Saint Paul Outside the Walls made the request. They intend to use it as the capitular seat for the university. His Holiness Pope Boniface wants the love of learning to be cultivated in all Christian cities. In Rome he has already promoted the Sapientia, the university for the Urbe's scholars."

"Is Boniface behind the studium?" Dante asked with some alarm. "Who commissioned the mosaicist?"

"The commission was given to Ambrogio, a Comacine master, who lodges with the brothers of Santa Croce."

"Who is paying for the work?"

"Not the city . . . I believe the college of the studium pays directly."

"Are the members of this teaching college so rich?"

The secretary shrugged. "Some of them are well-known in their trade. . . . Perhaps they earn enough, or have other sources of money at their disposal. Messer Teofilo, for example, with his shop, is certainly not poor, given the prices we pay those damn apothecaries . . ."

Dante suddenly looked up and took a step toward the secretary, who drew back. The man had suddenly remembered that the prior was also a member of the apothecaries' guild. He bit his tongue, cursing himself, as he sought desperately to find a way to mitigate what he had said. But the poet was thinking of something else. "Teofilo? Do you mean Teofilo Sprovieri, with the shop at the Fontana della Morte? Is he a member of the studium?"

All of a sudden the shrewd face of the apothecary was before him, cast now in a different light. A more sinister light, if the man had anything to do with that hypocritical specimen of a Pope.

The secretary quickly scanned his documents to make certain before nodding in affirmation.

Dante reflected in silence. When he looked up at last, Messer Duccio was still waiting, gripping the account book as if it were the family fortune. "You may go," he told the secretary. "But I have need of your services. A detailed report on the members of the studium: who they are, where they come from, their political affiliation, their vices, their wrongdoings both known and concealed . . . everything."

The secretary went out.

Dante, perplexed, gazed distractedly at the few objects in his cell, trying to gather his thoughts. The idea that Boniface might be planning a university in Florence, which he would then control through his acolytes, worried him.

He walked to the door, and with an abrupt gesture summoned the guard who leaned idly against a column of the cloister. The guard gave him an annoyed look as if two orders in the space of a few minutes were too onerous for a man like him.

Dante waited calmly for him to get close enough, then dealt him a violent back-handed blow. "Useless sluggard, I want my orders obeyed with the speed of thought itself. More quickly, if possible. And it better be possible, if you know what's good for you," he hissed, landing a kick as the fellow spun around to escape another slap.

"Summon two bargellini to escort me to Santa Croce immediately."

The stunned guard nodded as he rubbed his cheek. The poet watched him run to the guard's quarters. He had seen the man glance at his throat, his eyes sharp as a blade. Perhaps he should be more circumspect, he told himself. He would not be prior forever.

IT WAS market day, and stalls were set up near the old city walls. Dante had decided to cut through those crowded aisles. To his chagrin he soon realized he would have been better off following the Arno, avoiding that filthy rabble and their dubious wares. Cavaliers and sluts, noblemen and pickpockets seemed locked in a lewd embrace that spanned the streets of the city once devoted to San Giovanni.

He felt a dull rage as he watched that humiliating spectacle.

"Try to stay close to me," he called to the two bargellini who were following him. But though they shouted and threatened the crowd with their pikes, they were engulfed almost at once in the sea of heads that surged from one wall of houses to the other. It seemed that all the flesh of Florence, pack animals included, had decided to mass in that tangle of narrow streets between the baptistery and the church of the Franciscans.

He forged ahead alone, struggling to make his way through the throng, keeping as much as possible to the edge of the street to avoid the copious horse droppings. He had thought that the badges of the prior's office would be enough to clear a path for him, but once he lost contact with the armed guard, neither his biretta nor his gilt cane made any impression on the mob. On the contrary, these insignia seemed to attract the insolence of those vulgar commoners. Twice already he had narrowly avoided a stream of urine that had erupted from the windows overlooking the streets, and he suspected an offensive intent behind those mishaps.

He made a mental note of the houses from which they had come. The lairs of those dogs the Donati, his enemies. Soon he would find a way to avenge himself. Taking advantage of the temporary shelter provided by a moneychanger's awning, he stood on tiptoe to look for the bargellini. But the scoundrels seemed to have disappeared.

Someone grabbed his hand. Startled, he tried to wrench himself free, but the person clenching his wrist resisted with unexpected force. A woman, covered in rags, her long white hair hanging over her humped back.

"What the devil do you want from me, you old hag?" the poet shouted. "A coin!" she cried, keeping her head lowered, as if she dared not look him in the face. "In exchange for your fortune."

"Mind your own fortune, witch. You have need of some."

"A coin. A coin for your fortune," she repeated. Her voice, firm and sonorous, belied her decrepit appearance. She forced open the palm of his hand and began to scrutinize it. The crowd slipped around them now, parting like a wave breaking against a rock.

At least now the badges of the priorate were being respected, the poet thought.

Yet the glances of the passersby were focused not on him, but on the woman. It was she everyone was trying to avoid.

"Let go of me. I don't believe in your claptrap."

"A coin to know when you will meet your ruin."

"Who says I will meet my ruin?"

"You. You, who are trying to bring ruin upon yourself." Dante tried again to free his hand, but the woman would not let go. "You exposed the face of the dead man," she went on.

"What . . ."

"But a dead man will not speak to you."

Dante was taken aback. Automatically he reached for the purse attached to his belt and took out a copper coin.

"Tell me about the dead man."

"He will guide the living."

"Guide them where?"

"To the land of the other dead. You should not have exposed his face."

Dante was baffled. Like all fortune-tellers, the old woman spoke in a way that was vague and obscure. Still, she seemed to know something about the previous night's tragedy. "Why are you telling me this?"

"So that it may give thee pain." All of a sudden the woman released her hold, drew back a step, and was quickly swallowed up by the moving throng.

Caught by surprise, Dante hesitated a moment too long before deciding to follow her. By then he found his way blocked by an impenetrable wall of bodies. "Who was that woman?" he asked a moneychanger who stood at the entrance to his stall. He was sure the man had witnessed the scene. "Who is she? Speak, I am a prior of Florence!"

The man did not seem too impressed. "It was old Martina. Don't pay any attention to her, she's crazy. She lost both her sons at Campaldino."

Dante stood still a moment longer, letting the restless crowd jostle by. The reference to the mosaicist must have been a coincidence. Or maybe one of the bargellini had talked about what he had seen in the church, and the story had gotten around. He shrugged and resumed his laborious journey to the convent.

He cursed himself for having paid heed to one of the many hopeless wretches who play at being witches and sorcerers. Florence was full of them, just like the *bolge,* the madhouses of the Inferno.

My fortune for a coin . . .
The devil take it!

AT LAST he reached Santa Croce. The Comacine master had taken lodgings at the convent of the Franciscans, in the wing the brothers made available to wayfarers.

The father custodian was not overly surprised by his arrival. When he learned of the death of his boarder, he did not seem too upset. Perhaps his composure was simply that of a soul practiced in dealing with the fragility of human life. Maybe he had grown accustomed to the transitory nature of the presences in the building, and death, after all, was merely a way, like any other, of leaving a place. Yet Dante continued to wonder about whether he too might have had previous knowledge of his death, like the old woman at the market.

"His cell, did anyone enter it?" he asked.

"I did not see anyone. But the door is not guarded. Come, I will show you Master Ambrogio's quarters."

Ambrogio's cell was situated at the end of a narrow corridor that led directly to an interior courtyard. A corner of the colonnade opened onto the side entrance of the church. Anyone would have been able to enter without being noticed, taking advantage of the comings and goings of the faithful.

The furnishings of the room were very plain. The master had slept on a plank bed, and a board affixed to the wall had served as his desk. On the desk were a wooden box of quills and several clay ink pots. One of these had lately been overturned, for the wood was stained, and an inky rag lay on the ground nearby. Among the papers stacked there he found a letter of mandate, bearing the papal seal, summoning the master to Rome to undertake certain consolidation works in the monastic complex of Saint Paul Outside the Walls. There was no date, but the document appeared to be recent.

"Did Ambrogio go to Rome before coming to Florence?"

"I believe so. He spoke about the Holy City as if he knew it quite well."

Dante went back to studying the letter. This detail seemed to confirm his earlier idea that the mosaic might have been intended as a celebration of the Centesimus. Again he wondered what had been planned for the part that had not been completed.

"Did you notice anything strange about his behavior? Was he afraid of something? Did he seem worried?" he asked the father custodian.

"No, I would not say so. He was very engrossed in his work . . . apart from the matter of the letter."

"What letter? This one?" the poet asked, indicating the contract.

"No, not that one. A few weeks ago he asked me if one of our brothers might be leaving to go north. He wanted to give him a message to bring to his fellow guild members. Perhaps a report . . . who knows?"

"And was the message sent?"

"Yes, just at that time a visiting father had to go to Mantua. The master gave him an envelope."

"And you have no idea what was in it?"

The friar shrugged his shoulders. Beside the plank bed was a large open chest, full of sheets of rag paper and parchments covered with architectural drawings: details of arches and trusses, sketches of mosaic decorations, and plans for flooring all jumbled together indiscriminately. A guild master would never have treated the tools of his trade in such a way. Someone must have rummaged through there, without bothering to put things back in place. What could that someone have been looking for? Maybe what he himself had been unable to find in the church: the complete cartoons for the mosaic.

He sat down on the straw pallet that covered the bed, and began carefully examining the drawings. He hoped to find at least one preliminary sketch, if not the actual detailed plan for the huge mosaic. But there was absolutely nothing concerning the work that, Dante was certain, had been the cause of the master's death.

Perhaps whoever had rummaged through the dead man's papers had found what he was looking for.

He was ready to give up. On one of the last sheets was a magnificent sketch of a polychrome stained-glass window. Idly, he held it up to the light to admire it. He turned it over, and his attention was caught by a mesh of faint marks, now brought out by the glancing light from the window. Delicately touching the surface of the parchment, Dante thought he could feel grooves left by a point. Something there must have been scraped out.

Curious, he got up and went over to the box of quills. As he had hoped, it also contained a piece of charcoal. He began to rub this over the entire surface of the parchment, in light, consecutive strokes. Behind him the father custodian craned his neck, trying to figure out what he was doing.

Slowly, as if by magic, the outline of the original drawing became visible. It was not the departing colossus portrayed in the mosaic, but something even more surprising.

It was a ship, a galley with its fo'c'sle festively decked out. The rows of oars were clearly visible, as was the square sail, stretched taut by the wind. There was a second sail unfurled in an unusual position below the keel.

Dante peered intently, the better to perceive every detail. Perhaps it was merely a preliminary sketch. Perhaps the draftsman had thought of locating the ship lower on the page and had later modified the initial plan, moving the entire drawing higher up.

Yet he did not believe this other sail represented a change of mind. It appeared to be connected to the keel by a mesh of ropes, as if Ambrogio had wanted to indicate the real possibility of maneuvering it.

It was absurd. A joke.

But why play a joke on a material as precious as parchment? Then, too, he had never heard it said that the Comacines took an interest in shipbuilding. They were famous as architects, builders in stone. Even Arnolfo di Cambio had employed them for all of his buildings in Florence.

As he was asking the father custodian to have the other papers transported to San Piero, he noticed one more detail. In the sky, over the bow of the ship, two small marks could be seen: a minute five-pointed star and the name Venus. Venus, the morning star, luminous ruler of the third heaven, one of the nine crystalline heavens.

He rolled up the parchment, carefully, so as not to smudge the charcoal that had revealed the secret drawing.

He was about to leave the room when his gaze again fell on the quill box and ink pots. Beside them was a glass vial he had not noticed before. It was empty, but bringing it to his nose he immediately smelled the bitter, unmistakable odor of *chandu*.

He had promised Sprovieri that he would go back and pay him a visit. He decided to honor this commitment. At once.

As he stepped through the door he spotted the lost bargellini arriving; they were out of breath. The glitter in their eyes was evidence that they had stopped in some tavern: it was for that purpose, then, that they had fallen away from him, taking advantage of the confusion of the market. He clenched his teeth in anger, but, remembering the murderous gleam in the eyes of the priory guard, said nothing.

3

The same day, toward noon

THE APOTHECARY seemed happy to see him again. "I see you have recovered, Messer Durante. Just as I promised," he noted with ill-concealed pride.

"And just as I promised you, I am back to pay my respects and renew an old friendship."

"I am glad. So my potion had a beneficial effect?"

"Absolutely, and I again thank you for it. Did it have a beneficial effect on the others too?"

"What do you mean?" Sprovieri asked, a sudden wariness behind his cordiality.

"Ambrogio, for example, the Comacine master. Did he not turn to you as well?"

The apothecary let a moment go by before responding. "Yes, of course," he said, as if he had just remembered.

"Was he, too, suffering from unbearable pain?" Dante pressed him.

Again Sprovieri did not reply immediately. Then he nodded in assent. "Although not the same kind as yours. There is bodily pain and spiritual pain, and for some souls the latter is more terrible than the former."

"A suffering of the mind . . . perhaps caused by the immensity of his charge?"

Sprovieri stared at him questioningly.

"Saint Jude. The enormous mosaic in the apse," the poet continued. "I have seen it. So colossal as to cause your heart to tremble."

"Ambrogio is a consummate artist, a master of his craft. It is natural for great men to undertake great works and be consumed by the task. I was happy to provide him some relief. I am fond of him."

"How did you come to know him?" Dante asked, struck by the fact that the apothecary spoke of the dead man without any special emotion. Was he not aware of the crime?

"He is part of a small circle of men who have been my companions since I came to your city. Scholars, whose friendship makes me feel honored . . . as does yours."

"A circle of scholars here in Florence? You must be very fortunate, Messer Sprovieri. I, though I was born here, have never been able to find more than five estimable men. And three of them are already dead."

The other smiled. "Oh, it is certainly not Plato's Academy! We are merely a small group that meets from time to time in the evening, after having completed our respective offices, to talk about virtuous matters. We try to share amongst ourselves that angelic bread that each of us has attained through his own studies. We are all masters in our trades, who have come to Florence because of the *studium generale*."

Dante pretended ignorance. "I did not think there was a university in Florence."

"And yet there is. At least in the parchments and deeds by which King Charles of Anjou founded it, more than thirty years ago. But before long it will appear not just on paper, but in all its actual splendor. For now, our classes are held in temporary locations in all four corners of the city, but soon the studium will have a definitive seat."

"I have heard of plans to that effect. Is it not Saint Jude, in fact, the old parish church at the new walls?"

Sprovieri nodded. Again he made no mention of what had occurred there the night before. He appeared to be completely in the dark concerning the tragedy.

"A college of learned men in my city . . . I would be truly honored to debate some of the new ideas with all of you, and subject my meager knowledge to your scrutiny," Dante went on. "Furthermore, it would be extremely discourteous on the part of one of the Commune's highest authorities not to pay his respects to the men who are about to confer prestige upon Florence."

The apothecary remained silent a moment—too long a moment it seemed to Dante—his eyes half-closed, his face a feline mask. Then the cordial smile that he had seen earlier reappeared. "I am certain that they will all feel honored by a visit from the prince of Tuscan poets, and that you will not find it entirely beneath your powers to take part in one of our conversations. When will you come?"

"This very day, if you like. Your words have kindled a desire in my heart. If that does not disrupt your plans, of course."

"No, on the contrary. This is a better day than any other. We were thinking of convening today. I shall meet you at vespers, in the tavern behind the big fountain on the road to Rome. Baldo the Crusader's tavern. There you will find yourself in the Third Heaven."

"The Third Heaven?"

"It is a figure of speech we use among ourselves, an inside joke among scholars. But you will certainly appreciate it. The love of knowledge that stimulates us when we approach the angelic doctrine is such that each of us seems to ascend to the heaven of the star Venus. But that is not all. You shall see."

Dante remained silent, absorbed in thought. Perhaps it was only a coincidence that Ambrogio had been killed while working for the studium. But maybe, he thought, it is simply the insufficiency of our senses that keeps us from recognizing an orderly plan behind the apparent fortuity of events. He would have liked to question the apothecary further, but decided he should reflect first. There would be time, later on. On the way out he paused a moment at the door. "Messer Teofilo?"

"Yes?"

"What does your magical potion contain?"

"I do not know, Messer Alighieri. The person who gave it to me did not reveal it."

"And you did not try . . ."

"I studied it carefully. But I was not able to learn anything, except that it is composed of five different substances."

Dante shook his head. He sensed the man was lying. For a moment he imagined him in shackles in a subterranean dungeon of the Stinche prison. How long would he hold out with his secret against the strappado?

And how long had Master Ambrogio held out with his?

4

The same day, toward vespers

A PAINTED copper plate hanging from the portico attracted
drinkers to the tavern known as On the Road to Jerusalem.
The sign represented the shield of an imaginary nobleman, rendered by a painter of no pretensions. Six heavily armed horsemen
were depicted in the background; in the foreground, a goggle-
eyed Saracen's head, cleanly severed and bloody, seemed to observe
every customer. The image was divided in two by a red cross.

"A fair treatment for those Moorish dogs," Dante thought
as he looked at it. It was the only thing there that met with his
approval.

The tavern had been formed by enclosing the supporting
arches of a large Roman edifice with ashlar walls. The upper part
of the ancient structure, which must have been imposing, had
been broken in two, apparently from some collapse, long ago.
Only a corner of the remains, still standing and rebuilt into a
squat, crenellated tower, conveyed an idea of the building's original height. The rest had gone to ruin, and it was amid that ruin
that this bit of the Orient bearing an insignia of the Holy City
had settled in.

There was something sordid about the structure now, not
least the wooden hovels that surrounded it. All around, vast fields
stretched away from the encroaching city, the new growth that

clung close to the new wall. Dante looked around, irritated. Why would men of learning have chosen to meet in such a place, instead of in any one of the convents within the old walls? What could possibly draw them here, if not a desire to avoid the glances and honest curiosity of their townsmen? What was there to hide about a studium?

Even the name of this place seemed ill-chosen. After the defeats suffered by Christians overseas and the slow reconquest of Palestine by the Mamelukes, Jerusalem had become a sacred and at the same time sorrowful symbol, and its name most inappropriate for the sign of a tavern.

HE CLIMBED the disjointed steps of the arcade and went up to the door. He heard a confused clamor from within, as if a great number of people were in there, despite the late hour. Nobody in that city seemed to fear the curfew, the poet thought with annoyance. Resolutely, he pushed open the door and entered, making his way through the servers and customers milling about in the wide space between the tables, which were arranged along the perimeter of the room. In the center of the room, a great copper cauldron bubbled over a crackling brazier, flanked by spits of meat turned by wretched children hunkered on the floor. Slaves, bought for a few coins from some poor family in the countryside, Dante thought in disgust.

The air, dense with smoke from the lanterns and brazier, hung beneath the trussed ceiling before escaping through an opening in the roof. The babble of voices, the dull clatter of tableware, and the shouts of the servingmen reminded him of the hubbub in the market that morning; he worried that his headache would return and begin tormenting him again.

He was already thinking of leaving when a voice stopped him. "Over here, Messer Alighieri, come! Take your place in the Third Heaven!"

The poet turned. In the far left-hand corner of the room, the apothecary, seated among several other men, had risen to his feet and was waving an arm at him as a sign to approach.

Dante headed toward them with deliberate slowness. He wanted his movements to be stamped with that gravitas that the ancients held to be innate in judicious men. Besides, that way he would have an opportunity to study the group before joining them at the table.

At the same time he sensed that every detail about himself, from his garment to the way he walked, was the object of their assessment. The men around the table, with their unfamiliar faces, all appeared to be protected by an invisible barrier. Although the room was crowded, the seats closest to them were vacant, and the few customers who sat nearby seemed quieter and more composed than the rest. Everything about them testified to their superior status, from the excellent quality of their garments to the tableware, laid out on an ample cloth. The polished surfaces of the neatly arranged tin plates and cups reflected the tongues of flame from the brazier. Not for them the crudely chiseled wooden trenchers on which lesser customers were served their food, and instead of tavern benches, they were seated on elaborate, high-backed chairs.

Teofilo continued motioning to him, but the others did not move. They waited until the poet reached them and then got up together, bowing their heads in a silent sign of deference, measured yet polite.

Dante bowed his head in turn, astonished at what he saw: the entire corpus of the art of physiognomy was there before his eyes. A dog, a fox, a monkey, and a lion in human clothing were all staring at him intently. Along with a horse, an eagle . . .

Never before had he come across such a precise correspondence between the animal species and the various human character types, that correspondence he had read about in the books of the old philosophers. Well then, so this heterogeneous group made up the society of learned men of whom the apothecary had spoken. There could not be many scholars in Florence, and yet none of those faces was known to him. They must be foreigners, like Teofilo, he thought, studying them.

"What a delight for all of us to see you here, Messer Durante," the apothecary said, rousing him. He turned to the others. "Dante Alighieri, the poet. My teacher and friend."

Dante parried this compliment with a gesture. Strictly speaking, he had no right to the title of teacher, for he had never taught. But deep down he felt flattered: it was only right that the profundity of his knowledge be recognized. "It is I who thank you for the invitation, Messer Teofilo. And for the company of your friends, to whom I hope I shall not be unwelcome."

"Whatever are you saying, Master! It will be an honor for all of them to make your acquaintance, starting with the man beside you, to your right." The apothecary pointed to a strongly built man who towered over the others by more than a handbreadth. The gentle eyes of a spaniel gleamed in his face, beneath heavy eyelids. "Augustino di Menico, natural philosopher, student of Creation's most intimate secrets. He has just returned after spending several years in the remote, infidel city of Tripoli, where he worked with the pagan writings of the Arabs, translating them into our language. A master of alchemy and a great authority in ancient languages, as is moreover his neighbor, Antonio da Peretola, jurist and notary, a renowned scholar of both laws, civil and canon," he continued, pointing to the next man, whose face bore the sharp, shifty features of a fox. Da Peretola responded with a ceremonious bow.

"In the service of the Curia, I imagine," Dante said, trying to conceal his distaste.

"Head of His Holiness' chancellery. At one time," the fox confirmed. His standing and prestige were displayed in his heavy gold chain and the rings adorning his fingers, and in the richness of his black robe, interwoven with gold threads, which contrasted sharply with the sober dress of his companions.

"Bruno Ammannati, teacher of God's sciences," Teofilo resumed, indicating the third man, who sat a little apart, as if the Franciscan tertiary habit that he wore dictated a certain reserve, especially in a place devoted to revelry. A constantly changing, intelligent face, on which the monkey had left a clear mark of intelligence, but also of ambiguity.

Dante was not surprised to find a cleric in a tavern: it seemed that the pleasure-loving Frati Gaudenti of Bologna were spreading throughout the rest of Italy, he thought, studying the man from head to toe. A quick glance was sufficient for him to notice that the cloth of the friar's habit was much finer than is usual for members of his order. If the theologian sensed the poet's mistrust, he did not show it, but instead returned Dante's greeting with pointed courtesy.

"And this is Iacopo Torriti, from Rome, our newest member. He is a surveyor and architect."

"And a mathematician," the man hastened to add with a certain self-importance.

Dante recalled having heard of him: he was one of the great Arnolfo di Cambio's assistants and had come with him from Rome when the construction of the new cathedral had begun. He scanned the architect's ungainly form, seeing the majesty of the horse in his elongated limbs and face, and a restrained vitality that seemed ever on the point of manifesting its full power. His hands seemed born to wield stone. Perhaps that was not all they had wielded.

The sixth member of the group approached, inclining his head and anticipating Teofilo's introduction. He was a vigorous man, with a thick mane of dark hair tied up at the back of his neck and the sharp, menacing mouth of a lion. "I am Veniero Marin. Your servant, Messer Durante. I hope to be honored by your friendship as I have been by that of these learned men, after my bark abandoned me on these shores, though I could not offer them any particular philosophy in return for theirs," he added with his gentle Venetian cadence. "My science is that of the sea, and a galley's deck is my cathedra. Places that often give birth to a different vision of terrestrial things."

Dante felt an instinctive liking for this man and his straightforward manner. He must have been around the poet's own age, even though his face, scoured by the wind, was engraved with a web of wrinkles that made him appear older. He brought a note of warmth in that assembly of cold pedants.

"The science of the winds and seas borders on that of the motion of the stars. And, like it, is advanced by precise calculation and the correct measure of things," Dante replied, smiling, as the man studied him with his clear eyes. "Just as in the better-known, though certainly not more ancient, sciences. Did not our Savior choose His earliest companions from among a populace of sailors and oarsmen?"

"Messer Veniero is not a fisherman. On the contrary, he was a valiant captain in La Serenissima's navy," Teofilo corrected him, as if to reclaim the role of master of ceremonies that his companion's impetuousness had usurped. "But he had some conflicts with the Doge's administration, and had to request asylum. This explains his presence here among us, so far from the sea . . ."

"By all means tell him that I am here to escape the executioner," the Venetian interrupted. His eyes had suddenly lost the gaiety that had animated them. Dante was surprised to hear those bitter words. Veniero responded to his silent question. "It is not advisable for a seafaring man to let his eyes linger too long on the women of the land, not even in our most serene Venice. Least of all, on the wife of a member of the Council. Only the sirens of the sea are conceded us, with their flesh that tastes of fish," he exclaimed, bursting into a thunderous laugh. He seemed to have recovered his good spirits, but in his eyes a trace of shadow remained.

At the end of the table, there remained one man, a young man with long, thick black hair that fell to his shoulders. The eyes of an eagle blazed in his face, which was already beginning to age, as if from wakeful nights of study—or some deep unrest. He waited motionless, like one of the large Byzantine mosaics that Dante had seen in the churches in the Po delta. During the introductions this man had not once taken his eyes off the poet's face.

Now, like the Venetian, he spoke without waiting to be pointed out by Teofilo. "You know me, Messer Durante, and I know you," he said. "Even though this is the first time our paths have crossed. I am Francesco of Ascoli."

This was entirely unexpected. Glancing around, Dante saw the others regarding the young man with the greatest deference. "Messer Cecco has been chosen chancellor of the studium," Teofilo said briefly.

Francesco Stabili, known as Cecco d'Ascoli. It was said that all the knowledge of the stars was in his hands. The greatest astrologer of his time, according to the followers of his science.

He opened his arms and the poet responded warmly, placing both hands on Cecco's shoulders and grasping them tightly. "Oh,

I know you for certain, Messer Cecco, and I salute the great doctor and astrologer in you," he said with sincere enthusiasm.

"And I salute in you the *dolcissimo* poet, indeed the greatest among the greats," the other replied with a smile, as he in turn embraced him. "I have wanted to meet you for some time. In all of Italy they talk of nothing but your new style, the *dolce stil nuovo,* and its sweetness. If the Emperor Frederick were alive, he would certainly want to hear you, to relieve the cares of state with your verses."

"If the Emperor Frederick were alive, you would be at his court to illuminate the course of his realm with your science. You, the favorite pupil of Guido Bonatti," Dante responded with a bow.

"The master of the science of the heavens," Cecco added in a reverent tone, pointing a finger skyward.

"And of the rites of magic," the poet replied, pointing to the ground.

"As you wish."

Dante waited another moment before disengaging himself from the embrace, then sat down at the only empty seat, certainly meant for him, letting himself lounge against the chair back.

That group of men was to found the university of Florence, he thought, and not one of them was Florentine. And death had already visited them.

"So this is the Third Heaven. The heaven of loving spirits. Of wisdom and learning, as Teofilo made known to me," he said then, without addressing anyone in particular. "But why choose such an unusual place to meet? I know that you do not yet have a seat for the studium. But surely while the restoration of the church is being completed, the Commune would let you have a room in San Piero, or in the chapter house of some convent . . ."

He thought he caught a rapid conspiratorial glance among the men seated there. "If you will be patient a moment, you will quickly understand, Messer Alighieri," the apothecary said, gesturing toward the back of the room, where for the past few minutes the crowd had been growing more excited. From it the faint sound of a tambourine could be heard, slow and sensual, and a metallic jingle, as of small bronze cymbals. A female figure appeared, greeted by ovations from the tavern's clientele. A forest of hands and bodies rose up around her and began swaying wildly, shouting vulgar exclamations, and the din of wooden platters rhythmically pounded against tables.

Dante gave Teofilo a questioning look.

"It is Antilia, the dancer who has made Messer Baldo's tavern famous as far as Rome," the apothecary explained, he too caught up in the sudden excitement.

The poet looked around. So this hovel was renowned even in Rome? And Florence, no longer his but another, unfamiliar city that had suddenly sprung up beyond the circle of the old walls. A new Babylon without the magnificence of the ancient one. With new idols . . . like that dancer, having come from who knows where, a drifter with painted eyes.

"Antilia? A curious name, surely not found in the canon of our saints," he merely observed.

"Antilia would not be admitted to the canon of saints even if her name were Mary Magdalene, believe me," said Veniero, laughing.

"Still, even though she is not in the canon, I think you, too, will appreciate her endowments, both manifest and concealed," Teofilo added with an ironic expression.

Dante listened distractedly, staring toward the indecorous spectacle at the back of the room, trying to catch a glimpse through the wall of bodies. He studied the figure at the center of so much attention, a woman with a dark complexion and impressive limbs.

A cry of pain was heard, followed by a resounding burst of laughter. From the other side of the room a stocky man with only one arm had grabbed a drunken customer's groin with his single hand and begun dragging him toward the door while the poor wretch screamed like a stuck pig.

"Our friend the tavern keeper has had to resort to the 'crusader's hold' again tonight," Bruno said, winking.

"The crusader's hold?"

"Are you not familiar with this charming discovery that comes from across the seas, Messer Alighieri?" Veniero joined in. "It is one of the arts that the Moors have handed down to us along with their commentaries on Aristotle. When our men, in their chain mail coats, reached the shores of Asia for the first time, they instilled fear and confusion in those sons of Satan, who had thought themselves invulnerable. But the perfidious infidels soon perceived that there was a weak point in the Christians' body armor, with consequences that you can imagine and of which you just saw a demonstration. With such a grip, Baldo, despite his missing arm, is able to get the better of men who are bigger than he, and so maintain an enviable order in his tavern."

While they were speaking, a drum had joined the chorus of instruments, its deep, powerful voice rising above them. As if this were a signal, the dancer began to move with a regal gait toward the table of the Third Heaven, breaking through the waving hands that surrounded her like the figurehead of a galley plowing through the sea. Her face, half hidden by a veil, revealed her utter contempt for the bawdy admiration of the rabble.

Yet Dante sensed a falseness in this contempt, in the way that she offered herself to the gaze of the crowd as if she were forced to. He was sure that deep down she was flattered by the very gestures for which she feigned disgust, that she was playing a role.

The rhythmic music of the drums and platters grew even louder as Antilia approached, making a wide arc around the empty area between the tables. The poet's detached curiosity was metamorphosing into a faint shiver of pleasure as she came toward them, ignoring the common rout that idolized her.

The dancer was swathed in a thin silk veil, richly embroidered with a design of peacocks' eyes, that lent her the graceful beauty of an exotic bird. Dante was certain that he had never seen a fabric like it in the shops of Florence.

She reached their table and stood there, swaying her hips slowly and jingling the metal disks tied around her wrists, staring at them with glittering jet-black eyes. She bent her head back, voluptuously arching to expose a neck adorned by a tumble of slim gold rings. Then she raised her shoulders as if she were about to move away again, shaking her breasts and splendid hips until her entire body began to sway on her slender ankles, also encircled with gold. She spun around once, then a second and a third time, lifting her arms toward her face in a parody of an offertory.

Dante looked fixedly at that magnificent face with its oriental features, expertly painted with a thin veneer of carmine that gave her the luster of a copper statue. Her movements reminded him of a panther's—a beast he had seen once, years ago, in the menagerie of the Sultan's ambassador. Her dance seemed like the celebration of a rite. A blasphemous rite, given the shamelessness of the officiant, yet one rich with a strange spirituality.

He was fascinated by her. If ever a creature had danced in the terrestrial Paradise, it must have been in that unique way. Lilith must have danced that way; thus were men lost in their earliest temple. In the expression on Antilia's face there was no trace of the wantonness with which she had just offered her body to their gaze. She wore a celestial smile. The poet was surprised to think that a messenger of God had actually arrived in that sordid place of pleasure, one of the angels who had walked the streets of Sodom, inviolable even while surrounded by a frenzy of unclean desires.

As she spun faster, the layers of her mantle loosened, then flared out like an extraordinary corolla, gradually unfolding before the eyes of the dumbstruck spectators as the music soared to a feverish crescendo over the throbbing beat of the drum.

Dante, caught up in the swelling wave of desire emanating from the other men, rose to his feet, as if compelled, pulled upward, by her mantle's ascent as it revealed that body in all its splendor. Against the taut muscles of her naked belly beat a golden pendant hanging on a slender chain.

Dozens of eyes stared dazedly at the fine down that now appeared, gently outlining the arc of her pudendum. The woman continued spinning ecstatically, blurred in a cloud of peacock eyes. Her arms, still raised above her head, vibrated from the tension. It seemed as if the whirling would never end. Then all of a sudden the music stopped, and at the same instant the dancer abruptly ceased her dizzying rotation, without effort, as if she were totally weightless. The mantle floated back down over her naked body. Clasping the veil around her hips, she remained motionless for a time, catching her breath, apparently unaware of the spell she had cast on the room.

Dante had turned to stone. Suddenly rousing himself, he snapped his mouth shut—it must have been open throughout the entire spectacle—and felt overwhelmed by shame. Clearly the *chandu* still ruled his brain; what else could cause a prior, a member of the Florentine Council, to have a reaction typical of simple-minded men? He sat down again, confused, hoping that no one had noticed.

———

I⒯ WAS Teofilo who broke the silence. "Now you understand why we usually refer to our small group as followers of the Third Heaven," he said, keeping his eyes fixed on the woman, who, still wrapped in a dreamlike silence, now retreated to the back of the room and disappeared behind a curtain. The members of the circle began talking and laughing again, but joylessly, as if each was waging a secret battle against the demon of lust.

"I understand," Dante said quietly. "And it is not difficult to imagine which amorous sensations the goddess's messenger brings you . . ."

Now that the excitement had diminished and he was once again master of his feelings, he was appalled. A slut, that was who the tutelary deity of the future *universitas* of his city was! A triumphant whore who wandered freely through the taverns without clothes and without the stamp of her infamy. Someone in the Commune would pay for this manifest corruption. What a wonderful allegory of the times, he said to himself, suppressing a scornful smile. A prostitute elevated to the heaven of the goddess of love.

Veniero's booming voice interrupted his thoughts. Of all of them he seemed the most at ease. "What do you think of what you have seen, Messer Durante? Does it not seem to you that the wisdom of these learned masters also shines forth in the good judgment with which they pursue beauty, which is so great a part of the universe? I say that as one who has sampled the beauties of almost all of the ports of the Mediterranean."

"Who is that woman?" the poet asked, trying to give the question an indifferent tone.

A spark of desire gleamed in Augustino's eyes as he answered. "She arrived in Florence recently, from distant lands. Did you see her features? They say she was among the refugees of St. John of Acre, the few who escaped that horrendous massacre. Alone, with no other possession than her singular beauty. It is in the East that she must have learned the movements of her dance, which has nothing in common with our country dances."

"She does not appear to be a descendant of Latin people."

"No. Perhaps her family were Greeks from Byzantium. Or Jews. Or slaves captured in Anatolia. Not even she knows—or she does not want to say."

"Well then, Messer Alighieri," Bruno Ammannati chimed in, fixing him with one of his mischievous looks, as if trying to provoke him. "Does a desire not arise in you as well to draw closer to our hall of learning?"

Dante was certain that all of them, beneath their apparent detachment, were anxiously awaiting his response. "Your assemblage seems more like a court of love than a convocation of learned men," he replied evasively.

"The woman whom you admired is the cause of that, Messer Alighieri," Antonio da Peretola said. "Moreover, do not your very own verses, which I am honored to recall, seem written for her?

You, who know well how to converse of Love,
Oh, listen to my ballad of dismay,
That speaks of a disdainful lady, who
With all her worth has snatched my heart away.

Dante flushed, recognizing the opening lines of one of the ballads he had dedicated to Beatrice. He was outraged that someone would consider it fitting to repeat them in praise of the worldly beauties of a dancer. He was about to respond vehemently, but he restrained himself. Perhaps Antonio had not meant to offend him, but rather to pay him homage.

"Furthermore, even the great Solomon subjugated his wisdom to his desire for the queen of Sheba, and did so without hesitation and without losing any of his glory," Iacopo, the architect, put in slyly. "Perhaps you might find inspiration here to add to your poetic laurels."

"If the rigors of my office, with its many obligations, did not tear me away from the sweetness of conversing about love," Dante replied.

"But our conversations are not only about love," Cecco d'Ascoli said calmly. "The fruit of science is the revelation of that which is concealed from our intellect owing to Nature's jealousy. Inquiring into such mysteries is the true mission of the scholar . . . and the purpose of the studium."

"Yet of all topics of discussion, none appears more worthy than love of being analyzed by the patient toil of our reason," Iacopo insisted. "And you, Messer Alighieri, will agree with that."

They all nodded, ready to add their commentaries to those of the architect, whose view they obviously shared. Augustino in particular seemed on the point of saying something.

"Nothing more momentous than love. Not even a crime?" Dante asked suddenly, forestalling him.

There was silence.

Then Bruno spoke. "A crime?" he asked. "Do you think that a crime can in some way be a subject for learning? How is that possible, given that crime is, on the contrary, the perfect opposite of reason, Messer Durante, as Socrates and Plato maintained?"

Dante let his gaze slide over them. "A crime is an evil act, but not one foreign to the soul. Crime has pursued us since the first act of human insolence, in Eden. And since the first homicide, when Cain led his brother to the pasture." He stopped for a moment, to appraise the effect of his pronouncements. "But I also think that there is no machination of the mind that reason and virtue cannot decipher. Because the murderer leaves the stamp of his own spirit on the victim's body, along with that of his hands.

And the victim calls his killer to him, through some secret, mysterious attraction. Thus the living man and the dead man are a mirror of one another."

"Are you certain of this?" Ammannati said.

"I am. Give me a victim and I will show you the offender, as surely as the great Archimedes could balance the entire world on a single point."

"What do you mean?"

"I mean that every victim chooses his own killer and creates the conditions of the crime, so that the crime is modeled on him, not on the killer. The victim is linked to his killer like the stars to their heaven. Thus in planetary motions, according to Ptolemy, the apparent inversions of the celestial bodies at the edge of the *primum mobile* are realigned in the regular interconnection of their epicycles. Likewise, the assassin's basest machinations remain linked to the erring orbit of his sinful career, precisely calculable by a mind that does not err."

The poet felt the attentive, perplexed gazes of all the men upon him. "Not willing evil, God's power illuminates our minds to enable them to oppose it," he concluded.

They seemed bewildered, and Dante wondered how much of his reasoning they had understood. Very little, he was sure, except perhaps for Cecco, the astronomer. He relaxed in his seat, pleased with the perplexity he saw on their faces. In the end, it was not difficult to deal with these strangers, even if they were of a certain level of culture.

This time it was Augustino who broke the silence. "From the way you speak, Messer Alighieri, one would say that your interest in crime is not limited to theorizing; you must follow its twists and turns out into the streets of the world as well. Now that you are prior, perhaps you will have the opportunity of pursuing one of these crimes of which you have spoken with such fervor," he added in an innocent tone. "Has some such crime already been committed, perhaps?" he continued, smiling, as if venturing an absurd hypothesis.

"That is exactly what has happened. And this crime that I am pursuing is, in turn, dogging you."

At those words, a sudden silence fell. Even the general racket in the tavern grew quieter. Out of the corner of his eye Dante saw that Baldo, the tavern keeper, had moved closer. From that distance he could not possibly have overheard their conversation, yet there was no doubt that he was observing them closely.

"A man has been killed in an atrocious manner in the church that is to be the site of the studium. Master Ambrogio, the mosaicist."

There was no reaction to his words. One by one Dante studied those masklike faces. He would have expected some show of sympathy, of horror. Of surprise, at least. Was that wall of impassivity a living testimony to the imperturbability of sages? Or was it proof of the sages' knowledge of the crime? Those men must already know what had happened. And one of them knew more than the others.

All at once the spell was broken. The faces of those around the table were suddenly animated by the expressions of astonishment and grief that he had expected, while a chorus of exclamations conveyed to their corner the feelings of the rest of the tavern's clientele.

"Ambrogio dead?" Cecco d'Ascoli said at last. "How? And why?" He appeared distressed, but Dante sensed a false note in his emotion.

"The Bargello and his men are groping in the dark," he answered. He waited a moment before going on, continuing to gaze steadily around the table. He was more and more convinced that the men seated there had known about the murder and that there was a purpose behind their pretense of ignorance.

Of course, the idea that those scholars might have been actors in such a terrible crime seemed absurd. Yet, how many times had he experienced the most unpredictable duplicity in men's conduct?

"You have not answered my question, Messer Alighieri. How did the master die?" Cecco asked again.

"Ambrogio was buried alive." Briefly the prior described the scene in the church. "But it is possible that the victim had time to compose his own epicedium, even if only with vague marks," he concluded.

"Marks?"

Dipping a finger into the dregs of his cup, Dante traced on the table the letters he had found scratched on the wall behind the corpse. Suddenly he stopped.

A fragment of the vision induced by the apothecary's mysterious potion had superimposed itself on his recollection of what he had seen in the church. A detail that his mind must have secretly picked up and suggested to him in his dream and that now appeared in the light of certainty.

As he sat, shaken by the discovery, he heard Teofilo's worried voice. "Master, are you ill?"

Instead of replying, he in turn posed a question. "How many of you knew the mosaicist?"

The men exchanged a quick look. Again it was Teofilo who replied. "I think I can speak for all of us, Messer Durante. We all knew the master, and we all honored his greatness."

The apothecary spoke calmly, but the men's expressions showed that the question had unsettled them, above all because of what it might imply.

"You told us about the Bargello's dim conclusions," Teofilo went on. "And yours?"

"At first, not much more discerning, even though my capacity for analysis is certainly greater than that of the unskilled bargellini," the poet replied. Perhaps it was only his impression, but it seemed to him that those words were met with relief. "Until a few seconds ago," he added, and waited another moment. "When the luminous hand of Minerva cleared my mind."

"What do you mean?" Teofilo asked.

"A thing that seems evident to me." With his finger Dante slowly retraced the marks on the table. "Does it not seem to you that when Ambrogio scratched these three brief vertical marks, followed by what must have been the beginning of another, incomplete word, that he must have been trying to write III COELUM, the Third Heaven?"

Again his words were met by silence. "That would be an extraordinary coincidence, would it not, Messer Alighieri?" Augustino said at last, in an offhand tone.

Dante decided to humor them. If they wanted him to reveal his intent, he might as well do so immediately. "I would be offending your intelligence if I thought that none of you had already arrived at the same hypothesis."

"But what is to be drawn from such a hypothesis?" Iacopo asked in his lumbering voice.

Without giving Dante time to respond, Cecco d'Ascoli entered the discussion. "Yes, Messer Alighieri, I, too, believe that the inscription was not accidental, and when you put it before us, I arrived at the same conclusion. But accepting the hypothesis that Ambrogio was invoking the Third Heaven, did he do so to summon punishment upon us or to ask us to avenge him? And, in the former case, did he mean to accuse all of us or only one of us? And in the latter case, against whom should our anger be directed?"

"And if lastly, *tertium datur*, neither of the two cases is accurate?" Bruno interrupted. "If the Third Heaven has been called into play not by the victim but by his killer, and therefore refers to something completely different, to which heaven should the dying man's last gasps be assigned? What do you think, my friends?" the theologian concluded, without addressing anyone in particular.

"And on this rock the little vessel of our genius shatters," Augustino murmured.

Dante paused before speaking, absorbed in thought. The summation outlined by his interlocutors was precise. He went back to studying the faces that were staring at him. Behind that wall of politeness, someone was throwing down the gauntlet to challenge him.

But he was prepared to accept the challenge. "The killer thinks he can get away with the crime by hiding behind this insane riddle. But Florence has placed the sword of justice in my hand, and I will not lay it down until I have cut off his head," he said, emphasizing each word.

Apparently satisfied, they watched him impassively, like sated cats. They reminded Dante of those brokers for the wool guild, whom he had seen many times along the streets of Florence arm in arm with their buyers, and for a moment he was seized by doubt.

HE TOOK his leave. The curfew bell had already rung, but no one around him seemed to care, as if everyone in the tavern enjoyed a safe-conduct.

At the door he ran into the tavern keeper, who looked as if he had been waiting for that moment to approach him. The man seemed anxious to tell him something, yet in the end he only bowed awkwardly and mumbled a few words of farewell. He seemed to be keeping an eye on the members of the Third Heaven as he spoke, and they, in turn, did not appear to miss a single gesture of his.

Dante walked quickly through the streets of the Oltrarno, deserted with the coming of night. Back at San Piero, on the stairway leading to his cell, his strength suddenly failed him. He had to pause halfway up the flight to catch his breath. He fell upon the bed still clothed, stopping only to unstrap his shoes and cover his head with a nightcap.

He thought about everything he had seen and heard. About the church where the murder took place. About the mosaic that Ambrogio had not completed. About his ghastly funeral mask. Was there some relation between the two things? The one illuminated by his art and the other marred by his suffering? And why had the mosaicist been killed in that way, transformed into the same material as his work?

He slipped into sleep, lulled by the clinking of little bronze disks that still echoed in his head.

5

June 17, toward sunrise

RISING FROM his bed was a struggle, and he had to use his hand to screen his eyes from sunlight coming through the window. Dreams and recollections were still muddled in his head. For an instant he was afraid that the flashes he was seeing were some new effects of the apothecary's potion, but the tavern's white wine and acrid air were enough to explain his stupor.

He lay down again, fixing his eyes on the rafters, trying to check his dizziness. The room was swirling around him like Antilia's garments. He squeezed his eyelids tightly, to shut out the piercing rays of light that were assailing his brain, as his nausea gradually diminished. Finally, cautiously, he got up.

He cursed himself for his imprudence. A prior of the Commune of Florence should have conducted himself with greater sobriety, should never have indulged in such debauchery. He hoped his colleagues would never learn of the incident.

He spent over an hour preparing his papers for the first meeting of the Council. He was still busy outlining the *incipit* of his oration in his mind when the report he had requested on the members of the Third Heaven was brought to his door. As he had imagined, the men were all guild masters, and held degrees issued by prestigious universities.

The oldest was the friar, Bruno Ammannati. Following in the footsteps of Saint Francis, founder of his order, he had spent many years in Palestine, trying to convert the infidels. The youngest was Iacopo Torriti, the architect. All of the men had come to Florence at different times during the past year and had begun teaching individually, each one with his own group of students, after being confirmed as instructors by the Commune and obtaining a teaching license. They were in contact with the *scholae* of Santa Croce and Santa Maria Novella, but were not dependent on them in any way. Even Teofilo Sprovieri, who for the most part practiced his skills in his shop, occasionally gave lectures on pharmacology at the convent of Santa Maddalena.

As for the captain, Veniero Marin, though it was noted that he frequently mixed with the others, he did not appear to have a practice of his own. The members' sources of income were not known, but it was suspected that they resorted to loans and usury. Each member's name was followed by the street where he usually resided.

"Are you sure of this?" Dante asked the official standing before him, pointing to a sentence on the page.

"Yes, prior. They all came here from Rome."

"Notable travelers, one would say. And the dancer? Why is there nothing about her?"

"But . . . she is not part of the studium. Therefore I did not think you would be interested . . ."

It seemed to Dante that the man's words held an innuendo. "Everything is of interest to the Commune's authority," he retorted coldly. "Justice must keep watch over every questionable individual."

The man, intimidated by the prior's inquisitorial tone, stammered. "We . . . we do not know much about her. It appears that she comes from abroad. The watch guard at Porta al Prato recorded her entry . . . sixty days ago. She declared her status as free, and it does not . . ."

"What?"

"It does not appear that she practices prostitution."

"And where does she live? I don't see that indicated."

"In the tavern . . . I imagine. She is not subject to any restrictions on her movements, although her questionable reputation is well known to the district guard, who keeps an eye on her," the official said, as if wanting to excuse himself for that omission. He seemed relieved when the poet dismissed him with a gesture.

DANTE PLACED the report in the cabinet, intending to study the information more closely later. Then he set out for the council chamber. Walking along the loggia, he breathed in the fresh morning air, sniffing the scent of wood smoke and baking bread. He struggled to put the images of the night out of his mind, to concentrate on the speech that he must give to the Council. He would have to be persuasive, if his hopes of a political career were not to be frustrated.

He would begin with a celebration of divine liberty, citing Aristotle's *Ethics,* and then his *Politics.* But Antilia's body and Ambrogio's mask insinuated themselves between him and his carefully planned words. And evil ran rampant through his mind.

His feet struck an obstacle that almost knocked him flat on his back. It was a man who lay huddled on the ground, his head partially wound in rags as if to conceal some foul disfigurement. "A coin," he whined, trying to detain the poet.

"A coin, and I will reveal your fortune!"

"What? Again!" Swearing, Dante kicked him away. He knew that ugly mug: he'd seen it many times among the beggars who hung around all day in front of San Piero Scheraggio, the parish church in his district. The man was a former thief; his fingers had been cut off.

"Go away, or I'll have you thrown in the Stinche!"

"Your fortune, sir, for a coin!" he heard the beggar cry, his tone insolent now as he moved off.

As if a few coins would really be enough. . . . They were all eager to predict his future in that city, he told himself, shrugging.

THE COUNCIL'S meetings were held in the old refectory of the convent. When he made his entrance the other five members were already in the room, seated around a long table. They were busy studying a document and talking animatedly.

Seeing him enter, the prior of the Wool Guild cleared his throat. Dante had the impression that he wanted to attract the others' attention, to warn them of his presence. Then he spoke. "Here before us is a papal bull, containing His Holiness Pope Boniface's requests. The papal nuncio himself, through a representative, has submitted it to the Council." He began to quote: "Most noble city of *Florentia*, most beloved of our heart, pupil of our eyes and pearl of our realm . . ."

Dante was irritated by the delicate way they were passing the bull from hand to hand, as if fearful of touching a parchment that had been touched by the pope. He had promised himself he would resort to persuasion rather than invective, but their timid attitude, their willingness to give in, sparked his ire. When the document reached the man seated next to him Dante tore it away with a brusque gesture and tossed it on the table.

"Get to the point, Messer Lapo. We are all familiar with the subtleties of Caetani's prose. What is the purpose of studying his words as if they were the utterances of a new Evangelist? What does he want?" Dante burst out. He knew nothing as yet about this request, and had the unpleasant sensation that the others had deliberately kept him in the dark.

"The noble Caetani, His Holiness Boniface VIII, asks us for assistance in the form of money and troops for his undertaking in Tuscany."

So that was the point, finally. He was familiar with the issue. The city of Lazio, following the example of Palestrina, had rebelled against its papal vicar and had proclaimed itself a free commune.

"All in all he is requesting only about a hundred crossbowmen and some cavalry . . . perhaps we could comply without stretching our commune's finances too far . . ." one of the priors suggested hesitantly.

"Our finances are not what is at stake, Messer Pietro," Dante replied harshly, "but rather our freedom and that of those who place their trust in Florence. Should we now offer our neck to the yoke of that contemptible simoniac Boniface?"

"Boniface a simoniac? Be careful what you say, Messer Alighieri, lest you come to regret it. And lest you drag all of us along with you in your undoing. The White faction has no interest . . ."

"The White faction is my party also. You seem to forget that. And it is in your interest that I propose to act. But there is also a greater purpose that must guide us: the salvation of our city."

"But we are only talking about a hundred crossbowmen," the prior of the Exchange Guild interjected in a conciliatory tone. "Perhaps we could satisfy Boniface's requests without depleting our own defenses . . ."

"Do not delude yourselves: this number is not small," Dante retorted. "It appears that you are not aware of the neglected state of our troops after years of the most wretched leadership. If at this moment we were to sound the martinella, who do you think would show up at Campo di Marte to fight our battle? A few thousand down-at-the-heel shopkeepers, whose last practice drills took place at least three years ago: ill-disposed, ill-equipped, with no officers, no training, no discipline, and no stomach for battle. Adept at fighting only with their bare hands, stupidly savage in striking the opponent when he is down but incapable of standing up to the attack of a well-organized army. Since the time judicial regulations excluded the nobility's offspring from leading the army, the district units have ended up in the hands of wool-carders, upstarts, sons of bitches . . ."

"Messer Alighieri!" Lapo Salterello got to his feet, shouting. "From the way you speak of them it appears that Florence's citizens are no longer your people! As though you yourself were not the offspring of merchants and money changers, not to mention worse!"

"Blasted scoundrel!" Dante leaped to his feet in turn and lunged for Lapo's neck. He felt hands restraining him, as the others quickly intervened.

He was barely able to scratch the man before he pulled back with a stifled cry.

"You scratch like a cat, Messer Durante!" Lapo whimpered, pressing his bloodied nose.

"I attack like a tiger. I leave the cats to mice like you!"

His heart in turmoil, the poet looked around, enraged, blood throbbing in his temples. Slowly he began to calm down, his eyes still fixed on Lapo. "Yes . . . perhaps it is best that we resume our task." He picked up the parchment again, his fingers still trembling. "You said that we are only talking about a hundred crossbowmen. But our troops who bear the crossbow are the only real military body in Florence. To assign them to Boniface would mean dismantling the backbone of our defense. It would also mean exposing our men to the corrupting influence of Caetani: he could buy them, then return them to us, serpents ready to bite our hand at his command. Or else keep them outright, forcing us to look for others. Think what a heap of florins we would have to draw from our funds to hire mercenaries from Genoa."

This observation made an impression. Even Lapo Salterello, though still scowling at him, seemed to be considering his words.

"Perhaps it would be best to reflect some more. We can stall for time," Messer Pietro murmured.

It was a start, Dante told himself. At least he had been able to sow a seed of doubt. He knew that he had struck the right note; he hadn't had to resort to Plato and Aristotle. How much more sonorous was the voice of gold than those of virtue and reason!

"Yes, we can tell the pope that we will provide him with the crossbowmen as soon as we have finished reinforcing the new walls," Messer Duccio added, sounding relieved. Released from the anguish of having to make a decision, everyone appeared more serene.

"Have you heard the news about Porta al Prato?" Lapo asked. "It seems that a crowd of lepers was seen approaching from the north, headed toward Rome. They are hoping that Boniface's Jubilee will cleanse them of their sores. Who knows how many of them are impostors and agitators. The prior of Calimala should give the order to reinforce the guard, to prevent them from coming into the city."

"They should all be put to death," Messer Pietro said harshly. Beneath his fierce tone fear was audible. "Unfortunately, they are covered by the Church's dispensation."

"Do you know what they are saying in Padua, where the quarantine ward was emptied? That it was the Ghibellines, acting through several mercenary friars, who spread the word among those forlorn vagrants that they would find the cure for their illness in Rome. They want to use this foul mob against enemy cities."

"And we have to treat those cursed hordes as well. An underground vault is already prepared for them at Maggiore Hospital, and it might not be sufficient. The lepers atone for their sins through the disease that devours them."

Dante was thinking of other matters. The news of an army of lepers seemed to him to be a tale. But the last assertion struck him. It was a banal idea, product of an obtuse mind, yet it touched on a point that he had dwelled upon at length during the course of his studies in moral philosophy.

"Do you really think that illness is a punishment for not acting virtuously?" he asked, speaking mainly to himself. "And if so, what wrongdoing was punished by the agonizing death of the master mosaicist at Saint Jude?"

An embarrassed silence fell in the room. Not expecting a reply, Dante went on. "I have learned that a *studium generale* is about to open in Florence. A faculty of arts like that in far-off Paris. And at the instigation of Boniface, no less. Did you know anything about it?"

"Nothing," Messer Pietro replied. The others also shook their heads. "But in any case, it is the Church's affair. The Commune does not finance that type of school, but only schools for those assigned to workshops. Still, it is a good thing that a *universitas* is finally springing up in Florence. That way our fellow townsmen will no longer have to bankrupt themselves to send their children to Padua or Bologna. Or to that den of heretics, Paris."

Dante threw him a sidelong glance. He had studied in Paris as a young man. And, moreover, at the Faculty of Arts, the school to which the city owed its renown for free inquiry. What did the bumpkin mean by his allusion?

He got up abruptly, gathering his papers. He had had enough of that company.

―――――

As HE LEFT the Priors' Palazzo, he saw a man staring up at him from the bottom of the stairs. Despite the heat, the man was wearing a tunic of white wool, and his face was covered by a veil to protect it from the fierce heat of the sun, in keeping with the custom of desert peoples. As he approached, he raised the veil, revealing his face. It was one of the members of the Third Heaven: Augustino di Menico, the natural philosopher.

He approached the poet with an affable smile—and an icy gaze that belied it and put Dante on his guard.

"Greetings, Messer Alighieri. I came here to the piazza to meet my students when I saw you and wondered if you would like to come along with me. It is rare in this city to be able to enjoy the learned conversation of a fellow philosopher of your stature. One who has studied with the Parisian masters, what's more."

It seemed they were all privy to his studies. "Perhaps you have formed too lofty an opinion of those masters," Dante replied curtly.

They had moved away from the stairs in the direction of the loggia of Orsammichele, where the cloth merchants' carts stopped to load before setting off for the markets in the North. The dung left by the dozens of horses that filed through that narrow passageway had fermented in the atrocious heat, attracting swarms of flies that circled crazily. Despite the torrid sun, the street teemed with men, their faces, like Augustino's, protected by veils.

"It was not to discuss the founders of our knowledge that I claimed your attention, Messer Alighieri," Augustino went on, waving away a cloud of insects, "but, rather, to learn more about your thinking concerning the crime that you are called upon to judge."

Dante did not answer at once. He wondered about the reason for this great interest. Perhaps simple curiosity, perhaps a sense of guilt. He decided to humor him. "There was little to be seen in the church. Nothing more than what I reported."

"Really?" Augustino seemed disappointed. "I thought your superior intellect might have glimpsed a light where our insufficiency would have groped in darkness. But perhaps my opinion has been influenced by what I have heard said about you."

Dante clenched his teeth. He glanced away, as if interested in the people around them. "However, I have an idea about the little I learned there," he said turning back and looking hard at Augustino.

"Which is . . . ?"

"That the members of the Third Heaven already knew many of the same facts—perhaps all of them."

Augustino paused before responding. "I imagine that you examined the mosaic the master was working on with great care," he said.

Dante brushed away a fly that had settled on his cheek. "Did you see it, too?"

"The colossus? Yes, once, shortly after Ambrogio had begun working on it." Augustino did not add anything further, but waited for the poet to resume the conversation.

"It would seem to be a sacred representation of Nebuchadnezzar's dream," Dante said cautiously. He did not mention any details of the work, nor the fact that more than half of the wall remained incomplete. "It is a symbol that is all too transparent," he concluded.

"The work was not merely the translation of that episode into a play of line and color. You are missing the secret meaning that inspires it. Behind it lies a more complex idea, one that the Comacine master was attempting to render visible through his art."

"So, then, you also believe that he was killed for this reason?"

"Is it not so?"

Dante shrugged. Augustino waited. "I think it is so . . . of course. A murder may be done to avenge a past action, or to prevent a future one. In the latter case, therefore, to eliminate the *proprium,* the victim's most profound identity. And what more than his work embodies an artist's *proprium*?"

They were approaching the arcade of the market. The philosopher stopped and bent down toward one of the bronze tubes of a fountain shaped like a wolf's head. Dante also took a sip of the tepid water. He felt the burning thirst of his fever rekindling.

"I think you are right," Augustino said. "Perhaps Ambrogio was wrong to want to modify the plan."

The prior wiped his lips on his sleeve. "Was the theme of the work not determined by the consigner and therefore, ultimately, by those of you who make up the studium?"

Augustino again gave him a little smile. He seemed to want to ration out his information, to maintain his advantage. "That's right. But originally our idea was quite different. I saw the charcoal sketch on the wall, drawn by a pupil of Cimabue: a celebration of plants and animals, an *arbor vitae* in the style of the magnificent one in the basilica of Otranto, in the southern kingdom of Naples."

"So what happened then?"

"The master requested and was given permission to replace the theme with another of his choosing. He refused to measure his skills against such a grand work. Or, at least, that was the reason he gave."

"And you did not believe it?"

"I have the impression that master Ambrogio was not a man who would refuse to test his skill against anyone in his craft. On the contrary, his opinion of his abilities was so lofty as to verge on blasphemy. He said that he would make Saint Jude the center of the world. No, I think the reason for his decision was something else."

Dante reflected in silence. Why would that marginal passage of Holy Scripture have so impressed the mosaicist that he would change his design and risk coming into conflict with his consigners? And above all, if the opinion that Augustino had expressed about him was correct, why would he have passed up an opportunity to measure his skills against one of the greatest works of Christianity? What had been the significance of that colossus?

Only Ambrogio could have answered that, he thought, and Augustino seemed to read his thoughts. "It would be necessary to question the deceased," he said suddenly. "If only that were possible."

"And do you think it might be?"

The philosopher did not answer: he seemed reluctant to venture rashly down that path. But he had not lost the desire to challenge the poet. "It would seem impossible, but are you not attempting to interrogate his spirit, at least?"

"The dead are interrogated through patient analysis, Messer Augustino, by gathering and carefully examining the traces their passage has left in our world. Assisted by the light of reason, which, if properly guided by virtue and knowledge, never errs."

"I think the concept is correct. But be careful, for there are others who secretly travel the road that leads to conversing with the dead, for different reasons. And encountering them can be a mortal danger. There are those who believe that it is simpler to evoke the defunct through thaumaturgical power, snatching them from the realms in which they dwell."

"Those realms are the realm of God. Are you perhaps speaking of necromancy? Of black magic?"

Augustino lifted his shoulders and said nothing.

"Do you think that the spirits of the dead can be forced to speak to the living? And do you consider yourself capable of forcing them, or believe that someone known to you is?" Dante pursued.

Augustino had turned pale. He was staring past the poet's shoulder as if he saw a ghost. Dante threw a quick look behind him, to see if someone was spying on them. But the piazza was strangely empty, like a city stricken by some great calamity. Perhaps the realm of the dead resembled that grimy stone pavement.

"Watch what you say. We are within the Church's territory here," Augustino said then. He pointed to a procession of monks who had appeared at the corner of Via degli Acciaiuoli.

"So there are no necromancers in the Church's territory?" Dante pressed him.

"More than anywhere else, perhaps."

"Even in the lodgings of men of the cloth?"

"Brother Francis counted more devils in the consistory than among the infernal legions."

"In the Third Heaven as well?"

Augustino did not answer. He pulled his garment around him as a gust of wind suddenly swept through the piazza, stirring up a cloud of dust. He lowered his veil over his eyes. "*Tibi benedicat Dominus,* brother. We shall resume our conversation when you return to the Third Heaven."

THE PHILOSOPHER hurried off, after taking his leave from Dante with a quick nod. The poet remained there thinking over Augustino's words, his obscure allusions, and the accusation of arrogance he had directed against the dead man.

He realized that he himself knew very little about Ambrogio, apart from the fact that he had been a great artist. Had anyone known much more than that? The most likely person would be a fellow artist. The tall figure and equine features of Iacopo Torriti came to his mind. Torriti was the only one who had been acquainted with the Comacine master before his arrival in Florence.

Or at least, the only one who admitted it.

HE KNEW the architect would be at the huge construction site of the new cathedral, working in front of the baptistery. Dante covered Via dei Calzaiuoli at a rapid pace, heading for the piazza of San Giovanni. At that hour the street was cluttered with vendors' stalls, a sea of colorful tents with only a narrow passageway left through the center.

Before the doors of the baptistery the earth had been leveled for more than two hundred yards, as far back as the ancient circle of Roman walls. Massive supporting structures rose from this ground, divided into three naves marked by huge pillars. The perimeter walls had already been erected up to the level of the windows; toward the transept, the structure of the apse, with its three niches, was nearly complete. There the great Arnolfo had already positioned pillars to support the cupola that would crown Christendom's greatest church.

The poet entered the building site, picking his way around the wheelbarrows and trying to avoid all the tackles that seemed to orbit overhead like the trajectories of an armillary sphere gone mad. Inside the dream of the future cupola, at the geometric center of the great brick octagon, were long tables resting on trestles. From a distance he recognized the architect, bent over a series of drawings.

Dante came up behind him. He remained silent for a moment, admiring the skill with which Iacopo sketched the detail of an arch with a few chalk marks while explaining it to the master mason at his side. The perfect circle of sky framed by the roofless drum seemed like God's vigilant eye overhead, intently watching what was being built in His name so that Babylon's arrogance would not be repeated.

The architect turned his head. For a moment he seemed annoyed to see Dante there, then his face lit up in a faint smile and he stood up. "Messer Alighieri, it is an honor to welcome a prior of the City to our humble building site. I am sorry that Master Arnolfo is not here today to confer upon you the distinction that you merit. I imagine that you have come to inspect the status of the works."

"Actually, I was looking for you, Messer Iacopo. Although seeing the impressive grandeur of your work," Dante added, raising his eyes skyward, "is certainly a singular inducement to publicly sing the praises of Arnolfo and you who assist him."

"You were looking for me?" Iacopo said, ignoring this encomium. He seemed concerned.

"Yes. I want to know more about the master who was killed. I believe that of all the members of the studium, you must be the one who knew him best."

Iacopo raised his eyebrows. "Of course, Master Ambrogio and I practiced the same trade. His association, the Comacine Guild, is not much inclined to fraternize with nonmembers. During the time we worked at the building site in Rome, we often came together. But we were not friends, if that is what you want to know. Then, too, it was not for very long. One day he departed unexpectedly, suspending his work. I did not expect to see him again in Florence, when I came here with Arnolfo."

Dante looked at him. "What do you think of his art, Messer Iacopo? Was he really the best mosaicist in Italy?"

Iacopo paused, then said, "Ambrogio was certainly a master of his craft. Boniface himself charged him with decorating the walls of his sepulchral chapel, in Saint Peter's," he said curtly.

"But you don't approve of his style, is that right?"

"Times change, Messer Durante. A new style has come down, from France. Master Ambrogio was still bound by the old rules, by the persistent repetition of established formal elements. A style that is perhaps suited to the majesty of emperors, but not very fitting for our time, marked by the rise of common folk. Besides, you have seen his mosaic in the church. You must have noticed the rigidity of his line . . ."

"The unfinished mosaic . . . I was told that the original design followed a different theme, a representation of the tree of life, an *arbor vitae,* as an allegory of Creation. Do you know why the master changed his mind?"

"No. And I am not even sure that he ever began working on that subject. Early on, after having assumed the task, he let quite a few days go by without starting anything, while he wandered around the church, absorbed in deep meditation."

"As if he were unsure about what to depict?"

"Yes. Or, rather . . ." The architect broke off with an embarrassed look, as if he regretted having broached the topic.

"Or, rather?"

"As if he were afraid."

"Of what?"

"I don't know. But I think it was something that followed him here—from Rome."

Dante reflected on those words. "And do you think this thing, whatever it was, was to be the subject of his depiction?" he asked finally. "What he wanted to reveal in his work?"

Iacopo cast a nervous glance around him and seemed suddenly anxious to get back to his work.

"You have an idea of what it might be, have you not?" the poet persisted. When Iacopo did not reply, he grabbed him roughly by the shoulder. "Is it not so? Do not forget that the Commune has the power to force those who are reluctant to speak."

"There was a rumor going around in Saint Paul's basilica, where we worked . . . a rumor about the death of Celestine V . . . the hermit pope," Iacopo said nervously.

"Of course, everyone has heard it. Murdered on Boniface's orders."

The architect appeared genuinely astonished. "No, Messer Durante. Certainly not by his orders. In Rome it was whispered that Boniface had reacted to the news with a fit of violent rage, and that for three days he railed against Death for having snatched away his quarry."

"Quarry?" Dante exclaimed, taken aback.

"Some secret knowledge that the old pope had acquired and taken with him to the grave."

Dante was not convinced. This had to be one of the numerous tales that circulated within Boniface's corrupt court, spread by his followers to protect the pope from discredit. "What did they say it was?"

"They didn't. Perhaps Ambrogio knew something. And perhaps he was not the only one."

Dante tried to make some sense out of what he had just heard. "Not the only one? Who are you referring to?"

"During the course of our work, several members of the Curia were also lodged in the convent attached to the basilica of Saint Paul. A group of jurists who were working on a particular assignment on behalf of Boniface . . ."

A name crossed the prior's mind. "One of them was Antonio da Peretola, the jurisconsult of the Third Heaven? Is that what you mean to say?"

Iacopo nodded. "Perhaps he can be of greater use to you, Messer Durante. He was certainly closer than I to the source of those rumors."

Dante stepped aside to make way for a load of bricks that was being hoisted up by a movable arm connected to a counterweight. His attention was captured by the apparatus: one of Archimedes' simple levers, but constructed on a gigantic scale. A Comacine specialty.

"You have a number of these here, from what I see."

"That is true. They are the very lifeblood of vast construction projects."

The poet looked around. The only thing that remained of the old church of Santa Reparata was the outline of the perimeter walls, and they would be hidden beneath the new floor. He looked up, imagining what the structure would be like once it was completed. A temple worthy of giants erected for such dwarfs . . .

Iacopo had followed his gaze. "When it is covered, at the cross formed by the pillars, it will be Christendom's largest church. Arnolfo's masterpiece. Thus, through these walls, Florence's name will spread all over the world."

"Florence's name is well-known by this time, even in hell, Messer Iacopo," Dante muttered. "There is the city that rises upward, but there is also another that burrows into the depths, almost as if wanting to dig a passageway to Lucifer."

The other, surprised, stared at him in silence.

ANTONIO DA PERETOLA, the man with the face of a fox, was lodging at San Marco, in the convent's guest quarters. Perhaps by that hour he would have already returned from his lecturing at the Franciscan *schola,* the prior hoped.

In fact the man was there, busy making notes in a thick manuscript. He seemed engrossed in a laborious comparison of several volumes that lay open around him.

When he saw Dante he broke off immediately, closing the manuscript on which he was working.

"Good afternoon, Messer Antonio," Dante greeted him. "And I apologize if my coming has interrupted your work," he added.

Peretola, having risen from his seat, inclined his head in greeting. "Nothing that cannot be put off till later," he said, motioning the visitor to a bench from which he hastily cleared off a heap of parchments.

"Moreover, the Commune's pursuit of justice at times imposes uncivil ways, for which I hope you will excuse me," the poet continued, settling himself comfortably.

"On the contrary, it is a pleasure to see you, Messer Durante. Your renown has reached as far as Rome. Your love poems flow even from the mouths of those who, like myself, reserve their attention for other areas of the spirit. And apart from our pleasant meeting in the Third Heaven, I am pleased to speak with you . . .'For it is possible to recognize, simply by talking, if a man is wise . . .'"

Another citation of one of his poems. It seemed that the members of the studium were all truly his admirers.

The poet flushed, seized by a burst of pride, and was about to recite the rest of the sonnet, but he restrained himself. Something in the other man's eyes warned him not to lower his guard. Inside the muzzle of this fox lurked the teeth of a wolf. So he merely offered brief thanks. "I am here to ask for your help in my investigation, Messer Antonio," he then said. "I have heard that you lived in Rome before coming to Florence, in the convent adjoining the basilica of Saint Paul Outside the Walls."

"That is correct. It was there that I was taken in, having just returned from overseas."

"You, too, were in the Holy Land?" Dante asked, surprised.

"I thought you knew that. I was among the retinue of the Cardinal of Liège, the last apostolic nuncio in St. John of Acre. I fled with him when the city fell, and when I reached Italy, Pope Boniface kindly chose to make use of what little learning I have for the glory of the Church."

"Did you know Ambrogio, during your stay in Rome?"

"The Comacine master? Yes, but we were not on familiar terms. He was engaged in some work in the basilica; I don't know what. I think I met him occasionally, taking a walk in the cloister."

He spoke the last sentence casually, as if he wanted to stress the superficiality of their acquaintance. Yet he was taut as a crossbow string, and, Dante thought, careful to gauge each word. Perhaps this was simply his jurist's mentality, alert in any case to nuances and subtleties. Or perhaps it was the defensiveness of someone with something particular to hide.

Dante decided to tackle the subject head-on. "Could the master have learned something dangerous during the course of his work in Rome?"

"I have no idea. Something for which he might have been killed?" Antonio's foxlike face showed genuine surprise.

"Something that might have been revealed in his work here in Florence?"

"The convent of Saint Paul is part of the benefices of the Templar commendam of Rome. At the time it housed a commission of jurists, of which I was a member, charged by Boniface to prepare the doctrinal support for a bull that he is planning to issue. There was nothing that might justify a murder."

"A bull? On what subject?" Dante asked, paying greater attention. Suddenly the reason for which he had come seemed of secondary importance.

"The supremacy of spiritual power over temporal power. Better yet, the assumption of the latter by the former."

"In a word, a legal justification for Caetani's tyranny?"

Antonio looked him in the eye. "You do not sympathize with Boniface's just claim of primacy over the Empire? And yet you are of the Guelph party . . ."

Dante did not reply. Instead, he pointed to the closed manuscript. "Is that where your supporting arguments are assembled?"

"Yes. I was the commission's secretary, and I have all the proceedings and transcriptions. Based on those, I am preparing the text of the bull. God has granted mankind a Sun, the Throne of Peter, to govern and illuminate the territories of the Empire. *Unam Sanctam:* this is to be the Church's destiny, and this is written in my documents," the jurist declared proudly, as if he harbored no doubt whatsoever about the excellence of the resolution he supported.

"Yet men's actions, illuminated by God, have placed a second Sun, a temporal one, side by side with the spiritual Sun, in the person of the Holy Roman Emperor. You seem to forget that."

"Your theory, Messer Alighieri, equates the brilliance of the Sun created by God to a light that, though strong, is lit by men. And this is an assertion that is . . ." He seemed unable to find the right word.

"Foolish, perhaps?" Dante jeered.

The other shrugged. "No, not foolish. Perverse."

"I will succeed in convincing you of the contrary. But let us get back to Ambrogio's death . . ." the poet resumed. Time was running short. He regretted having given in to his political passion. "Did you know that the first design for his great mosaic was different from the one he was working on?"

"No. Why would he have changed his mind?"

"I was hoping that you would know. I have heard that the reason may have been connected to his stay in Rome. Perhaps something happened during that period, something that you, too, witnessed."

"I was intent upon my research, Messer Alighieri. And you, who are likewise a man of scholarship, know all too well how such activities can isolate and alienate one from the world. But on second thought, there is, in fact, something I can relate to you, with regard to the deceased master. It was rumored that he was once sent away from a church that he was decorating, and that his work there was destroyed, because those who had commissioned him became aware that he had portrayed the apostles with the faces of the imperial family, from Barbarossa to Corradino. But perhaps this was merely gossip."

Dante saw that the jurist was not about to reveal anything further. Possibly because he truly did not know anything more. Or maybe because every fox always keeps an escape route at the back of his den.

He took his leave. Ambrogio's ravaged face kept flashing before his eyes; however, he could not neglect his other duties. Disconsolate, he thought of all the examples of pettiness that he had witnessed in Florentine assemblies: the enthusiasm with which they approved stripping the defeated; their infinite caution when dealing with the arrogance of the great. If only there were a few other men like him in this cursed city . . .

But it was useless to think about it. He shook his head, rubbing his hands across his damp brow. His mind returned to the mosaicist's death.

He would solve that mystery. But he had to return to the church where the crime had taken place. By himself.

On that first visit he had been accompanied by other people, and his vision had been blurred by migraine, his sensations distorted. He had not heard the subdued voice with which places speak to the spirit. Had he also been unable to see? He must have overlooked essential signs and traces.

After the sun set, he would be able to move through the streets more freely. His position as prior of Florence gave him the right to travel about after curfew. Then he would proceed.

6

The same day, after curfew

A T EACH turn of the narrow passageways, Dante stopped to listen for the measured tread of the patrol. But the streets of
the ward were steeped in silence. The only sounds he heard came
from within doors: occasional bursts of laughter, soft cries, whis-
pers wafting from the windows of lower floors.

The noises of concupiscence. His mind recorded every detail.
He would write up a meticulous report for the Commune, urging them to curb such decadence.

A suffocating fog had risen, just as on the previous night. He
felt exhausted by the time he reached the church, and his garments
were limp with sweat. The building was plunged in darkness: a
vague mass barely distinguishable from the shadowy countryside.
Only the bell tower stood out sharply against the hazy aura around
the moon.

He picked his way through the debris in front of the door.
Running his hand along the stones of the wall, he groped his way
in an obscurity barely lightened by the faint glimmer of the moon
coming through the window openings. At least his memory of
the pit in the center of the nave was vivid enough, and he skirted
it without any difficulty.

There might be some torches in the apse, left there by the
bargellini. When he reached the semicircular area in front of

the shadowed mosaic, he took some tinder and a flint from his purse. Beneath the scaffolding was an oil lamp that he hastened to pick up.

He had just begun to strike the flint when a violent shove from behind made him shout out in surprise. Someone, bursting out of the shadows, had collided with him on the run. The flint fell to the ground with a metallic sound and skittered on the stone pavement as he struggled to keep his balance. Quickly his hand flew to the hilt of his dagger, but his mysterious assailant had already disappeared. He remained motionless in the dark, his ears straining to catch some sound.

When he was certain that he was alone, he got down on his knees and began groping for the flint and the lamp, still attentive to the slightest noise. He could feel a slick of spilt oil and hoped there would be enough left in the lantern.

Could the intruder have been a thief? But what was there to steal in a deserted church? Or perhaps someone, like him, had come to inspect the scene of the crime. As he fumbled around in the dark, he had the feeling that there was a second body nearby.

At last he found both lamp and flint, and managed to strike a light. He brought the lamp close to the exact spot where Ambrogio had been killed, and carefully explored the floor; then lifted the small circle of light and began to reexamine the unfinished mosaic. Little by little the flame revealed several details of the colossus, but the figure as a whole did not emerge.

Yet something was different. He noticed a little heap of tiles and some lime dust on the ground, and immediately above them, conspicuous marks on the surface of the design, toward the center, as if someone had tried to obliterate that part of it. But this destructive act must have been interrupted, for the erasure was incomplete. Dante raised the lamp as high as he could, rising up on tiptoe. What at first glance had seemed to him a random web of scratches was in fact a precise design: a pentagram.

The figure of the pentacle. The most powerful thaumaturgical symbol.

The design had been etched forcefully, hurriedly. He looked around. In the center of the nave was a hinged stepladder that had been left open by the restoration workers. He dragged it over to the mosaic and leaned it against the wall, then set the lamp on top of it. Unencumbered, he began to examine the diabolical marks more closely. With his fingers he brushed the grooves cut into the plaster: someone must have repeatedly passed a steel point along the wall—maybe a sword or a dagger. Rising once more on his toes, he was able to reach the highest point of the engraving. Whoever had scored the wall must have been more or less his height.

He had once seen one of those evil signs in a book of magic spells seized in the house of a man suspected of witchcraft. The man had been caught evoking the shades of the dead and had been handed over to the Inquisition, along with all the documents that were found with him. It was said that he had been transported straight to Rome in fetters, in a tumbrel, and no one had ever heard anything more about him.

At that time the poet had held the office of magistrate for the residents of San Piero, and he himself had signed the statement delivering the man to the ecclesiastical authority. But he had seen to it that the documents were held for one night at the public offices, so that he could read the *Grimorio,* the Book of Shadows, for himself, and thereby learn as much as possible about the sorcerer's diabolical art.

The book had been written in a strange language made up of indecipherable signs and numbers—perhaps an arcane tongue spoken by demons. He had understood little of it, other than the impression of total mental confusion, of a depraved reversal of the natural order in the exposition of each theme. Only a few details seemed comprehensible: images of stars and constellations and geometric figures, and among these the pentagram had occupied a position of prominence.

It had fallen to him to interrogate the wizard and he had done so at length, trying to wrest an explanation from him. He had ordered him released from the cords with which the bargellini had begun to dislocate his joints, but once free, the man produced an unintelligible singsong, a demonic invocation accompanied by a strange dance. Dante had struck him violently in the face when he realized that the dancer was drawing a boundary around himself, painted with the blood from his lacerated feet, a magic circle that shut him off in his depravity.

"You strike me because I am in your hands," the prisoner murmured then, repressing a grimace of pain. "But if you were in mine I would open your eyes to the truth, instead of closing them by fire as you are doing to me."

"If I were in your hands it would mean that the world was upside-down, and that the Antichrist's legion was controlling the earth," the poet replied sharply.

"And yet that legion carries with it the secret of good and evil, the fruit that makes us similar to God. Come, enter the legion whose name is the name of my master." As he continued speaking words mixed with bloody drool, the man leaned toward him. "Bring your ear close to my mouth. I will reveal to you the word that moves stones and throws open the door to the realm of the dead."

His eyes had glittered in the dim light of the underground dungeon. Was it the reflection of the torch set into the wall? Or a flash of the madness that had taken possession of him?

Dante stepped back, horrified, putting his hands over his ears as the man, leering hideously, went on murmuring.

For years he had reproached himself for that act of cowardice. He had not had the courage then to put his faith to the test. And now he saw the pentagram again.

So it was true that rites of necromancy were being practiced in Florence, under the unseeing eyes of its government. But why had the symbol been drawn on the wall, contaminating the mosaic's biblical allegory, rather than on the ground, where, it was said, sorcerers traced it for their rituals?

Again he examined the mosaic closely. The engraving had marred the left leg of the colossus. The tiles that lay in that little heap of lime dust were terra-cotta.

Something glittered among the fragments. Dante picked it up. A dagger with a short blade that he did not recall ever having seen in Tuscany. It resembled in miniature the billhook that peasants from his native countryside used for cutting and pruning: good for grafting a vine, but also for resolving a question of honor without witnesses, should the need arise.

There was something engraved on the horn handle. The poet held the weapon up to the lantern. It was a cross. The cross of the Templars.

He looked around uneasily. No, there was no reason to think his assailant was a thief. Only now did he realize that he had not heard the man's footsteps moving toward the church exit. Perhaps he was still there, hiding and ready to strike. He hoisted the lantern as high as he could, but its dim light revealed only a forest of dark shadows. The place appeared deserted.

And yet he was certain that the man had never reached the door. The dark pit of the collapsed vault yawned in front of him. Maybe there was a way to descend into the abyss, or maybe the crypt itself had a secret exit. Cautiously he approached the brink of the pit, keeping the lantern raised over his head.

For the first time, he examined the rubble closely. A pile of debris could be seen beyond the edge, fragments of stone and ashlar, similar to rough-hewn steps. He ventured closer, to determine whether someone might have passed through there. To his surprise he discovered that it was not the remains of the floor, but the top of a stairway that descended into darkness below. Clutching the dagger in his fist, he placed his foot on the first step.

The flight wound down in a spiral along the tufa walls of a vast circular excavation. This excavation narrowed as the stairs descended, forming a dark funnel, as if an appalling beast had forcibly burrowed into the damp earth, seeking a lair in which to escape the light.

He moved with caution, careful to keep his shoulder to the wall, listening to the echo of his own footfalls, amplified by the bizarre dimensions of the place. He felt that he was surrounded by a moving crowd, a clamor of voices that chased one another into the depths. In the midst of that confusion, he thought he could make out the sound of water.

From a fissure in the wall, a small underground stream flowed across the steps and then down into the void. After a moment's hesitation, Dante leaped over the muddy little rivulet, praying that the steps would not give way under his weight. He felt he was crossing an implicit boundary, as if the little stream had been a warning not to go any further. The lantern flickered as he landed, illuminating the descent more clearly.

The sides of the pit were no longer solid rock. Dozens of loculi of varying dimensions pitted its surface, a horrific honeycomb filled with human remains. The lamplight, fanning out over these recesses, seemed to bring defunct limbs within them to life.

Empty eye sockets followed the poet, and skeletal hands reached out from the burial niches, as if an entire infernal legion had been awaiting him there.

He felt his knees give way.

This must be an ancient burial ground. He went down a few more steps, fear tightening his throat. Then he paused, trying to overcome a shortness of breath that had become unbearable. A yellowish haze rose from the earth beneath his feet. All of summer's torrid heat seemed to have stagnated in that place.

He forced himself to overcome his fear with reason. The figure that had collided with him in the nave had been a living being: the fact that he had fled immediately afterward was proof of it.

On his first visit, when he had nearly fallen headlong into this abyss, he had thought that the crypt might be an ancient Roman cistern for collecting water. But Christians must have later transformed it into one of their catacombs outside the walls, far removed from pagan eyes.

After the Church of Saint Jude had been built on the older structure's foundations, this burial ground must have lain forgotten, until the vault collapsed, opening up that dreadful maw once again.

Or perhaps the tomb was one of those that the Etruscans had scattered throughout their ancient realm. Enormous examples had been found in the region of Maremma. In any case, it was the work of men, not demons.

Still, if the inferno had a form, Dante thought, it could not be much different from this.

He resumed his descent, reassured by the light of reason. Even the air seemed to have cleared somewhat, as if a faint ventilation welled up from below.

———

THE STAIRCASE came to an end against a blind arch, closed off by a brick wall. Someone, at some time, must have decided to block off this path to the bowels of the earth, perhaps to prevent explorations such as his from going any further. Or, perhaps, to imprison forces that might otherwise run rampant over the Earth.

The bottom of the crypt was a circle at least ten yards in diameter. Its floor consisted of irregular slabs of basalt, eroded by time; water trickling from above had collected in a well in the center of it. On the last few steps someone had left numerous candle stubs. He picked one up. It had been lit recently: the wax was still pliable and gave off a faint aroma.

Fear of his unknown assailant seized him once again. It was not possible for someone to have escaped through there. He raised the lamp again, looking around with greater attention. The lamp's flame continued to flicker. Cautiously he moved toward the source of the draft of air.

He examined the wall more closely. It was imposing, constructed of irregular blocks of stone, evidently the remains of the older building's foundation. There was an area of darker shadow at one point. It was a niche, a passageway just large enough for a man to pass through. He went closer, holding his lamp to the opening, and saw that the narrow passage led into a more spacious cavity, defined by regular walls.

Although he could not judge its extent exactly, he was certain that this space was larger than the one he had just left. As his light gradually picked out new details, the structure's plan became clearer. He was in an underground gallery dug out of the rock, at least four yards wide and enclosed by a barrel vault. At various points the vault had been reinforced by pillars and brick arches. He could feel a viscous sludge beneath his feet; from it came a strong odor of putrefaction. It must be clay from the banks of the Arno; in winter, the swollen river must rise and fill the gallery. Now, during the summer, the gallery was dry, the passage open.

He continued his examination, and marveled at what he saw. This was an impressive work, worthy of the skills of its ancient builders. And now it was part of the realm of evil. How many of those subterranean structures were there, in the Commune's territory? Beneath how many churches, beneath how many convents did similar excavations extend?

The candles in the crypt were evidence of a disquieting habitation, of rituals so ignoble that they could not be performed in the light of day. Had the Comacine master himself taken part in those rites?

Dante took another step or two. He was certain that the mysterious visitor had fled through that passage, but it was too late to think about pursuit. He was about to turn back when he detected movement in front of him. Along the walls and against the pillars of the arches he had noticed shapeless masses, lying like heaps of rags. Now they were slowly rising from the ground.

He leaned against the wall, horrified.

It was thus he had always imagined the reawakening of the army of the dead, on Judgment Day. But this resurrection had something dubious about it, as if it were a wretched parody. In place of bodies cleansed of their sin, he saw limbs marked by the most horrendous sores, clumsily wrapped in bandages soaked with blood and pus.

He felt his heart stop. The horde of foul lepers was not on its way to Florence, as they feared at San Piero, but had already spread through the bowels of the city.

Summoning all his courage, he moved ahead, threatening the foremost one with his dagger. But the man paid him no heed. He continued to grope toward the prior, ulcerous arms outstretched, his ugly mass of a face scored by a mournful smile.

"Stop, fiend, or it will be the last step you take on this earth!" Dante shouted.

"Messer Alighieri, do you not recognize me?"

That voice stirred something in his memory. Cleaving the air with his blade, to create a steel barrier between himself and that devil, he answered only, "I do not know you."

"But you do, Messer Alighieri. Giannetto of San Piero. Giannetto, the beggar."

The man had now stopped, and stood quietly before him, within the circle of lamplight. He began unwinding the bloody bandages from his head, and Dante slowly lowered his weapon. It was Giannetto, the beggar he had stumbled against in front of the Priors' Palazzo. Giannetto, who had offered to tell his fortune. Meanwhile the other creatures had fallen back, as if their curiosity were exhausted, and were crouching on the ground once more.

"Welcome to the realm of true seekers, Messer Alighieri. Are you, too, seeking a roof for the night?" The man smiled sarcastically, revealing jagged teeth.

The poet had not sheathed his blade. A feeling of rage replaced the horror he'd felt a moment before. His hands were still trembling. He flung himself forward and grabbed the beggar by the neck, violently knocking his head against the wall. It was the man's terrified eyes, rather than his plaintive cry for pity, that stopped him.

He released his hold. The beggar remained slumped against the wall, in pain, trying to catch his breath. Dante, panting himself, rubbed a hand over his eyes, trying to erase what had happened. "Why are you covered in these foul cloths? And those others, perhaps, are . . ."

"Them?" Giannetto retorted, indicating the bodies huddled around them. A few had moved, half-raising their heads, then lain back down again, as if a brawl were not an unusual sight in that place. "I see you have been fooled by the Secret Guild," he went on, getting back on his feet.

"The Secret Guild?"

"That's right. The Guild of the Ciompi, of the lowest specimens. It is not registered anywhere, not even in the list of the Commune's lesser guilds. Yet I assure you that it exists, as you can see. The grandees of Florence live in their palazzi and their towers. But in the streets there is another court, which lives in their shadow. We who subsist on charity need to feel the light of grace close by."

Dante looked around again. For some time Florence had been infested by beggars, who descended upon the city like flies on a horse's carcass. Bogus pilgrims, bogus cripples, bogus victims of deformities, bogus blind men, bogus crusade veterans mixed in with the truly disfigured and truly maimed, true lunatics and true convicts, all united in an army of whiners, fortune-tellers, and miracle proclaimers, men whose only real cause was to stir up trouble.

Yet he had seen worse in the north, as a student in Paris. Those dregs of the human race had formed a league strong enough to actually bargain with the French king for control over entire quarters of the city. Now Florence, too, would plunge headlong into the chaos that was spreading throughout Christendom.

"But you are all afflicted by foul diseases. . . . How is it possible that you are permitted to beg freely, under the eyes of decent citizens?" he asked.

"None of us is really afflicted by the disease he pretends to have. The watch guard knows it, but is content with collecting a handful of coins from us each day to let us beg. Believe me, Messer Alighieri, we thieves are in good company, here in the City of the Florin."

Dante let an instinctive nod of agreement escape him. Really, there wasn't much of a difference between those who hung from the gallows of Florence and the cheering crowd that watched. Perhaps this miserable scoundrel could be useful to him. "Did you see anyone fleeing, a little while ago?" he asked.

"I noticed somebody coming down from the church."

"Who was it? How was he dressed? Did you see his face?"

"No, I am sorry I cannot be of help to you. He was running in the shadows."

"Might one of the others have seen something?"

"No one pays much attention to other people's affairs, here at the Guild. Then, too, it happens frequently that someone comes down from the church. We take no notice of it."

Dante grabbed him by the shoulder. "What do you mean? Do the workmen know about this passage?"

"There are no workmen, Prior. I went up there more than once, to assess the . . . situation. The only person I saw at work was the master mosaicist, the one who was killed. Besides that, no work was being done there. I was referring to the others."

"Whom?"

"The men who meet at the bottom of the cistern for the ceremony. I thought you knew that."

"I know nothing about it. What ceremony?"

"More than once, always at night, I have seen a group of men holding a clandestine meeting at the bottom of the catacomb beneath the church. We avoid that side, so as not to disturb the sleep of the dead, but their voices reach us."

"What do they say?"

"It is impossible to understand: jumbled words, arguments. . . . At times they pray."

Dante rubbed his chin, puzzled. The pentagram, drawn in front of the altar to evoke demons . . .

Suddenly he raised his eyes to the beggar. Giannetto's ugly snout poked out of the bandages like a rat's from a hole in the wall. A doubt crossed his mind: this might be a trick, a tale told to mislead his imagination. Maybe the master had been killed by one of the bogus lepers, who had come up from the cavern to rob him. The Comacine masters were renowned through all of Europe, and the amount of their commissions was common knowledge. Not even Giotto had been so richly compensated for his work.

Perhaps Giannetto himself, with his innocuous look and toadying ways, was concealing bloodstained hands inside those bandages. He should arrest them all, he told himself. Well, now he knew where their lair was located. He would return.

"What lies beyond there?" he asked, pointing to the darkness before him.

"The underground passage comes out beside the Arno, near the Ponte Nuovo."

The poet leaned against the wall in silence.

Only after a time did he realize that Giannetto was still staring at him. He seemed to want to tell him something more, something for which he could not find the words.

"I would like to ask a favor of you, Messer Alighieri," he said at last, rubbing the back of his neck, as if to remind him of the blows he had received.

"What is it?"

"You are a writer, are you not? Speak of me, I beg you."

Of course, the prior said to himself. That is what we all want, even the most wretched among us: that the light that illuminates our name not be snuffed out. And if we were able to visit the land of the dead, would this not be their request as well?

"In exchange I will reveal something that will be of use to you," Giannetto went on.

Dante studied him. What could this wretch know that would be useful?

"Something that might save you," the beggar continued, fixing his beady eyes on Dante.

"My fortune? Again?"

"Be prepared to flee. Your party is done for."

The poet pricked up his ears. What could such human wreckage know about Florentine politics?

The other seemed to be aware of his distrust. "One of the soldiers whom I pay for protection has a relative in the pope's army. Boniface is preparing to set forth for our city with the apparent aim of bringing peace, but in reality he means to plunder, and to topple the Commune in favor of the Blacks. For us beggars, any change of fortune among the parties matters little, but for someone like you it could mean life or death. Flee, before it is too late."

He feared the story might be true: it was not difficult to imagine the continual flow of information that a man like Giannetto might gather, living in the streets. Out of the corner of his eye Dante saw two of the crouched figures rise up and head out. He noticed Giannetto's suspicious look as he followed their movements. Before disappearing, one of them turned around. For a moment Dante thought he discerned a familiar face, but he could not place it. "Who are they?" he asked Giannetto.

"Two men I never thought to see here in the Guild."

"Well?"

"I do not know. For some reason they are trying to pass themselves off as two of us. They have fooled the others, but not me."

Dante looked again toward the two tattered figures, but they had already disappeared into the shadows.

7

June 18, morning

D ANTE HAD the Bargello urgently summoned to the Priors'
Palazzo.

The man arrived out of breath and visibly annoyed. Without
his usual armor, he seemed smaller.

"What is so important, Messer Alighieri, that you have to tear
me away from my duties?" he said at once.

The tavern is where your duties call you, you sot, the poet thought,
but said nothing. He turned over in his hands the strange dagger
that he had found in the church. "Are there Templars in Florence?" he asked.

"What?"

"Wake up, Bargello! The Order of the Poor Knights of Christ,
known as Knights of the Temple. White cloaks with conspicuous
crosses. Do you know if there are any in the city?"

Finally the Bargello seemed to understand. He shrugged in-
differently. "Oh, that so-called sect. So powerful, and then they
lost the Holy Land, pretending they wanted to die for the Holy
Sepulchre. They also got rich trading with the Moors. Haughty
and arrogant, greedy as Jews, troublemakers . . . No, the Commune has never allowed them to settle in the city. Besides, we already have enough usurers," he ended with a sardonic grin.

Dante could not help smiling. For the first time he found
himself agreeing with the man. Then a thought made his blood

freeze. Was that scoundrel alluding to the slanderous accusations against his father, Alighiero? He clenched his fists, advancing toward the man. "What do you mean by that?" he shouted.

The captain of the guard quickly drew back. He seemed genuinely surprised by the prior's reaction, as well as frightened. "Nothing more than what I said," he replied hastily. "There are no Templars in the Commune's territories. Their closest commendam is in Aquila; from there they trade with Capitanata and the other territories of the Kingdom of Naples . . ."

"I, too, am aware that no official presence of the order is recorded. What I want to know is whether, in the course of your inspections, you have ever come across signs of their secret presence—perhaps members in disguise."

It was a hopeless question, Dante thought. That man would not notice a herd of unicorns if they trotted under his nose. But he was surprised by the Bargello's response.

"No, not Templars . . . but there is someone, I think, or at least there was. In disguise, as you say."

"What do you mean?"

"It was said, in the past, that among the Franciscans, even those in Florence, there was a faction, a group of advocates for the Empire, that secretly adhered to the Order of the Temple. But no one knows for certain. It was just talk. You would have to get inside the monks' heads. They go at one another's throats, yet nothing gets leaked to the outside. As if Francis and Sister Poverty were still to be found inside the walls of their convents . . ."

He did not know anything more. Dante dismissed him, irritated by his impertinence. He was fed up with that stock of clichés about the friars. Only persons who had frequented them as assiduously as he had could know their perfidies and virtues inside out. Few virtues, innumerable perfidies.

THE BARGELLO had just left when the guard came to inform Dante that a stranger was requesting an audience with him.

"Did he say who he is?"

"No, but he claims he knows you."

The poet felt the muscles of his jaw contract. That infamous Manetto with his demands again. He glanced around nervously, looking for a way out. "Not now. Ask him to come back after the Council session."

"Always running, Messer Durante, aren't you? Like at the rout of Campaldino!" a mocking voice called out.

Dante wheeled around like a dog whose tail has been stepped on, ready to bite. A man with a broad, smiling face stood before him, looking at him, with his fists on his hips. He was dressed in rich traveling clothes, too gaudy and ornate to suit the Commune's regulations against extravagance. Everything about him proclaimed him a foreigner, including the slight Sienese inflection of his voice.

"It has been many years since you have seen my ugly mug, but has love changed me so much that I am no longer recognizable?" the newcomer continued in a playful tone.

Dante looked at him closely, shielding his eyes from the rays of sun coming through the arches of the arcade. "Messer Angiolieri . . . Is it you? But were you not in prison?"

The other burst out laughing. "By dint of much tear-shedding, I persuaded my old man to settle the debt with the usurers, and I have been out for three years now. As for that scoundrel I slashed with my dagger, he withdrew his infamous charges thanks to bribery. But if I had not saddled up in a hurry, I would be in irons again. A roll of the dice betrayed me again, and this time the old man will not listen to excuses. Especially after having read that little sonnet of mine in which I said I wanted to see him burn. I just had time for one last quickie with my Becchina, and here I am a fugitive in your free city . . . in which I hear you have begun a splendid ascent. A prior, no less. You, a poet! In Siena they barely stop short of cutting out our tongues. Is it really true what they say? That a new Athens is rising on the banks of the Arno and that there are more scholars here than in the entire library at Alexandria?"

Dante opened his mouth to speak, then shut it again as the other hurried on enthusiastically.

"Then, too, your taverns . . . truly splendid! Not like the sordid rat holes frequented by my fellow townsmen. I have seen the one run by a certain Baldo, who keeps open house outside the ancient walls. Do you know it? There is gambling there, did you know that? And beautiful women as well."

"Cecco," Dante was finally able to say. "The Commune here is not tolerant toward those who run gambling houses, nor does it smile on dissolute behavior in general. In the city of the Baptist, it is virtue that we seek to establish as the basis of our actions. Be careful not to get yourself in trouble. You do not know what hell is like, if you have never visited our prisons. And as for Campaldino, my formation retreated only a little, and only at the beginning of the day, later returning to the attack and trouncing Arezzo's audacity through the force of our efforts."

"It may be as you say. Perhaps I did not notice that you were not bolting with your Florentines because I was too busy bolting with my Sienese! But why concern ourselves over the miseries of war, when agreeable vistas of peace are opening up to meet our hopes? I read your *Rime* and your imprecations against the beautiful Pietra. So, then, has the wound inflicted on your heart by Beatrice healed? Is it then true, as I have heard it said among poets who write of love, that even Dante Alighieri has returned to the realm of flesh and corruption?"

Dante reddened and did not reply. He looked around, in search of some pretext to take his leave.

The other seemed to notice his embarrassment. He was about to utter a further sarcasm, but then suddenly changed the subject, resuming his more playful manner. "I attended your investiture at San Piero. An impressive ceremony, really. Heavenly power combined with terrestrial authority. I rejoiced over my good fortune: a powerful friendship is the best viaticum for someone in exile."

The prior stiffened. "You, too, were in San Piero, on the ides of June? When did you arrive in the city?"

"Three days ago. Just in time to witness your triumph."

Or to be on hand on the night of the crime, Dante thought, studying the man, who went on jabbering as he glanced around. Part of Piazza Maggiore could be seen from the arcaded roof-terrace, but the view toward the Arno was obstructed by the imposing base of the bell tower that Giotto was erecting.

"It seems that your city is growing by leaps and bounds, Messer Durante, just like the arrogance of you Florentines. But in Siena we have laid the foundations for Christendom's grandest cathedral. From its rooftop we will give you Florentines the fig and on down to the pope in Rome," Cecco said, making an obscene gesture for Dante to see.

Dante could not resist smiling. He could picture Cecco railing from the top of a great bell tower, making that indecent gesture of contempt.

"Speaking of Boniface, he is raising quite a lot of money with this business of the Jubilee. I, too, will end up tagging after that crowd of idlers swarming down through the valley of the Tiber, making the clerics richer. Yes, in ten years this city will be unrecognizable."

"It is already unrecognizable," Dante muttered. "And it is not a change for the better. So you are familiar with Baldo's tavern?"

"Even better, I am lodging there. That one-armed scoundrel demanded a fortune to put me up, but I mentioned your name and he quickly softened. It seems that you are truly an important man in your city. Or at least you are in Baldo's tavern," Cecco added with a sarcastic smile.

He continued studying Dante mockingly, as if he were in some way master of his old friend's fate. The prior felt anger rising inside him. Insufferable versemonger! Cecco had even had the gall to taunt him in his rhymes, with his provincial immorality. Dante suppressed a savage reply. "So, what wind brings you to Florence? Besides the need to avoid the authorities, as you said," he asked instead.

"Can you not guess? There is an assembly of learned men in your city. There will be a fine Jubilee of scholars, with that studium of yours. I came to offer my services and my erudition."

"You speak in riddles, like a Jewish Kabbalist. What could you hope to teach in a faculty of arts? It does not appear that dialectics and rhetoric are wanting in you, but as for making them the subject of disputation . . ."

"And who says that I am preparing to hold forth on those obscure disciplines, Messer Alighieri? In Siena I learned some other lessons that were quite different! *Three women came round my heart* . . . as they did to you. And they illuminated me."

"And who might they have been, in your case?"

"A woman, a tavern, and a pair of dice."

Dante stared at him with an icy gaze that the other endured impassively. "The gender of dice is masculine," he retorted.

"Until it is weighted with lead. Then it becomes feminine and, like a woman, bends to the commands of its master."

"Do you know what I wondered, Cecco, as soon as I saw you?"

"No, what?"

"I wondered what animal you resemble, of all those that the science of physiognomy envisages."

"Have many such animals come your way lately?"

"Many, but not yours."

"And what would that be?"

"A basilisk," the poet said, turning serious.

"But the basilisk does not exist!"

"Nevertheless, it poisons and kills as if it existed, just as slanderous words do."

8

The same day, after dusk

DANTE MADE his way to the scholars' table without hesitation. By this time it was clear that this corner of the tavern was in fact a kind of private area. All the men he had met previously were there, lined up in their seats. They got to their feet, silently returning his greeting. Though they eyed him curiously, no one seemed inclined to be the first to speak.

As always, it was Teofilo Sprovieri who broke the silence. "Here you are again in the Third Heaven, Messer Alighieri. We were hoping that you would do us the honor of returning. We are anxious to hear your conclusions concerning the matter we talked about the other evening," he said, offering Dante the chair next to his own. "If there are any."

Dante thought he perceived a shade of irony in the apothecary's tone. He was about to respond in kind, but was forestalled by Cecco d'Ascoli.

"My friends, why do you ask our welcome guest to dwell on such an unpleasant subject, when luck affords us the privilege of availing ourselves of his views on much more lofty topics of learning? Tell us instead what new literary works you will be undertaking, in the periods of respite from the responsibilities of government."

"I am considering a poem about the bread of knowledge,

which is distributed to whoever wishes it, as in a banquet," Dante replied.

"A banquet?" a voice asked, making him turn around. Cecco Angiolieri had appeared behind him. One would have thought that he had been hiding under the table until that moment, or that he had mimicked the stealthy step of a thief, a trick learned during his repeated visits to prison. "And would it be open to everyone? Not just to scholars?" He looked around, as if to draw the others' attention to what he was about to say. The impudence with which he had approached the table did not seem to bother anyone. On the contrary, Dante thought he saw looks of amusement, as if Cecco's witticisms were well known.

"Do you not think, Messer Alighieri," Cecco went on, after a quick acknowledgment of the company present, "that your table might be reduced to an insufferable bunch of beggars and free-loaders? And what areas of philosophical inquiry will you deal with in your work?" he added, sitting beside Veniero and pouring himself some wine in the Venetian's cup.

"All of them," the prior replied coldly, stressing each word. "Systematically and by subject. From the structure of the cosmos to the secret impulses of the spirit. And I shall end with the most sublime virtue that we have been granted to attain."

"Which?"

"Justice." Dante looked around, his gaze lingering on each of them. They all seemed struck by his last words.

"Of course, justice is cardinal among the virtues," Antonio da Peretola, the jurist, commented. "Your plan, however, brings us back to that gloomy subject that Cecco d'Ascoli was hoping to avoid. How will you deal with the causes of crime?"

"That's right, Messer Alighieri," Bruno Ammannati joined in. "I would like to know that. And what better occasion for discussing it than our mosaicist's death? It is the opinion of many that if a strong personal motive can lead to a crime, an equally strong will can resist committing it. If this is true, then Ambrogio was murdered either by a weakling or for a very powerful motive."

"I think that is so."

"What would you say to the theory that the Comacine master may have been killed by his own guild associates?"

"For what reason?"

"A very strong one, undoubtedly. Pride in their guild, which the victim was aiming to deride. You have seen the mosaic and its five parts composed of materials of decreasing value. I am certain that in that representation Ambrogio wanted to allude to the five greatest mosaicists in Italy." Ammannati turned to the others, as if seeking their approval. "You will recall how he was in the habit of extolling his work by comparing himself with the four men who shared the art's glory with him: Buondelmonte, Martino, Giusto da Imola, and you, Messer Iacopo. Last, but not least, certainly."

Hearing his name spoken, the architect responded with a faint smile, just barely bowing his head in a sign of appreciation. Ammannati, the friar, continued, "He made no secret of the fact that he considered himself superior to the others; at times his words even bordered upon disparagement. I believe that his decision to mix those disparate materials in his portrayal of the ancient colossus—whose body symbolized the totality of the art—was a clear allusion to a hierarchy among the artists."

"It is true," Cecco d'Ascoli confirmed. "I recall quite well how he often unfavorably compared the others' ability to his own. But to think that for that reason . . ."

"You are all familiar with the rigid regulations of the stoneworkers' guild," Ammannati continued. "Each member was very rigorously forbidden to defame any of his fellows, under the most severe penalty. And it would not be the first time that the members of a guild have cruelly punished those who violated its rules. You should know this well, Messer Alighieri, if what they say about the Florentine dyers is true."

Dante nodded. The expedition that the Calimala Guild had organized, even going as far as French territory, to put to death two dyers guilty of having revealed trade secrets was well known throughout Italy. Afterward the news had been circulated as a warning to all the others. Still, a death as horrible as Ambrogio's seemed a disproportionate punishment for mere rivalry.

Nevertheless, the theologian seemed convinced of his hypothesis, which had the advantage, moreover, of diverting any suspicion away from the members of the Third Heaven, with the exception of Iacopo Torriti. Observing the onlookers' faces, it was clear that each of them—except Torriti—would gladly welcome this solution.

"On what facts do you base your hypothesis?" Dante asked warily. Deep down he had his doubts about the validity of the theory, but by encouraging discussion of it he might be able to gather some further clue.

"Consider the way in which the mosaicist was murdered," Ammannati replied. "With the prime material of his craft, quicklime, as if the killer wanted to demonstrate the fact that the cause of the crime should be sought in the victim's art itself."

"But do you really think that rivalry in the guild satisfies the requirement for a very strong motive?" Teofilo joined in, sounding unconvinced.

"You are forgetting the second condition: a weak spirit. Feeling one's own dignity affronted can easily drive a man to crime if he is not staunchly grounded in Christian truth. In some men, moral weakness can be transformed into a weapon, creating an unexpected physical vigor. It is not necessary for the revenge to have been carried out by the entire guild. A single offended man may be responsible for it. Find the name of the man who recognized himself in the terra-cotta tiles and you will have the guilty party."

"Very difficult to do," Antonio da Peretola interjected. "None of those artists has ever been to Florence. Except you, Messer Iacopo. Though your masterly skill excludes you from suspicion, of course," he hastened to add.

From the moment Bruno Ammannati had begun to put forth his idea, Dante had been thinking about the shadowy figures he had glimpsed in the underground chamber. Individuals who had never been seen before, according to Giannetto. It seemed that none of those present was aware of that detail.

Or else they did know, and were trying to point him in that very direction.

"Still, they all worked in Rome, together with the sublime Giotto, to beautify the Urbe for the Jubilee," Bruno persisted. "And the rivalry that exploded here might have originated there. As for the fact that none of them was ever spotted in Florence, what with the bustle of pilgrims and postulants, soldiers and merchants, I think it is totally irrelevant as an argument *adversum*."

"Whom do you think master Ambrogio held in greatest disdain?" the poet asked.

The others avoided answering, exchanging confused glances, as if they hesitated to formulate an aesthetic judgment that could be tantamount to a condemnation.

"Your theory could explain why Rome was depicted. But why not locate the colossus there, if the mosaic has to do with an episode that occurred there? And what city is portrayed at the right-hand side of the work?" the poet went on.

"Perhaps I know its name," Antonio da Peretola murmured, drawing the others' attention. "Damietta." Dante was startled. "Damietta," the other repeated in a more certain tone. "With a great stone gate and four lions. Baldo told me."

"Are you sure it was the tavern keeper who spoke to you about it?"

"Yes, I am certain of it. And besides, who else among us could have knowledge of such a distant land? Unless he has traveled overseas . . ."

The poet glanced around, looking for confirmation of that hypothesis, but no one seemed to have anything to say.

"Would you summon the inn's proprietor to our table?" the prior continued. Toward the back of the tavern, Baldo's head could be seen bobbing among those of his guests like a pumpkin tossing about on the sea.

Veniero, who up until that moment had remained silent, stood up and walked over to the tavern keeper. They chatted for a bit. Dante saw the crusader turn his eyes in their direction more than once, with a bewildered expression. Then the two approached.

Baldo stopped, leaned on the table and looked the poet in the eye defiantly. His one hand, covered with a heavy, green cloth glove, gripped the oak tabletop. "I was told you wish to speak with me, Messere."

His grip on the table seemed to tighten: the man's entire strength was concentrated in his surviving limb, as if nature wanted to compensate him for the loss that men had inflicted on him. But what surprised Dante was the sight of the other arm, what remained of it. From a slit in Baldo's doublet, just below the shoulder joint, the stump emerged like a wing tip, protected by a brass pan, probably part of the tavern's cookware.

"Does my Grail amuse you, Messere?" Baldo asked ironically, bringing the stump close to the poet's face.

"Were you wounded at Damietta?" Dante asked, forcing himself not to look away. He was annoyed by the display. Did the tavern keeper think he could impress him with his miseries? As if he too had not witnessed bones broken and heads rolling in the dust, at Campaldino.

"No, Messere. It was at Acre that death began stalking me. But I have seen Damietta all right, during my travels."

"And is it true that its walls are adorned by a great, white stone gate, crowned by four lions?" Antonio interjected. He seemed to be looking for confirmation of the statement he had made.

"It is as you say, Messere. An enormous gate, as wide as the gate of hell, with four lions topping it, ready to sink their teeth into those who try to enter by force. But they would have done better to put four dragons there, to guard that den of infamy."

The man seemed overcome by violent emotion. Suddenly he began to sing, in an ill-tuned, croaking voice.

> *Per te venit hac tribulatio*
> *O quam pravo ducti consilio*
> *Exierunt Duces in praelio*
> *Damiata tu das exilio*
> *Maledicta fatorum series.*

A startling silence had fallen over the tavern. Dante saw more than one person's eyes begin to grow moist. Everyone, even the tavern's most humble patrons, seemed to be mourning still the tragedy of the crusade. Damietta, flower of the Nile, where Christian forces had experienced a scorching defeat. A martyred city that had been recaptured and lost twice thanks to the crusaders' determination to remain within its walls instead of retreating to a more defensible position.

The massacre of those defenders, left on their own, waiting for reinforcements that never came. The ugliness of the retreat, the responsibilities shirked. The foolish pride of the Templars, who had wanted to join battle alone, certain of their invincibility, their superiority to the troops that had fled. The savagery of the triumphant Moors.

After fifty years, the bitterness of that defeat and its unresolved disputes still poisoned Christianity. Dante remembered that when he was a child, on *Calendimaggio,* the first of May, the people of his city would sing the glories of the Florentine unit that had taken part in that ill-fated mission.

"Did you hear?" Antonio exclaimed, comforted by Baldo's words.

"Yes . . . it could be," the poet admitted. "But in that case, the mosaic—with its fivefold oddity—would appear to depict the abandonment of the city rather than the city itself."

"Perhaps I can help you, gentlemen."

All eyes turned toward Veniero. The captain was seated to one side, apart from the others in the group that pressed around Baldo.

"You have heard the song *O quam pravo ducti consilio,* whose lyrics mislead you with a base implication. The defenders were betrayed. I, too, was overseas. Before I left the navy, I often transported groups of pilgrims on their way to Jerusalem. And often on board it was the fall of Damietta that was criticized and denounced. There were five protagonists involved in this tragedy: the French, the Lombards, the Teutons, the Genoese—and the Order of the Temple. And there was always a dispute over which among them bore the greatest responsibility for the defeat. Perhaps Master Ambrogio wanted to represent these same five forces in his mosaic, assigning each of them a degree of merit in proportion to the material he chose . . ."

"Branding the one that in his opinion was responsible for the betrayal with lowly terra-cotta," Antonio joined in. "Perhaps there is someone who did not wish to be accused of cowardliness in a Christian church . . . where the general chapter of the studium will rise."

"Going so far as to commit murder?" Dante asked.

The question went unanswered. But it was the facts that spoke, with their evidence of death. Meanwhile the others had fallen upon this new track, animatedly discussing various hypotheses. The prior, distracted, followed the debate in silence. To point to the French or the Lombards as the responsible parties was like not accusing anyone. Then too, why choose the image of an elderly man, if the subject of the mosaic was betrayal? Age had always been a mark of wisdom and virtue, of detachment from passion. Why would Ambrogio have turned that symbol upside down? And why direct the man toward Rome?

The conversation around him began to languish. Dante turned to the tavern keeper, who remained beside him, his one hand still clutching the tabletop. "You said that death began to stalk you at Acre. What did you mean?"

The man clenched his teeth, and suddenly released his grip on the table to scratch the brass shoulder cap, as if he felt a sharp pang in his stump. "Messere, you are opening an old wound. But I will answer your question. As my companions and I were defending the last walls, under the torrid pagan sun, I was wounded by a venomous arrow. I saw it coming toward me and just had time to shield myself with my hand. The arrow pierced my glove. The poison quickly began to course through my veins, just as the hordes of Moors were coursing over our bastions. My body could not hold out, weakened as it was from battle, and succumbed . . ."

Baldo's voice was cold as ice, as if the events of that terrible day were again before his eyes. "The surgeons of the Order determined that there was no other hope for me but to amputate the hand. And with only the help of lotus, I offered my wrist to their instruments." He gazed proudly at those grouped around him, and they shivered as each of them relived in his own body the torment described by the one-armed veteran. "But the poison of the infidels was too quick: the gangrene spread to my wrist, then my elbow. And so I exposed my arm to the knife three more times, as they pursued the poison. This," he concluded, shaking the stump, "is my fifth arm. As compared to the one that nature gave me."

"How did you manage to survive?" Dante had seen some of these dramatic amputations, both on the battlefield and in Florence's hospitals, and rarely had they ended well. That this man had endured four such operations and now enjoyed good health was a miracle.

"I owe my salvation to the protection of my lucky star," the crusader finally answered.

The poet looked at him, bewildered.

"Its rays . . . healed me. Along with prayer."

Dante went on staring at him, wondering what he might be holding back. Then he addressed the Venetian. "Messer Veniero, do you know anything about a miraculous star that heals arms that have been cut off? Have you encountered it in your voyages?"

"Alas, no, Messer Alighieri. I fear that such a star is not to be found in any heaven," the man questioned replied sardonically. "But if one existed, I would like very much . . ."

Veniero broke off suddenly. Antilia had appeared in the back of the tavern, and was walking toward them.

SHE WALKED slowly, wrapped in her peacock mantle, which now fell to her ankles. She stopped at the table, alongside Dante, as Baldo hastily stepped aside. The poet stiffened, seized by a sudden surge of shame. For a moment, the image of Beatrice passing along the streets of Florence had superimposed itself on the dancer with the supple hips.

Now, at last, he was able to observe more closely the majestic body that had so excited him.

Her bare feet, the toes adorned with shining gold rings, peeped out from beneath the turquoise border of her garment. Her coppery skin recalled the radiance of an ancient statue, and made the whiteness of her large teeth and darkness of her eyes more striking. Languidly she tossed her head, making her gold pendant earrings quiver. Then with a graceful movement she sat down next to Dante. As she did so, the edges of her mantle parted for an instant, revealing her naked glory.

Dante's face blazed. The cognoscenti of the Third Heaven had certainly caught a glimpse of that splendor, judging from the stir around him. None of the other customers appeared to have noticed; all were engrossed in their wine, or perhaps they simply did not dare raise their eyes toward that august company.

Even so Antilia sat there, perfectly still and perfectly at ease. The poet grew terrified at the idea that someone outside the studium, one of those tavern-haunting bargellini, perhaps, might see him and report him—Messer Alighieri, newly elected prior of Florence, at table with a dancer in a dubious locale!

Suddenly Antilia, who had remained for some minutes completely immobile, turned her head, letting her gaze wander over the faces of the men around her. Last of all she looked steadily at Dante, who stared straight ahead, trying to ignore the power of those eyes that burned, yet without any heat, as though she were scrutinizing a piece of furniture in the room.

Finally he turned toward her. The high cheekbones, below eyelids elongated with kohl, gave her an indefinable expression, as if she were lost in a distant space and time. He had seen a face like this once, at the homestead of a farmer. This peasant had turned up a sculpture while plowing his field: a fine marble head—the likeness, some said, of an Etruscan noblewoman.

He compared Antilia to all the beautiful women he had

known, to the women he had loved. None had been as lovely as this dancer, except for Beatrice, with her celestial smile.

"So then, Messer Durante, it appears that Antilia has struck your fancy," Cecco Angiolieri said with a sly smile, after carefully observing his fellow poet.

"Just so, and yet you have not told us what you think of her beauty," Antonio da Peretola interposed. "One would expect a livelier enthusiasm for her feminine graces from a poet who writes of love as you do. You have dedicated charming verses to all kinds of women. Why not gladden our hearts by doing as much for her?"

"My verses are inspired by the love that quickens the spirit, not the frenzy of the senses. They celebrate the nobleness of woman and her proximity to God, not her visible attributes, which only confound the eyes."

"We fully understand your reluctance to trot out your verses at the table of a tavern," Cecco Angiolieri spoke again. "And certainly the craft of the polished poet does not lend itself to an extemporization such as that which we are asking of you. And so I would like to help you, by reciting something of yours. And you tell me if these verses do not seem written for her.

> *Who dares to meet without dismay*
> *This lovely maiden's arrowed gaze?*
> *It wounds me till I weeping pray*
> *For bitter death to bring me ease.*

He delivered these like an actor, directing them at the dancer, who listened intently. Dante wondered how much she had understood of those words recited in a language different from her own, written for another woman. Antilia had not taken her eyes off him. All at once she began to sing. From her slightly parted lips came an intensely rhythmic dirge, the melody sorrowful, the words incomprehensible. It rose in pitch, soaring to the tavern's vault.

Dante listened, enchanted. This was not any Christian language that he knew; nor was it Hebrew, or the learned tongue of the barbarous Moors. Her shoulders lifted as she sang, and the edge of her mantle slid down, baring her neck and revealing a sinuous tongue of flame that rose from secret depths, curling up around her breasts to kiss her throat. He looked again and saw it was a scarlet serpent with a crested head, like a basilisk's, etched into her very skin. He thought of the monster's hidden nest and was filled with unbearable excitement.

Now it was he who sought to meet her eyes. But Antilia's gaze had become evasive. She broke off her song abruptly after one agonizingly prolonged last note. Then she rose slowly, turning for a moment to look at the poet, and moved off toward her refuge beyond the curtain at the back of the tavern.

The eyes of the Third Heaven followed her. Cecco Angiolieri was the first to open his mouth and that was to make a sly allusion to the charms they had glimpsed beneath the thin veil of silk. But no one paid any attention to him.

"You should be flattered, Messer Durante. Antilia sang for you. This is the first time such a thing has happened," Antonio said enviously. "We had thought, in fact, that she was mute."

Dante reddened. Her profound gaze had spoken of unbounded distance, and the scarlet serpent plunging into her body had taken root in his heart.

9

THE COLOR of copper still filled his eyes when he awoke. He must dispel it; it was the sign of an immoral and pernicious attraction. That woman brought misfortune, he was sure of it.

Dante tried to concentrate on public business. No meetings of the Council were scheduled for that day, but he knew instinctively that this was no time to absent himself. Three beasts were devouring Florence: cowardice, ambition, vice. The other five priors, driven by these, were capable of anything. It was up to him, with his wisdom, learning, and intuition, to save the city.

But Antilia's body continued to haunt him.

He listened intently to the sounds outside his cell. There were no voices, no footsteps. Was the convent deserted? He left his cell and quickly checked all the others. There truly was no one there. Perhaps the Priors had returned to their homes. Well, he could take advantage of the situation to attend to the crime at his leisure.

He had explored the church and walked the streets of the surrounding area. He had sought out and observed the possible perpetrators. He had not yet examined the body of the victim, except superficially.

The corpse should still be at Misericordia hospital, in the care of the chief physician. Maybe that drunkard had discovered something useful in the course of his postmortem examination.

He pictured the old doctor, a fraud and a sodomite. Another product of the corruption of the times. He knew nothing of elementary astrology, physical medicine, the science of fluids and humors—he had no skill in any subject, simple or complex. He had risen to his extremely important post only because he belonged to a family of newly rich upstarts, who bled the public coffers. He would fight to keep it, too. But sooner or later, Dante would see to him. The doctor was on his list. Like that cursed Bargello. Like so many others.

He went out with a quick step. He didn't meet a soul, either in the courtyard or on his way to the door, confirming that the place was empty. Another sign of decadence, when policy was made not in the Priors' Palazzo, but in the homes of the powerful or in clandestine huddles. What purpose would the new building that was under construction serve? A hollow shell, useless grandeur to mark a faded justice, like the triumphal arches of the ancient Romans.

There was the usual workday crowd in front of the arcade of the Orsammichele market. He was surprised to recognize Augustino and Antonio among the throng, talking to a third man whose back was turned. They had seen Dante, and made haste to approach him, while the unknown man rapidly moved off without showing his face.

"Messer Durante! Are you out on your official duties?" Antonio asked.

"Or still searching for the killer?" Augustino put in.

"Both, given that my duty as prior is to battle against evil."

"And has your pursuit of the quintuple enigma erased the magnificent Antilia from your memory?" Antonio continued. Something hidden underlay his tone; perhaps he was still irritated by the favor the dancer had bestowed on the poet.

"Yes," Dante cut him short. "Even so, our meeting here is fortunate, for I think you can help me. I want to know more about your plan to establish a studium. Who charged you to come to Florence? Is it true that the idea for the studium came from Pope Boniface himself? For so I have recently heard."

The two men exchanged a hurried glance. Then their eyes turned back to him. "No one, Messer Durante," Antonio replied. "No one summoned us. His Holiness encourages the establishment of universities in order to propagate thinking favorable to his cause in his contention with imperial theologians. But he in no way determined our intention. Each of us arrived in Florence on his own. It was here that we came to know each other, and it was here that we felt the void that the absence of a studium created, the lack of means to diffuse the learning that we love so much."

"I understand. A laudable undertaking, were it not tainted by Ambrogio's death."

The two looked quickly at one other once more, but chose to ignore the allusion. "There are four great universities in Italy," Antonio went on. "The Studium Florentinum will be the fifth."

"The fifth," Dante murmured. That number kept coming up continually. Five artistic masters, the pentagram traced on the mosaic, five possible traitors . . . and now five universities.

His mind began to wander. He was reflecting on that haunting number. Every relationship that he could think of revolved around some other number: the oneness of the true God, Adam and Eve, the immense, unknowable Trinity, the four horsemen of the Apocalypse, the four evangelists, Nature's four foundations . . .

However hard he tried, he could not remember any significant group composed of five elements. The seven sages, the seven wonders of the world, the nine heavens, the twelve apostles . . . as if five were really an abominable number, interdicted from the mathematics of God's creation.

Was there no group of five objects? Or five conditions? Or five ages, the most obvious possibility. Suddenly he recalled the interrupted phrases, the words that he had sometimes heard whispered in the quiet halls of the *studia* and in the *scriptoria* of convents, and, later, in the tales told in taverns and post houses of Via Francigena by pilgrims coming from the north or lands overseas. The Fifth Gospel. The Five Evangelists.

Might Ambrogio have wanted to celebrate James, who, if the tales were true, had written the First Gospel, the oldest one? The brother of Jesus the Savior himself, that shadowy figure who was ever present yet constantly denied in Church history?

But why resort to the metaphor of a colossus? Each evangelist had his own attribute, well established through time and in the work of painters and illuminators. And why should the fifth Gospel have been symbolized by terra-cotta? Was it not absurd to apply a hierarchy of value to the word of God?

"Why do you shake your head, Messer Alighieri?" he heard Augustino say.

Dante roused himself. "I was thinking about the mosaic. About that inexplicable allegory."

"Yes, truly singular. A biblical inspiration. Most singular of all, that such should come from Master Ambrogio," Antonio interjected.

"Why is that?"

"The Comacine master certainly did not concern himself deeply with religious matters. I would have said he was more of the school of Epicurus. The delights of Eros were likely not repugnant to him. He often had a woman's name on his lips . . ."

"What name?"

The other hesitated a moment before replying. He seemed embarrassed. "Oh, a name you know quite well. Beatrice."

Dante grabbed Antonio's arm, forcing him to draw closer. He recalled the jurist's words during their meeting in the cell at San Marco. "Was it not you who told me about the master's imperial sympathies?"

"Yes . . . or at least so it was whispered, in Rome," Antonio replied, struck by the question. "Do you think there might be some relation . . ."

Dante did not answer. He was thinking.

Four metals and a material that was lowlier, but tenacious. Fragile, yet enduring. The bronze and iron of the ancients were dust, like they themselves. But the Romans' bricks were still there, in arches and in basilicas, to attest to the Empire's grandeur.

The friable terra-cotta on which the remaining hopes of a great structure rested. And in a Florentine church, no less, in the city of the empire's enemies. A smile came to his lips: if that were really the meaning, what subtle perversion had animated that project! Not even Cecco Angiolieri would have been able to conceive an act so irreverent. A mockery.

His blood began to rise, as in the times when he would remonstrate with Guido Cavalcanti during those Florentine nights spent chasing after the young wives of elderly husbands.

The two men seemed intrigued by his expression. But the poet did not want to deal with their questions. Not now. First he had to learn what he could about the murdered man's body. "I bid you good day, gentlemen. Unfortunately my official duties compel me to take my leave. I must put the affairs of the Commune before my own," he said, and turned his back.

10

The same day, around midday

Dante passed through the door of Misericordia hospital with his head lowered, though not one of the group loitering beneath the portico—hooded members of the confraternity of Hospitallers—showed any interest in his arrival. They were busy drinking by turns from a small jug as they leaned against the side of the cart that transported the dead.

He mounted to the upper floor and made his way along the former convent's loggia until he came to the chief physician's cell. He entered without knocking and stopped in the doorway, his arms folded.

"Greetings, Messer Durante," the man inside said after a moment's surprise—and, Dante thought, suppressed annoyance. He had been busy counting some coins in an iron box. Now he hastened to close the lid and jumped up to greet the poet. "What brings you to us, interrupting the onerous duties of your office? I hope that it is not some ailment of the body, yours or that of a relation. In that case we will hasten to provide care and remedy."

The doctor was a thin man, with sharp features. A vast mane of white hair fell down the back of his neck, brushing shoulders that were draped in a rich silken robe. His eyes were cold, devoid of any sign of intelligence, and clouded by the indulgence of more than one deadly sin. While still at the door the poet had begun to recite a silent prayer to ward off the evil eye, followed by a rapid petition to the Virgin Mary.

The other must have noticed, because his thin lips broadened in a mocking smile.

"Damn him! Damn him three times over!" the prior thought. "I want information about the man killed at Saint Jude," he said aloud. "What have you learned from your examination of his body?"

The chief physician had fully recovered his pompous air. "Nothing. He died." He seemed genuinely surprised. "What should I have discovered?"

Dante closed the door and moved slowly toward the man until he almost touched him. He spoke in a low voice. "That he is dead is news that has spread through all of Florence. It is the human condition to travel a brief distance on this earth, in accordance with God's will, and then return to dust. But at times the natural extent of that distance is shortened by men's iniquity, and this is one of those times. So then one would expect that the Commune's chief physician would notice something more than a simple lack of respiration."

"When I had the corpse delivered to you I sent orders that a scrupulous examination be made," the poet persisted.

"But that is the very task I myself personally carried out, in observance of your orders, prior." The physician's use of his title seemed to imply that he had acceded to Dante's wishes only because of his office.

"You did well. So then?"

"His spirit separated from his body violently, owing to suffocation."

"What else?"

"Nothing. There were signs of blows to the head, but no wounds. No other signs, aside from . . ."

"Aside from?"

"A superficial wound on his chest, inflicted with a pointed object. A scratch of some kind, a design . . ."

"Let me see. At once!" Dante cursed himself for not having personally examined the body the night it was found.

"The body is laid in the vault, near the chamber of the incurables . . ." The chief physician wrinkled his nose in aversion. "It is a simple scratch . . ."

"Anything can be significant. Take me there." The prior threw open the door and was already in the loggia. Reluctantly the chief physician followed him.

Hurriedly they passed through large halls given over to the care of the sick, carefully skirting the rude wooden beds. Linen sheets were stretched between them, creating small cubicles crowded with relatives who had come to sustain their loved ones. In the back of the last hall was a door leading to a narrow staircase. From there they descended into the subterranean floor of the building, which was divided into two sections. The area facing the river, on the other side of the brick wall in front of them, was the Commune's prison; it was entered through a low doorway. The other section, the one they were now passing through, housed the dead and sheltered the dying—more to conceal them from view than to give a last refuge to their suffering.

Another hell.

This vault, the abode of the dying, barely illuminated by the few windows opening to the street above, was polluted by an unbreathable miasma, made even more noisome by the fierce outside heat. The low space was littered with plank beds, on which lay shapes barely human, wrapped in rags. Other bodies leaned against the walls, their heads sunk on their chests. A few of the moribund still had the strength to stay on their feet, and dragged themselves about here and there, in a random flight from death. But there was an undrawn border, near the back wall, that none of them crossed. Against that wall were the benches that held cadavers awaiting burial. Between them and those still living there was only a band of empty space, a kind of allegory of the river marking the boundary of the realm of the dead.

The living and the dead together in a wheeling final dance, Dante thought. Perhaps it was just as well that that ghastly spectacle was removed from the sight of decent citizens. Perhaps the ancient Persians were right, perhaps there really was a realm of darkness concealed from God's luminous eye: a place where even His power yielded to the baseness of the flesh.

He recalled the murky atmosphere of Saint Jude's crypt. What difference was there between the dying bodies he saw here and the decomposed, mummified ones that lay at the bottom of that infernal funnel? Perhaps in a few hours the ones before him now would be like those others, defunct and at rest until Judgment Day.

Each time he descended a stairway he discovered a city of suffering, a *via crucis* beneath the ground, of which this station was the last and worst.

The chief physician had donned his doctor's mask, with a long protuberance at the nose that made him look like some obscene marsh bird. It was filled with herbs and essences to overcome the horrific stench of dead and living flesh.

Dante swallowed the bile that had risen in his throat. "Where is the master's body?" he asked.

The other pointed to one of the benches near the wall. Ambrogio's nude corpse, partly hidden from view: a figure stood over the murdered artist, bent down as if to observe him. For a moment Dante thought it was one of the mortally ill, trying to discern his own future in the dead man's face. But this figure's garments were white and clean and whole. The robe of a Dominican: a visitor from the world of the living.

Hearing the sound of their footsteps, the monk turned suddenly and quickly moved away from the body.

"Who are you and what are you doing here?" the prior demanded brusquely.

For a moment the man hesitated, no doubt deciding how he should reply.

The poet stepped closer, and under a faint ray of light recognized his face. "You are Noffo," he said. "Noffo Dei."

One of the Florentine inquisitors, associated with Boniface's faction, in the service of the pontifical legation. Dante had often seen him in the company of Cardinal d'Acquasparta, the apostolic nuncio, always walking just a step behind him. One of Boniface's spies. One of those who should be banned from Florence.

But there was no proof of his treacheries. Not yet.

"Brother Noffo requested to see the cadaver." The chief physician's voice was muffled by the mask.

"To bring the solace of Christian mercy." The Dominican broke his silence. He stood motionless in front of Dante, his head sunk into his cowl, hands tucked into his wide sleeves. "I know you, too, Messer Alighieri, and pay homage to your office, your erudition, and the steadfastness of your faith."

"That the head of the Inquisition should come himself to dispense such mercy is a source of hope for all of us. That strengthens the faith of humble sinners such as I am. But is the examination of mortal remains part of the last rites? I thought that your task was the care of the spirit, and that the care of the body was reserved for the sisters of mercy," the poet replied with irony.

The Dominican remained impassive. Dante moved closer. He was anxious to know what Noffo had been looking at when they had surprised him. Ambrogio's chest was marked by several abrasions around the heart, drawn from one shoulder to the other. They must be the scratches to which the chief physician had alluded. The cuts were studded with drops of coagulated blood, yet they did not appear particularly deep. Nor could they have been inflicted to shorten the master's life, but rather to intensify his pain.

Dante forgot the presence of Noffo and the doctor; he no longer heard the moans of the dying or smelled their rotting flesh. There was nothing in the room but that lacerated skin, which his spirit explored like a traveler. The assassin had carved five lines. Their intersections formed a pentagram. That symbol again. That cursed number.

He raised his eyes to the friar. It was hopeless to attempt to wrest information from him—it would be easier to break into a tomb and interrogate a cadaver. Only with a red-hot poker in his eyes would this man speak, he thought, and perhaps one day that could be arranged.

Too many questions about the Church's role in this affair were still unanswered. Master Ambrogio's sympathies had lain with the empire. And the name of Beatrice had been on his lips. That name could explain a lot of things—even the presence of an inquisitor in the house of the dead.

But it would be pointless to demand explanations from Noffo Dei when a prior of Florence could go directly to his superior, Cardinal d'Acquasparta, the pontifical legate in Florence.

II

The same day, in the afternoon

THE OFFICE of the papal nuncio had been munificently housed at the Commune's expense in a wing of the convent of Santa Maria Novella. When the retinue that accompanied Cardinal d'Acquasparta had entered Porta Romana at the beginning of the year, applauded by the curious crowd that lined both sides of the road, everyone had believed that a great mediator had truly arrived in Florence, a man who would subdue hatred and bring peace to the city in the name of Christian brotherhood.

Only Dante had remained apart, uneasy, like a prescient Trojan at the sight of that great wooden horse. *"Timeo Danaos et dona ferentes,"* he thought. "I don't trust these dogs, even if they are smiling at me." He did not like anything about the man or his court. The cardinal's physiognomy marked him as a lecherous sluggard, and his face was imbued with the hypocrisy of the Curia. And when he made the grand gesture of refusing a cup filled with gold florins in the Council chamber, the sinister flash of greed that lit up his eyes did not escape Dante's notice. He had refused the money so as to gain a great deal more of it later on.

The poet did not like his devious secretaries either, flatterers like the inquisitor Noffo Dei, who had come to lodge with him and were quickly dispatched into the streets of Florence in search of no telling what. And he especially did not like the two dozen mercenaries armed with crossbows and pikes who, despite his opposition, expressed in a meeting of the Council, had been authorized to follow the high-ranking prelate within the city walls, and who had transformed Santa Maria Novella into a kind of outpost for Boniface's troops, a lion's claw thrust into the lambs' pen.

Hastily he summoned his "family," twelve district guards who had been assigned to defend him and to deal with any disruption of public order.

"What the devil is it, Messer Alighieri?" one of the other priors shouted. "Is there a rebellion? Where is our guard?"

"Nothing that should disturb your sleep, Messer Lapo," Dante replied. As he was going down the stairs he heard one of his colleagues furiously asking the Bargello why he was rushing off with his men.

He stopped at the foot of the priory stairs, waiting as the guards lined up in two rows in front of him, panting under the weight of their mail. He had demanded that they equip themselves from head to toe, bearing full weaponry, and that they don a complete suit of armor bearing the Commune's insignia. Six of them had shouldered heavy Genoese crossbows, shaped like fanciful steel monsters—useless in a clash in the narrow city streets, but impressive.

Intimidate the enemy: this is what Dante was determined to do. Up till that time he had preferred to make his moves discreetly. The depravity revealed by Ambrogio's death had made him wary of involving the Commune in that crime. But the circumstances were changing now: the evil he had uncovered made it necessary to cross paths with an authority as powerful as his own.

He had dressed himself in his full official regalia. He placed himself at his soldiers' head and ordered them to march toward Santa Maria Novella. He wanted Acquasparta's spies, who were certainly posted around there, to have time to announce his arrival.

———

RAPIDLY HE traversed the distance that separated his lodgings from the pontifical nunciature. At every step of the way the hubbub and the crowds continued to increase, as if all of Florence had decided to convene at the door of the papal vicar's quarters. Finally his escort had to force its way through the throng of clerics, merchants, armed guards, and especially beggars, bawling and flaunting their miseries, as well as flocks of children fleeing from their schoolmasters or their fathers' shops. A cloth merchant leaning against his doorjamb with his arms folded seemed to be enjoying the spectacle.

"Why the devil are all these people rushing and bustling about like this?" the poet asked.

The other did not seem too impressed by the prior's badges of office or by the armed guard following him. "Priestly business, Messere," he replied. "Today is a day of public audience at the cardinal's home. Given that it is now *his* home, is it not?" he added with a sarcastic smile.

"Santa Maria is and will remain the home of Florentines only, rest assured of it."

"It may be as you say, but it should also be understood by the cardinal, who holds court here."

"But why have people flocked here in such great numbers?"

"Indulgences will be granted today, and above all prebends and viaticums for Jubilee pilgrims."

A foreboding thought crossed the poet's mind. Perhaps he would be better off choosing another time to request an audience. But his task was urgent; he could not worry that it might be ill-timed. Then, too, it was not just any of the Curia's attachés he wanted to meet with, but Acquasparta himself. All this confusion might therefore play out in his favor.

Meanwhile he and his retinue had arrived in front of the church's still incomplete facade. There the territorial sovereignty of the Commune ended and the Church's jurisdiction began. He ordered the guards to line up in front of the entrance, then set out alone toward the cloister to the left of the building.

The vast square space, surrounded by porticos, had been opened to the townspeople for this day of audience and was teeming with men and women crammed together, waiting for who knows what. The poet shoved his way through to the staircase, trying to protect his robes and cursing the judicial regulations that prohibited him from making a clean sweep of that rabble.

With a leap he cleared the first step, which was strewn with wretched drop cloths on which peddlers were displaying their wares. Recovering his balance, he began his ascent with some difficulty, taking care not to collide with those who were coming down.

He had to back up more than once so as to allow those descending to pass, but then he took advantage of an opening created by a group of corpulent Lombard merchants who were ruthless in their approach, making their way up the stairs like pikemen assaulting enemy ranks. Sailing in the wake of these battletroops, Dante was finally able to reach the top of the staircase, where armed guards were questioning petitioners before admitting them to the low doorway behind them or sending them back, deciding each man's fate according to some mysterious criteria of their own. A crossbowman clad in imposing armor, massive as a cathedral bell, appeared to be the supreme authority. Seated on a cask, the scoundrel passed judgment with a grunt or a vague wave of his hand, at times merely raising his eyebrow.

Pressed back by the mob that surrounded him, Dante had time to study the man. The petitioners coming from the left were systematically favored with respect to the others. As if, in the crossbowman's view, the left were the side of the meritorious, while the right, by some strange inversion of the universal norm, were the side of the outcasts. Dante forced his way to the left, and with a final exertion reached the foot of the cask.

"I am Dante Alighieri, prior of the city of Florence. I request an immediate audience with Boniface's vicar," he said in the most solemn tone he could muster, standing squarely before the man and drawing himself up to his full height. The crossbowman remained calmly seated.

His name and office must not have made any particular impression. The man merely studied him from top to bottom. "Wait," he said curtly, "you and the entire Commune of Florence." He uttered those words with a contempt that spoke volumes: this was how Boniface's hirelings felt about the city. His accent betrayed his foreign origins. He must be one of the cardinal's French mercenaries.

Bending one knee, Dante lowered himself slightly so as to be level with that brazen face. "Announce me to the cardinal at once! Your ill will and your indolence are obstructing a mission on which the triumph of justice may depend, as well as relations between St. Peter's Patrimony and the noble Commune of Florence. You will be hanged, you and the rogues that attend you, when . . ."

"Go fuck yourself, Messere," the other interrupted without so much as making a move to get up, accompanying his words with a yawn. *"Vade et repetito,"* he felt obliged to add.

"Repete, you idiot!" Dante shouted. "Announce me, you bastard, or tonight you will sleep in the Stinche!"

The other looked at him as one might look at a madman. Then he seemed to finally become aware of Dante's lavish clothing. His eyes lingered on the symbols of the priory, as a guard bent down to whisper something in his ear. Perhaps he had recognized him, or else he had noticed the escort of bargellini deployed at the entrance. The man was puzzled now, but did not yet seem inclined to yield. Then, as if swayed by a sudden feeling of sympathy for the angry petitioner fretting before him, he shrugged. "Since you seem to think you are a big shot, maybe it is just as well that you go in to see the Cardinal: he will be able to put you in your place. Go on. But be careful not to annoy him."

Dante passed through the door without even being aware of it, shaking with rage. To be permitted to pass through a door in his own city, of which he was prior, thanks to the concession of a villainous Frenchman! Had his gaze fallen on someone at that very moment that unfortunate bystander would have been turned into stone, so poisonous was the anger in him now. This is how the Gorgon must have been born.

AN OFFICIAL of the Curia accompanied him along a short corridor, then beyond the open loggia to the edge of the construction. A man stood there, his back to the poet, contemplating the city. His head turned slightly, and Dante glimpsed his profile with its coarse features. A landlord, contemplating his estates.

As the friar who had announced him retreated silently, the man turned around. Tall and bulky, with a broad nose that drooped over his upper lip, he would have made a magnificent model for the portrait of a decadent emperor. A Commodus, perhaps. Or a Nero, had he not been completely lacking in that youthful spark of madness that must have illuminated the Roman tyrant's features. The cardinal's face showed nothing but the prolonged practice of intrigue and corruption.

"And so we meet, Messer Durante. We have wanted to make your acquaintance for some time. This does not mean that we do not already know you in spirit, through the medium of your love poems," the lofty prelate began.

"Has my art risen to the attention of the Church?" Dante asked with a hint of pride.

"And yet your ideas, and, even more, your actions, have not always inspired our paternal benevolence. We might have hoped that a good Christian such as yourself would show a greater understanding of our aspirations, which are those of Pope Boniface. *Ergo,* those of God."

The poet's eyes flashed, and his fists tightened. He let a moment or two go by before responding. "That is an overstrained syllogism, Your Eminence," he replied, trying to maintain an even tone. "I draw a distinction between God's infinity, the Church's majesty, and Boniface's mortal span. Moreover, I have had occasion to oppose the pope's aims through my counsel, words, and actions, even before donning the garb of prior."

Acquasparta's face twisted into a scowl. "It appears that your obstinacy has not diminished, even though the responsibilities of your role should induce you to adopt more conciliatory ways. What inspires such confidence? Are you really so certain that belonging to the White faction sets you above the whims of fortune? Now, your back is covered, thanks to the protection of the Cerchi family, just as years ago you escaped justice thanks to the arm of the Cavalcanti. Indeed the manuscript of your worthless book, *Fiore,* with its obscene deriding of the clergy, is among the investigations undertaken by the Inquisition."

Dante remained impassive. Deep down he had known that sooner or later someone would link those allusive sonnets to him, even though he had been careful to have them circulated only as anonymous copies. But confronted by these cursed hypocrites, he would retract nothing.

"It appears that my fellow townsmen have a more flattering

opinion of me, given that they have entrusted me with their fate," was all he replied.

"Perhaps your fellow townsmen do not know as much as we know. We wonder why a man who has so badly administered his own affairs should excel at managing the public's business. And now we have received word that you are investigating a crime. Ruin seems to follow you, Messer Alighieri, as a dog's shadow follows the dog."

"Or as death's footsteps follow the tracks of those hated by Boniface, in his Christian cities."

The cardinal leaped up, his face purple. "How dare you! Such insolence! Associating His Holiness' name with villainy is an act of foolish arrogance you will regret. You seem to forget that the only reason you are not in chains is the benign patience of the Church."

Eyes blazing, he shoved his ring in the prior's face, striking him on the mouth, ordering him to kiss it. Dante jumped to his feet, his hands reaching for the other man's throat. The prelate instinctively drew his head into his bulky shoulders, like a turtle defending itself from a crow, and the prior's fingers were unable to breach the folds of flesh. Meanwhile the prince of the Church, having overcome his initial shock, began mustering his strength to call for help, his eyes glassy with terror.

The poet released his hold with his right hand, groping on the desk to find something with which to strike the man. Acquasparta in turn locked his arms around the poet's waist and began dragging him toward the door. In the clench, the handle of the concealed dagger pressed against Dante's ribs. Dante grabbed the weapon and turned it toward his adversary's neck.

"You would dare . . . such a thing! In the house of God's vicar! You would dare bloody the threshold of Peter's house!" the cardinal said in a whisper, his voice cracked and breathless, the point of the dagger against his throat. "You will not get out of here alive . . . never!"

"Nor will you get out of Florence alive!" Dante hissed into his ear. That ugly appendage was close enough to bite off, and the poet was sorely tempted. Meanwhile he was rapidly weighing the debits and credits on the scale that fate was offering him. His own life versus the elimination of one of the most bitter enemies of Florence's freedom. He could finally get rid of that venomous man, crush the head of the serpent that had deposited its eggs in his city. Boniface, deprived of his *longa manus* in Tuscany, would have to abandon his goals there.

Then the act appeared to him in all its enormity. Sacrificing his own life did not matter to him, but Acquasparta was nevertheless God's vicar. Then, too, cutting off the head of the hydra would serve no purpose, when a hundred others were lying in wait with their jaws wide open. Slowly he loosened his grip, then took one step back. The other started breathing heavily, as he felt the poet's hold slacken, massaging his throat where finger marks were quite visible. He slumped onto one of his thronelike chairs. The poet also sat down, facing him.

"Repent . . . mortify your rage before our humble magnanimity and you will once again be our son . . ." the cardinal said. Every trace of his hypocritical holiness had vanished. Now he appeared as he truly was: a politician intent on a duel with an unyielding adversary. He had lost the first round and was trying to muster his forces to attack again. "And then? What brought you to these rooms, besides the perfidious desire to offend our sacred person?"

"Why is the Church taking an interest in a mosaicist's murder? Why did you send that hireling of yours, Noffo, to spy on the remains?" Dante rejoined, his voice also cracked and breathless.

"I have nothing to explain to you. The Holy Roman Church determines what is good and what is evil, and decides when and how to intervene," the cardinal replied pompously. Gradually, his color was coming back. "A heinous crime in a sacred place is always the object of its attention. And of that of the Inquisition, in cases where diabolical traces are evident."

"And you have recognized such traces in the mosaicist's murder? Is that it? You think it was a devil who killed him? Beelzebub's talons tormented Ambrogio's poor body? What is it you really fear from this death? And before that? What might you have feared from his life?"

The other did not seem to notice the prior's scoffing tone. He approached the window, as if seeking air. Then he turned around, a flash of cunning in his eyes. Having dropped his curial mask, he appeared now merely as an astute merchant, prepared to buy and sell.

"What should the Holy Church have to fear from the death of a wretched artisan? Or from his life?"

"He was not a mere artisan, but a great master of his art. A Comacine master. With Ghibelline loyalties, what's more."

The cardinal maintained his attitude of indifference. Dante thought back to the contract for the restoration of Saint Paul's convent that he had found in the dead man's cell. "The man had also worked for Boniface, in Rome."

"And so?"

The poet thought he caught an uneasy note in the last question. He decided to try a lunge. "The master's death was linked to his art—everything leads me to that conclusion. In fact, it is the opinion of a number of persons who have seen it that through his last work he may have wanted to transmit a truth he had learned in Rome—a city from which he fled in great haste to take refuge here."

He paused to appraise the effect of his words on his adversary. "A truth he felt had to be revealed through the power of his art. Remember that the church of Saint Jude was to become the seat of the Florentine *Universitas*. Beneath that image great scholarly debates would take place. And if the Church had not appreciated . . ."

"And what do you think this truth so displeasing to the Church might be?" The pontifical legate's eyes had narrowed to slits.

"Do you mean to say that you do not know?"

"What is this truth, Messer Alighieri? What was it that the Comacine supposedly wanted to portray?" the other repeated, his eyes now almost completely closed, his face beaded with sweat.

Dante let another moment go by before responding. "It is possible that he intended to set in stone a symbol of the Swabian imperial family."

The cardinal's eyes suddenly flew open, and a contemptuous smile curled his lips. "This miserable hypothesis is the entire fruit of your brilliance? These are the results of your investigations? And what harm could come to Christ's triumphant heir from a recounting of dead men vanquished and erased by time?"

The sarcastic tone had the effect of a lashing. Without thinking, the prior abandoned all prudence. "Vanquished but not erased. Perhaps the Comacine artist did not mean to celebrate only past generations, but also the current one."

"What do you mean? What generation are you alluding to? Are you insane?"

"You are forgetting Beatrice, Manfred's fifth child. The last heir of Frederick II."

The face of the prince of the Church seemed to have turned to stone. He quickly stood up, and from his full height, looked down at the poet. Dante settled more comfortably in his seat, straightening the folds of his garment. Acquasparta's voice became strident, without any pretense of affability. "You speak of a legend! There is no fifth child! Manfred, that bastard, had only four descendants, all of them male, and they are all dead!"

"But if the legend were true? Perhaps this is what the Comacine master learned in Rome, and what he wanted to reveal."

The Cardinal lost all control. "There is no Beatrice, I tell you!" he sputtered.

"Perhaps that is so, but the power of legend often surpasses that of reality. If the imperials decide to introduce a Beatrice as the legitimate heir to the imperial crown, Boniface might find more than one obstacle on his way toward complete dominion of Italy."

"That is a lie . . ."

Dante felt he had made a breach in the man's assurance and carried on, implacable. "After Manfred's defeat and death in Benevento, his sons were captured. There were four of them. But they say there was also a woman with the king. A woman who carried his seed in her womb and who was able to escape with the imperial treasure."

"How did you come to hear this tale?"

"The Church is not the only one with eyes and ears. And perhaps my intellect is sharper that you think," the poet snarled.

Abruptly, something in Acquasparta's attitude changed. Dropping his arrogant tone, sounding even conciliatory, he said, "You are completely on the wrong track, Messer Alighieri. And I would not hesitate to leave you to your error, were it not for the fact that our beloved Florence might suffer harm in being led astray by a city ruler. Do not defy our power. It is not worth your while. Instead place your trust in the Church's magnanimity. Indeed, we offer our cheek for a conciliatory kiss. Boniface can be munificent, even toward his enemies. We are aware of your domestic difficulties. Take refuge beneath our sheltering wings and you will find not only the faith of your fathers, but also the help that you need. No usurer in Florence is able to be as generous as we are."

Dante approached, more of a mind to bite than to kiss. "Do you think that in exchange for my temporal salvation I would be willing to betray the Commune's liberty? And sooner still, betray the truth?"

"The Church is well aware of men's frailties, because it has been their compassionate guardian since the time of Peter's betrayal. The spirit that inspires us is not measured in years, but in millennia. We know how to wait. In the end you will come back to us, and it is up to you to decide whether to do so as a prodigal son or in chains. You are made of dust, like all of us. You sail in the heavens of the muses, but your little vessel shatters on the swell of a few florins."

The prior leaped to his feet. "Only God is the guardian of my destiny! Not even Boniface has authority over it, as long as Florence confronts him with her head held high. As for me, I will continue my investigation, and my voice will rise even louder, to stop your designs on our liberty!"

"Go ahead and follow your own path, Messer Alighieri. But it will not get you anywhere. Ambrogio did not flee from Rome for the reasons you believe. Nor was he killed for them," the cardinal said, dismissing him with a gesture.

Dante started to leave, but when he got to the door he stopped, detained by Acquasparta's strident voice. "We have had a report about the dancer who performs in the crusader's tavern. It appears that you have taken an interest in her, and knowing you, it is easy to guess what kind of passion attracts you to such a whore. But indulge in no poetic illusions: that woman is dangerous, a vessel of lust perpetually on the point of overflowing."

The poet hurried down the stairs, heedless of the throngs that continued to stream in. He fought his way through the mass of bodies, shoving, stamping, and punching as if the Furies themselves were circling overhead, or as if the Four Horsemen of the Apocalypse were galloping at his side. Every muscle in his body was tensed to the point of spasm. He had the feeling that a crossbow's arrow might rip into his back at any moment. Only after reaching the street did he slowly begin to relax.

OUTSIDE, he found his guardsmen loudly jesting with passing servingmaids. Irritated, he dismissed them; they impressed nobody, but they made him conspicuous, and to carry out his next project he must attract as little attention as possible. He would go on alone.

Quickly he turned into a side street, looking around cautiously to make sure that no one was following him. He made rapid progress, keeping close to the facades of the buildings. Meanwhile, he thought over what had just taken place.

Acquasparta had denied everything. But could the fact that he had arrived in Florence immediately after the Comacine master's arrival be a mere coincidence? Perhaps Ambrogio, fleeing from Rome, had left some evidence of his intentions behind, and the pope's men had followed his trail, like hounds on a scent.

IF HE HOPED to escape men's notice, he would have to conceal the insignia of his office, he realized. He halted at a stall. "Give me a length of cloth, any kind will do," he demanded imperiously of the shopkeeper. Intimidated by his arrogant manner and his official garments, the merchant hastened to offer him a scarlet fabric that still smelled of dye. He seemed surprised at the payment that Dante hastily tossed on the counter before he moved off.

Around the corner, the poet took off his biretta and wrapped it carefully in the cloth, along with his gilded staff. Tucking the bundle tightly under his arm, he continued on his way bareheaded, under the fierce heat of the sun. He had gone scarcely a hundred steps when a sudden faintness accompanied by vertigo forced him to stop and lean against the wall.

He closed his eyes and waited for the fit to pass, and remembered that he had not had a bite to eat all day. Only Baldo's wine, he scolded himself, shaking his head at his own folly.

In his excitement over recent events, he had forgotten the demands of the flesh, and now his weakened body was taking its revenge. Shading his eyes with his hand, he spotted a sign for a small tavern at the other end of the street and headed that way.

"What can I get for you, Messere?" the host asked solicitously. Displayed on the counter were several trays with cheese and prosciutto, as well as platters of vegetables. The man followed the poet's eyes.

"I see that you appreciate my food. You will not regret your choice. Sit down," he invited him cheerfully.

Dante collapsed on a bench. "Bring me something, anything you have," he said glumly. "And some wine. White."

He set his bundle on the table and put his head in his hands. He must think of a convincing speech to accomplish the task that awaited him—an ordeal he would have paid anything to avoid. His creditors seemed as numerous as the flies in that dirty tavern.

"Here you are, Messere!" The host's voice took his mind off his worries. The man placed a wooden platter in front of him, containing slices of dark bread soaked in a reddish slop. On top were two slabs of cheese with a thick, moldy rind. "And here is some wine, true nectar of Saint Dennis!" he exclaimed, setting down a moist earthenware jug.

"Dionysus," Dante muttered.

"Saint Dionysus?"

"No, Dionysus the god."

"By God, Messere, you are right; the other was Saint Damian."

The prior dismissed him with a nod and looked around for a spoon. He resigned himself to using his fingers, and after having rolled up his sleeves, scooped up and swallowed a dripping mouthful. Not so bad, aside from the mold on the cheese, and not too different from what the kitchens of the Priors' Palazzo dished out, he thought as he fell upon the wine.

He was beginning to feel better. He would have liked to linger a few more minutes to rest, but the swarm of flies that had descended on the remains of the slop had become intolerable. He gathered up his bundle and left, after dropping a coin among the leftovers.

THE CARDINAL might be wrong about everything else, but he was damned right about Dante's being in need of money. The image of Manetto came vividly to mind, his pointy, weasely teeth, his coarse, bilious complexion. And Manetto was not his only creditor, only the most irksome and impudent one.

The closer he got to his destination, the darker his mood grew. By the time he turned into Via dei Cambiari, he could have killed any man with just a glance, so great was his rage at the world. The effect of the rude tavern meal, but also of what he saw around him—the narrow, unassuming street that was Florence's true pulsing heart, with its merchants' stalls, warehouses, and, above all, the establishments of the city's most prominent usurers.

It was not the first time he had passed through one of those doors. After his father's death, the fortunes of the Alighieri had gradually diminished with the decline in land values of the properties that comprised the family patrimony. The revenues had been reduced to almost nothing, withered away by bad harvests and the demands of tenants and sharecroppers.

In the early days of his government career, more than one moneylender had come forward spontaneously, offering to cover his expenses. Contributing to the election of a member of the Council of One Hundred was worth a great deal, in terms of favors owed.

But then he had begun rudely chasing away those who came to harvest the fruit of their investment, and they, not receiving the patronage they had hoped for, became eager to have their money back instead. With full interest. As time went on, it became increasingly difficult for Dante to obtain a loan, even when resorting to his brother Francesco as a pledge.

Slowly he made his way down the street, then stopped before the small shop of Messer Domenico. The size of the shop was deceptive: it always contained a great deal of ready money, thanks to Domenico's association with the prestigious Bardi family. Who would have guessed that behind this simple wooden doorway, covered only by a threadbare piece of cloth, sat one of the greatest economic powers of the city—perhaps of the entire Empire?

The poet was still plucking up the courage to enter when from behind the shabby curtain he heard voices approaching. Before he could step aside, Veniero came out of the shop, accompanied by the moneylender. The two men seemed to be in good spirits. Messer Domenico was escorting the Venetian out with unusual courtesy, touching his elbow lightly, while the other took his leave with equal ceremony.

Dante was taken aback.

Seeing him there, Messer Domenico assumed a hurried, impatient air, clearly anticipating Dante's mission. The man had rapidly sized up the bundle that Dante held so tightly under his arm. Did he think the prior had brought something to pawn?

Damned bloodsucker, Dante would throw his insignia in his face, as soon as they were alone.

Veniero, meanwhile, broke into a broad smile, as if he were pleased at the encounter. "Messer Alighieri, I see that your business takes you on the same path as mine. Are you also in search of florins?" he asked briskly.

"But with little hope of obtaining them. Gold does not often go hand in hand with poetry. I imagine you know that," Dante replied, his eyes following the usurer, who had hastened back inside.

"For that matter, it does not often accompany a life at sea either, I'm afraid."

"And yet is not the sea the repository of all riches?"

"If that is true, then for me its coffers have remained tightly shut, and now I must seek treasure on land," the other rejoined, pointing to the door of the shop behind him.

Dante would have liked to know what lay beneath the surface of that cheerfulness, which was perhaps not as forced as it seemed. The Venetian played down his expectations, but Dante had quite clearly seen the flash of cupidity in Messer Domenico's eyes as he bade Veniero good-bye.

Certainly the consideration the captain had enjoyed was not what that avaricious dog kept in store for those unfortunates who came to grovel for a loan. No, Dante would swear that Veniero had gone there to offer, rather than to ask. He said to the Venetian, "Still, even if the treasure chests remained shut, the water routes lead to the realms of riches. And who better than a mariner like you could have plied and exploited them?" he persisted.

Veniero froze, then grabbed him by the arm. "For God's sake, Prior! I do not deny having attacked a few prosperous Saracen vessels in my day, or boarding a Genoese ship or two, before the changing tides of my fortune stranded me here among your hills.

Of course, several years ago I could have armed a war galley all on my own, and Messer Domenico would not have had the pleasure of making my acquaintance." The man seemed to brush away a dark thought. "Nevertheless, my life is rich not only in virtue, Messer Alighieri, but also in a certain folly. And that is the source of my misfortune."

"As it is for everyone. Where do all our misfortunes originate if not in folly? Yet I would not describe being overcome by love a folly, except for simple minds . . ."

"Ah, what I said to you in the tavern. . . . Still, it is not love that brings me to a usurer's shop, but a more sinister demon," Veniero interrupted him, bursting into laughter. "Gambling, Messer Alighieri!" he added quickly, seeing the poet's puzzled expression. "And its ill luck."

Dante nodded, smiling in turn. "I am not surprised, if that is your second passion."

"Not the second. And you, have you never been tempted to try your luck? It would be an honor to test my skills against yours. I am sure you would be a formidable player."

"As I presume you would be a great navigator. Placing one's trust in dice or the sea requires the same courage."

"Did you ever go to sea?"

"Never for long voyages. I think the stable continuity of terra firma more suited to my nature."

"And yet you are a man of study and erudition. If you banish Poseidon's realms from your horizon, access to the fourth part of the globe—the most extensive part—is closed to you."

"The most extensive part—and the most unstable and uncertain. God in His design separated the water from the land, and assigned the latter to man and the former to fish. I prefer to stay on the side created for man. Then, too, what did you learn from your voyages, Messer Veniero, that I should envy you?"

The seaman suddenly turned serious. "I learned the shocking diversity of places and people."

"One might think that you reached the Happy Isles that are the subject of legends."

The Venetian shrugged. "La Serenissima's commands were clear: my galley was to protect cargo ships bound for Palestine against Saracen pirates. And this I did, for many years. But one time I took aboard my vessel an agent of the Republic who was returning from Jerusalem. He bore specific orders directing me to place myself at his service. He was an elderly man, yet still sound. He ordered me to set sail for the west, toward Morocco. For more than a month we sailed along the coast of Africa, until we reached the Pillars of Hercules."

"And did you go beyond them?"

"Yes."

Dante leaned toward him. "What did you see?"

"To the south, on the equatorial line, the stars of the other hemisphere. Such a splendor of light, so different from ours! There too God has left His mark, announcing the coming of Christ. There is a constellation of four large stars that form a perfect cross."

Dante listened wide-eyed. "What else did you see?"

"Mountains of water, and enormous fish, and horrendous monsters with tentacles that reached over a ship's broadsides to snatch the sailors at night. That was all. The nights were cold and the days were very hot. Perhaps I should have hanged one of my enemies from the prow, to have better fortune!"

"That is true. Even the Greeks thought human sacrifice propitious for navigation. But what was your passenger looking for?"

"He was a scholar. Are you familiar with the secret of the magnetic pole?"

"Are you referring to the metallic needle that always seeks the north? The one brought from China by the Amalfitani? It is an instrument well known by now."

"Yes. But perhaps you do not know that its position gradually diverges from the north at an increasing angle as one moves toward the west. The elderly man's task was to measure that deviation at each degree of longitude. The result of his work now lies in the archives of Venice, another weapon in the battle against the infidels," Veniero replied, with a bitter twist to his mouth, as if the memory of that adventure aroused painful feelings. Or perhaps it was the name of his lost city that saddened him. "Days of hard work and misery, consumed in idiotic research," he added after a brief pause, in a derisive tone.

"Why do you say that? To advance one's knowledge is the most noble of undertakings. Do you not believe . . ."

"I do not believe anything, Messer Alighieri; nevertheless, I am certain that I have no need of those numbers to command a galley meant to attack the Moorish coasts. But perhaps you learned men are cut from another cloth. You detest empty spaces on your maps and always need to fill them up with marks. You would sell your soul to discover an insignificant, useless truth, just like that elderly man. He had studied the customs of the people of the East in great depth. During the long nights of the voyage, as we sat by the stove in the quarterdeck, he would tell me what he had learned about their religions and about the demons they were able to evoke. Strange cults that have reached our shores as well, arriving in pilgrims' knapsacks, like the contagion of leprosy. These are peoples who worship stones, proud of their beliefs and passionate about their strange faith. As much in their way as Messer Bruno."

"Bruno Ammannati, the studium's theologian?" Dante asked. Ammannati, too, had come from abroad, according to the priory secretary's report.

"Yes, the very one. Have you ever listened to one of his sermons, at the church of the Quaranta Martiri? I assure you they are very dramatic. Even Master Ambrogio was fascinated by them. I often saw Bruno and Ambrogio together, engrossed in intense conversation." The captain smiled. "Maybe the Comacine master was religious. Your city seems to attract pious souls—like Angiolieri." He spoke these last words with obvious sarcasm.

"Indeed, Messer Cecco," the prior said slowly. "A bizarre poet and equally peculiar man, don't you think?"

"Of course, but perhaps more sensible than many others."

"That may be. Did you know each other before?" Dante tossed out the last observation in a seemingly distracted way, as if thinking of something else. But he was certain that Veniero was paying strict attention to every word.

"No, Messer Alighieri. I am a seafaring man. Nevertheless I quickly discovered in him a certain affinity with my own way of thinking, which makes him dear to me. We share the same passion, and it is certainly not a passion for poetry. It is that affinity that may give the impression of a longer acquaintance. But now I really must bid you farewell; I do not wish to steal precious time away from your administrative duties. Or other business," Veniero finished, with a mischievous gleam in his eye, glancing toward the moneychanger's door.

Dante gazed after him as he left, then entered the usurer's shop with a determined step. Domenico was seated behind a worn pine counter that was covered with documents and ledgers.

He made no move to get up, merely nodding at Dante. His eyes slid down to the scarlet bundle, then rose again; he studied Dante with a haughty air. "Do you wish to offer me a pledge in pawn, Messere?"

The poet bit his tongue. He could not afford to have a falling out with Domenico just now. The dog was his last hope. He tried feverishly to remember the conciliatory speech he had prepared, but all that came to his mind were words of insult and invective. And then there was Veniero, and his unexpected presence there. To the devil with Manetto and his demands, he told himself. There would be time to deal with that.

"The Commune's authority needs to confer with you, Messer Domenico, regarding a criminal matter."

The man's expression quickly changed. "Criminal . . . matter? What do you mean, prior?"

The poet noted with satisfaction that Domenico had at last pronounced his title, and with the obligatory deference. "You have certainly heard about the murder in our city of the Comacine guild master. The Commune has charged me to find the guilty party."

"And you are looking for him here?" the usurer stammered.

"Wherever he may be hiding. But for now there is something else I want to know. What business did Messer Veniero, a citizen of Venice, come to conduct with you?"

"None . . . not yet. He merely asked me if I would be willing to accept a letter of credit."

"And what was your response?"

"That it would depend upon the solvency of the guarantor."

"And what did he say?"

"He . . . said not to worry on that account. That his guarantor is sound throughout the Empire's territories."

Dante, thinking hard, said nothing.

"However . . ." Domenico cleared his throat and his face assumed the cunning expression natural to his trade. As always, he was ready to sell out anything and anybody. Now it was the prior who would have to ingratiate himself. "However it seemed strange to me . . ."

"What did?"

"So much talk of guarantees and empires, and then he ended up asking me for an advance on a pledge. A gold ring," he said with a contemptuous sneer, drawing the item from under the counter and showing it to Dante. "They are all alike, these seamen," he concluded, winking at him with an air of complicity.

Dante snatched the large ring, which was covered with small, almost indistinguishable marks, and examined it closely before handing it back to the moneylender. "Indeed, they are all alike. I will be back to see you again, Messer Domenico. We have other things to talk about as well."

He started to leave, followed by the usurer's puzzled gaze. As he passed through the narrow doorway he bumped into the doorjamb with his bundle and let out a curse.

12

The same day, late afternoon

DANTE ENTERED the small, dark nave of the Church of the Forty Martyrs and approached the altar, keeping near the wall so as not to attract attention. Toward the back, near a simple altar surrounded by wooden pews, a rudimentary wooden platform had been set up. Behind that makeshift pulpit stood a man preaching to a small group of the faithful, who crowded around him.

There were not many people, perhaps a few dozen souls, both men and women. Some were scattered here and there among the columns, listening to the sermon; others were seated on plain wooden benches; still others crouched on the floor. All were listening, and on the faces of all of them was an expression of wonder. The simple faces of these country folk drew Dante's attention even more powerfully than the man who was speaking to them. They seemed enchanted.

"Messer Durante! Come, share the bread of angels with us."

Bruno Ammannati had interrupted his sermon and was now looking at Dante with an inspired expression. One or two of the congregation cast a suspicious glance at the newcomer, but were quickly reassured by the preacher's familiar tone.

After that brief greeting, Bruno, too, seemed to forget about him. He returned to his oration with fervor; his shining eyes were raised to heaven. Judging from a note of finality in his voice, he must be coming to the end of his peroration. Even so Dante had no difficulty recognizing its source. Bruno referred to the successive stages of man's life on earth. The poet was certain he would reach the point of exalting the third or future age, the Age of the Spirit, the liberation from the weightiness of the flesh and of matter, the elimination of vices and egoism in a society of equals in which the Church, renewed by the animating influence of the Holy Spirit, would at last become a model of liberty and justice.

Those commoners with their credulous faces were the ideal terrain in which to sow dreams. Yet another fruit of the great tree planted by Joachim of Fiore, the fanatical monk who more than a hundred years before had tried to renew the Church through his prophecies.

Animatedly, Bruno continued to fill his verbal landscape with images of salvation. How could a sophisticated theology teacher lose himself in these crude visions, meant for simple spirits? Was it similar nonsense that had aroused Veniero's interest?

Dante lost interest; his mind began to wander. Then something—a change in the preacher's rhythm or in the tone of voice—recalled his attention.

The monotonous tale about the grandeur of the future age, with its indefinable aspirations and extraordinary expectations, had given way to a darker theme. Suddenly, the light of God had disappeared, making way for a turbid, malevolent obscurity.

Bruno was no longer guiding his listeners' thoughts and dreams toward a distant future. Instead he had turned to man's remotest past. Gradually, as the evocation proceeded, his words retreated further and further from Joachim's theories. Now the theologian was speaking about the Age of the Angels, who had rebelled against God, and of the Giants, who had been born from the bones of the angels and had dominated the Earth, oppressing it with their might. Of the Age of the Prophets, who had received the gift of sight and had died blinded by what they had seen, and of the Ancients, who had erected extravagant monuments, bloodying the earth with their battles. Finally, he spoke of the Last Age, of those who would inherit the earth if they were able to evoke the extraordinary forces of the four races that had preceded them, those races whose bodies now rested underground, awaiting the Awakening.

Upon hearing those words a murmur ran through the congregation. Dante caught a comment or two, about the enormous bones found on a farm in the Mugello. But Bruno paid no attention to these interruptions.

"Those who have come before us lie in their graves, not dead but sleeping," he declaimed with his eyes half closed, as if he were looking within himself for evidence of his own words. "It is possible to reawaken them and sit with them at God's banquet. It is possible to do so. It is possible. *It is possible!*" he repeated three times, as his voice rose to a shout. "The stars, the visible form of the ancient, sleeping races, will indicate the moment to the Master through their movements. Starting with the evening star, the quintuple symbol of our Lady of Angels."

Dante was scandalized. There was nothing Christian about Bruno's words: they were the shameful ravings of darkness. Men had been torn to pieces by the Inquisition for much less than this, in fact. How was it possible that such teachings were being imparted in a church? He recalled Veniero's words, and was convinced that the Comacine master had fallen into the same trap. If it were true that Ambrogio shared this perversion, perhaps what he had wanted to portray was the five ages of a world abandoned by God. What other members of the Third Heaven had followed him along that path of perdition? Mentally he reviewed again those men whose faces wore animal masks. Someone skilled at calculations, a master of the heavenly science . . .

He went back to studying the faces of the congregation, wondering what consequences Bruno's distorted cosmology might have on them. They looked like sleepwalkers, like men under the influence of a narcotic. Now the preacher was intoning an unfamiliar psalm, and his congregation responded in antiphony, mumbling phrases in unintelligible Latin. He was able to make out just one formula, repeated several times: *"Mater salva nos!"* This "Mother" was not the Blessed Virgin, but a woman unknown, with a name that sounded like the hissing of a snake.

Again he glanced around. He heard no other reaction to the preacher's blasphemous words. No objection, no sign of dismay. Instead, an abject chorus that prostrated itself, mindlessly invoking a void.

Only one man, he noticed, remained silent, unmoved by the formulas of this ritual. He stood slightly apart from the others, on the opposite side of the nave, his face sunk into his cowl. Just as Dante looked his way, he turned his head slightly, revealing his face. A shiver ran down the poet's back, and he instinctively drew back behind a column.

Even in the dim half-light he could not have been mistaken. It was the man he had caught examining Ambrogio's body. Noffo Dei, the inquisitor.

What must he do now? The friar's presence meant that the Church was aware of what was taking place in the Quaranta Martiri: Bruno was doomed. And so, perhaps, was he, Dante. He would have liked to melt into the marble. He did not know whether Noffo was already there when he came in. In any case, it was too late to do anything about it now. That rogue would be able to accuse him of collusion in Bruno's heresies.

He could not afford to place such a weapon in the cardinal's hands. Perhaps he should leave at once. Or . . . he could interrupt the mad rite by stepping forth and accusing Bruno of homicide— of the murder of Ambrogio. Have him arrested by the civil author- ity, snatching him from the hands of the Inquisition, saving the madman from death at the stake.

He was about to reveal himself when his glance fell on the theologian, who was staring at the corner where Noffo Dei was standing. He saw a look of collusion pass between the two men. It was unmistakable. Bruno was aware of the friar's presence there, and yet he had not ceased or even faltered in the proclamation of his insane heresy.

Was he seeking martyrdom? Or did he feel secure enough to mock the executioner? For a moment Dante was tempted to be- lieve that the cult of Fire Asiatic plague had taken deeper root, in- fecting even the highest levels of the ecclesiastic hierarchy. He looked again in the inquisitor's direction. The man evidently did not wish to intervene: he turned and moved slowly toward the door, keeping to the shadows. Near the door he brushed against a group of women.

Then Dante, watching Noffo, saw her, half hidden behind a column in a side chapel. She was wrapped in a long garment of deep blue cotton and her face was hidden by one of those cotton masks noblewomen wore outdoors for protection against dust. But when she rose on tiptoe as if to see better, the slight move- ment was enough. He recognized her, with that indefinable in- stinct of a man in love.

Now she, too, moved toward the door, with her supple step. Had the inquisitor given her some sign as he passed? A sign of complicity, like the one exchanged with Bruno? Perhaps Noffo had come to keep watch not on Bruno but on the woman.

An inquisitor, a heresiarch, and a slut. Three cards drawn

from a perverted tarot deck, dealt out in a holy church. He could not comprehend the relationship between them.

He waited a few moments in the doorway, then ventured out into the street. He saw no trace of the friar, and Antilia was far off.

DANTE UNWRAPPED his biretta and put it on, lowering the veil. He walked along, following Antilia. The dancer slipped through the crowd unnoticed, her beauty concealed beneath her loose-fitting cotton robe and mask. She walked quickly, unaffected by the heat, which was intense. The shadows of the buildings were lengthening. By this time they had crossed the entire quarter, but she continued on her way, heedless of the exertion and the swarms of insects.

She reached a fountain and stopped to drink. As she lifted her mask, she turned her head and he saw the black eyes flash. Then she continued on her way. He followed her without paying any attention to the route, all his concentration focused on not being discovered. Only now, at the sight of that fountain and the apothecary's shop beyond, did he realize where she had been leading him. At the apothecary's door she paused once more and glanced around as if she suspected her movements were being observed. Fortunately, at that moment a wagon laden with barrels passed by, hiding him from her view. Unfortunately, by the time it moved on, she had disappeared.

Dante was uncertain whether to follow her into the shop or wait until she came out and continue trailing her secretly. He decided to wait and ducked behind a column of the arcade at the corner, chasing off with threats and invective the beggar he found squatting at its base. The man gave Dante a surly look, moved just a few yards away and sprawled on the ground again, his hand stretched out in supplication.

There was something unusual about him. Another of those swine from the secret guild? After his encounter with Giannetto, the poet looked differently at a world that earlier he had simply brushed aside. The beggar, not he, was master of the street, like a dog that has marked the corner with his urine. He recalled Giannetto's sinister prophecy, his apparent certainty in predicting disaster for the Whites. What did that pack of derelicts know about Florence's future, about his own destiny? He felt the earth shift beneath his feet and was aware of an acute pain in his left eye.

He resumed watching the door. Suddenly a commotion broke out behind him. A second beggar had accosted the first, insulting the other man for having invaded his territory. He recognized Giannetto's voice, and turned around as the two came to blows. The stranger quickly got the upper hand: with a roar he hurled himself upon Giannetto, landing a violent kick on his side. Giannetto screamed in pain and slumped to the ground, his hand pressed to his broken rib.

Dante hurried toward them. Not that he had any intention of intervening in a fight between two beggars, but in the scuffle the interloper's garment had opened at the chest, exposing a hard polished surface, leather or bronze: a cuirass. He wanted to make certain of it, but seeing him approach, the armored beggar leaped to his feet and ran down the street, dodging into the crowd of curious passersby who had already gathered, and vanished from sight—but not before directing an obscene gesture at the poet.

"I am a prior of Florence, you animal! Save that for your bitch of a mother!" Dante shouted. "Miserable Thersites!" A young man wearing the uniform of a bargellino emerged from the crowd and set off in pursuit of the fugitive.

"Who was that scoundrel?" Dante then asked Giannetto, who was still hurling curses and obscenities at his adversary.

"I don't know," the man replied with a painful grimace that accentuated his rat-like expression. "Someone new, who has been hanging around here for a few days begging without the guild's permission. There have been many like him, for some time now, come from who knows where."

"Many?"

"Yes, too many. Curse them!"

Dante leaned against the column, taking deep breaths to calm his agitation. Then he made his way past the struggling onlookers toward the apothecary's shop. Teofilo, standing in the doorway, appeared to be waiting for him, and stepped aside to let him pass. Dante strode in: given that circumstances had decided the matter for him, he would interrogate the woman now. Quickly he glanced around. "Where is . . ."

"Antilia? Is she the one you are looking for?" Teofilo asked with a mischievous smile. "She was here a little while ago."

"Where did she go?" Dante asked, bewildered. He certainly had not seen her come out.

"She left, did you not see her? We heard shouting outside, and I thought it would be wise for her to leave without attracting attention. You know her particular situation, the risks . . ."

The poet nodded briefly. Teofilo was hiding something. "What was she seeking here?" he asked abruptly.

The apothecary paused, as if he could measure out how much truth to speak as precisely as he calculated how much potion to administer. "What everyone seeks in my shop," he said finally.

"Everyone?"

"Everyone. Including you, Messer Durante."

"Your meaning escapes me."

"How to free oneself from pain. Or . . ."

"Or?"

"How to unleash it. Pain is the prime mover of our actions. This is what the great Aristotle was thinking of when he imagined his celestial system."

"No, you are wrong. It is love that moves the heavenly spheres. It is the desire for the supreme heaven, immersed in love of the divine essence, that determines the rotation of the lesser ones, since each heaven wishes to experience the infinite joy of illumination at every point." But he spoke distractedly, as if repeating a lesson. He was thinking about Antilia.

This game of allusions irritated him. He opened his mouth again to question the apothecary, but Teofilo spoke first. "And yet, Messer Durante, do you not think that Algos is the god that dominates here on earth? Is it not on his account that we fight, love, create, and die? You yourself confirm it, according to Aristotle: if the first heaven rotates frantically to be with God at every point, its search for that absolute joy presupposes its own deficiency, in other words, pain?"

He spoke in a low voice, as if he feared that his god of pain might be listening. The poet shrugged. He had no desire to enter into a theological debate. He was convinced that Teofilo had started the discussion only to distract his attention from the woman.

"Did Antilia request that medicine of yours?"

The apothecary burst out laughing. At once he became again the jolly soul from the tavern. "It is called *chandu* . . . Oh, no, nothing so serious. She was merely looking for a soap that would preserve the beauty of her skin. But who knows, perhaps for a woman the struggle to protect her beauty is a fundamental source of pain . . ."

Dissatisfied, Dante continued looking about him. Antilia had headed for the apothecary's shop immediately after hearing

Bruno's sermon; if there was a significance in that, Teofilo's words did not explain it.

"Last time you told me that your drug *chandu* was made up of five elements," he said, changing the subject. "Do you truly not know what they are?"

The apothecary started slightly, and his eyes flew to the iron-bound chest, as if to reassure himself that it was securely locked. "Its composition is a secret, Messer Durante," he said evasively. "You experienced its effects. You are therefore in a position to accurately judge its merits."

"The mosaicist was killed because he was preparing to reveal the five parts of something. So why not the five elements of the mixture . . . which he might have learned from you—or stolen from you. You say that I myself can judge its merits. That is true, and I consider its merits to be extreme, capable of inducing someone to kill in order to obtain it. Or in order to defend it."

The apothecary suddenly looked worried.

"Is it not perhaps with that potion that Messer Bruno drugs the disciples of his cult, of which you too are a member?" Dante persisted.

"You don't think . . ." the other stammered.

"Why should I not?"

Teofilo hesitated for another moment, then abruptly raised his right hand, his fingers forming the recognition sign of the apothecaries' guild. *"Auxilium peto,"* he exclaimed.

It was the formula by which a guild member asked a fellow member for help. Dante automatically replicated the gesture, forced to respect the oath that bound him. *"Auxilium fero,"* he replied.

Now Sprovieri appeared more confident. He grabbed Dante's arm, gripping it tightly. "We consider that secret to be important, and rightly so. But it is not the only secret under the sun. Other, more important ones exist, and perhaps it is well for a confrere to know them."

"What do you mean?"

"Who knows, perhaps you could actually help me . . . perhaps your learning . . ." Teofilo remained motionless for another instant, as if overcoming one last uncertainty, then went over to a cabinet. He opened it and took out a small, perfectly square box made of the dark, precious African wood favored by the pharaohs. He busied himself briefly with one of its sides. Dante heard a faint click and saw him lift a small peg. The box sprang open, revealing within it a round object of yellow metal. Teofilo picked up the object almost fearfully and handed it to him.

It was a gilded metal circle, engraved with faint writing in a foreign alphabet. Very similar to the ring that the poet had seen in Messer Domenico's shop—the pledge of the Venetian seaman.

He balanced the object on the palm of his hand. "Is it what it appears to be?"

"Yes, Messer Durante. It is gold."

Dante continued turning the ring in his hands. He looked up. "Where does it come from?"

"Perhaps it would be more accurate to ask from *whom* does it come. These rings appeared in Florence some time ago, accompanied by a rumor. A tale, perhaps."

"What tale is that?"

"That this gold does not come from the bowels of the earth."

"Do you mean that someone . . . produced it?" the poet murmured, carefully re-examining the ring. Then he brought it to his lips, brushing the metal with his tongue. "If what you say is true, the Commune's finances are in grave danger. Every method known for recognizing the dross in a forger's coin would be hopeless."

"So then, do you not think that this secret is greater than the secret of my drug?"

"From whom did you get this ring? And what alchemist has knowledge to effect the transmutation? A member of the Third Heaven? Tell me!" Dante pressed him. He was about to repeat the recognition gesture, but suddenly checked himself, hiding his hand. "I do not want you to respond to the oath of the guild, but to the authority of Florence."

"I do not know, I swear to you! It was Ambrogio who gave it to me, shortly before he was killed. But he told me no more than I have told you." He seemed shaken, as if the dead man's name had evoked his ghost as well. "The secret is not in my possession—I myself am in search of it," he added.

Dante reflected on his last words. The drug was certainly extraordinary, but what was its value compared to the miracle Teofilo had just shown him? And who was there in Florence capable of achieving it?

"The gold circlet . . . Can you lend it to me for a while?"

"Of course, Messer Alighieri," the other replied, handing it to him. "Do you think you can discover its origin?"

The prior did not answer. His mind was elsewhere, and with unintended discourtesy he walked out of the shop without bidding the apothecary good-bye. He felt excited by the revelation and the new prospects it opened.

TEOFILO FOLLOWED him to the doorway. As soon as Dante was out of sight, he closed the shop's door. A faint rustling sound behind him made him turn around. One of the wooden panels of the cabinet against the wall opened and Antilia stepped through it. Teofilo's eyes ran over the charms that appeared beneath the delicate folds of her garment like a statue of Venus half hidden, half revealed by her drapery.

She had removed her traveling mask and her face shone out in naked beauty. A single drop of perspiration rolled down her perfect forehead.

"Did you hear?" he asked her.

Antilia nodded, staring at the ebony box still lying on the counter.

"I revealed nothing," Teofilo added, with a quiver in his voice. "When . . . when will you set off?"

She was silent.

"May I not come with you?" The apothecary went over to her and raised his hands to lightly touch her shoulders. She watched his movements without emotion. The man began to loosen the ties of her garments, slowly baring her copper-colored body.

13

June 20, in the morning

"CURSED MERCHANTS. Worthless men," Dante hissed to himself, pacing the vestibule of the offices of Calimala, the cloth merchants' guild, the most important in Florence. Rich, arrogant, and insolent. At least half of the Commune's functionaries were more or less openly in its service, and those who were not feared it. "They dare to keep me waiting. I would have them all hanged, if there were a hangman around."

He had barely been able to gain admittance even to this antechamber, and that only by invoking his authority. In the space of half an hour he had seen corpulent merchants, rough laborers, and other rabble go in before him, and his anger against those upstarts had welled each time. It was because of people like them that Florence had become what it was. A city that could have been a new Rome, given the wisdom of its laws, and another Athens, thanks to the splendor of its art, had been transformed into a second Babylon. There was no public office that was not sold, no law that could not be passed to the tune of florins, no sentence that was not commuted in accordance with the judges' interests.

Calimala was housed in the Old Town and the chamber looked out onto yet more new construction. An imposing edifice was rising on the other side of the street, replacing some ancient hovels. There was something unsound, he thought, about the ostentatious display of these new buildings growing up in the midst of vineyards, to be occupied by the teeming masses of country folk coming to the city to seek their fortune, a hidden flaw like an invisible fracture in the bronze of a church bell, that only a trained ear can hear before the bell suddenly cracks. And the poet's ear, refined by the muses and by his familiarity with the voices of the ancients, perceived that dissonance clearly, like the roar of a distant waterfall.

"City of thieves," he repeated, moving away from the window.

Finally a servant dressed in the guild's flamboyant livery summoned him curtly and led him without ceremony to a room on the upper floor, which overlooked the arcade that spanned the Old Market.

A man with an air of authority was seated behind a tall desk, surrounded by smaller desks occupied by a dozen or so accountants who were busily recording the commercial proceedings of the companies and merchants in large ledgers. "What can I do for you, prior? Is the Commune taking an interest in our guild?" the director asked. He spoke in a cold, droning voice: the same he would have used to address the lowliest of his subordinates.

"The Commune takes an interest in what is good for Florence—and what is not. Today it is concerned with the latter."

The director was caught off guard. He had expected the usual request for favors, or for money. "What does that mean?" he asked, with a show of displeasure.

"I have the duty of conducting an investigation into the murder of Master Ambrogio."

"The Comacine mosaicist . . . I have heard. But I do not see what it has to do with Calimala . . ."

"Neither do I. Not yet, at least. But I am exploring various paths to arrive at the truth."

"And one of these paths has brought you here?"

"Calimala is the guild in which all branches of knowledge converge, they say. Act, decree, dispose: is not this your motto?"

The director nodded, not looking convinced.

"In any case, I am here to speak with one of your members," Dante went on. "Flavio Petri, the Genoese."

"The master dyer? And for what . . ."

He did not complete the question. The look he saw on Dante's face did not invite discussion. With a few short words the director ordered one of the secretaries to escort the prior to the dyer's vault.

THE VAULT was located in a vast basement with a low arched ceiling. It was cluttered with large copper vats, continually boiling, and mortars for crushing and mixing. Dense vapors made the air almost unbreathable.

Flavio Petri was alone. When Dante entered, the master dyer was pouring a substance from a glass beaker into one of the cauldrons. He spoke briefly with the clerk who had accompanied Dante, then came forward.

A pair of lively coal-black eyes gleamed in his wrinkled face. "What can I do for you, Messer Durante?"

"I wish to draw upon your wisdom in a particular area."

"Everything I know, little as that may be, is at your disposal."

"I do not underestimate your learning. You are the most knowledgeable natural scientist in Florence—in Italy. Perhaps throughout the Christian world."

The other inclined his head slightly, with a reserved smile. He waited for the prior to continue.

"What do you know about the fabrication of gold?" Dante struggled to pose this outlandish question in a casual tone, and was amazed at the serenity with which the Genoese responded.

"I have heard a thing or two, in the course of my long life. An epic search that would make your pulse throb, but one too often based on delusion. Men have devoted years of sleepless nights to it . . . I do not know if it can be called divine, this desire to penetrate nature's matrix, for it is also tainted by more worldly desires. That is the uncertainty that man's conscience is unable to resolve each time his mind wrests another secret from creation, no matter how small."

"But do you believe it can be done? Or that it has already been done?" Dante persisted, ignoring the old man's moral reflections. Flavio Petri shrugged, his gaze fixed on a distant point.

"There are those who say it can. I have met men of all kinds who swore they were in possession of the secret. Scoundrels and tricksters, for the most part, incapable of providing even the most superficial evidence that they knew anything whatsoever of the alchemist's great art . . . except, perhaps, one man."

"And what did you learn from him?"

"He was one who truly possessed an alchemist's skill, and he told me there were five steps by which copper could be transmuted into gold. Copper: that was the crux of his secret. The force that generates gold comes not from the sublimation of lead, as many think, but from the fire concealed in copper."

"And . . . did you put this theory to the test?" Dante asked eagerly.

"I did not ask to know the theory in its entirety. The secret of gold is the secret of kings. Too many who boasted of knowing it have been killed by those who wanted to know it . . . or who did not want anyone else to know it."

Dante was puzzled. He had listened too often to tavern tales, of the philosopher's stone, among other marvels, and all had proved completely unfounded. "So you heard about this process long ago, during your travels. In distant lands, I imagine," he said, with a hint of irony.

The master dyer looked him in the eye. "No, Messer Durante. I heard about it recently, in your own city. And it was not just talk. I will show you what was found by a local fisherman, at the bottom of a skiff abandoned on the coast of Pisa. One of our agents was curious about it and sent it back to the guild hall."

He opened a drawer and took out a reddish stone as large as a walnut. "Look. Have you ever seen anything like this?"

Dante studied the object closely. "Is it copper?"

"An apple of the Hesperides," Flavio replied mysteriously. "Yes, it is copper. Extremely pure."

"And this can be transformed into gold?"

"Perhaps." The Genoese continued rolling the nugget between his fingers. "Copper is found in nature in the form of fine filaments intermingled with imposing masses of rock and soil. This is an anomaly."

"And how do you explain this anomaly?"

"I cannot explain it. It might represent the first stage of the transmutation. There is a mountain of knowledge in Florence, and it is growing at a staggering rate. Our towers now rise to the sky. Church domes broad as meadows multiply over our heads. Machines never seen before are invented to assist these vast constructions. Perhaps someone has plucked again the fruit of the tree of Eden."

"Yes, truly someone may have eaten of that fruit. What do you think of this?" Dante answered, drawing the gold ring out of the purse he carried at his girdle. The other took it in his hand and examined it curiously. "Yet another one of those rings . . ."

"You have seen others?"

"Yes . . . at least two others, very similar to this one."

"What can you tell me about the metal? Is it gold? Natural gold, I mean . . ."

Flavio gave him a quizzical look, as he brought the ring over to a slab of black jasper on the counter and began rubbing it on the stone with gentle strokes.

"Yes, it is gold," he said then, carefully observing the subtle streaks that the metal had left on the slab. "Untainted by any impurity. But I cannot tell you if it is the work of nature or of man: no touchstone exists for that."

"Where did you see the other rings?"

"They appeared in the guild's coffers, somehow. That is all I know. Nor would I tell you more, even if I knew. Calimala's affairs are under seal, and the seal is death."

He gave the ring to Dante, who was about to reply when his attention was drawn to a large sheet of folded paper that was lying on the workbench beside the vats of dye. On the side that was visible he recognized the blue of waterways and the ocher of mountain chains. He went over and picked it up to examine it more closely, noting Petri's look of irritation as he did so. Indeed he had the impression that the master dyer would have torn the sheet out of his hand had he dared.

"I recognize the city of Paris, with its turreted island. Is this also useful to your work?" the poet asked lightly.

"The knowledge of geometric principles falls within my province. Exercising it is one of the ways in which I serve the guild. The precise recording of roads and boundaries is important for commerce, as are many other kinds of knowledge. But I would ask you to say nothing of what you have seen," the master dyer added, this time taking the sheet of paper out of Dante's hand and carefully refolding it.

Surprised by Petri's behavior, Dante admonished him. "Why should knowledge of the configuration of any place be kept secret? Why conceal the appearance of the world? To do so would be to conceal the face of God!"

"The roads of the world are not merely the nerves that connect the various parts of its vast body, they are the veins through which riches flow, Messer Durante. To know them is to be able to draw freely upon this lifeblood, safe from the envy of rivals. Then, too, who knows, perhaps the configuration of the world is truly splendid and terrible like the face of God, and like it must be veiled if we are to avoid being blinded."

"You are probably right, Messer Flavio. Yet they say that at the last moment of seeing, before plunging into darkness, the eyes of those condemned to blindness experience a miraculous flash that reveals to them the true form of things. Perhaps it is precisely that flash that all of us are seeking."

The old man lifted his shoulders as he said, "Yes, before the darkness."

HE BID farewell to the master dyer and returned to daylight and the crowded street, his ideas no clearer than before. At the corner was a small tavern. He sat down on a bench outside, under the awning that shaded the doorway, and the innkeeper poured him a measure of tepid white wine that did nothing to allay his burning thirst. The glitter of transmuted gold flashed before his eyes, cutting through the vapors that rose from the street, the miasma of human and animal waste.

Was it really possible to fabricate gold so pure that it fooled even the eye of an expert like Flavio Petri? He should alert the master of the Mint. He stretched and rolled his head from side to side to relieve the torpor caused by heat and wine. His thoughts continued churning in his head.

What would happen if an enormous number of florins were

actually put into circulation? At first, a seemingly benign increase in wealth and public contentment. Debts forgiven, taxation ended, a universal freedom from need. The Land of Plenty.

Followed by disaster, the loss of any standard of value once gold became as common as sand. A new age, like the one Bruno Ammannati yearned for. But one of despair, truly the Last Age.

He must have spoken aloud, for the tavern keeper hurried over, thinking he had called for another round. The heat had become intolerable.

"That may be their plan!" he shouted suddenly, leaping up and overturning the bench. He tossed a coin at his startled host and raced off in the direction of Ponte Vecchio.

"Was that man not Messer Alighieri, the new prior?" one of the customers asked. "May God protect us!"

14

The same day, around noon

THE PRIORY secretary's report on the members of the Third Heaven had included the locations where each of the directors of the future studium temporarily held his classes. Cecco d'Ascoli assembled his students of medical astrology in the small capitular room of the abbey of San Sisto, in San Frediano.

From the time he had seen him in Baldo's tavern, Dante had meant to meet with him alone, to confront the issues that divided them. For years they had carried on their debate on the nature of astrology from a distance. But now that he had heard the preacher in the church of the Quaranta Martiri, a confrontation was imperative. And why not now, when his imagination—warmed by the wine—was in the best condition to prevail?

He made his entrance as the instructor was observing the outcome of a debate between two students. Looking down from his cathedra, Cecco seemed satisfied by the progress of the discussion. The *sic* had already completed his argument, and the advocate of *non* was also about to conclude. The young man was reading, standing before his professor's chair, while behind him the other half-dozen students sat on a bench and listened, taking notes on their wax tablets. Beside him, his opponent for the day listened attentively, on the alert for any contradiction so that he might raise his finger and pronounce the word *nego*.

Dante was in time to catch the final remarks. The theme must have been the influence of the transits of Mars on the humid secretions of the lungs. The gusts of Mars, hot, dry planet of fire, stimulate the spirits in the body. And this, in the opinion of the speaker, was a sure cause of a reduction of fluxions and sputum.

His opponent had evidently argued for an opposite result: ". . . certainly misled by the evident eruption of seminal liquid and by the increase of amorous dreams that occur at the time of its transits. Yet it is known, moreover, that aridity fosters coitus, a hypothesis substantiated by the increased fertility of animal species in the hot season and by the well-known amorous impetus that characterizes the black peoples of Libya."

The young man had pronounced these last words in a compassionate tone, as if he wished to extenuate his opponent's error, which he was maliciously exposing. A burst of applause accompanied his retort. It seemed that his thesis had indeed convinced the small audience. Even the instructor made a slight show of approval, as if he desired to express his esteem, but without sowing the dangerous seed of arrogance in his pupils.

The students addressed ceremonious farewell greetings to their instructor. Only then did Cecco d'Ascoli become aware of Dante, who had remained standing near the door. He quickly climbed down from the podium on which the cathedra was elevated, opened his arms and kissed the poet on both cheeks.

"Messer Durante, welcome! If I had known that you meant to attend my class, I would have had a second seat brought into the classroom so that you might sit at my right hand and observe as my equal."

Dante returned his greeting. "I thank you for the honor, but I do not possess a *licentia docendi*. The courses I took in Bologna and Paris did not elevate my learning to that rank. Therefore my place is down below, amidst your students."

"I know that you excel at modesty as you do at wisdom, master. If you wanted one, there would be a place for you in the studium. And in this very area of astrology, in which I know you are extremely qualified."

Dante looked him in the eye. "Would you also receive me into the Third Heaven?"

The other stiffened. His affable expression and animated manner vanished. "Why not?" he said finally, after a pause that seemed interminable. "The Third Heaven is that of Venus, and you are a poet of love . . . and a very great one, I might add."

He took a deep breath, then unexpectedly began to sing *Love, that within my mind discourses with me,* continuing through the entire first stanza. The sweetness of the lines was enhanced by his fervent voice, as he marked the rhythm by tapping his hand.

After his initial surprise, the poet sang the second verse, and then Cecco sang again, intoning the subsequent stanzas to the end.

After a moment of silence, in which the harmony of the voices still seemed to echo in the room, the astrologer resumed speaking. "You rendered the terrestrial object of your passions immortal. Alas, the wretched times in which we live prevent it, but in another era your Beatrice would have risen to astral ranks by virtue of your extraordinary verses. As did Berenice, celebrated by Callimachus."

"It is not the wretchedness of our times that prevents it, but the fact that we are human beings. It is this that denies us the chance of ascending to the heavens, except through the portal of Peter and his angelic choirs," the prior replied, moved.

"That may well be. But you . . . What may I do for you?"

"There is a question that I would like to submit to your knowledge. It concerns the noble subject of astrology, but also a perverse criminal act."

The other came closer, his curiosity aroused. "Tell me."

"Do you believe that the influence of the heavens, insofar as it determines our destinies, is inevitable or accidental? Do the stars ineluctably guide our steps or, on the other hand, do they merely provide an initial impetus to our impulses, which are then governed by free will?"

Cecco d'Ascoli smiled slightly. "It is a question that is much debated, Messer Durante. But, if I may say so, only among weak minds. It has been established that the celestial bodies that orbit the heavens beyond the lunar sphere are perfect and incorruptible. If their motion were avoidable, it would be defective, and we would have an uncertain consequent from a certain antecedent, a perfect cause that gives rise to imperfect effects. And this is a contradiction from which our mind recoils. Ergo, our destiny is written in the stars to an exact degree."

Instinctively Dante raised his index finger. He did not actually pronounce the word *nego*, but his entire body leaned forward, as if he were engaged in a debate. "Yet if we were to admit that the influence of the heavens on our natures is inevitable, the ethical framework that supports all of our laws and customs, even our moral sense itself, would crumble," he replied calmly. "Even master Ambrogio's death could thus be ascribed to the timeless revolution of the planets, and the hand that brought it about would become merely an instrument, in no way responsible. Redemption would be futile, since there would be no guilt. Our own religion of salvation would be as vain as the pagans' idols."

Cecco d'Ascoli returned his gaze coldly. "Perhaps it has been vain."

"That is blasphemous! This is not what the great Ptolemy taught in his *Almagest*!" Dante shouted. "Nor Sacrobosco. Nor Guido Bonatti, your own teacher!"

"My knowledge is not based solely on their teachings."

By now the poet had drawn so close he could feel the warmth of the other's breath. "Did you perhaps go to Messer Bruno's pulpit and draw the nefarious dream of other gods from the wasteland of his mind? Do you, too, believe that the stars are the visible form, the manifestation of beings of inconceivable powers who preceded us on earth and then deserted it, but are now ready to make their return? And that through the observation of the stars it is possible to evoke those beings? Is this what you believe?"

"I too have listened to Messer Bruno's words," Cecco replied slowly. "These are not concepts that are part of our science. They come from afar, from the lands of the Orient where Ammannati practiced his preaching as a young man. But you should not attribute to them an importance greater than is due: they are not harmful to anyone who does not take them to heart." A smile lit up his face. His expression became conciliatory and his voice assumed its former warmth. "Come, Messer Durante, let us leave behind this perilous road that subordinates the radiant beauty of the science of the heavens to the miseries of this world. As for redemption, you know that it does not contradict my argument. In fact, the birth of Our Savior was precisely anticipated by stellar revolutions and announced by the conjunction of Mars and Jupiter in Pisces."

Dante softened his tone of voice in turn. "All right, then, yes, let us leave religion to the priests. But I have another argument to demonstrate the fallaciousness of yours. Does the influence of the stars, certain and incorruptible, also act on the minerals concealed in the earth's bowels?"

"Unquestionably. It is the influence of Venus that determines the antiabortive property of carnelian, just as Mars renders onyx a potent antivenin. And finally, is it not the sun that gives gold its properties of plasticity and luminosity?"

"Yet if the properties of gold are shaped by the force of the sun, how do you explain the fact that the mineral to which the greatest, most luminous star gives its nature is so rare?"

Cecco gave a self-satisfied little smile. "Who says that gold is so rare on this earth? Or that, if it is, it always will be?"

Dante remained silent, looking steadily at him.

"And in any case, even if the heavenly bodies are not gods, as ancient wisdom believed, nevertheless they truly have an enormously powerful influence, as we learn daily from the factual evidence of life's stormy circumstances. The wrath of Mars, the power of Jupiter, and above all, the irrepressible energy of Venus, the pentagonal star that batters the city's gates, these divine attributes, unlike the old divinities, are far from dead."

"The mistress of the Third Heaven," the poet murmured. The astrologer's words had called to mind a detail. Ambrogio had inscribed a tiny five-pointed star in his documents. And Bruno, in the church, had spoken about a quintuple planet.

Cecco nodded his assent. Then he began reciting, again marking time to the words and pausing briefly after each line.

> In the third orbit, Love's radiant star
>   Brings my soul anguish, while shedding its light
>   On her beauty, to others made dim and obscure
>   By death, yet before me still present and bright.

Dante listened in silence. "What lines are those?" he asked.

"A quatrain from a little poem of mine about the configuration of the heavens. These lines speak of the third heaven and its queen."

"Why did you call the evening star pentagonal?"

The other gave him an ironical look. "Surely you do not expect me to believe that you do not know why, Messer Durante," he replied in a tone of mock disbelief. "With your reputation as an expert on celestial motions?"

Dante reddened, injured by the observation. "No, certainly not. But why should Venus and love bring about anguish?"

"You are asking me? You really do not know why? Or do you not believe that Love guides the steps of Death? Why do you think that master Ambrogio was killed?"

"For the love of a woman?"

"The woman who is Truth."

"Why should the mosaicist have been a victim of the truth?"

"Are we not all, in one way or another? Are you not also truth's victim, Messer Durante?"

Dante thought of what he had read in the report on the Third Heaven. They had all come from Rome. But before that, they had all been in the Orient. Like Baldo, the crusader. And Antilia . . .

He had the impression that Cecco was using the dignified mantle of astrology to cover up something darker. And that Antilia might be something more than just a dancer. A shiver ran through him as he recalled her body. He had to see her. Now. Alone.

To learn more about her, naturally.

The same day, early afternoon

BALDO'S TAVERN was almost deserted at that hour; only two servers bustled around the great fireplace, bent under the weight of the fagots that they were piling against the wall. The crusader was sitting on one of the benches, drinking wine from a metal cup as he watched the workers' progress.

Seeing the poet enter, Baldo set the cup down on the table with a nervous gesture, spilling part of the contents. Clearly he meant to free his single arm to defend himself.

Certainly no decent citizen entered the door of a tavern at that hour, after the noon meal and before the end of the workday. Most likely Baldo thought he was dealing with a drunkard.

Dante scowled. He, a prior of Florence, received like a common tippler by a disreputable, one-armed nobody. His hand flew to his concealed dagger, as the ghastly image of the crusader's hold invaded his imagination. He had to be on his guard and not let Baldo approach beyond a safe limit.

"May I serve you some of my best, Messer Alighieri?" the tavern keeper said, forestalling his rebuke.

"I am not here to enjoy your wine," Dante replied. "I wish to speak with the dancer who performs in the tavern."

Baldo rubbed his chin and studied him slyly. "So you want my Antilia. My splendid Antilia." He gave a lascivious stress to the word "splendid."

"Your Antilia?" The poet had never considered the possibility that the woman might be a slave, purchased or captured in battle in her native East. Still, Christian laws did not forbid taking pagans as slaves.

"Did I say 'my'? Oh, forgive me, Messere. Surely it is because of the admiration I have for her. Antilia does not belong to anyone in this city. For many men this fact is the cause of great torment. And I am one of them," Baldo concluded, patting Dante on the shoulder.

The prior stepped back, both in fear of the crusader's hold and out of irritation at such familiarity. "I wish only to speak to her," he answered pointedly.

"Antilia certainly does not live in my humble abode, Messere. You must set your sights higher, if you wish to find her."

"Do you mean to say that she does not live here, in your inn?" Dante replied, surprised. According to his report on her, she should have.

"No. Undoubtedly she is under someone's protection, and it is to that person's house you should go, if you wish to speak to her."

"Tell me who her lover is, at once!"

"Messer Alighieri, as I have said, many are in love with the beautiful Antilia," the man said. "And I could even tell you their names, seeing that you share their table every now and then. Certainly I, too, am one of that number . . . and perhaps you are as well," he dared to add. "But her real lover, the only one whose love is requited, is not known to anyone. Discover him, and you will find Antilia."

"Do you mean to say that you do not know how to send for the woman who enlivens the nights at your tavern and who receives her livelihood from you?"

"You are mistaken, Messere. She receives nothing from me. I do not have the means. No, only a prince could pay for her."

Dante grew more and more astonished. "Is she not a dancer by profession? So then why . . ."

"I do not know. No one knows," the crusader interrupted him. "It was she who asked me if she could perform in my tavern, without any compensation. In fact, I had the impression that she herself would have been willing to offer me money to let her do so, if I had refused."

"But you did not refuse."

"No. I do not think there is a man in all of Florence who would have."

Dante was greatly disconcerted.

Baldo seemed to read his mind. "I am not a man of letters as you are, Messer Alighieri. But I have seen a lot, overseas, perhaps more than what is written in your books. And I have heard many tales recounted by our men who ventured farther than I, toward the lands of India, following in the footsteps of the great Alexander."

"What did you hear of India?"

"That in those lands some inhabitants honor their gods not with words or songs, but through bodily movement. Well, Messere, I think that Antilia, in some way, pays homage to her gods with her dance."

The poet tightened his lips. For a moment he was tempted to agree with that simple man's intuition. Hadn't he himself perceived something magical and ritualistic in the woman's motions the first time he saw her? If the idea had not been blasphemous, he would actually have admitted that there was something divine in her performance, that it was the rite of a priestess, not the dance of a whore. It was rumored that in the steppes of the Orient lived savage tribes of nomads whose princes and priests were women of marvelous, statuesque beauty. When they died, the rulers were buried in sumptuous tombs, with splendid jewels and other insignia of their greatness, and alongside them were laid flocks of courtiers, sacrificed so that these women would not have to face the terror and darkness of death's journey alone. These priestesses communicated with death during life, seeking answers after taking strange potions, calling the shades to assemble.

He wondered if Ambrogio had been a sacrificial victim of that foreign goddess, appointed her eventual companion on the journey toward the abode of the dead.

Baldo, rubbing his one hand across his forehead, said suddenly, "Sometimes I feel that the Moors' poison has not left me, that it is merely asleep, like a serpent awaiting May's warmth beneath a rock, ready to strike again."

"And is it the Holy Spirit that protects you? That strength of our fathers, witness to the divine sacrifice at Golgotha?"

The tavern keeper shrugged. "Overseas, I came to know many spirits."

Dante looked at him in silence. Then he dipped his index finger into the wine cup and traced on the table the pentagram that had been scratched onto Ambrogio's mosaic. The crusader turned pale, but remained expressionless, as if he did not understand. "Did you perhaps trade for the salvation of your body that of your soul?" the poet asked him.

Baldo did not reply.

Dante got up slowly. "And does your spirit demand blood sacrifices in exchange?" He had the impression that the one-armed man was trying to avoid his eyes. "And the others? To which spirits have they consecrated their faith?"

"The others? Who?"

"The scholars who have chosen your tavern as the altar for their rites. What do you know about them?"

"Nothing. They are men of learning. What could they have to do with me?"

"Much, if their science is that of intrigue. And in this you, too, might be a learned doctor."

Baldo paused, mechanically running a filthy rag along the edge of the table. Then he said, "I am not the only one."

The same hour, at the convent of Santa Maria Novella

IN HIS ROOM, Cardinal Acquasparta sat on one of his thronelike chairs. His face was turned toward a small window through which the Abbey's bell tower showed like a knife slashing through the blue sky. The bell was tolling nones.

Behind him he heard a slight movement and a sigh, as if someone wanted to attract his attention, but discreetly. Slowly he turned his gaze.

Noffo Dei was standing in front of the door. At a gesture from the cardinal he knelt down, kissing the ring that was offered him, the fall of his cowl around his shoulders revealing his tonsure.

The powerful prelate indulgently stroked the back of his follower's neck with his free hand. "What did you find out?" he asked, a hint of anxiety in his voice.

"What we already knew. The pentagram is clearly visible. It is his unequivocal message."

"Do you think that meddling prior has understood its significance?"

Noffo shook his head. "The prior is astute and intelligent. But he knows very little. As yet." He spoke the last words in a worried tone that did not escape the prince of the church.

"Do you think he is on the right track?"

"I am certain that he is not. He is confused, blinded by his perverse faith in reason. The stamp of the Sorbonne doctors can readily be seen."

"He, too, has been to Paris? But he must have been just a boy . . ."

"Their diabolical teaching with its misleading message has corrupted victims without number. And in our man that doctrine has grown into the insane conviction that human reason can penetrate all the secrets of nature and of human behavior. This is why he is now lost in a labyrinth, without realizing that its deviations and dead ends are created by himself as he proceeds step by step with his investigation."

Acquasparta gave a faint, cruel smile. "This gives us time to forestall the whore's moves."

"Do you think it is possible . . ."

"I do not know. But the last flicker of doubt must be snuffed out."

"I think so, too, Your Eminence. You will recall what I have already suggested."

The pontifical legate stopped him with an abrupt gesture. "You know that is impossible, in this city. Some priors are indeed on our side, but the time is not yet ripe for direct action. Such a remedy would be taken for what it is: a challenge to the Commune's sovereignty, and in its own territory, what's more. And we would find ranged against us even those who sympathize with Boniface, and excuses furnished to every hidden Ghibelline . . . like that Alighieri. Besides, you know very well that only the district watch guard can make arrests."

"We could accuse her of witchcraft and demand that the secular arm intervene."

"I have already considered that possibility. But if she has ventured to come to Florence, it means that she has trusted and perhaps powerful friends here. If we were to fail, we could find ourselves drawn into a public trial. And if everything we hear is true, and she were to talk . . ." The voice of the cardinal now cracked with rage. "How is it possible that she escaped surveillance, once she reached Italy? How is it that no one followed her movements, prevented her from crossing the border? How was she able to pass through the Church's territories to get here?"

Noffo shrugged. "We do not know. She appeared in Florence as if by magic. She is thought to have traveled by ship. Perhaps on board a Genoese vessel . . . those pirates will do anything for money. That Sienese scoundrel, Cecco Angiolieri, is also in the city. He quickly joined the company. They were expecting him, evidently."

"I have read his writings," the cardinal said with a leer. "He is the right man for them."

"Perhaps he is the right man for us as well. A few florins, and we shall have him in the palm of our hand."

"I know about your plan, but have you weighed the consequences thoroughly? If you were to be discovered . . ."

The inquisitor shook his head. "Nothing could ever be traced back to your person, nor to Holy Church."

Acquasparta began to pace back and forth across the room, circling around Noffo, who stood motionless. Then he halted. "Do it then," he said.

"It is already done. I was counting on your approval."

15

The same day, late afternoon

THE BARGELLO had turned up at his cell again. Dante was be-ginning to think that the man was a jinx. And the captain's worried expression did not reassure him. Clearly, he had found something to be uneasy about, again.

"What is it this time? Whenever I see you I never know whether I should be pleased with your conscientiousness or curse in anticipation the reasons that bring you to me."

"There is something that you should know . . . you, at least."

"Why? Because I am a poet?"

"No, the poetic art has nothing to do with it. But per-haps. . . . In any case, it is something serious."

"Tell me."

"This morning the servers in the kitchens were putting away the vats of wine reserved for the priors . . . so they say."

"So they say?"

"If you ask me, they were looking to have a drink at the Com-mune's expense, those rogues."

"Well then? Did you come to discuss the sobriety of the palazzo's servants?"

"No. As they were moving the vats, they say, one of them fell and broke."

The poet went toward the man, making a show of straightening his shoulders. "Do you wish some help in cleaning the wine cellar?"

"No, of course not." The Bargello reddened. He held out his hand which he had been keeping behind his back. "In the pool of spilled wine, a servant found this."

Dante almost tore the object out of the man's hand. It was a cloth pouch, filled with something soft. The fabric was wine-soaked, and a strong odor permeated the cell.

After briefly examining the outside of the little bag, he took his dagger and began cutting into the fabric.

"Is it perhaps a curse, prior? A spell cast by black magic?" the captain of the guard asked worriedly.

Using the tip of his blade, careful not to touch anything with his hands, Dante drew from the pouch a tangle of rotted leaves and flowers.

"Maybe something to spice the wine, some clever notion of the vinedressers?" the Bargello ventured, looking dubiously at the sodden clump.

Dante approached the window to examine the matter more closely. His face turned somber, a sharp furrow creasing his forehead. The pain in his temples had returned and grown worse. "Get rid of all the wine in the wine cellars, Bargello. It is best that Florence's priors drink water, at least for a few days."

"What is it? Do you know?"

"It is datura, thorn apple. The leaves of the plant and its flowers, the most toxic part."

"Is it . . . a poison?"

"Yes. In strong doses it can cause death, but diluted it is perhaps even more harmful."

"Why?"

"It unsettles and clouds the brains of those who should be vigilant. It causes dreams and visions. A perverse mind must have thought of using it against those who govern Florence. A poison that merely killed us would have brought about a grave, though surmountable crisis, for the Commune. To drive us silently to lunacy, on the other hand, to propel us into the darkness of illusions without our being aware of it, is truly a diabolical act. See to it that you maintain absolute silence about this nefarious deed. Those who contrived it must not know of our advantage."

"And what will you do?" the Bargello asked.

"I must carry on with my investigation. If I can catch one of the heads of this hydra, I will have all the others."

Once the captain had left, Dante succumbed to a frenzied agitation. So, was the evil actually spreading from Saint Jude's subterranean chambers to penetrate the halls of government as well?

He was furious. He stormed back out to the piazza, his head on fire again, and off toward Baldo's tavern. He refused an escort offered at the door by the startled Bargello, citing secrecy as an excuse, and his need to move about more freely.

But in truth those were not the reasons he wished to go unaccompanied. Antilia's body was still dancing before his eyes. He wanted to interrogate her alone, after her performance. He told himself repeatedly that his only objective was to punish the wrongdoer. And perhaps it was so. But a sense of guilt was already settling within him.

He felt like Jacob, wrestling with an angel in the night. Inwardly he struggled and squirmed like a wayfarer who has fallen into the pool of dark water where he is destined to drown.

NOT ALL of the members of the Third Heaven had assembled when he reached the tavern. Teofilo's place was empty. On the table was a huge jug of wine, from which those present had already helped themselves. Dante filled his cup as well, after having greeted them all individually, by name. He was about to ask after Teofilo when Cecco d'Ascoli's ringing voice forestalled him.

"How often we have spoken about love in the past few days, Messer Durante! And yet the minds of such learned men as we should be concerned with things far more solemn. In your opinion, then, what is this force that seems to prevail over every rational intent?"

"More importantly," Bruno Ammannati interjected, "is it correct to speak about a force? Or would it not be more accurate to define love as a weakness of the mind induced by the precipitous flight of vital spirits? Is love something that is added to the soul, like a virtue emanating irresistibly from the beloved object itself, or does it, like an incurable illness, deplete the mind?"

As they spoke, from the back of the tavern came the sound of the drums announcing the dancer's appearance. Dante turned from Ammannati toward Antilia. Was it love, this feeling of confusion he was experiencing, this desire to fuse his flesh with hers, to lose himself in her as in a whirlpool? Was he the same man who had trembled at the very thought of Beatrice? And if he had changed, was the force of love so great that it could transform a man's very nature in such a perverse way? Was this the force that had driven our progenitors from Eden?

He seized his brimming cup of wine and took several long gulps.

"You have of course read the canzone of your friend Cavalcanti: 'A Lady Asks Me.'"

It was still Cecco speaking. His voice sounded distant to Dante's ear, as if he and all of them had suddenly stepped aside to make way for Antilia. He was certain that her dark eyes were seeking his, that among all of them it was he to whom she would dedicate her dance. Even so, he felt hatred toward all others who desired her, who slowed her movements by reaching out to her.

He was about to stand up and proclaim his authority as prior. He would summon the guards, he would have that den of vice closed down, have that slut dragged to Maggiore hospital. Where did she hide, and with whom, when each night she fled from Baldo's tavern? He wanted to know, and he would drag the secret out of her as soon as she had finished that obscene performance.

The one-armed crusader had brought her from overseas; he was the root of it all.

"For example, Messer Durante, our Antilia," he heard Augustino say. "Her presence undoubtedly ignites heat in men's bodies and predisposes them for copulation. This occurs by operation of the luminous rays that emanate from her body and penetrate the ocular cavities, dilating the mucous ducts through the action of their heat. It is a virtue that is characteristic of the female nature. Any shapely woman who exposes herself to a man's eyes generates the same reaction, which is at the root of reproduction. But how do you explain the attraction that a woman is capable of exerting even when she is absent? Do our fluids retain over time the impressions and modifications that her emanations have impressed on them, as a liquid retains the shape of the container into which it is poured?"

Antilia had changed direction. Tonight she had decided to end her performance at the table of some tipsy merchants who were seated near the hearth.

Dante roused himself with difficulty and turned his attention once again to the man who had spoken to him. "Of course, Guido's canzone . . . I believe that love is a stirring of the heart. But that it does not originate from a radiant influence, as the infidel Al-Kindi would have it in his treatise. Love is a virtue inherent in those of noble spirit, who cultivate it from the moment of its birth—just as virtue is inherent in the mineral matrix of a precious stone. All a woman does, with her beauty, is activate this latent virtue, which in order to develop needs only to be awakened. This condition should satisfy your doubt as to how a woman can exercise her attraction even when she is absent, or even after her death, as I myself have experienced. You know about the divine Beatrice."

"So in your opinion the *spiriti amanti,* spirits of lovers, really exist? But why are only a few individuals familiar with this science of love, when all men are predisposed for reproduction?"

"Because the science of love is the supreme science that sustains the progress of learning in all branches of knowledge. As you also believe, moreover," Dante replied, glancing around at all those present.

"We?" Cecco said.

"Of course. When you named the college that is to be the foundation of the studium the Third Heaven, did you not intend to appeal to love as your lord and prime mover, after God? Did you not select the celestial Venus as the mistress of your meetings?"

The others glanced at one another, as if weighing his words.

"However, you overlooked one important truth when you chose Venus, not Minerva as the muse of your assembly. Love is an illuminating force, but if it is not controlled it leads to perdition. You broke the bread of knowledge together under the sign of Venus. But under the same sign, Ambrogio was murdered."

Dante picked up his cup again, which someone must have refilled meanwhile, gulping down another copious swallow. He felt the heat within him grow more intense, as if his viscera were on fire.

Veniero spoke, "Messer Alighieri, your argument is certainly suggestive. For me, however—since I am less erudite than you, though I have visited many more ports and traveled many more seas—a woman is like the wind that can swell the sails and speed a voyage—or shatter the mast when a squall breaks out. She is the force that we men require to cross the sea of life, and that we try to catch in our sails." He turned his gaze toward the dancer, who was moving away. *"Nec tecum nec sine te,"* he concluded.

The poet drained another cup. The cooled white wine, mixed with acidulous water, provided him an instant of relief as he drank, but could not quench the flames inside him.

"How would you interpret this verse then, Messer Alighieri? *Cometh from a seen form which being understood . . ."* Augustino recited. "Do you mean to say that Cavalcanti reduces the origin of love to pure vision? And that therefore it is not possible to fall in love, if you are apart from the love's object? But then how do you explain the passion of the troubadour Jaufré Rudel, who died of love for a woman he had never seen?"

"And that such a vision must be 'understood,' or rather traced back to something already known to us?" Antonio added. "But then how do you justify Adam's love for the first woman, Eve, about whom he could not have known anything?"

"And what a love, Messeri, judging from the consequences!" Cecco Angiolieri exclaimed. Up until that moment he had remained silent, his face expressing growing disgust, as if their talk were nothing but tiresome chatter. "Given that we are all still paying for our progenitor's deeds, one is tempted to wonder if he would not have done better to devote himself to the solitary art of Onan."

"Your blasphemous derision does not help us advance along the path of truth!" Augustino retorted.

"I say Cavalcanti is mistaken, and greatly so," Cecco snorted. "Love does not come from vision, as fine Florentine intellects like Guido, Lapo, and the others would have it. It comes from touching and pinching and sucking and lapping and smelling and shrieking and writhing in bed and tearing one's hair out in despair. Perhaps I, too, might modestly recall some verses of my own. But I fear that Messer Alighieri might take offence were I to compare my Becchina, with her grace, to the Selvaggias and Beatrices, with their *souls*."

As the discussion about love poetry continued, Dante felt his thoughts become more and more turbid, as if slime from the seabed had risen up to muddy the clear waters of his mind. The rigorous order of his arguments often broke off in disorder, and he found it hard to find the exact words he sought. His mind, on the other hand, was brimming with illustrations and hypotheses. His thoughts seemed to outstrip his tongue.

It was a sensation that he had experienced before, especially in his youth, when on Calendimaggio, he would indulge in the celebration of Venus and Bacchus with his comrades of the brigata d'amore. Since he had embarked on a political career, however, he had always been very careful to stay sober, at least in public, even on the First of May.

Perhaps it was merely a passing agitation that another sip of Vernaccia would calm, helping him regain his balance. He raised his cup again.

He wanted to reply to what seemed to him to be fallacious . . . but what was the proper order for his arguments? Or should he perhaps illustrate a premise? He tried to stand up and fell back on the seat. Someone behind him must have pushed him down. Who had dared to take such liberty? An acute pain smote his brain, radiating from his left eye. He needed some of Teofilo's potion. He would get up again, but first he had to shake off that annoying jester who had climbed up on his back and was jingling his bells in his ear. He reached his arm behind his neck, trying to nab the fellow before the others became aware of the rude prank of which he was the object.

Finally he was able to stand up. He tried to straighten his cloak, which was greatly hampering his movements, so voluminous had it become. Meanwhile a strong wind had arisen, sweeping through the entire tavern, knocking against the walls and ceiling. The flames of the braziers flickered dizzyingly, and the plank floor swayed beneath his weight, as if he had suddenly grown in size. Yet his mind was perfectly steady. There now, he had recomposed his arguments concerning love, and the fallacy of Cecco Angiolieri's reasoning appeared in all its obviousness. He mustered his forces and delivered his *sic probo*.

"That is not so," he was finally able to say.

The members of the studium seemed like spectators at a play, their gazes remained fixed on him, waiting for a further clarifying word. Their eyes were like opaque glass.

He felt a hand rest gently on his shoulder and heard a voice he thought he knew. He would have turned around to see who it was, but first he had to free his cloak which had got itself caught on the chair. He did not wish to appear clumsy in the eyes of these outsiders. He was about to turn when he remembered that he had to complete his argument against Cecco.

"That is not so," he repeated, and felt that he had been stunningly conclusive.

The voice whispered in his ear again. "The air here in the tavern has become so heavy, do you feel it too? The smoke from those damn braziers is shrouding everything. Would you not prefer to come outside, where you can breathe more easily?"

That queasiness he had begun to feel was caused by the braziers, of course. He tried to move forward, while the hand behind him moved to assist him. Supporting himself against the table, he started toward the door. Then he paused, picking up the cup again. He wanted to drain it before leaving. But it must have been glued to the table, for he was not able to lift it, even with the help of his other hand. Another of that cursed tavern keeper's pranks.

"Hideous cripple!" he shrieked. "Damn you!"

Outside, the damp, warm wind hit him in the face like a slap. He felt the beads of sweat on his neck condense and turn to ice. The ground on which he set his feet was soft and yielded under his steps like a horsehair mattress. Those damned Florentines, with their muddy streets. Now that he could move freely, he was able to see the man who accompanied him. Of course he knew him.

The other set out at a good pace. Swaying, Dante caught up with him, grabbing him by the arm. "Now the meaning of the *veduta forma,* seen form, is clear to me. Of course, it is so. *Quod erat demonstrandum.*"

He continued gripping the man's arm. A shadow of annoyance passed over the man's face as he gently tried to extricate himself, but the prior tightened his hold. "It is the sensitive soul, on which love's mark is imprinted. This is why love persists even when the woman who has generated it disappears. Just as in sleep, where the recollection of breathing persists. This is why we can love someone we do not see. This is why we can love someone who has died."

"Perhaps you would enjoy studying the effects of love, Messer Alighieri, rather than its causes," the man said after a brief silence. By now he had given up trying to free his arm. His voice softened. "You have written much about love. Come with me to Paradise. The best of the five."

Swaying, Dante took a few steps in the direction his guide was indicating. That number five again. Why did that cursed number keep resounding in his head? He was annoyed by the way this man's body kept bumping into him and interfering with his movement.

"The best of the five. What . . . what are you referring to?" he asked.

Veniero's face came close to his. The seaman seemed to be searching the depths of his eyes, as if to make certain he was in a condition to understand.

But the poet understood everything. "The best of the five?" he repeated, his voice unaccountably slurred.

"There are five houses of love in Florence, Messer Alighieri. And each is situated in the vicinity of one of the city's gates. You should know that, as prior."

"Priors do not go to brothels." Five gates. Five whore houses. What was Florence becoming, under the corrupt Boniface? Did no one devote himself to works of wisdom and virtue anymore? "Paradise? Lady Lagia's house . . ." he said. Now he understood, it was all clear to him.

"Are you familiar with it?" Veniero asked in an ironic tone. "I thought only Angiolieri was a connoisseur of such places."

All of a sudden the poet rallied, as if he had conceived a new idea. He began to run, catching his companion completely off guard. Veniero hastened to catch up with him, seized him again by the elbow, and steered his course toward a narrow sidestreet.

"Why that way?" Dante asked. He still felt disoriented. "Paradise is in the opposite direction."

"The circle of the old walls: this is what connects the houses . . . a circle. And a circle can be traveled in both directions, Messer Alighieri," Veniero replied.

The poet was certain that those words concealed a profound truth. But he was unable to grasp what it was. The captain must truly have been an expert navigator, even through land routes. Strange: a land-bound man, guided by a man of the sea.

The cooler nighttime air and the walk were beginning to dispel the fog in his brain. He remembered the drawing he had found among the Comacine master's papers. "Messer Veniero, do your galleys have sails beneath the keel as well?" he asked.

The mariner stopped abruptly, staring at him. He withdrew his hand, and Dante seized by a violent fit of dizziness, had to clutch for that arm again as he squeezed his eyelids shut, waiting for the world to stop whirling.

"No, of course not. The ship's bottom works are submerged in water. What sense would it make to have a sail under the keel?" the Venetian explained with deliberate slowness. "What gave you such an idea?"

"I saw a ship with sails down below."

"Where?" Veniero's voice reached him from a far distance. Even so, Dante was aware of his curiosity. "Where?" the captain repeated.

"Among Master Ambrogio's papers," the prior replied, rummaging in the inside pocket of his garment. Then he remembered that he had left that parchment at San Piero.

"A fanciful notion. Ambrogio was a great artist and builder, but he knew little about marine matters. Or he might have been imagining some curious allegory. It was among his papers, you say?"

A LIGHT glimmered in the distance. Dante recognized the two lanterns marking the entrance to Lady Lagia's establishment, which—like Baldo's tavern—was built on the remains of a Roman villa. All the houses of ill repute seemed to spring up from the ancient fathers' ruins, like worms from a cadaver.

But in this place the changes were less evident. The structure's original design had been preserved: a series of spacious rooms on the ground floor, aligned along the sides of a square courtyard, with a portico on the outside. Above these was a second level, divided into narrow cubicles.

They entered the ancient *impluvium*, which had been transformed into a drinking spot, and crossed what remained of the
old paved floor. Beneath their feet a painted ship surrounded by
black dolphins was completing its disintegration in a centuries-
old shipwreck, trampled by clients' horses. Around the fountain
were symbols of the constellations and the seven planets in their
orbits, half obliterated by time and neglect. A complete zodiac in
decay, extending along the entire surface of the courtyard.

Dante felt dismayed. On how many nights had he passed those
signs without heeding them, his awareness and his senses blinded
by lust? The heaven of Paradise . . . but was there really a paradise
somewhere, besides that obscene stone parody where strumpets
slept with fly-by-night lovers? The marble tiles had disappeared
here and there, but the course of the stars was still visible; here, just
in front of him, the curving orbit of Venus could be made out. The
goddess journeyed through her heaven naked, straddling a star.

He crossed the circles of Mars and Jupiter, then Saturn and
the dustlike specks of the fixed stars, and passed beyond the great
circle of the ecliptic, as far as the opposite wall, with its archways
leading to the ancient storehouses. On his right rose a narrow
brick staircase.

He started to ascend. It seemed to him that sarcastic laughter
accompanied his steps. Abruptly he turned around, thinking Veniero must be behind him. But it was someone else, hidden in
the opening of an archway, who watched intently a point on the
other side of the courtyard. He was wearing the livery of the
Bargello's men. They were spying on him, those cursed guards.
He retraced his steps with some difficulty and, assuming a menacing look, approached the man.

The man did not appear concerned. There was a bluish glimmer on his face. Dante stopped, uncertain, passing a hand across
his forehead. "You?"

The unknown man did not say anything, but merely returned his gaze.

"I wanted to thank you," the poet murmured, holding out his hand. "The other night at Saint Jude . . . It was my lucky star that placed you beside the abyss."

The other inclined his head slightly. As he moved, his resplendent hair glinted through the shadows. "We are wherever we are summoned," he replied, as he continued looking up. "Up there. They are waiting for you," he went on.

"Who summoned you?" Dante asked.

But the man had turned away and was moving off along the path of painted stars, toward the stables.

A YOUNG woman appeared at the top of the stairs, as if she had been waiting for him there. She was barely more than adolescent, and her long hair fell loose in a triumph of dark curls that spread out above her shoulders like a martyr's halo, framing a sharp face. She was staring at him brazenly, her head cocked to one side, her lips curled in a vulgar smile.

"So I see you are here yet again, Messer Alighieri. You seek my bed once more, after all," she addressed him brusquely, loosening the ties of her garment and displaying her breasts. Her voice cut like a blade.

Dante stopped abruptly, two steps below her. The girl approached and leaned over him, brushing against him with her breasts. The poet was aware of a muddled odor, the coarse scent of a winded mare mingling with something artificially sweet, one of those cheap perfumes sold in the markets of the Oltrarno.

"Pietra," he stammered. "Is it you?"

"Yes, it is I, Messer Alighieri. Or must I call you prior?" She leaned nearer to him, seeking his mouth.

Dante drew back instinctively, avoiding contact with her naked skin. The young woman gave an angry start, tossing her black curls and moving close to the wall again, almost as if she wanted to pass through it. She watched him with a mixture of rage and tenderness. Then she held out her arms to him again, drawing him to her.

Again her perfume invaded his nostrils, and his desires reawakened at the touch of those seeking hands, whose coldness and warmth he knew all too well. But this time he would not give in. He pushed his arms against her, rejecting her. "Go away, Pietra."

"Oh, Messer Alighieri, do you not need to console yourself for your wife tonight? So then what brings you to Paradise?" she sneered.

A fresh fit of dizziness clouded his sight. "I . . . I do not know."

The girl's gaze seemed to soften, but a sly gleam lingered in her eyes. "The mistress does not want anyone to leave here unsatisfied. Come," she said, holding out her hand.

Dante set out after her along the corridor, trying to keep pace with her light steps. But the girl ran off, as if in a great hurry, and disappeared around a corner after throwing him a quick look.

Dante thought she'd wanted to make sure he saw her. After a moment of uncertainty, he decided to follow. He rounded the corner and found himself in the building's other wing. Here the cubicles gave way to larger rooms, more sumptuously furnished, with good wooden beds instead of lowly straw pallets. Although all of the chambers were empty, when he passed by the open doors he could see that a small lantern had been placed in each, barely lighting the space inside, populating it with shadows.

He could not find Pietra in any of them. His footsteps on the wooden floor resounded in a confused echo, and under it he heard a metallic clinking, a sound he was certain he knew. The wine still muddled his thoughts, and he found it difficult to make sense of his surroundings. Why was he there? What was the meaning of all this lunacy? Where had Pietra led him, pretending to run away? Was she, too, an angel, or had Mercury appeared to him in her guise? Was he dead, and were those rooms the ante-chamber of Hades?

He continued on toward the back, as the clinking noises grew louder. Fragmented images flashed through his clouded mind, impossible to grasp. Then, as he reached the last room and stopped in the doorway, his memory cleared. Vertigo seized him, but it was not from wine. He remembered the nature of that sound even before seeing what it was.

HE STAGGERED into the room and sank down on the side of the bed, staring at the sight before him. Kneeling on the floor, her arms outstretched toward an object on the ground before her, was Antilia. The little bronze disks on her fingers jangled rhythmically as she intoned a chant in her strange language. Among all of the unfamiliar words he thought he recognized one—the same sibilant name invoked in the church of the Quaranta Martiri.

The woman broke off upon hearing him enter, hastily spreading a veil over the object in front of her before she rose. He thought he glimpsed a statuette: a pagan idol, before which she had been performing an unknown rite.

She stood before him, dressed in a simple yellow silk tunic that hid none of her beauty. The gold circles that adorned her elegant neck and ankles had chimed like bells when she stood up, and they continued jingling now, moved by her shallow breathing. She seemed exhausted, as if she had been praying thus for hours.

"What are you doing . . . here?" Dante mumbled. "Here . . ." he repeated, indicating the room with a vague gesture. He would have liked to get up, but his legs did not seem to want to obey him. He remained seated, as the woman took a step toward him.

"Here . . ." he said for the third time. Or maybe he only thought it, or his voice was muffled in the dense air. Here in a brothel, that was what he meant to say. Whore. And how could she be there, if he had just left her . . .

Antilia moved closer, holding a hand out to him. She had an uneasy expression, with no trace of that indifference to men's lecherous gazes that had so struck the poet at their first encounter. She seemed more human, as if the substantial panther within her had fled, leaving only its shadow. Her face shone, more copper-like than ever in the lantern's warm glow.

With her fingers she began lightly touching his face, slowly, with tenderness, like a blind woman trying to trace an unseen lover's features. Her eyes seemed even blacker: two bottomless pools of darkness. Dante rose up toward her, without noticing the sudden ease with which he had accomplished that movement. She reached a hand behind her back, loosening her garment, which slid easily down her shoulders, leaving her naked.

There it was again, the scarlet serpent, coiled on her belly, writhing up toward the curve of her breast. The creature's eye seemed to stare at the poet as Antilia moved even closer. Discernible on her breath was the acrid odor of *chandu*.

Dante felt the mattress resisting beneath him, smelled the sweat in the crumpled bedclothes, as Antilia's body pressed against his, as she clung to his limbs with all the desperation of a soul afflicted by solitude. Her hands moved down to seek him. And the prior yielded to her touch and sank into her breasts, and then her belly, and thought no more.

He made love to the dancer with the painted face, a woman who became every woman except the one she really was, the one he did not know, behind the copper mask. In the darkness

of that room, Antilia overlay the memory of another woman, a
woman now lost.

SLOWLY HE came to his senses, and pushed away that body whose
weight had become oppressive. He felt that he was suffocating, as
if the whole building were on fire and the flames had entered the
cubicle. As he stood by the bed trying to straighten his garments,
wordless and unsmiling, he felt the dancer's eyes on him, staring
out from the shadows. He turned toward the wall, to escape
them, then he faced her again, defeated.

Antilia stared at him in silence. She had risen from the bed
and was standing motionless in the center of the room, triumphant in her nakedness. The serpent gleamed, its lifelike coils rippling as she breathed. Her body, covered with a sheen of sweat,
shone in the lantern light, as if all the moisture of that sultry night
had adhered to her bronze flesh. The poet could still smell the
pungent odor of her skin in his hair, in his beard, beneath his
nails . . .

"Who are you?" he whispered.

She pointed her forefinger toward her breast. Even with that
slow gesture, the gold circles vibrated, emitting their metallic tinkle.
"Beatrice."

Dante gasped. "How do you know that name?" he managed
to say. "Who told you? Pietra, that slut . . ."

"Beatrice," the woman repeated. "I want my remuneration,"
she added, but in a toneless voice, as if she did not understand the
meaning of what she was saying, and was simply repeating sounds
in an unfamiliar language. She began to weep silently, but she remained upright, standing her ground in the middle of that room.
"My remuneration."

His head was hurting again. A slight ache, not the iron grip of other nights, but the faint touch of an old enemy who does not want to be forgotten. The muscles of his face twisted into a grimace. He felt Antilia's sorrow envelop him like the coils of the serpent she bore on her skin.

The lantern's flame seemed to trace a putrid luminescence around her, similar to the glow of decomposed weed that he had seen rising to the surface in the Po delta. As if the dancer were not really there and he were not there, either. Two apparitions, meeting in a mirror.

That image had descended into this abyss of sorrow from a different heaven. Paradise is an inferno turned upside down. How mistaken Plato had been, however great he was, when he imagined that our souls descend from the stars. No, the soul only wants to return to where it has never been. She wanted her remuneration.

A whore, like Pietra.

He leaped to his feet and fled down the corridor. It was Pietra, he was sure of it, who had revealed that name to her. To ridicule him, to get her revenge. The name echoed in his brain. He hated her, that slut.

The girl was once again at the top of the stairs and seemed to be waiting for him. She stared at him with her hard gaze, like a guardian at the gates of hell.

"What did you tell her about me, you damned slut? And what does she want?" Dante asked. "How must I compensate her?"

Pietra ignored the insult. "She is a strange woman. She has strange desires."

"What does she want?"

The girl experienced a moment of uncertainty. "Time. She said she wants some time."

"What does that mean?"

"She wants some time," she repeated. "That is what she told me to ask you for. You're the scholar, you should know."

Dante was trying to understand, nervously glancing around at those walls steeped in lust.

Pietra looked at him a moment, then a vulgar laugh again came to her lips. "So then, Messer Alighieri, did the red-skinned whore succeed in making you forget your little Pietra? Or do you still have that other one in your head? You cannot forget her, can you? She has been dead for ten years and she is still in your thoughts. And she never even knew you were alive!"

"Shut up, you whore! What do you know about love?" Dante shouted, slapping her.

She touched her lip, where a thin trickle of blood appeared. "She never loved you, she never loved you!" she screamed in his face, as a few drops of blood soaked into her robe. Then she burst into tears. "Nobody loves you. You will end up far away, alone."

Dante felt like he was sinking in a well of sorrow. He was gulping down that bitter water like a drowning man. As the girl fled down the corridor, sobbing, he went slowly down the stairs, with a heavy step.

When he got to the bottom he looked up at the stars. He saw lamplight at the door of a cubicle; it moved to the end of the covered passageway, borne by a vague shape. Shadows of shadows. For a moment, the little flame, moved by a puff of wind, illuminated a bare cheek. Then shadows submerged it, and the face disappeared.

His melancholy increased. He did not have the courage to ask himself if the woman with the lantern had been Antilia. On his hands were reddish streaks. It must be the carmine that turned her skin such a glorious bronze. Angrily he wiped his fingers on his garment.

BACK IN the courtyard, he passed through the orbits of the seven planets and sank down beside the ruins of the fountain. The water gurgled. He dipped a hand into the small pool, then brought it to his forehead. The cool touch fully restored him to his senses. The effects of the wine were wearing off as the deepest hours of the night waned. His thoughts were beginning to clear, although a flurry of images and female faces kept racing through his mind.

Again he raised his eyes toward the place where he thought he had glimpsed Antilia, but the entire wall was now shrouded in darkness.

He twisted his head around, looking hopelessly for a reference point: the four sides of the building were identical, their rows of windows masked by drapery.

For an instant he felt an impulse to go back upstairs and search all the cubicles. He could call upon his authority in order to do so. He glanced toward Porta Carraia, quickly estimating the time. If he hurried, he could reach the Palazzo, alert the watch, and come back with half a dozen bargellini before daybreak. He would order those scoundrels to turn over every pallet and look behind every curtain.

But he had a feeling he would never find the woman. Just as at Teofilo's shop, when she had disappeared without a trace. He got up and walked to the entranceway. He turned around to glance one last time at the windows, then went out into the street.

In front of him stood a man. Instinctively the poet's muscles tensed and he raised his guard. But he was reassured as soon as he recognized Angiolieri.

"Cecco, so you too know about Paradise?" he said.

"This one and many others, from here to Siena. But this one is the most divine of all."

For a moment they just looked at each other. Why should

Dante be surprised to find Cecco there? Cecco might have followed him and Veniero when they left the tavern. And besides, his presence in a brothel was not uncommon.

Yet Dante suspected that the man was there for another reason. He wore a strained expression, different from that which you might expect to see on a satisfied client.

"Do you know why I have it in for my parents?" Cecco asked out of the blue. The prior was surprised by the question. "Just think, I tried to kill my father. I threw him down the stairs in his house, and the devil only knows why he didn't break his neck."

"Because you are a madman, Cecco. That's why."

Angiolieri raised his chin and narrowed his eyes, as if he were reliving the scene. A smile rose to his lips, and became a sneer. "You don't get it? Not with all your learning?"

"It is difficult to follow a crazed horse, especially when it gallops at breakneck speed," Dante muttered.

"And yet I am not mad. Even though I wrote that melancholy assailed me with such force as to bring me close to death. Do you want to know why I did it?" Cecco sidled up to Dante, almost touching him. He lowered his voice. "I am afraid that he will eat me up."

"What are you saying?"

"The old man. He is a devil. He is capable of devouring a whole suckling pig at supper, just to do me harm. He spends the earnings of three vineyards in a single day. He will leave me nothing. He says he will eat it all by the day he dies. It is all futile, because he will outlive me in any case. He has the devil on his side."

Dante could not resist a smile. But it was not Cecco's father he was interested in. "Why did you come to Florence?"

"I told you. Things were not going well for me in Siena. I had to get away as quickly as possible."

"But why to Florence in particular?"

"Doesn't everybody come here? Is this not the city where everything flourishes? The florins in the cash boxes, the height of the towers, the bellies of the women? Where everything grows and multiplies faster than Our Lord's loaves and fishes? If Christ had been on the banks of the Arno instead of on that puddle of a lake, Tiberias, he could have served his followers pheasants and deer tongues instead of crusts of bread. Here there is work for me too, I am sure of it. Need and necessity are the two horses that pull my wagon."

"You do not mean to tell me that you have come here looking for a job?"

"So, then, it is really true that an undeserved reputation pursues me! Oh, if you only knew how my character has changed since the time we were at Campaldino . . . and yet that is precisely my intention: to offer a helping hand in an honest venture from which I can make a small profit."

"So your character has changed. . . . And your ideas, have they changed as well?"

The Sienese gave him an enigmatic look. "In '89, at Campaldino, I risked my neck for the Guelphs. And what did I get for it? Poverty and exile. This time I have decided to cast my own dice."

"The feminine kind?"

The other nodded slowly, studying Dante as if he were trying to read his thoughts. "Are you not aware of what is being planned in the city?"

He seemed to think that Dante should be informed about something. But what? Which ideas of his had changed? "You were left disappointed by the Guelph party, you say," the poet ventured. "Do you think that the imperials would be more generous?"

Cecco did not answer, waiting for him to go on.

"The large Ghibelline families have consolidated their strength in their estates to the north and have no intention of descending below the Po Valley. In the south, in the Kingdom of Naples, power is in the hands of the French, who are on Boniface's side, albeit reluctantly. The Colonnas and the Orsinis of Rome hate Caetani and will contest him, but only to restore their own personal power—certainly not to open the Urbe's doors to a foreign sovereign. Then, too, who would lead the endeavor, after the disaster at Tagliacozzo? The wretched Corradino died without leaving any heirs."

Cecco remained impassive, as if these observations did not disturb him in the least.

"Because there are no heirs to the imperial throne, are there?" Dante went on. "Or am I wrong?"

The Sienese glanced for an instant to the windows of the cubicles. Only a flicker; then his eyes returned to Dante, with the same indifferent expression as before. But it was enough for the poet to cast a rapid look in the same direction. He saw nothing, yet all of a sudden Paradise seemed illuminated by a different light. Less sordid, but more menacing.

The army of bogus lepers mixed in with the pilgrims heading for Rome: were the exiled Ghibellines assembling in Florence, along with tricksters and schemers like Cecco, to place themselves under the command of a secret queen? That whore? Perhaps the men that Giannetto said he had seen in the beggars' shelter were the vanguard of an armed force that was meeting secretly in the crypt, and he had mistaken their clandestine plotting for the celebration of an occult rite. While Giannetto was imagining demons and witches, they were consulting their maps, determining rallying points, readying caches of weapons . . .

"Cecco, do you know the church of Saint Jude, outside the walls?"

The other burst out laughing, finally showing some sign of

life. "You would be better off asking me if I killed the Comacine master. And if you were to pose this question to me, I would give you two answers: *sic et non,* as in the debates of those pundits of the Third Heaven. No, I did not kill the mosaicist. Yes, I know the church. But many people in Florence are familiar with it, believe me."

"What do you mean?"

Cecco chewed his lip. He seemed torn, perhaps mindful of their old friendship. Then suddenly he spoke. "A new era is in the making, for Florence and perhaps for all of Italy. Think of your own interests, Messer Alighieri, if you want to seize Fortune's mane as she gallops by." Then he moved off, passing beneath an opening in the arcade. Dante saw him heading toward Porta Carraia and he slowly followed along the same street.

Seize Fortune's mane . . .

He had never been able to do so, in the first half of his life. Not even now was the blindfolded goddess willing to grant the new prior her sweetest favors. The path of greatness, not happiness, awaited him. And glory is achieved through virtue, not fortune. He wanted to shout this in the Sienese's face, but by now Cecco was far off.

He sat down on a milestone along the side of the road, still slightly dizzy. Follow the path of virtue. . . . But what should he do if his hypothesis proved to be the truth, if Antilia's copper mask were merely an expert ruse to conceal her most noble features, giving her time to unleash the revolt? She herself had uttered the name Beatrice. Her own name. Who would ever have thought to look for the last Swabian heir beneath the roof of a tavern, or within the walls of a brothel?

What was his duty? Run to the Palazzo and denounce the Ghibelline plot? Come back with soldiers, surround Paradise and have Antilia shackled? Forcibly wring a confession from her, then hand her over to the executioner for decapitation, as they had done to Corradino? Prevent a whore from ascending to the imperial throne?

He shook his head.

That woman was simply a dancer who had come from overseas. It was not possible for a queen to stoop to prostitution. Cecco was delirious, or else he was poking fun at all of them. Maybe he was drunk.

16

DAWN WAS beginning to break, and strands of subtle pink streaked the cobalt of waning night. The white speck that was Venus sparkled like the diamond on Lucifer's forehead, obscuring all other stars.

Perhaps he should wait for them to open the gate. He could demand that they do so now by identifying himself and exercising his authority, but then everyone would be aware of his movements.

When he reached the portal, he found it already open, with a group of armed guards lined up in front of it. After a moment's uncertainty he decided to pass through. Should there be a problem, he would make himself known. He took a few steps and found himself surrounded by pikes. Robust arms seized hold of him.

He tried to protest, struggling and shouting out his name. He heard a voice order the guards to let go of him. The Bargello had appeared among his men as if by magic.

"You, too, out on a nocturnal reconnaissance, Messer Alighieri?" he asked him when they stood together. "A satisfying reconnaissance, considering where you have come from," he added with a crafty smile.

"And you, what are you doing here with your men?" Dante retorted, ignoring the insinuation.

"My duty, Messer Alighieri. It seems that someone is determined to infiltrate the city. The guard has been doubled."

The poet grumbled something and continued on through the archway. The other made no move to go after him, but merely followed him with his eyes.

Dante wearily crossed the endless-seeming stretch between the gate and San Piero. He reached his cell and collapsed onto his bed as the first light of dawn came through the window.

Despite his exhaustion, he was unable to fall asleep. Thoughts and images darted about in his mind like trapped birds. His gaze went racing from the writing table to the small bed and then to the window opening, then at last it paused for a moment on the cabinet in the corner. It seemed to him that he could see through the wood panel to the vial hidden among the clothing. There must still be a trace of the green liquid left.

HE WAS about to drift off at last when he was roused by a harsh laugh. He turned quickly, and there standing beside his bed was Guido Cavalcanti. He was dressed in a long tunic, and his tenuous body glowed like a hollow trunk in which a fire had been lit. The flames illuminated his skin and shone through the fine wrinkles on his shadowed face.

Guido watched him and laughed again, as if he could read his friend's very thoughts. Dante felt overcome by a river of love.

"*Salve,* Guido. What brings you here? Tell me your news!"

"I am dead. And in death I have gained valuable experience. I want to talk to you about it."

Then Dante saw that his friend's strange garment was like the livery of a confraternity. A crest was embroidered on the front, five colors repeated in vertical stripes.

Guido noticed his gaze and pointed to his heart. "There are

five monsters lurking in your path," he said. Then he sketched a pentagram in the air. His finger left a trail of blood, like the marks on Ambrogio's chest.

"What are you trying to tell me?" Dante asked uneasily as the crimson trace drawn in the air slowly vanished.

"We who are deceased are blind to the present, because existence is in the present and that is denied to us. But we can see far into the distance, as if our vision were magnified by those lenses they grind in the land of Arabia. And I can see your destiny as though I peered through such a lens. You will wander the earth for twenty years, and then you will know clammy death, which bores into the bones and viscera with its fevers. But I do not wish to sate you with the knowledge of future things: it is for you to discover them, one by one, painfully. I will tell you no more and I will answer no further."

"Continue!" Dante exclaimed. Why was his friend speaking to him in riddles? Why was he leaving him in such apprehension? "You are an arrogant bastard, like all your stock!" he shouted angrily. "That rogue Giannetto is alive, and he knows more than you do!"

Guido glided over to the window. He raised a finger toward the heavens, pointing to the most luminous of the stars that shone in that square patch of sky. His wrinkles had become more accentuated, limned in fire. His features were barely recognizable, blurred by the radiating brilliance that consumed his face as it devoured his body. Dante was dazzled. The lapping flames reached out, ready to consume him. Then he woke.

Trembling, he rose from his pallet and sought the open window and the star of his dream. It was dawn. High above the horizon, scarcely dimmed by the first tenuous streaks of blue light, Venus shone in all her brilliance.

Dante was bewildered; he knew that his friend was not dead.

Why, then, had Guido appeared to him in that guise? Why had he sketched the shape of the pentagram, and why had he pointed at Venus?

Since Guido was alive, it could not have been his soul that had visited Dante's sleep. An incubus must have assumed his friend's form in order to deceive and assail him. Thus, it was said, the devil breached the fabric of the human mind, seeking its weakest points.

He washed his face and his senses, fogged by illusion, slowly became alert again. His logic, strengthened by right judgment and the grace of God, could not be deceived by diabolic powers. There had to be another explanation.

He thought back to what he had learned from the book of Artemidorus, the Greek who had studied the secrets of dreams. The day's images, distorted and corrupted by the vegetative soul. Something we already know, without knowing that we know. A dream is nothing but a memory.

How many tales had he heard, how many heated sermons had he listened to, about the dead man who returns to visit a living friend, to tell him about the regions of the hereafter? His sleeping mind must have drawn upon those memories in order to formulate the dream.

The unsolved mystery of the five parts of the mosaic might explain Guido's strange attire and the pentagram traced in blood. Even Cecco d'Ascoli had spoken of Venus as the pentagonal star.

His sleeping mind must know answers that his waking mind did not, for now, in the light of day, his ability to link the images of the night seemed to fail him.

Frantically he reviewed everything he knew about astrology. A rapid search turned up Guido's Bonetti's treatise, buried in a pile of papers. Distractedly he leafed through the outsize pages, looking for something that might give concrete form to his vague suspicions. Tables, the calculation of the ephemeris, the planetary motions . . . properties of the zodiac. There it was, under his eyes, drawn by the sure, mechanical hand of some uncomprehending copyist: the cycles of the planet Venus. A complete study of its conjunctions with the sun on the great ecliptic. Every eight years the sun and Venus approached each other five times in their circular movement, and the trail of such conjunctions formed the vertices of a perfect pentagram on the celestial vault. The quintuple star—as the ancient Babylonians had discovered. Now he understood that sibilant sound, the name invoked by Antilia and the others: Ishtar, the Babylonian goddess of love, who grants her devotees carnal ecstasy. The morning star of the East, who demands bodily sacrifice from her priestesses, ordering them to copulate with strange men.

Slowly a picture formed in his mind, of actors making their appearance to fill an empty stage.

He put his head in his hands, forcefully pressing his temples as if to slow the confused assembly of his thoughts. "If at least you, Father, might help me," he caught himself thinking.

"You have called me to be your guide," Virgil's beloved voice replied. "Why?"

"Because of all masters, you are the greatest!"

"No. You chose me because I am dead. And the dead do not cast a shadow."

The sound of heavy footsteps outside, followed by a rapid series of firm knocks, diverted him from his dreams. By now he knew those signs.

"Messer Durante, wake up."

The poet hastened to open the door and found the Bargello standing before him, armed and breathing heavily. Now, in the clear light of day, made joyful by birdsong, this man with his battle gear seemed more than usually grotesque. Nevertheless, something in his expression kept him from appearing ridiculous.

It was fear. His eyes were bloodshot, and the part of his face visible beneath his helmet was ghastly pale. "Come quickly. Another body."

"What?" Dante exclaimed. "Where?"

"Near Porta Romana, the shop of Master Teofilo, the apothecary. The dead man may be he."

"*May* be?"

"You must see with your own eyes, I tell you. It is like the other time."

DOWNSTAIRS was a guard armed with pikes, waiting to escort him, but Dante, unencumbered by armor and weapons, raced ahead of them to Teofilo's shop. He found the door open, watched by a single bargellino who held his pike across it to keep out the curious. Quickly he moved aside to let the prior enter.

The body was hanging in front of the brick oven, strung up by the neck from one of the chains of the ceiling lamp, the hands, tied behind the back, still tensed from the victim's attempt to free himself. Maybe it actually was Teofilo. The garments on the corpse were his, and so was the ring that adorned the right index finger. But the reason for the Bargello's uncertainty was obvious: the head was entirely covered by a hard yellowish substance. On the floor, near the body, lay an overturned copper cauldron; the sticky remains of the material used for the murder—candle wax—still coated its sides. An obvious replication of the first crime: wax was a base in the preparation of many medicines, therefore a primary material of the victim's art. Here too the same ritual, the same obscene liturgy, to obliterate the face that renders us similar to God.

The molten wax had oozed across the tormented features in a thin layer: they could be seen as though through a dark glass. To be certain, with his dagger's point the poet lifted an edge of the mask. It really was Teofilo the apothecary. He loosened the garment that covered the apothecary's breast, disclosing the same five slashes that had marked Ambrogio: a pentagram. The wounds were superficial, no visible sign of any blow. The scalding wax had been poured onto the poor man while he was still alive. Teofilo must have followed his murderer's moves until the end, when his eyes were blinded by the blistering liquid.

"Do you still deny that a sorcerer is at work in our city?" The Bargello spoke behind him. The dead man seemed to scream his agreement, his mouth open in a supreme howl.

Dante felt nearly delirious.

Until that moment all his attention had been centered on the harrowed corpse. Now his eyes flew to the double-locked chest. It was open. On the floor in front of it were scattered the pages he remembered seeing neatly bundled inside. The flask of *chandu* was gone.

Eagerly he gathered up the pages, only to find that all except two of them were blank. The first contained only a brief phrase. On the second were marks, hastily drawn, representing several numerical sequences, whose meaning he was unable to comprehend. Perhaps the killer had taken the completed part of the apothecary's treatise along with his precious drug. A further search turned up a scrap of timeworn parchment with traces of faded colors. The remains of a drawing or a map.

There was nothing more to find, he was certain of that. He went back to examining the written page.

"What does it mean, prior?" the Bargello asked. The man had followed all his movements, and was now breathing down his neck, straining to read those few words. *"Non in trigono nec in tetragono . . ."*

". . . sed in pentagono secretum mundi," Dante finished impatiently. "In the pentagram lies the secret of the world."

"But what does it mean?" the captain of the guard repeated.

The poet shrugged. He wondered if the criminal had acted alone. Perhaps more than one pair of hands had destroyed those two lives. And yet his mind recoiled from the idea of some murderous partnership: the two crimes followed a pattern, and in that pattern the absolute individuality of a single killer stood out.

The person who had killed two people had done so for one reason, even though he had concealed it in a forest of symbols. Everything had started with the murder of the mosaicist, and it was impossible that there not be a relationship between that and the death of Teofilo. Another possibility flashed through the poet's mind. The murder of the Comacine master might not be essential to the chain of events, but rather a mere digression on the criminal's path.

But such a hypothesis would belie all of his convictions. The Philosopher had taught that, in fact, every event is determined by a Mover. It was an assertion that Dante had never doubted. The temporal order of any series of events must follow a necessary logic. Therefore, the first act of violence must have been a starting point for the second act, and so on, in a ghastly chain. If on the other hand the perpetrator's true object was to destroy Teofilo, then Ambrogio's horrible end had been merely a tragic prologue, a sinister comedy, staged to deceive.

Dante had been searching for a motive for the murder of the Comacine master. Now that Teofilo was also dead, he had to discover an element common to both crimes—an element that pointed to the killer.

There was such an element, he thought. Gold. The gold ring that Ambrogio had given to Teofilo, fabricated, perhaps, by exploiting a terrible secret. The gold that was furtively circulating in Florence, the gold that glittered on a woman's flesh.

He had to speak with her. Alone, this time, and without letting wine betray him.

Suddenly he recalled Antilia's mysterious disappearance from that very shop.

"Who discovered the crime?" he asked the Bargello.

"It was my men," the other replied, with a hint of foolish pride in his voice. "They were passing the door on their rounds and heard a suspicious commotion inside. They quickly entered . . ."

"A commotion? They caught the murderer in the act? Where is he?" Dante nearly shouted.

"There was no one there. But they said the killer must have just fled, because the victim was still writhing in his death throes."

"Fled? The shop has only one door onto the street. How could they not have seen him, those damned idiots?"

"I tell you there is a diabolic power behind all this!"

The poet was no longer listening. His eyes scanned the shop, studying every detail. The stone walls appeared to be solid, and were completely visible, except for an area behind the herb cabinet. He seized a corner of the cabinet and shook it, testing its weight.

"Help me move this, quickly."

The Bargello joined him, looking puzzled; then a gleam of intelligence shone on his stolid face and he threw himself upon the cabinet, trying to drag it away. "It seems to be riveted to the wall . . ." he gasped, red from exertion.

Dante's forehead was damp with sweat. The two of them pushed and pulled, with all their strength, but the cabinet wouldn't budge. Beside himself, Dante swept a row of containers to the floor and began striking at the exposed space in the center of the back panel with the handle of his dagger. A hollow sound responded to his blows. "There is no wall behind here," he cried.

"Break through at this spot," he ordered the bargellini, who had begun crowding into the shop.

Was it only his imagination, or was someone moving on the other side of the wooden partition? There must be a mechanism that opened it, but he did not have time to look.

The bargellini attacked the wood boards with their swords. The seasoned oak resisted, breaking up slowly in a hail of splinters, then cracking loudly as the structure began to give way. Gesturing to the men to move back, Dante shoved the cabinet with all his strength. The last ceramic jars fell to the floor, shattering noisily, the cabinet yielding at last, and the prior tumbled into the small room that lay concealed behind the shop. It was empty. There was nothing in it but a high, narrow window. A torn curtain hung from a corner of its frame.

"He must have fled through there. Quick, follow me!" he shouted. He grabbed the edge of the window opening and hoisted himself up.

Supporting his chest on the sill, he peered through. On the other side was a vast space, dimly lit. Carefully he squeezed his way through and let himself drop down.

He blinked, trying to adjust to the darkness of his strange new surroundings. The room resembled the belly of a vast ship, populated by crowds of specters clad in robes that stirred faintly in an imperceptible draft. A closely strung series of ropes ran for a hundred yards from one end of the building to the other; on them hundreds of multicolored fabrics had been hung to dry. The dense, humid atmosphere, saturated by the vapors of the dyes, was almost unbreathable.

He had stumbled into a tiratorio. The chamber was being used by some dyer for stretching and drying his treated cloth. Dante, bent over on his knees, was overcome by nausea as he struggled to catch his breath. All the while his mind was busy, tracing a map of Teofilo's shop and this room behind it, which for some reason the apothecary had kept connected to his own establishment, and about which his killer had known.

"Do you see him?" the Bargello shouted.

The closely packed fabrics interfered with his line of sight. And except for the slight rustling, the tiratorio was absolutely still. The building's architect must have provided openings, arranged to generate that faint current of air he could feel on his face. There must be some other way out of there, he thought with alarm.

Rapidly he passed through the rows of steaming cloth, inspecting the narrow aisles between them. Just as he decided that the killer must have fled, he noticed movement ahead of him. By now his eyes had adjusted to the shadows. He thought he could make out a bulge among the fabrics, proceeding slowly toward the opposite side of the building. Someone was escaping, using the sheets of material as a shield.

"Bargello, come quickly with your men! He's still here!" he shouted, and sprang toward the still rippling sheets, dagger in hand, wondering what he would do with it if his adversary drew a sword.

Yet something inside him reassured him: that man did not kill with a sword—if in fact it was a man. Antilia had once disappeared into that same space.

Meanwhile the movement behind the fabric had shifted to his right, crossing the ropes of drying racks diagonally. Dante saw a figure dart from one row to the other, then vanish behind a wall of cloth. The leap had been very quick.

Something moved nearby a few rows over to the right. Was the killer circling around so as to surprise him from behind? Hastily he turned and began pushing his way back toward the entrance, roughly shoving the drying sheets aside.

Then to his relief he saw the guards, there at last, climbing down from the narrow window. The Bargello's thickset body filled the empty space between two rows of fabric. He stood still, panting, but at least he had arrived.

"Watch out, he is running toward you!" Dante yelled.

But the mysterious adversary again reversed his course and made straight for Dante. The bulge in the fabric came billowing toward him like the charge of some ferocious beast. Terrified, the poet remembered a boar hunt he'd witnessed in the wooded hills near Fiesole. The shrubs had swelled in just this way an instant before their quarry had hurtled out of the underbrush and into his horse's side, slashing the poor animal's belly with its deadly tusks.

A shudder went through him. The bargellini were chasing the shape but, encumbered by their pikes, were unable to overtake it. The fools, they were beating the game before them, chasing it straight at him. He dropped to his knees, gripping his dagger with all his might and waiting for the impact of the onrushing foe.

Then, as if by magic, just a few steps away, his assailant stopped dead. Dante waited, breathless, for him to spring. Suddenly a large piece of fabric, taking on a life of its own, rose up from its supporting rope and fell upon him. He felt the clammy material wrap itself around him and thrashed about, trying frantically to free himself. Two strong arms gripped him tightly. He struck out desperately with his dagger, but the fabric hid his target. His nostrils filled with the acrid odor of dye—a scent he had never associated with danger or death. Terrified, he thought that a blade would slice through his flesh at any moment, that nothing could save him.

When the unseen arms released their grip he toppled to the ground. He was still aware of a body's mass over him, but no blow came. Then the presence was gone. The beast had only wanted to clear the way, push the hunter out of its path.

He struggled to extricate himself from the wet folds that entangled him, while trying to get to his feet.

Again there was someone beside him. Two hands clutched him, then pulled away his shroud. One of the guards had rushed to his aid. Nearby stood the Bargello, looking stolidly amused.

"Let me be!" the prior gasped. "Don't let him get away!"

"Who? We have not seen anyone."

"I tell you he was in here . . . he cannot have vanished yet! Look for him!"

The men glanced around, bewildered.

"Spread out among the drying racks and go back along the aisles, we have to surround him," Dante bellowed at them.

The bargellini turned toward their captain, who nodded. As they hurried to obey, the poet rushed toward an aisle in the center of the room, where he was sure his assailant had headed. But the man was not there. And the bargellini had found no one, either, in their reconnaissance. The sheets of fabric swayed faintly, stirred by the drying chamber's draft. The killer had vanished.

17

The same day, in the early afternoon

SIX MEN sat around a table in high-backed, carved chairs, drenched in the intense light that streamed in from the tall windows of the chapter house of San Piero.

A large sheet bearing the Commune's insignia passed from hand to hand. It had already gone around the circle several times.

"The number is . . . high," said one of the six, a small, thin man who almost disappeared in his lofty seat. "Perhaps . . ." The hand that held the parchment trembled softly. The man, aware of it, hastened to steady the sheet with his other hand.

"We must be prepared for anything."

"But so many. . . . And then the names. . . . Many are in Boniface's good graces."

"Do you think there are too many? That we should show clemency toward some?" Dante pressed him. "That we should pardon those who have brazenly violated our laws? Those whose evil works have helped transform the Commune from a noble city, worthy heir to Rome's greatness, into a den of thieves and panderers, and whose brawls and feuds have stained its streets with blood? Those who have flung open the doors of the temple of civil war?" The poet was silent for a moment, his hands clenching the arms of his chair. "Those whose irresponsible behavior will be used to justify Boniface's designs upon our freedom?"

An awkward silence descended.

"No . . . certainly not." The other prior said at last, confused. "But to banish the Donati as well. . . . Are they not your own relations?"

"My wife is a Donati. What of it?"

The other, embarrassed but not silenced by this answer, persisted. "There are forty-nine . . ."

"You are mistaken. There are fifty. I added a name in my own hand. The last one."

The small prior held the list up to his eyes, scanning it anxiously. Then he looked back at the poet, whose cold voice had stung like a serpent's tongue. "Must we really . . ."

"It is essential. For the welfare of Florence." Dante rubbed a hand over his forehead, trying to drive back a sharp stab of pain behind his eyes.

There was another moment of silence, as the priors began passing the parchment around again, pausing first on one name, then on another. As they finished reading, each in turn gazed intently at the poet, looking for some sign of doubt, a shadow of uncertainty on his angular face. But he remained impassive, meeting the others' eyes resolutely.

"All right, then, as you say." The man who spoke was the oldest there. He dripped hot wax onto the parchment and, after a moment's hesitation, pressed into it the huge signet he wore on his finger. "What's done is done," was all he added, passing the list to the man on his right.

One by one the other priors repeated his gesture, almost as if they wanted to spare themselves anguish by acting swiftly. The fifth man held back the document for a moment before passing it on to the last. "Fortunately, our mandate expires on the ides of August. I plan to make a pilgrimage to Rome for the grand Jubilee. I wish to distance myself from this city; there is something evil here. And what will you do afterward, Messer Durante?"

Irritably, Dante snatched the parchment from his colleague's hands and hurriedly applied his own signet. "I do not know. I cannot see the future. But I agree with you about one thing. The devil has indeed been walking the streets of Florence, ever since . . ."

"Ever since when, Messer Durante?"

Dante did not reply. He sat rapt, as if experiencing a vision. Then he roused himself. "Make sure the order of banishment is communicated to the chief magistrate so that he may see to its execution. By tomorrow none of those on the list should remain within the circle of walls."

As he was going out he almost collided with the Bargello, who was waiting outside the door. In his hands the captain gripped a small bundle tied with a string. "I came to confer with you, prior. You ordered that any detail that may have a possible relation to the crime be reported to you."

"Is there something new?"

The captain of the guard turned his eyes doubtfully toward the other priors. He looked back at the poet, and read in his face the command to keep silent, to reveal nothing to the others seated there.

Dante waited until his colleagues had dispersed, then he hastened to question the man. He felt that he did not have much time: the look of suspicion that some of the priors had given him as they were leaving the room had not escaped him. What did the others know of this matter? What could that fool the Bargello have said? Was it possible that one of them was involved in a conspiracy—for he was now almost certain that there was a conspiracy in Florence.

"Well then?" he pressed him.

The Bargello untied the knot and opened the bundle beneath the poet's eyes. Inside was a page containing a list of names. "This is the register of those entering the Porta di Francia. My guards write in it the names of everyone who passes through the gate, for the toll. And today they notified me of the entry of two suspicious people, mixed in with the pilgrims stopping off on their way to Rome."

"Who are they?"

"They claimed to be merchants from Padua. They took lodging at Ceccherino's tavern, the one that . . ."

Dante knew very well what they said about Ceccherino and his clientele. The French called it the Florentine vice—he had learned that as soon as he arrived in Paris.

"You would not be concerned about the fact that two more pederasts have chosen to come to Florence," he said harshly.

"My commander at the gate comes from Siena, and he recognized them. They may well be Paduans, but they are certainly not merchants. He remembers them well: they supervised the workers at the construction site of the new cathedral in his city. They are both master builders."

"Like Ambrogio?" As he thought this over, he glanced at the date on the registry page. "But this occurred more than a week ago! Why did you wait so long to inform me?"

The other reddened, embarrassed. "The register is checked every ten days. . . . My man could not imagine . . ."

The poet hastened to moderate his tone. If even the Bargello knew of these Comacine masters, then what Giannetto had said must be true. But were they the same two men he had glimpsed in the subterranean chamber? And why were so many associates of this powerful guild arriving in Florence?

"Where are they now?"

"Do not worry, prior. My man is experienced. We are watching them, as we are required to watch all who enter the Commune's territory under false pretenses. They have been followed as far as Ceccherino's, where they are lodging."

"I want to know where they are right now, at this moment!"

"Still there, resting after their journey, I imagine . . ."

"You imagine? You *imagine*?" Dante glared. "And what else do you imagine?"

"I did not think it was appropriate to do anything," the captain of the guard stammered. "We considered them harmless enough. Everyone says that the Comacines are Ghibelline sympathizers, but in our Commune they have not been guilty of any offense . . . We knew of no wrongdoing in which they might be involved . . ."

"Aside from two atrocious crimes!"

Upon hearing those words the Bargello recovered his confidence. He straightened up, thrusting out his chest. "But no, Messer Alighieri! I have further news than this for you. The person responsible for the apothecary's murder was arrested an hour ago."

"What?" Dante exclaimed.

"My men caught a known swindler, a certain Giannetto, who usually begs at Santa Maria Novella. He was at the Lungarno market trying to sell some glass containers that were recognized as coming from Messer Teofilo's shop. Now he is in the Stinche, undergoing the strappado. He says he is innocent, a claim we may well disregard. You are mistaken in suspecting the Comacines."

Dante pictured Giannetto's contorted face, questioned under torture at the hands of the bargellini. He knew the scoundrel had had nothing to do with the crime—at most he might have robbed the shop, no doubt left unguarded after that first investigation. He was about to order the Bargello to release the wretch, then changed his mind. Perhaps it was fitting that Giannetto spend an unpleasant hour or two, given his immoral life. Later he would intervene, before the bargellini actually killed him. But that would take days.

Besides, better to let the Bargello think he accepted Giannetto's guilt. He did not trust the man, who was still watching him, waiting. Perhaps the captain was simply a fool; even so, he might know more about the two crimes than he let on. Perhaps he was in Acquasparta's pay. No, the prior would seem to accept his theory—for now.

"If it is as you say, at least one of our problems has been resolved. Thanks to your diligence."

The captain of the guard looked incredulous. Dante realized he had been too quick to agree. It was possible that the Bargello had merely suspected Giannetto's guilt, without being entirely convinced of it. And if so, that he was neither in Acquasparta's pay, nor entirely stupid, he thought as he took his leave.

As he passed under the portico he saw a group of pikemen in the Cardinal's ornate livery marching down the center of the courtyard. They were escorting a man dressed in the pale habit of the Dominicans. In bright sunlight he appeared much smaller, even more gaunt, than he had in the half-light of Misericordia's subterranean vault.

On that occasion Noffo Dei had been dealing with the dead. Here, among the living, he seemed withered, ill at ease, out of place.

Dante paused behind a pillar, to think and prepare himself for the encounter. So the wolf had come to the sheepfold—with his pack. Who had permitted those armed thugs to enter the Priors' Palazzo? He experienced a moment of uncertainty: perhaps he should turn back and assemble a guard of his own before approaching the inquisitor. But the man had already seen him, and now moved swiftly across the courtyard, as if fleeing the sunlight for the protective shade of the portico.

"I am pleased to meet you in the setting of your official duties, brother," he said, ostentatiously holding out the crucifix that he wore around his neck. Dante barely nodded, ignoring the gesture.

The other quickly withdrew the cross, not commenting on the other's failure to observe the ritual.

"Are you here to confer with the council?" Dante asked him.

"Not with the council but with you, Messer Alighieri, who are the council's noblest voice."

"A nobility that comes from an ability to resist flattery, Brother Noffo. What do you want here?"

The inquisitor's sallow face flushed for an instant; then he reverted to a diplomat's mask. "Perhaps it is best that we discuss these matters in your chambers, away from indiscreet observation," was all he said.

Dante nodded and led the inquisitor to his cell.

They sat down opposite each other on the spartan stools provided by the convent. Noffo threw back his cowl and wiped his damp forehead with a cloth he removed from a small shoulder pouch.

His demeanor had suddenly changed. The shadowy atmosphere of the cell seemed to revitalize his forces. The man grew larger in darkness. His eyes lost all trace of their former hypocrisy, recovering the icy expression of the torturer. Instinctively the poet felt for his dagger.

"I regret that I am reduced to requesting an audience from you, Messer Alighieri, going against the Church's customs and my personal convictions," the inquisitor began. "I believe that the good shepherd should follow the sheep lost in the night, in a blizzard or in the desert. But if the sheep has become a wolf, has pretended to be lost to lure the shepherd from the flock, then the shepherd must run home and arm himself."

"That is a sinister allegory, brother. Might I be the sheep in wolf's clothing? Or is it the entire city of Florence, which I represent?"

"You represent nothing, Messer Alighieri. And soon enough you will know the precise measure of that 'nothing.' But for now, you hold an office that compels our attention. And it is for this reason only that I have overcome my just pride, following the example of Our Lord when he washed the feet of the unworthy Judas."

"What has brought about such condescension? Do you perhaps want the order of banishment revoked?"

Who could have informed that cur of a decision that was to have remained secret until it had been carried out? But it was useless to rack his brains now. Any of the other five priors might be in the Cardinal's service.

The monk's face twisted into a grimace. "The Church does not harbor any concern for the fate of men who are squabbling within the circle of the walls. Nor is it asking for any repeal of the expulsion orders: soon it will be our hand that opens and closes the gates of Florence, and all righteous men will be recalled to their city. No, that is not the reason that brings me to you."

"Then what is it?"

"I am requesting that you arrest a woman: Antilia, the dancer who performs in the tavern on the road to Rome."

Dante let a few moments pass before he replied. He wanted to study the other man's expression, to understand what he had in mind. But the inquisitor remained impassive. "Why?" he asked.

"So that she may be prevented from doing any harm, and be transported to Rome in chains, where she will be tried for her wrongdoings. And so that she may give back what was not her due."

So the cardinal had decided to reveal himself. Dante's tangled web of hypotheses—now rewoven into a rational scheme—was finally being confirmed. There was only one reason why Boniface would want to get his hands on an unassuming dancer: if behind her carmine mask were concealed Beatrice of Hohenstaufen, legitimate heir to the last holder of the imperial throne.

All other theories faded in the face of that implicit admission. Was this, then, what Ambrogio had wanted to reveal in the future site of the studium? It had to be. "And what is the charge?" he asked.

"Witchcraft and acts against nature," the monk replied, in an indifferent tone. It was obvious that not even he believed the empty formula.

"The charge of trafficking with demons fits almost any act contrary to God's will. In the end any crime involves Satan's participation, whether as bystander or active participant. Therefore the authority of the Commune requires greater details to take such a grave step, especially when it involves a woman of royal birth."

Noffo Dei's face again bore beads of sweat. "Not that legend about Manfred's daughter again. . . . You are as obstinate as a mule. I told you that that is not the charge being made against the woman."

Dante sneered. "Yet I see that my assertion does not surprise you. Why else would you want her to be handed over to you? Surely not because she is a witch," he pursued, moving closer. The monk had turned pale. "What are you accusing her of? Tell me what the real charge is!"

"I told you, we are accusing her of theft."

The prior frowned. Theft? The gold ring that Teofilo had entrusted to him and that was now hidden away in his cell at San Piero flashed before his eyes. Identical to others that were circulating in the city, Messer Flavio had said. And similar in its color and brilliance to Antilia's bangles. Was it possible that there was no greater mystery behind her disguise than the banal deception of a thief? It was absurd. It could not be so. "What do you mean?" he asked.

"The woman is in possession of something that belongs to the Church."

"What is that?"

For a moment Noffo seemed uncomfortable. "I . . . I cannot tell you."

"In Florence, questioning without manifest evidence of wrong-doing is not permitted. Do you think you are in Rome?" the poet retorted.

"I cannot tell you because I do not know what it is."

"What?" Dante exclaimed, astonished. "What do you mean? How can you accuse her if you do not even know what she has stolen?"

"We know that someone revealed a secret to her. It is this secret that she has stolen from St. Peter's patrimony."

"I can believe that His Holiness has more than one slippery secret!"

"The secret regards not Boniface, but his predecessor."

"Ah, Celestine. No doubt, then, the woman knows the names of his assassins. And for this you would like Florence to put her in irons?"

"What prattle is this about assassins? A blasphemous word to associate with the serene death of a holy man!"

"Even the walls know that Celestine was murdered!" Dante shouted. "But not how," he added slyly. "What other secret could the Curia value so highly? Unless . . . the woman possesses knowl-edge of the transmutation of gold? Is this what she took from you?"

The monk did not deny it. For a moment he seemed about to disclose something further, then he straightened his slight shoulders with an abrupt gesture. His face resumed the cold, impassive expression of marble.

"That is all I had to tell you," he declared, and he stood up. "We trust that our order will be performed expeditiously. It is your final opportunity to correct the opinion we have formed of you."

Dante said nothing, but as the man left, he made an obscene gesture at his retreating back. "I will not hand her over to you, you dog," he thought.

HE WAS furious. He had had that viper in his hands a second time, and again he had let him get away without extorting any certain information from him. There were indeed sinister rumors regarding Celestine V's death, and the truth had somehow escaped Boniface's clutches. Perhaps now there was a breach in the wall of silence that the Church had erected around that affair.

He remembered Iacopo Torriti's hints regarding the relations between the two pontiffs. The architect had simply reported hearsay. But Antonio da Peretola might know much more about it. During his years spent in the service of the Curia he must have seen and heard many things in the corridors of the Lateran basilica. Celestine's death had certainly been a subject of gossip in that nest of vipers. He had failed with Noffo: he must make da Peretola talk.

He paused halfway along the portico. He wanted to give the inquisitor time to reassemble his escort and leave, before he himself proceeded. His eyes were still fixed on the courtyard when he heard his name shouted. He turned just in time to avoid a collision with Messer Duccio.

"There you are at last!" the Commune's secretary exclaimed, breathing heavily. "One can never find you."

He had taken a large scroll from under his arm, and was awkwardly trying to unroll it.

"Perhaps because I am occupied with the city's affairs," the poet replied coldly, not deigning to glance at the sheet the other placed under his eyes.

"But the priors must not leave the palazzo during their term of office . . . You know that."

"That is the rule. But life loves exceptions," Dante said shortly. "What is it that is so important?"

"The location must be decided."

"The location of what?" The prior took the sheet at last and examined it. It looked like an architectural drawing, the plan for a building. A long structure divided into many smaller spaces. A convent, perhaps, or a new hospital.

"The superintendent of roads insists on locating it at the Guardingo opposite the future priory. He says that will be the center of Florence before long, and an appropriate site for such a place, open to all citizens engaged in public affairs, as well as to all outsiders passing through, so that they may bear witness to civic virtues when they return home."

Dante continued studying the plan. He was about to ask a question when the man anticipated him.

"The plan was done by a gifted artist, to accommodate fittingly our citizens' contributions. He derived it from a similar plan of the Romans'. Their emperors always saw to it that nothing was lost. And now we Florentines will do the same."

The poet listened, his eyes on the drawing. Of course, the entry gallery was perfectly recognizable. And it would be imposing, judging by the number of rooms that opened onto it. Perhaps there was still some hope for his city. Only in France had he seen something similar. There, the kings had for some time displayed their treasures, collections of jewels and court paintings, to glorify their rule. And Florence was certainly not inferior to France in the brilliance and talent of her artists. Here, not kings but private citizens would bring prestige to the city by lending their private treasures to the place. In Italy, only the pope would have a comparable collection, but this one would be the first to be open to the public. A temple to the muses: a museum, that was the right name for it.

He looked over the plan again, pleased. "Each room should display the examples of one artistic style, so that the eye may enjoy all of humanity's highest endeavor by passing through its history systematically. Yes, I, too, think that the most fitting site is in front of the Palazzo Comunale."

"Arnolfo di Cambio, who is supervising the building of the cathedral, was also consulted," Messer Duccio added. He seemed struck by the poet's far-reaching views.

"The great Arnolfo? You did well to call upon his enlightenment."

"You see . . . it does not seem fitting to me to have the entrance open onto the piazza. It would be better in the rear."

"Why?"

"I do not find it seemly that our administrators should run into some lout with his breeches lowered."

Dante looked at him, baffled. "Why the devil should someone lower his breeches in a museum?"

"I do not know what museum you are talking about. But I think it would be difficult for someone to relieve himself with his breeches up."

The poet tore the sheet out of his hands, hastily examining it again. "It is a urinal! You want to put a public urinal in front of our town hall?" he exclaimed, turning red.

"Of course, that is precisely the idea. It would be a source of great revenue, the tax on urea . . ."

"You want to collect piss and make a profit on it? And in front of the Priors' Palazzo?"

"But urine can be used for tanning and bleaching . . . Even the Roman emperors saw to the collection of urea . . ."

"Go to hell, Messer Duccio, you and your urea! Pass the biretta around, if that is what you have in mind!" Dante shouted in exasperation, shoving the man aside and heading for the doorway.

But he stopped abruptly. "Submit the plan to Messer Lapo Salterello, my colleague," he said. "He has received many in his lifetime, and now he will have a chance to review one for the Commune."

Then he hurried out. Once in the street he made a mighty effort to calm his rage. And suddenly he remembered what he had to do. There was still time before the curfew, while the streets leading to San Marco teemed with people idling about now that the bells had announced the end of the workday. He quickly made his way through them to da Peretola's lodging. Filled with confidence, he imagined the crowds parting with fearful respect as he passed.

THE JURIST was in his cell, at work among parchments and manuscripts that lay heaped on his writing table. He was busy as ever, making annotations.

As Dante entered, Antonio raised his eyes. "What can I do for you, Messer Alighieri?"

"Reveal more of what you know."

"With regard to the papal bull? Are you convinced of your error . . . the strange theory of the two suns? We could take up . . ."

"With regard to Celestine V."

Antonio's face darkened, as if that name sounded inauspicious to his ears. "Resurrect that vile pope?"

"Vile or saintly, according to . . ."

"Celestine was no saint, believe me. But neither, perhaps, was he a villain. What do you wish to know?"

"Information that only someone well-acquainted with the Church's affairs can give me: someone like you, Messer Antonio. That it was not Boniface who killed Celestine, contrary to what everyone believes."

The other hesitated an instant. He seemed flattered. "That is correct. I do not deny that sooner or later he would have done it. But later, just so. After having come to know his secret—the secret that the hand of the real assassin snatched from him instead."

"So Celestine, too, had a secret. And you know what it was?"

Antonio cleared his throat. "No one knows. Just before being elected, Celestine made a long journey to Lyons. There he was a guest for several days at the city's Templar commendam. From there he went on to accept his investiture to the sacred throne. But it is said that he left Lyons bearing a knowledge that led to his death. It is this secret that Boniface is searching for. Or at least so they believed in Rome."

"But why is he convinced that Antilia knows it?" the poet said, half to himself. "Unless he believes that she was involved in that crime . . ."

"The dancer? I don't understand," Antonio said, puzzled. Then he added, "Nevertheless, do not forget that the Church's sources of information are indirect but effective. If they believe a dancer was involved in the death of a pope, then perhaps she really was."

Dante listened, thinking hard, toying with a cord on his garment. "Messer Antonio . . ."

"Yes?"

"The convent of Saint Paul Outside the Walls, in Rome, where Ambrogio and Iacopo worked and where you played a role in drafting Boniface's bull. . . . It, too, is a Templar commendam, you said."

"Yes. Like the one in Lyons, if that is what you mean."

"That is exactly what I meant. When you were there, did you hear any talk about a mysterious figure, perhaps a pentagram, associated with the secret?"

The jurist's eyes lit up all of a sudden, as if those words had called to mind a forgotten detail. "Yes, I heard that too. The secret had the allegorized form of the number five. Does that suggest something?"

Dante shook his head. The five parts of the mosaic, the marks on the corpses, the five elements in the nepenthe from Asia, the five heirs of the emperor Frederick. . . . That number did not merely suggest a death message. It bellowed it.

HE FOUND himself back on the street without remembering how he'd gotten there. He was preoccupied, filled with unease. This crime fascinated him. But was it right to shine the whole light of his intellect on the evil act of a single individual, neglecting the leadership of an entire people?

The stairs of San Marco's guest quarters led to a side alley off of the piazza on which the churchyard opened. The throng of idlers around him seemed to grow; their babble was deafening. He would have liked to return at once to the Priors' Palazzo, to assure himself that the order of banishment had been carried out, but his progress was maddeningly slow, hampered by the tightly packed crowd moving in the opposite direction.

The surge of strangers' bodies against his almost lifted him off the ground, sweeping him toward the end of the street, which widened into a square.

There, above the sea of heads, he spotted a flurry of colorful drapery, hoisted like sails at either side of a wagon that stood at the entrance to the piazza. Figures dressed in gaily colored garments were leaping about on that makeshift stage, applauded by the milling crowd.

The last thing he wanted was to be hemmed in by those idiots, watching a band of foolish tumblers. He tried to slip into one of the shops along the street, but the workday was over and all of the doors were locked. Before he could think of another escape, he found himself right up against that cursed wagon.

"Messere, it is a great show!" someone next to him shouted, shaking his arm to get his attention. The man must have recognized him, and seemed pleased that a prior would share the evening's excitement with him. The poet removed his hand from his arm.

"What is so wonderful in all this quackery?" he said coldly.

"The struggle between the angels and the devils!" he explained with undiminished enthusiasm. "To save man from Hell . . . Look!"

He grabbed his arm again. Dante resigned himself to watching the scene.

At the center of the stage a kneeling youth held a cloth puppet made to resemble a naked man. It had a crudely drawn face, goggle eyes, black holes for nostrils, a toothy mouth agape in what might have been a laugh, a sneer, or a scream. The puppeteer was the only person on the stage wearing workaday clothes. At his left was a small group of performers got up in flamboyant tunics and grotesque masks; they pranced about yelling imprecations and waving pitchforks hung with strips of scarlet cloth. On his right, an equal number of angels wore white tunics adorned with gold cloth wings, and expressions of sanctimonious bliss; they sang hymns of praise in ungrammatical Latin.

The man beside him spoke again. "The angels are trying to snatch the dead man's soul away from the devils. Look!"

There was now a great commotion coming from the left. A group of devils had surrounded the puppet and were stabbing him with their pitchforks, piercing his linen skin. Streams of sawdust gushed from the wounds. The puppet's head swung violently, yet his expression of doleful astonishment, stamped on him by his maker, did not change, as if he knew nothing about the otherworldly contention of which he was the object.

Meanwhile the angels had redoubled their celestial invocations and now began capering about, excitedly flapping their artificial wings. Far from conveying seraphic ardor, in their disorderly frenzy they looked to Dante like a pack of Harpies swooping down on the dead puppet's body. Whatever the pantomime's objective might be, he thought, the angels and devils would do well to hurry up, given that the object of their attentions was disappearing in a hemorrhage of sawdust.

"See how the Seven Capital Sins are trying to strike a blow? But the Seven Virtues will not let them strike him, that poor man!" the peasant exclaimed, appearing not to miss a beat of the agitated clash.

"And why should he be saved from hell, that puppet?" the prior asked, intrigued by the man's theological certainty.

"Don't you understand? He confessed his sins, he repented!"

"And that is enough to save him? A few little tears?"

"Of course, if the angel is willing. Now his fate will be decided, up or down," the other replied, pointing in turn to the festoons of painted fabric on either side of the stage. Dante's eyes followed the man's finger. What at first sight had seemed to be mere scraps of colorful cloth now, upon closer examination, appeared to be a kind of stage set. On the left, the same primitive hand had sketched the mouth of a cave, which opened onto a desert tableland dotted here and there with fragments of rock and scrawny shrubs. At the back of this cavern could be seen a riot of scarlet flames.

The cloth on the right was painted pale blue, randomly scattered with whitish shapes—evidently crowds. A series of concentric circles near the top of the sheet drew the eye toward a nearly invisible point, to which the leaping and fluttering angels obviously aspired. The latter were fervent in their attempt to pull the puppet up with them, though with his dull-witted air, he seemed unable to understand what was best for him. Dante narrowed his eyes, trying to make out what the players had drawn in the center of the circles' vanishing point. It appeared to be a flower, a white rose.

"That is Paradise, Messere!" the man felt it his duty to explain, following the direction of the poet's gaze. "See the orbits of the stars? The circles?"

He seemed very pleased to be able to help a prior interpret the scene's complexity. Dante threw him an icy look. "And why is there a flower in the center of the heavens?"

"Oh, well . . . That's where God is. That's why!"

"But why a flower?"

"Why not?" the other snorted.

Dante looked away, irritated by such impudence. He was thinking about the flower, *Fiore,* of which he had written himself: anything but a habitation of God. And yet Paradise might really be similar to that staged tomfoolery. Lady Lagia's Paradise certainly was. Who knows, maybe the players' performance had been inspired by a stop at the whores' place. The circular orbits, the heavens, Mercury, the Moon, the Sun, Venus, the third heaven . . .

At that moment one of the Sins, who had been leaning over

to grapple the puppet, suddenly turned and leaped toward the audience with a snarl. An exclamation of fright rippled through the mass of spectators. Even the man beside Dante cried out. As for the poet, he jumped back, thoroughly startled: the devil's mask, with its savage features, strikingly recalled Ambrogio's hideous death mask.

Perhaps the faces of horror are always similar to one another, though their manifestations differ, he told himself. The paths of sin are extremely wide-ranging. Perhaps he should explore all the places of crime, summarize them in a coherent pattern, draw a map of the city of sin and brimstone, the boundaries of Dis's underworld.

People continued crowding around, laughing at the puppet's tribulations. Lust had begun obscenely tickling his nether region, while Gluttony pretended to gorge uncontrollably in front of him. Dante looked around, his eyes scanning the faces of that bellowing crowd. What difference was there between those faces and the one of painted cloth and sawdust? If the Seven Sins were to come down off the wagon and walk through the city's streets, they would encounter nothing but men as blind as that puppet. How was Florence any different from the crude hell drawn on the fabric swaying in the breeze overhead? The cavern of Hell was like a walled city that took in the depraved. A circle encompassing every possible kind of savagery.

He shook off those gloomy thoughts. The first shadows of evening were falling. In his mind the fragments of a new work were beginning to form a pattern, just as the tiles of Ambrogio's mosaic had outlined the unfinished figure.

But meanwhile he had to proceed with the investigation, setting aside his impulse to search for the two disguised Comacines. By now, thanks to the Bargello's carelessness, they must have taken cover somewhere. No, it was the Third Heaven he had to return to now—one more time. There, he was convinced, he would find the root of these crimes.

He thought back to the lectures he had heard in Paris: he recalled the old debates about Universals for which he had developed a passion, in the intervals when he was not composing his *rime,* his love poems for Beatrice.

"No," he thought. "Collective entities do not exist. Universals, like Plato's idea of 'horseness,' the characteristic common to all horses conceived directly by God in the realm of ideas, are merely mental abstractions."

There could not be a blind, impersonal killer; he was certain of it. One single identifiable individual had killed, and that single individual must be identified. Who was it? And why had he killed? And above all, why in that barbarous way, in both cases? These were the three answers that he was searching for, and his logic told him that he would succeed in arriving at all three solutions at the same time, or not succeed at all.

His forehead was burning. A new intuition came to him. So far, he had been looking for a single answer to the three enigmas. But whoever had stained his hands with blood might have been driven by a diabolical motive, and might have chosen his method for a different reason. It was possible that thus far his investigation had failed because he had based it on his conviction that there was a logical similarity between the form of the crime and the mind of the killer. The brutal details of the murders had suggested the practices of a satanic cult. The victims' unnatural positions had seemed to him a hideous subversion of the Christian precept of eternal rest; in them he had seen the killer's determination to dominate the bodies of his enemies even beyond death.

What if the killer's motive had been something else? What if he was trying, in his own perverse way, to complete the work that Ambrogio had left unfinished?

18

The same day, at dusk

FOR THE fifth time, Dante crossed the tavern's low doorstep and approached the table around which the members of the Third Heaven were gathered. As he did so he scanned this corner with a rapid glance: all the members of the studium were seated at their places, speaking in low voices. There was tension both in the air and on their faces, where every crease appeared more pronounced. They seemed to have aged several years in the span of a single night. Only Cecco Angiolieri seemed at ease, and was sniggering with his neighbor. By this time he had been accepted among them in every respect, the poet noticed.

As he observed their expressions, the idea of a council of learned animals came to him again, with Cecco as an interloping basilisk. But Teofilo's empty chair stood as a reminder that one of those animals was a savage beast.

Even Baldo seemed upset, and had not hurried over to the table with his usual solicitude. On the contrary, he seemed to want to keep his distance. Dante had to call for wine several times before the crusader finally decided to serve him.

The poet drained his cup in one gulp.

Cecco Angiolieri was the first to speak, addressing the prior abruptly in his usual mocking tone. "Well then, have you begun that *Convito*, that *Banquet* of yours? That epitome of wisdom, of which you spoke before?"

Dante called for more wine. When the crusader had refilled his cup, the poet took it in both hands and for some moments remained motionless in that position, his lips compressed. Then he roused himself. "No. The work that seemed so fitting just a few days ago lost all interest for me over the past several hours. I am now thinking of a very different book."

"And what will this new one be about, Messer Alighieri?" Veniero joined in.

"Something you are experienced in. A journey."

"A journey? I did not know that you had discovered the joys of traveling along with its dangers. What lands do you mean to describe?"

"I will write about a city. A city of suffering. And I will systematically describe the enormous evil and very little good that I found within its walls. The endless delirium of crime and the glory of virtue that opposes it. This will be my work, the *Summa Criminalis*. In vernacular verse, in keeping with modern usage."

"Good and evil, virtue and wrongdoing? That will turn out a most frightening comedy!" Cecco Angiolieri exclaimed, bursting into laughter.

"Yes, a comedy . . . in some respects," the poet said absently. "But this is not the right moment for me to dwell on my work. I do not find here the usual joyfulness of your meetings," he went on, not addressing anyone in particular.

The men around the table turned toward him almost automatically, like clay targets on a carnival wagon, moved by wires.

"Naturally, the death of Master Teofilo has shattered the Third Heaven's harmony, depriving the crystalline vault of one of its stars. I understand your sorrow," the prior continued.

"First Master Ambrogio, then Teofilo," Augustino said in a low voice. "Teofilo too. . . . Why?

"Death makes a wide circle, sometimes, to reach its objective," Veniero remarked, without raising his eyes from his cup. "We see it veer to the right and then it surprises us on the left."

The others stared at Dante in silence. The animal character stamped on their faces had become more pronounced, as the turmoil within them found an outward expression.

"A sorrow made even more painful by the horror that still walks among you," the poet added coldly.

The tension heightened. A shadow lowered over their faces like a funeral mask.

Cecco d'Ascoli broke the silence. "The horror . . . among us? Do you mean the blind savagery that struck two of the studium's leading figures? The evil disposition of the heavens that brought about such a great loss?"

"I am referring to the individual among you who killed Ambrogio and Teofilo. Who with culpable malice and the power of an intellect inclined toward evil cut short those lives whose duration should have been determined by God alone."

He saw no reaction to that, beyond a slight shifting of their eyes, each man glancing sidelong at his neighbor, before staring again, blankly, at Dante. Evidently they already knew that a killer was sitting at that table, yet they seemed to accept the fact with indifference, or with the depraved solidarity of accomplices.

Again it was Cecco d'Ascoli who spoke. He had been resting his chin on his clenched fist. Now he roused himself. "You are right, Messer Alighieri, and perhaps that is what all of us believe. You are not the only one who has peered into the shadows of this mystery: our consciences have been troubled by what happened, and our intellects, like yours, have bent to the laborious search for the truth. But just as your intelligence has failed to come to a solution, our minds, too, are left without one, except for the bitter conclusion that death has halted the course of an ambitious project that would have brought glory to the city that took us in.

Teofilo's death, following that of the Comacine master, also marks the end of the Studium Florentinum."

"You mean to abandon the university?" Dante asked.

"Yes, Messer Alighieri," Bruno joined in. "But not just because of the tragedy that has befallen the Third Heaven. This city is not yet ready for the center of higher studies that we dreamed of. The Commune is not interested in having a center of learning here that does not further its narrow mercantile interests. Boniface has already decreed the establishment of the *Sapientia Urbis* in Rome. Padua and Bologna are too close, and their appeal to your young men is very strong. No, I fear that the Third Heaven would have become obsolete in any case, even without the intervention of Satan's hand."

Dante felt rage rising inside him. So it was this failure that saddened them, not the double homicide? He cast a glance toward the back of the tavern, looking for Antilia. A college of hypocrites guided by a sorcerer, their senses excited by a whore, their plans assisted by obscure divinities. And among them a murderer, or maybe more than one. Now they wanted to shut up shop. Just like that.

"You intend to return to your own cities then? And yet this city is at the height of its expansion; the new circle of walls will contain more than a hundred thousand people. The foundations for immense works have already been laid, and workers are coming from all over Italy to take part in the construction of the new Athens. The Commune will support your plan. Two new Comacine masters entered the northern gate, Porta di Tramontana, yesterday. Perhaps Ambrogio's work will be resumed and brought to completion."

He had not addressed anyone in particular, and at first no one responded. The poet continued scrutinizing his listeners' faces.

He was certain that at least one of them already knew about the last fact. Yet their expressions remained imperturbable.

Only Veniero acknowledged the news. "Two Comacine masters?"

"Then, too, this place will no longer be the same, when beauty has also abandoned it," Augustino said, as if he had not heard the prior's words. "Have you not heard that the divine Antilia is leaving Florence?"

Dante leaped to his feet. "The dancer? Are you sure?" he asked in a cracked voice. Then he bit his lips, upset over having revealed any emotion. "No one is to leave the city without the Commune's permission! Not until I have thrown the guilty party in the Stinche!" he exclaimed, with as much authority as he could muster.

"The woman is leaving. Baldo told us. And his dejected look is the highest proof of the truth of the news. As for the Stinche, surely you do not believe that her tender hands are stained with blood?"

That cursed tavern keeper had kept the fact from him. He would throw him to the Inquisition, just for that. Have them rip off his other arm as well. Let the cursed swine rot in prison, let death visit him for the fifth time. It would be the last time.

"Do you know where she is going?" he asked, as calmly as he could.

A shadow crossed Augustino's face, and he exchanged a look with the others. "Who knows . . . perhaps to her true love." There was a trace of sarcasm in his voice. "That devil . . ."

"Are angels and devils not the same thing, in God's timeless eye?" Bruno said. "Is everything not omnipresent in His mind? Does not Lucifer, though lost in hell, continue gladdening his ear with the lyre's dulcet notes, pouring out the honey of song? Is time not merely a pathetic illusion of ours? Are not our fallible senses our tormentors? Angel of heaven or devil from the earth's bowels, Antilia is bathed in radiance . . ."

"Because that which is above is like that which is below," Cecco d'Ascoli added. "The same fire that devours the belly of volcanoes blasts in the caverns of the heavens."

Veniero had fallen silent, and sat contemplating the bottom of the cup he gripped in his hand. Upon hearing those words he stirred. "And the depths of the sea are lashed by impetuous currents, like the torrents of air that swell the sails. Yes, truly, gentlemen, that which is below is like that which is above . . . I have seen it." He sank his face into his cup again, as if to dispel a painful memory.

There was a hidden meaning in these words, Dante was certain. The Third Heaven had begun to speak in allegories. "But even if there is no distinction in God's mind between what has been and what will be, by virtue of the omniscience imbued by the Holy Spirit," he answered, "our human limitation must acknowledge that two men have been killed, their passage on earth interrupted, their time stolen. And this is an act that screams to God for vengeance."

"But vengeance is mine and mine the forgiveness, the Eternal Father said. And He forbade anyone to touch Cain," Veniero murmured.

"His is the vengeance and His the forgiveness, but justice is ours. And so is the duty to restore a just order during the limited time we are allotted. It is that order that the criminal corrupts."

"You seem to set great store by the order of what is consummated on Earth, with all of its miseries. And yet . . ." Cecco d'Ascoli set his cup down on the table and stared at the torchlight reflected in the gleaming metal, as if that glittering illumination had wholly captured his attention. He placed a finger on the base of the goblet, and turned it in a slow circular motion, following its revolutions with his eyes. Abruptly he became alert once more. "And yet everything that lives is nothing but a pallid reflection of what is in the heavens," he concluded.

"Do you refer to the glory of God?" Dante asked.

"I am alluding to the infinite force of the luminous bodies that orbit above and sweep us into the vortex of their trajectory. They are the true foundation of the universe. They make us what we are."

"But in the vault of the heavens our spirit is unfettered. It is free to choose and to desire. Your reasoning is defective, and it is blasphemous. Look around you, even within this tavern: the dance of human limbs, the human heart's passions, its emotions, your own unforeseeable actions—are they not the highest proof of the truth of what I maintain? It is not a superlunary, preordained order that guides our volition. The force of the stars imprints us with only a faint inclination: we must assist God's plan with right action. And seeking justice is paving the way to fulfilling His will."

"You are wrong, Messer Alighieri. You limit the power of the stars to the inferior space of the universe in which fate has destined us to live. But just above our heads, and below our feet, that power explodes with a force that is multiplied a hundredfold. Has it not been demonstrated that rocks hold this power in the bowels of the earth? Is the diamond not king among minerals, because it is the one that lies hidden in earth's most profound depths, virtually combined with its very matrix? And does this not occur precisely because light beams, restricted on the surface, are magnified in the earth's core, just as the focus of a lens is located exactly halfway between the light source and its point of maximum radiation?"

"Do you mean to say that the virtue of the stars, exceedingly intense in the heavens, is weaker on the earth's surface and becomes magnified again as it descends into the depths?"

The astrologer brightened. "Of course, that is exactly how it is. *In interiore terrae erimus sicut deos.*"

"God separated light from darkness, land from water! And gave us light and the earth as our dominion, populating the darkness and the seas with monstrous creatures. The bowels of the earth are not the Promised Land, but rather Lucifer's den!" the poet exclaimed in a furious tone.

"And where else should the prince of angels have fled, if not to the place where everything converges, where the force of light is greatest?"

Exasperated, Dante was getting ready to demolish that absurd theory, when a thought crossed his mind.

He recalled the traces in the crypt of Saint Jude, the signs and incomprehensible litanies that Giannetto had spoken of. He stared at the astrologer's fine Roman profile. Had he, then, been the one to venture underground, in search of the radiant power of the stars? Was it his voice that had resounded in those horror-filled chambers?

And Ambrogio? And Teofilo? What power had claimed their lives?

So simple, so evil . . . It was not a conspiracy contrived against Florence, against the Church, or against the Guelphs. The Third Heaven was conspiring against God.

Slowly he rose from his seat, letting his gaze travel over the faces of those around the table. "Do you also stand by Master Francesco's theory?" he asked coldly. "All of you?"

Bruno leaped to his feet. He seemed about to reply, but whatever his argument might have been, it was drowned out by a sudden commotion at the entrance to the tavern.

A group of armed men had come bursting in, and the customers closest to the door were hastily moving aside, overturning benches and tables.

Dante turned, too, his hand moving to his concealed dagger. He looked around quickly, seeking an escape through the center of the room.

Then he spotted the leader of these invaders, and his anxiety subsided. A thickset man in heavy armor was barking orders left and right; meanwhile his searching eyes had lit on Dante. The poet walked swiftly toward him through the confused mob of customers.

"Perhaps it is providence that brings you here, Bargello," he said. Those men might turn out to be needed, if he wanted to stop the dancer—and the others—from taking flight. He was about to order their arrest, but the captain forestalled him.

"I am in need of you, Messer Alighieri, or rather of the Commune's authority. The Cerchi and the Donati are confronting one another near the Ponte Vecchio, in contempt of the proclamation of banishment and its orders. My guards and I are not enough: the presence of someone bearing the symbols of authority is crucial. I have brought your insignia from San Piero."

One of the bargellini approached and handed Dante his embroidered biretta and gilt staff.

"Could you not have called upon one of my colleagues?" the poet asked harshly, snatching the insignia from the guard's sweaty hands.

"I tried . . . but they . . ."

"They what?"

"They do not want anything to do with it . . . I think they are afraid."

"Afraid of a scuffle between some troublemakers?"

"No . . . they fear a revolt . . ."

With difficulty Dante suppressed the insults that rose to his lips. Oh, to be able to fully inveigh against such cowards . . . and against the insufficiency of the Bargello, who was not even able to put an end to a common commotion without disturbing a prior. Yet the man's face wore an anguished grimace; his eyes hinted at a situation graver than Dante could imagine.

Perhaps he would do well not to underestimate the danger. If the conflict between the Whites and the Blacks were to explode before the proclamation of banishment had rid the city of their factious leaders, all of Florence would be thrown into chaos, and Boniface would intervene. He might even appeal to the king of France for help, and that monarch, always eager to fill his coffers with florins, would comply. That must be avoided at all costs.

Hastily the prior donned his biretta and headed hurriedly toward the door, ordering the bargellini to follow him. As he was going out, he threw a last glance at the members of the Third Heaven, who had sat expressionless throughout the uproar.

He would return. Especially for one of them.

19

The same day, after curfew

THE BARGELLO had mobilized as many district guards as he could without leaving the gates undefended, along with the firefighting brigades. About forty men in all: that might be too many or too few, depending on what was taking place.

Swiftly they covered the distance to Ponte Vecchio, running at times, for as long as their strength and the weight of their armor allowed, with brief pauses to catch their breath.

"Do you know why they are fighting?" Dante asked during one of these pauses.

"Someone spread the rumor that a banishment proclamation had been issued against the faction leaders. The Cerchi and the Donati came down, armed, each to defend their own men, and to strike at their adversaries."

The poet clenched his fists. One of the priors had talked. And his unguarded words had been the seed of the revolt. Worriedly he cast a glance at the guards who were following him. If the members of the Cerchi and the Donati families had all descended on the piazza, the troops under the Bargello's command would not be enough. The Donati alone were capable of summoning five hundred armed men.

He should have called for the crossbowmen, or even asked for help from Acquasparta's mercenary guard. But then that viper would have been able to carry out the plan he had had in mind from the very beginning. Better to set fire to Florence, Dante thought. Then he remembered the lumber yards, hard by the mills along the Arno. If they were busy fighting flames to save their property, perhaps those troublemakers would calm down.

Quickly he discarded so desperate a scheme. As they rounded the final curve of the Lungarno, he heard the clamor; the nearer he drew, the louder it became. The torches of the warring parties could be seen in the distance. This nocturnal clash was strange, he thought, as he stopped a moment, bent over, breathless from running. It deprived the opponents of the pleasure of abusing one another openly, of choosing the most hated adversary from each other's ranks, of unleashing personal rancors with the excuse of political rivalry.

He wondered whether the universal disturbance had been deliberately provoked by someone wishing to cover up something more serious.

"Who started the riot?" he asked the Bargello, who stood panting beside him. But even before the man could say anything, he already knew how superfluous any response would be. Tension between the two factions had reached the breaking point long ago.

"The banishment orders against the faction leaders . . . a reckless action. . . . How will we get out of this?" the captain of the guard wailed.

"How can you expect to understand the Commune's politics, you fool? What do you know about what is stirring beneath the very soil you tread on?"

Even that idiot took the liberty of questioning his decisions. Would he have to convince him too, after persuading those other scoundrels, his fellow priors? He could barely restrain himself from slapping the man's reddened face.

Still, a sense of uneasiness was growing in him as well. His idea of a collective banishment had been a last attempt to salvage an already desperate situation. A risky move, made in the hope that the miracle of thirty years ago—when Florence survived the devastating conflict between Guelphs and Ghibellines—might be repeated. But that time peace had been brought about by colossal figures, like Farinata degli Uberti, and subtle minds, like Mosca de' Lamberti.

Who would save the city this time? The city's only hope seemed to depend on his strength alone. Surely this must be the mission of the Alighieri, announced to him by his guiding star.

"You simpleton, why was I was born under the sign of Gemini, if not for this?"

The Bargello, not well acquainted with astrological science, merely moved away a little, bewildered.

THEY FOUND the White faction, who had gathered behind the embankment of Ponte Vecchio's incline. They were brandishing their torches at the other side of the river, where the muddled mass of their opponents could be barely made out in the moonlight. Fewer than he had feared, the poet observed with relief. Perhaps it was still possible to get the situation back in hand.

"How do we know they are Blacks?" he shouted to the Bargello. They might also be the mysterious Ghibellines that everyone was talking about.

"We spotted their banner: Saint George. Ours upholds the Baptist," the other replied.

A few stones whistled by, grazing Dante and bouncing violently against the boards of the closed shops. Hurriedly he took shelter behind the mutilated statue of Mars at the top of the bridge. An intense light suddenly flared up from the other bank, as if numerous torches had been brought together to form a single blaze. Evidently the Blacks wanted to be quite visible. Some of them, in fact, had lowered their breeches and were showing their enemies their backsides.

A man appeared on horseback at the center of the crossing, a corpulent figure with a massive head framed by a thick white beard.

The poet's face twisted into a grimace. Even at a distance, halfway between the torches of Black and White, there was no mistaking who this was.

"Damn," the Bargello hissed, taking cover beside him. "Corso Donati, the leader of those brigands. Instead of trying to make peace, he is here to incite them against the Commune's authority. We ought to play the Pisan trick on him . . ."

"What do the Pisans do?" Dante asked distractedly.

"With the likes of him? They shut them away in a tower. Or they hang them from the lateen-yards of their galleys, covered with pitch so they'll last longer without decomposing. They bury them in the sky, those barbarians!"

Dante remembered the horrible end of Count Ugolino, walled up alive in the Muda tower with his sons. Corso Donati deserved the same treatment . . . That way he would be preserved for a long time, serving as an admonition to others.

An image flashed through his mind, as sharply as if a rock had struck him. How had he not thought of it before? They bury them in the sky. That which is above is like that which is below. Was that not what he had said? Could this be the Ariadne's thread that he had been vainly seeking? At that moment he saw everything with clarity: the pentagram, Venus, his knowledge of the stars.

He must return to the tavern immediately and have the guilty man arrested, have him tortured so that he would confess everything. It was him, it *had* to be him. He turned around to shout the order to the bargellini, then checked himself, stooping down again to take cover behind the shelter, now being hammered by a hail of stones.

Something, deep down inside, was holding him back. The use of torture as the primary way to get at the truth had always been repugnant to him. He would never resort to it in connection with a member of the Third Heaven. Not out of charity, no. The person who had committed those crimes had renounced his Christian nature, applying the celestial gift of the intellect to evil.

No, that was not the reason. The killer had challenged him. He had staked everything on destiny's scales. And he had placed a hand in front of Dante's eyes, certain that he would not be able to see.

That challenge must be fought and won through the use of reason, not with the executioner's irons. Even in shackles, the murderer would scorch him with his cold, contemptuous gaze if he had to admit that he did not know the reason for his crimes. For that was what he still did not know.

He thought he knew the guilty man's name, that name so long concealed in the roster of the Third Heaven. Perhaps the reason for the murders could be found in his lodgings. He had to find out at all costs. Abruptly he left the shelter of Mars' statue and began running toward the bridge.

"Where are you going, prior?" the Bargello's startled voice called out behind him. "The Blacks are over there! Have you taken leave of your senses?"

Dante had headed for the incline of Ponte Vecchio. Around him he heard the insurgents' increasingly angry shouts.

"Why are you running toward them? Are you running away? Are you fleeing, too?"

The poet kept on running. The Bargello would pay for those insults. But there was no time now.

A childhood memory came back to him, of expeditions across the bridge with his friends. He remembered the tanner's shop, in the middle of the arch, with its disgusting smell of horse piss. There was a staircase in the back that led up to the roofs of the shops that lined the Ponte Vecchio. From it he could cross the bridge over the heads of those scoundrels bellowing down below. It was years since he had thought of that staircase, but it was still there, though much more dilapidated than he remembered. He hoped it would support his weight.

From the other side of the bridge the Blacks had noticed his movements. At first, seeing him run out in the open and advance toward them, decked out in the Commune's insignia, they had retreated, afraid he was leading an assault of the guard. But when they realized that he was alone, they rallied. As he clambered gingerly up the rotting stairs, Dante heard them advancing through the shops.

He reached the top just as the first of them appeared at the center of the bridge, aiming a spear at him. He seized a loose plank from the ancient roof and hurled it, then leaped onto the adjoining roof. The boards creaked alarmingly under his weight, but held. From there with another jump he got to the next shop. Below him the Blacks, disoriented, experienced a moment of uncertainty, long enough to allow him to reach the last roof. He leaped to the ground behind them, and as they turned and came toward him with their spears, rolled neatly to one side.

He was no longer as agile as he had been, he thought with some anxiety as he got to his feet again, aching all over. He looked around, trying to orient himself in the darkness. To his left he saw an enormous shadow.

For an instant he thought it was a gigantic centaur bearing down on him. Corso Donati reached the bridge's incline at that moment and made his steed rear up with a violent tug on the bit.

His personal guard came rushing to his side, while three armed men in heavy cuirasses ran toward the prior with arms outstretched, ready to seize him.

Angrily Dante noted the tabards of Acquasparta's mercenary guard. He even recognized one assailant as the man who had insulted him on the steps of the pontifical legation. Those bastards had already started helping the Blacks, as he had long suspected. And now they were prepared to do away with him, so as to dispose of a witness to their rotten dealings.

He was done for, a mouse caught in a cat's paws. Then he spied a possible way out. On one side of the bridge's wagon ramp was a narrow flight of steps—he was sure it led down to the riverbank. He darted to that side, just managing to avoid a spiked club that grazed his head as a hand made a grab at his arm.

He shook himself free and plunged forward down the first steps. The guard, encumbered by his mail and swept along by his own momentum, stumbled into his two companions, who had halted at the edge of the dark ramp, and all three of them toppled over in a tangle of arms and legs, rolling down several steps before coming to a stop, their bodies shielding him from the continuing barrage of stones.

Meanwhile, Dante had reached the bottom and rushed straight for the floating mill over by Ponte alla Carraia.

"Cursed rogues!" he shouted back at the guards, who still lay near the top of the stairs. "Damned blackguards, sons of stinking whores!" he shouted with all the rage he had in him, raising his arm in an obscene gesture. "May you rot in hell, you bastards!"

Two of the mercenaries were still trying to get to their feet, while their big-bellied sergeant peered over the bridge abutment, his tiny porcine eyes searching for his prey. He was just in time to catch the poet's maledictions head-on. He curled his lips in an expression of loathing, baring crooked yellow teeth. "He's cursing us, that foreigner! He's putting a jinx on us! Seize the necromancer!"

The men crossed themselves rapidly and called on the name of Christ. Then they snatched up their pikes and hurried after Dante, who was running along the bank, his feet floundering in the low water, raising spatters of mud.

He ran desperately now, hearing imprecations and the clanking of armor behind him. A multitude of tinkers was crashing down the badly flagged slope. He did not slow down to look back, but bent himself wholly to the task of escaping.

He began to feel short of breath, and an acute pang gripped his side. His pursuers must be younger than he, he thought in despair. Yet he had to avoid capture at all costs, or Florence would be lost. That disturbance was certainly the harbinger of a general uprising against the Whites, as Giannetto, that cursed bird of ill omen, had predicted. Let the beggar be torn to shreds, in the Stinche. To hell with that useless being!

A few steps further on he saw a narrow opening in the brick wall that blocked his escape route on the right. He squeezed himself into it, hoping that his pursuers would overlook it as they passed.

Crouched inside the wall, his heart in his throat, he heard the clanking recede. An icy sweat coursed down his neck despite the summer heat. The pain in his side was tearing him in two.

Hoping he had been spared once more, he waited, motionless, afraid he would hear the rumble of footsteps and shouting returning. Sooner or later those scoundrels would realize that they had been duped and would come back. He had to make the most of his temporary advantage by finding a safer cover.

Hastily he considered whether it would be better to go back to the street and try to reach Porta Romana. But he was afraid that other mercenaries, led by that wild boar, might have already set out on his tracks. If the first three were to turn back, he would find himself trapped in the narrow brick passage without any means of escape.

Just then he glimpsed a shadow behind him. He turned around abruptly, ready to strike. In the darkness he recognized the face of Cecco Angiolieri. How was it possible? The man had been with him in the tavern a short time ago. He must have left right after him and somehow reached the other bank of the river. But how had he got there? Surely he could not know Florence better than Dante.

Cecco wore a leather cuirass and a plumed helmet and was brandishing a short sword of the type generally used for fighting on horseback. He looked like one of the Roman statues on the piazza of Santa Maria, come to life. Even in that situation he stood midway between the ridiculous and the appalling, Dante thought.

"Cecco!" he shouted. "So, then, this is the mission that drew you to Florence? The mission that is to change history? Pandering to the Blacks?"

The other raised his chin, as if to observe him better. "There is always a cozy nook for the panderer. And he is not forced to pay for what others must buy with ready cash. I am talking about that sweet flower that we hold so close to our hearts, you and I!"

"Do you side with the pope, Cecco?" the poet asked again, incredulous.

"What did you expect, Messer Durante? And so should you; listen to me," the other said, placing a hand on his shoulder.

Dante pushed him away with a brusque gesture. He wanted to add something more, then abruptly he turned and began running again. "I can't, my friend. I have an appointment with guilt," he shouted, as he went off without looking back.

"You would have been better off drinking that wine, you and the other priors. Now you would be dreaming, instead of having to open your eyes."

At that moment one of the mercenaries appeared, a crossbowman with his weapon notched. He dropped to one knee and took careful aim at Dante's retreating back.

Cecco Angiolieri's hand thrust the weapon upward, and the arrow passed harmlessly over the fleeing man's head. "No need. He has already dug his grave with his words," he said, indicating the poet. "Those are what will bury him."

BREATHLESSLY, Dante covered the remainder of the way. In the end, that disturbance was turning out to be propitious for his own cause. No one would be able to get through the combatants blocking Ponte Vecchio, and going by way of Ponte alla Carraia would take too much time.

He knew where to go. He recognized the cut-off tower right away, from the description given in the report on the members of the studium. There was no one along the road, which was bordered by blind walls broken only by the arches of windows, walled up since the time of the last riots. At the bottom of the tower's wall was a wooden door, bolted and reinforced with iron studs; there did not seem to be any foothold in the stone surface that would allow him to reach the small double window located at least twenty feet above.

For an instant Dante was at a loss. Then he leaned against the wood, testing its solidity. Despite its apparent sturdiness, the door rocked beneath his weight. Perhaps it was only latched. Or maybe the wood, as old as the structure, was worm-eaten. He pushed again; the door began to yield. He persisted, applying all his strength.

He heard a sharp click, a snapping sound and the door burst open, torn from its rusty hinges. He had to hold tightly to the doorjamb for support, so as not to collapse with it. Before him he saw a windowless room, empty. In the back of it rose a narrow flight of stone steps. The faint glimmer of moonlight coming from the open door was barely sufficient to allow him to orient himself in the small space. He spotted an oil lamp, set in a niche in the wall.

He took some tinder and flint from his pouch and lit the lamp. As soon as he was able to see where to put his feet, he climbed swiftly to the first floor. The old planks creaked beneath him. He hoped they were in better condition than the door. The room on this floor was nearly as empty as the first. There was only a simple wooden bed covered with a linen cloth that gave off a faint, clean fragrance, mixed with something else: the scent of female flesh. Evoked by that perfume, a vision of Antilia's naked body, displayed before him in all its splendor, filled his senses. So that was her refuge, with the man who had holed up in the decrepit tower. The secret lover, whom Baldo despised and perhaps feared. He could hear Pietra's words again. "No one loves you . . ."

He dispelled the apparition with an angry gesture. He would punish her, along with him. In a corner of the room stood a trunk filled with women's clothing. He sank his hands into that sea of silk, as if he were sinking them into Antilia's hair, and again her perfume filled his nostrils and her image took possession of his thoughts.

He was overcome by a fit of vertigo. For a moment time stopped. The symptoms of possession: they were growing in him. It is through the vegetative soul that demons find their way into the human mind, clearing a path where upright conscience is less vigilant. A diminished perception of time and space and an agitated imagination are the most immediate and most recognizable signs. But if he was aware of being possessed, would that be enough to save him from perdition? She had looked at him in the tavern. Is it not with a look that the basilisk kills its prey? Could he still escape the spell of that infernal priestess with the copper face?

He snatched up a fistful of her garments and sank his face into them, breathing deeply of her aroma. Perhaps her very clothing was steeped in some magic potion, the shreds of his conscience warned him.

He felt his mind losing the battle against the mirage. Then something unexpected jolted him out of his amorous delirium.

As his hands caressed her perfumed robes, he heard a sharp metallic clink. Something rolled onto the wooden floor. One of Antilia's bangles. Letting her garments slip back into the trunk, he bent to retrieve it. The extraordinary heaviness of the bauble impressed him.

That woman must truly know the secret of making gold, if she could afford to leave so valuable an object unattended in an open trunk. Without ceremony he tossed the contents of the chest on the ground, looking for more jewelry. Jumbled together with the precious silk and linen tunics were dozens of gold circlets like that one. The trunk was a treasure chest. With an effort he tipped it, spilling on the floor the glittering wealth of a kingdom.

A kingdom . . . so Antilia really was the descendant of the emperor Frederick II, heiress to the throne of Sicily. That was the reason she had subjected herself to that disgraceful performance in Lady Lagia's Paradise: anything to conceal her identity. Were the dancer's bangles recast from more ancient pieces? Had she been hiding a royal fortune in plain view? Anyone seeing those bracelets on a dancer would admire their beauty, but no one would ever suspect their preciousness, or that the woman possessed scores of them.

All the details of the affair were recomposing themselves in Dante's imagination, falling into place like the tiles of Ambrogio's mosaic. Acquasparta's hatred of the woman, his attempt to accuse her of heresy in order to be able to arrest her, the persecution of the Comacine master in Rome and then his murder. The murder of Teofilo, who had uncovered the secret of the gold and knew its provenance, and who had tried to deceive Dante by leading his attention along the illusory paths of alchemical science.

It was possible.

And yet some detail of that complex design must have escaped him.

Why hadn't Boniface's men made away with the woman, why had they wasted time destroying everything around her, hoping to conceal her identity, why had they kept the last Hohenstaufen hidden instead of eliminating her before she could reclaim in her own person the rights of the Swabian dynasty, wresting back the kingdom that her father Manfred had lost, with his life, at Benevento?

He raised the lamp and glanced up. There was a second set of stairs leading to another floor. He hurried over.

On the third floor he found another sparsely furnished room, this one with a simple table resting on two trestles, piled haphazardly with large sheets of linen paper. The poet picked up a page and held it close to the lamp. The paper was covered with an intricate sequence of lines drawn in charcoal, riddled with holes, as if an army of insects had repeatedly attacked the draftsman's work. The entire surface was grimy with soot.

He felt his heart leap to his throat in his excitement. He had found them: Ambrogio's cartoons, the preliminary drawings for the mosaic that the Comacine master had used to trace the outline of his work on the wall.

Feverishly he examined one sketch after another, but his excitement and the poor light made it difficult for him to grasp the picture as a whole. The detail of a leg appeared here, an arm there. The face of the elderly colossus was portrayed on one drawing, but all of the sketches had been muddled by a series of additional marks that hampered him from following their overall meaning. He gave up. There was only one way to figure it out.

He gathered the sheets into a bundle and looked around for something to wrap them in. A white cloth lay folded on a stool in the embrasure of the double window. He grabbed it and spread it out on the table, then froze in surprise.

What he had taken for a bedsheet was a voluminous mantle of fine white wool. Unfolded, it had the shape of a corolla: the outer side was covered by a richly embroidered cross extending from shoulder to shoulder, neck to heel. The cross of the Templars, identical to the one that adorned the dagger found in the church.

So then, not only was the dancer a descendant of the house of Swabia, but the Templars knew it and were protecting her. Or . . .

He struck his forehead with his fist. Now he recalled the words of Domenico, the usurer.

It was not the Order of the Temple that trailed after Antilia, held her hand in times of danger, caressed her copper flesh. It was one man alone. The one who dwelled in that tower.

The faces of the members of the Third Heaven whirled in his head. Hurriedly he wrapped the drawings in the mantle and ran for the door. Clattering down the stairs, he passed the second floor without a thought for the fortune that he was leaving unattended.

20

The same day, toward midnight

THE TORCHES left by the bargellini were still piled by the door. Dante lit one but the shadows were impervious to all but the smallest circle of light. Walking carefully within it he crossed the narrow walkway that skirted the abyss. When he reached the apse, the faint beam fell for a moment on Ambrogio's death mask, lying abandoned on the ground, bringing the Comacine master's last grimace briefly to life.

With some difficulty he clambered up the scaffolding and set his torch in one of the brackets fixed to the wall around the mosaic. Ambrogio had worked nights as well as days, hurrying to complete his work, as if he could smell behind him the hot breath of that hound of hell.

Dante unfolded the Templar's mantle and began rummaging among the sketches, looking for a starting point from which to reconstruct the design. He found the cartoon with the head of the old colossus and placed it over the corresponding part of the mosaic. On the scaffolding were a wooden mallet and a small bucket filled with rusty nails. Swiftly he affixed the sketch to the wall, then looked for one that would continue the story.

————

HE HAD been working for nearly an hour by now. The tesserae of the tragedy were beginning to connect in his mind as the sketches formed their unexpected pattern on the wall.

At first astonished by what they revealed, he was now keenly curious, as he realized how much the outline of the work differed from the initial plan. There was none of the airy lightness of Eden's birds, plants, and flowers. Ambrogio had not simply abandoned that earlier idea of an *Arbor vitae:* for him, that idea had never existed. With his masterly skill and extraordinary flair for color, he had given shape to a much more sensual image.

Could the secret that had to be concealed at all costs be that second human figure, to the right of the colossus, who appeared to be waiting for him at his journey's end? A female figure, her face luminous, of a woman about to embrace a long-awaited lover. So must Penelope have looked, welcoming Ulysses to her bed.

The woman was reaching an arm out toward the man. Unlike him, she was still in the prime of youth. And completely nude, as artists had dared to portray only Eve.

He recognized Antilia's face, her firm breasts, her triumphant womb. Her legs were strong as columns, but the ankles were slim and encircled with gold. Behind those pillars the artist had drawn the profile of a strange city, without walls or battlements but spiked with tiered towers like those found in the deserts of the East: a new Babylon, ruled by the queenly woman, who towered above it.

Between these two lovers there was water, cresting, jagged waves skimmed by strange birds, where gentle dolphins and the horrendous Leviathan swam. Across that barrier the woman's hand grazed the hand of the man who leaned forward to take hold of her. Within the semicircle of their arms were graduated lines marked by numerals, suggesting a solar clock. Below it, framed by a cartouche, were the words DECLINATIONIS MAGNETI-CAE GRADUUS.

HE APPEARED suddenly, from out of the shadows. He must have come up from the cistern, through the subterranean passage.

His eyes no longer had any friendliness about them; their blue irises glinted like ice crystals. He was moving toward Dante slowly, hands at his sides, but his muscles were as tense as those of a wild beast ready to spring upon its prey. He seemed taller now that he had discarded the mask of a humble exile: the blood of his corsair forefathers was again roaring in his veins. Wary of the crusader's hold, Dante jumped backward, putting his weight on his forward right foot, and prepared to land the Ghibelline kick. The other, guessing his countermove, suddenly changed his own stance: raising his arms to his chest, he held his palms out and stopped, as if to make his opponent understand that there was still time for words.

The prior accepted the tacit truce. He took a step backward and assumed a relaxed stance. Inwardly he was cursing himself for having gone there unarmed and alone, letting his impatience to learn the truth get the better of him. He had told nobody where he was going, nobody would come to his aid. His only weapon was the dagger in his secret pocket, but he doubted his adversary would give him a chance to use it.

"Better this way," he told himself. If God and justice were on his side, he would not need any help. He raised his hands in turn, returning the man's gesture, while out of the corner of his eye he looked nervously around the restricted circle of light for something to defend himself with.

"A strange place in which to encounter you, Messer Alighieri. Not in a scriptorium or a library, where one would expect to cross paths with a learned friend of words such as you."

"Perhaps. But for that matter, neither are we on the deck of a galley, or in a shipyard or on remote shores, where one would think of finding you, Messer Veniero."

"And yet there are more sea lengths and distant lands beneath these vaults than you would believe."

Dante looked at him, then pointed to the mosaic. "And there are also more words and meanings, and books beneath these vaults, than *you* would believe. But I imagine you know that."

"You do not seem surprised to see me."

"No. I knew we would meet. And perhaps this is the most fitting place."

"How did you come to suspect me?" the Venetian asked, after a long pause. There was sincere curiosity in his voice. He seemed not to know what to do, to be waiting for someone who might advise him or give him orders.

The poet turned his head slightly, indicating the mantle that lay at the foot of the scaffolding. "I imagine it is yours. You are a Templar."

Veniero gave a wan smile. "How did you realize it?"

"Not because of that. Nor because of the dagger you left here, when you tried to make your crime look like a perverse rite by tracing a pentagram on the wall. Messer Domenico, the usurer, made it known to me. He told me that you had offered him letters of credit that were guaranteed. Only Templar commendams can issue those."

"But how did you come to know about . . . this?" the captain asked again, indicating with a wide sweep of his arm the frescoes behind them and Ambrogio's mask lying at its base, screaming out against death.

"You yourself revealed it to me."

"I?" Veniero replied, astonished.

"You, with your own words. You told me about the human figureheads that at one time were placed at the prows of ships to propitiate the gods, to ensure a safe voyage. And is it not the custom of seagoing vessels to coat the bodies of condemned men with pitch, to preserve them as an admonition to others? And on the way to Paradise, you stated that a circle may be traveled in both directions. Ambrogio and Teofilo were on the same desperate path, and it was only by chance that one died before the other. That was what you meant when you said that the apothecary was the second to be killed only because death had chosen another path. But I was blind, until my mind was enlightened this evening at the tavern of the Third Heaven, when you compared the sea's currents to blustery winds and said that that which is below is like that which is above. That was the significance of the second sail in Master Ambrogio's sketch, was it not? A means of exploiting the currents of the sea. And you knew it, even though you pretended not to know."

Veniero nodded. "Yes, an ancient instrument invented by the mariners of Tyre to navigate the strong adverse currents at the Pillars of Hercules. They discovered that there is another current there, nearly two hundred feet below the surface, that travels in a westward direction, toward the ocean. And they invented a submerged sail to draw upon that force, as if it were wind."

His eyes gleamed at that recollection, as if the genius of those ancient mariners continued to stir his admiration. It seemed to Dante that the sound of the ocean breathed gently around him. He waited a moment before going on.

"But those are not the only reasons my steps took me here. I was guided by your own spirit. I told you that a crime reflects the mind of its author. Think of your companions in the Third

Heaven. Francesco d'Ascoli, with his faith in the abstract rigors of celestial motions, the absolute geometry of destiny. And Bruno Ammannati, the theologian, on his way to condemning himself to the stake, a blind guide to other blind men. Antonio da Peretola, at the mercy of his dream of uniting all men under the sign of the cross and for this reason willing to deliver Florence en masse into the hands of a tyrant. Augustino di Menico, convinced as the ancients were that reason alone can arrive at the truth and therefore destined to remain in darkness, outside the house of God. And Cecco Angiolieri, ravaged by the melancholy that pervades him like an inexorable poison. All of them could have killed, because of their passions."

Veniero had remained motionless, listening in silence, his arms crossed.

"Yet I did not sense passion in those crimes. They were marked by a different shadow," the poet continued.

"What was that?"

"Pain. The pain of a soul torn from its own land and cast out into the cold, in exile. That is perhaps the greatest pain, for which there is no remedy."

The Venetian lowered his head, as if to protect himself against those words. "You know my actions. Do you also know their motive?" he said then, looking up suddenly with a challenging air.

Dante turned toward the immense design, its missing portions finally revealed. The wavering light of their torches seemed to set in motion that vast sea. "Yes, now I do." His eyes ran over the graduated line that spanned the space between the body of the man and that of the woman, forming a semicircle as it joined the mass of rocks and rivers with the land on the other side of the ocean. "A new part of the world. After Asia, Europe, Africa and the fourth part, water. This . . ." He pointed to the dark city outlined behind the woman on the cartoon: the city with the strange towers.

Veniero moved closer, as if he, too, wanted to see better. "Yes," he said then. "It is an accurate work. Ambrogio was truly a master. One look at the secret archive of the commendam of Saint Paul, in Rome, was enough for him to understand everything. That secret had required years of research at the Temple. He wanted everyone to know. I offered him all of the gold, if he would keep silent. It was folly." Abruptly he drew a short sword from under his garments and held it against the poet's chest.

Dante felt the cold steel tip move dangerously near his throat and backed away, quickly followed by the blade. The mariner kept the deadly pressure steady, neither attenuating the threat nor rendering it more severe. His lips twisted at the corners, and the feral mask that Dante had seen at first replaced the refined, gentlemanly features he had come to know. His gaze was again the cold stare of a lion. All at once the poet felt sure he was doomed.

But the other merely toyed with his throat, as if he were in no hurry to put an end to their match. Perhaps, like a great actor, he did not want to leave the scene without an extreme display of bravura, without applause for his brilliance. And Dante, to gain time, was willing to give him that.

"Not one of the members of the Third Heaven ever suspected you. Nor did they suspect Antilia, concealed within the walls of Paradise as its most recent prostitute. But why Teofilo?"

"He knew the secret of metals. Of stones. And he suspected something about Antilia's origins. He had seen the pure copper she brought from her country's mines. He knew that such copper does not exist in the known lands. I tried to buy him too, with a vial of *chandu*. I hoped that, even more than gold, owning such a secret would appease his intellectual pride. But he wanted more . . . he wanted too much." The seafarer glanced for an instant at the woman in the mural. "He would have sought and found it. He, too, paid for his excellence," he added with a melancholy smile. "Perhaps the world belongs to mediocre creatures. Only they can go about with confidence."

Dante noticed a slight variation in his tone of voice, a conclusive note. Veniero was getting ready to strike him. Would he put his third victim on display as well, like a ship's figurehead? His thoughts raced as he considered what to do. He felt the weight of the dagger in his pocket. Maybe he could reach it before the other attacked him.

He dropped to his knees, as his hand flew to his weapon. Veniero, caught by surprise, hesitated a moment, giving Dante the time he needed to lunge forward, grabbing the seaman's right arm with his free hand and immobilizing him. His blade arced toward the Venetian's neck, tracing a semicircle.

It hit Veniero just below the ear, and glanced off something hard. A steel collar. In a flash the poet raised his hand again, this time aiming at the lion's heart.

He plunged the dagger in with all his might, but the other had jerked free of his grip, and the blade missed its deadly mark, sinking into Veniero's shoulder. Dante felt his adversary sag, as if his vital forces had deserted him.

He raised his arm once more, and someone grabbed it from behind. His left hand still clenched around Veniero's throat, he turned to strike this new enemy. It was Antilia. She was bent over him, but she was looking at Veniero. She showed no fear of Dante. Her eyes were filled with tears. The poet stood motionless, his blade raised toward the ceiling. He was panting from emotion and exertion.

At last Antilia looked at him. "I beg you, Messere," she whispered. She did not say anything more, merely fixed him with that distant gaze of hers. Yet a breach seemed to have opened in the wall of shadows that surrounded her. "I beg you," she repeated.

As if by enchantment, his fury subsided. He lowered the dagger. In his grip, Veniero still struggled weakly. He loosened his hold, allowing the man to breathe, then got up and backed away a step or two. The woman took his place over the mariner's body, sinking to her knees with the sinuous motion of a serpent. The prior was reminded of what a traveler in distant lands had told him about the mating dance of asps, a dance that could be seen among the desert dunes on moonlit nights.

Antilia had covered Veniero with her mantle and was trying to revive him, chanting over him in a low voice, an incantation of unintelligible sounds and words. She pressed him against her, rocking him gently, as if she wanted to transmit some part of her own vital warmth to him.

Then, as the Venetian began to recover, coughing and catching his breath, she rose and faced the poet.

"Take pity on us," she said. Her voice was cracked and she spoke the words with difficulty, like someone forced to express herself in a language she does not know well, in which she is terrified of not being understood. "Let us return. You understand the pain of exile. I have listened to you."

The copper-colored face, bathed in tears, gleamed in the torchlight. Dante noticed a slight movement from Veniero, who was slowly regaining his senses. The man had opened his eyes and was looking toward him. But his gaze seemed to pass through the poet's body to seek Antilia beside him. An unwavering gaze, without a trace of fear, yet expressing a profound grief.

Antilia continued to gaze at Dante, but this time it was Veniero, pale but calm, who spoke. His voice held no rancor. He gripped his wounded shoulder, stemming the blood with his hand. "I propose a pact, prior," he said.

"What pact?"

"I ask you for time. Just one hour."

"What do you offer me in exchange?"

The captain hesitated a moment. "You have discovered the secret, you know the fifth part of the world. But this knowledge, by itself, is useless, like knowing of Atlantis. To reach it you must have a map of the winds and sea currents that will enable you to avoid deadly whirlpools and massive rocks. This is what I offer you: the map and the pilot's book providing sailing directions to that new land." He fell silent. The woman also waited in silence, her eyes dilated with anguish. "One hour's start," Veniero said again. "Then you can resume your chase. A ship belonging to the Order awaits us at the shore. There is a full moon and the road to the seacoast is clear. When the tide turns, we will leave Tuscany."

Dante was unable to take his eyes off the Templar. Perhaps it was the devil's gaze that shone through his pupils. Antilia's face had moved closer to his and the two pairs of eyes watched him steadily. He felt dazed. Was it not the beast of the Apocalypse that was supposed to freeze men with its multiple eyes?

"Show me the map."

With an effort Veniero pulled several folded sheets from under his vest. "These belonged to Master Teofilo. He, too, wanted to chart the secret," he said, raising his eyes toward the wall. "Of course, with less ingenuity."

From among the sheets he drew the largest and handed it to Dante. The poet unfolded it and bent eagerly over the images that were revealed to him, stained with the blood that he had spilled. He recognized in their contours the shape of the world that he had studied with his teacher Brunetto. Mountain chains, long snaking rivers, vast oceans: Ptolemy's great work, transcribed on that parchment by a skillful hand.

And then there was the immense beyond. Dante studied the markings, comparing the precision of the representation before him with the allegory on the wall. So the ancients had been right: that body of water extending to the west—which his contemporaries' dwarfish intellect insisted on believing was an ocean—was indeed a river, only apparently boundless. Its other shore was clearly indicated, a track of lands, islands and gulfs that ran parallel to the shores of Europe and Africa. A massive territory shaped like an hourglass, or two huge islands linked by an isthmus.

The fifth part of the world. *In pentagono secretum mundi.* The land toward which the striding giant was headed, his eyes fixed westward. This was the secret that the Comacine master had tried to reveal through his work. Another continent that lay beyond the known seas.

The land of gold? Dante's gaze shifted to Antilia's bracelets, with their indecipherable marks. The woman seemed to understand instinctively what he was thinking. "Down there, this metal that troubles your dreams is plentiful," she said, her voice uncertain. "But for us it does not have the same value it seems to have for you. For us, this is wealth."

From under her robe she drew out a necklace of greenish stone with delicate reflections. Jade. "Take it. It is yours, if you let us go. It will make you immortal."

Dante continued staring at the map, as he distractedly held out his hand: it indicated not only geographic boundaries but also shipping lanes, the tracks of winds and currents, details of favorable landing sites and dangerous reefs, and the number of days required to complete the long journey and then sail along the coast.

Overcome by curiosity, he had forgotten his adversary. When the cold stones of the necklace touched his hand, he started back, defensive and alert. But Veniero had abandoned his hostile stance. He seemed merely anxious now, awaiting the prior's decision.

"I have it all in my hands. You, your secret, your accomplice. Why should I accept the pact you have proposed?" the prior said after a moment of silence, waving the map he still held in his hand.

"Because you understand suffering. You are not pitiless toward someone you have beaten," the Venetian murmured, lowering his head. Then he looked up again, with a nervous jerk. "And because an essential element is missing on those maps. What not even Teofilo was able to discover."

"What is that?" Dante asked.

"The vast sea is swept by constant adverse winds. It is these winds that have protected that land throughout the centuries. Only at one point, for a few degrees of latitude, do they blow favorably. Without knowledge of these any voyage is doomed to failure. One could wander for months or even years in a watery wasteland, without hope."

The poet considered these last statements. Perhaps the other man was assuming too much with regard to his nobility of soul. And perhaps he had not heard of the instruments of persuasion that lay in the Stinche's dungeons. Dante could learn the final secret without conceding anything.

Still, the look of the man suggested that he would be able to endure the most intense pain. Except, perhaps, for one thing, he said to himself, looking at Antilia, who stood behind her lover, silently invoking her gods. He imagined Veniero's torment seeing that body racked by the executioner.

But Dante would not be able to stand it, either. Angrily he brushed the thought away, as his curiosity began to get the better of him again. He wanted to stall for time.

He pointed to the maps. "How did you come into possession of these? Plato was the last person in the world to have heard about a land beyond the ocean, and even he spoke of it not because he had direct knowledge of it, but based on traces of an ancient tale . . ."

Veniero smiled faintly. "The Order of the Temple excavated for a long time among the ruins of the citadel of Jerusalem, beneath the ancient Temple. There were many among us who thought that we were looking for the treasure of the Israelites. The gold of the offerings, the Ark of the Covenant . . . and others actually imagined that we were in search of the Grail. Lunacy. There is nothing down there. There never has been anything."

A grimace crossed his face. A twinge from his wound, or the pain of lost illusions.

"No gods ever walked upon the earth. There are only mirages there. Stones calcinated by the sun and by the flames of sieges. Only a trace of the more ancient knowledge, preserved by the Jewish community of Alexandria. Fragments of maps. Indications of voyages to distant lands. Scraps of evidence that the Egyptian peoples possessed. It was along the Nile that they should have searched."

"Was this the reason the Templars fought for Damietta beyond all reason, even to the point of leading the Christian forces to destruction?"

"Yes. They had already found an incomplete *portolano* in Cyprus: a pilot's book showing the beginnings of routes toward the west. They knew that the library at Alexandria must contain the maps Ptolemy had drawn upon, and that those documents had been carried off by the Jews who fled when the city was destroyed by the Arabs. Slowly all those shreds of information were pieced together. In the Year of Our Lord 1294, a ship belonging to the Order set forth over a course indicated by our geographers. The route was calculated with Venus as its reference point."

"The jewel that fell from Lucifer's forehead," Dante added. "With its five points fixed in the heavens. The pentagram that you etched into your victims' flesh."

"You know it, too, then. Its steadfast motion is the simplest to follow in the heavens, even on seas where the compass begins to fail."

Dante gazed up at the mosaic. His torch, still burning, illuminated the central portion of the long arc of numbers between the two figures, leaving the farthest points in shadow. "Is the degree of correction in those numerals?" he asked.

The other nodded. The poet stared into those eyes that seemed to be seeing that distant horizon. He already knew the answer to his question. "Was it you who was in command?"

Veniero nodded again. In his eyes the recollection of those days still shone brightly.

Dante suddenly turned toward the woman. "And what about her? Is that where she came from, along with her gold and copper?"

The captain glanced lovingly at Antilia. "Yes, and she is its most precious treasure. Fortunate are the gods of that land who are honored by her dance."

"But why keep the secret? Why kill, and kill horribly, to conceal a revelation that could be of value to all of humankind?"

Veniero let a few instants go by before replying. When he spoke there was a touch of irony in his tone, as if he meant to mock the poet's innocence. Gently he took hold of Antilia's gold-encircled wrist, lifting it toward Dante's eyes.

"There is enough of this metal to fill the holds of a hundred of our galleys. Enough to satisfy the greed of all the kings of Europe and finance their wars for a thousand years. Enough to found a new empire . . . or to destroy an old one." He paused again, as if to make certain that Dante had understood his words. "To call Christ back to earth again. To light the flame of a new religion. To ascend to heaven and unhinge the very gates of the House of God. Do you really wonder why it is necessary to keep the secret? Why the Order of the Temple has tried to guard it at all costs? Why someone who put that secrecy at risk had to die?"

Dante stared at the map, motionless, as if a dream had torn the veil of the future for him. He felt a sudden heat flow through his veins. Everything seemed trifling and insignificant compared to the vision that inflamed his mind: Equip the biggest army on earth, rebuild the power of the Romans, make Florence the center of the world, sit among the great figures, prescribe a new law to make men's destiny conform to the words of the Gospels. Punish Boniface. "One hour of time in exchange for what you know," he said at last.

Veniero nodded slowly. For a second his hand moved toward the map as if to take it, but he checked the gesture. "Thank you, Messer Alighieri. The pact is fair. But if you keep the map, you will open the gates of hell. Your own intelligence tells you so," he said. Then he wrote a number, with a finger dipped in his own blood.

Dante clenched the parchment tightly. Nothing and no one would take it from him now. "What do we know about hell? What does our intelligence know of it? Only God's light illuminates our steps, not your ancient maps. If God hands us the key to this door, not to open it would be an offense against His will."

"You are using these words as a screen for your greed. But so be it, given that this day is yours. There will be other days, believe me. Remember: one hour."

"You shall have it. One hour."

They started toward the door.

"Messer Veniero!"

Veniero froze in the doorway, leaning on Antilia, who clung to his arm.

"Have you seen it, the new land?"

The Templar nodded.

"What . . . what did you see?"

"The coast, south of the equator. Its edge extending toward our world. An immense cliff that rises to the sky. It is there that we will return."

Dante raised his hand in a gesture of farewell. "One hour. And then I will come after you." As the two were leaving, he again called to Veniero. "One last thing. Did you ever encounter, in your voyages, a place where the waters rise above the level of the emergent land?"

"Never, nowhere."

"I knew it. I was right."

THE POET remained alone. He sat on one of the planks of the scaffolding, below the imposing figure of the woman awaiting her beloved. From outside came the sound of hoofbeats, galloping west. He wondered if Ambrogio and Teofilo's sacrificed blood would really protect that journey. He felt surrounded by shadows, as if a group of specters had gathered behind his back.

The map of the fifth part of the world lay open before him. In the flickering torchlight the parchment's surface, shiny with age, glowed like the gold to which it held the promise. Dante considered the dangers of that treasure, and Veniero's parting words.

He wondered with whom he might share so grave a secret.

There was no one. Only he in all of Florence was deserving enough to know it. No one else.

He held the edge of the parchment to the lantern's flame.

He stared at it for a long while, until the fire had consumed it. Behind him he thought he felt a friendly presence, observing his deed.

"Have I acted well, father?"

"Yes," replied the ancient voice that lived on in his soul. "But you will not be appreciated for it. You have veiled the eyes of your companions; you have poured wax into their ears. Because, like Ulysses, you want to be the only one to know."

June 22, at the first light of dawn

H E RACED down the road at full gallop, making full use of his spurs. A few miles from the walls of Pisa, the fugitives' track deviated toward the coast, leaving the road to the city behind.

Gusts of seawind blinded him, filling his eyes with tears. The well-trod wagon route came to an end several miles from the shore. An enormous marsh stretched out, its expanse broken by small rises and swamps and a few strips of sandy land. Stopping by the last small cluster of huts, Dante asked if there was a mooring in the area. The peasants stared at him dully for a long time before answering. Yes, they mumbled, there was a small dock, a little further on, along the shore. Yes, two strangers had come by, headed in that direction.

The night was retreating, releasing the marsh from shadow. He passed the last sand dune, his horse breathing hard, exhausted and covered with sweat. Below him was the sandy shore and the Tyrrhenian Sea, swelled by a rough surf. A summer storm lay just beyond the horizon, announced only by warm, damp gusts of wind.

He glanced along the coastline. On his left, toward the south, he spotted the port that the peasants had described, a simple timber-post mooring in a small cove, protected by a narrow strip of land. Around it a few wooden huts made up a small fishing village.

Then something else drew his attention. Further on, scarcely more than a hundred yards off the coast, he glimpsed the dark outline of a galley struggling to put out to sea, driven by a wind-swelled sail. The vessel, which flew no flag, was listing dangerously to one side. He tried to spur his weary horse in the direction of the ship. The animal balked and whinnied.

He was afraid the ship would succeed in gaining the open sea in the few moments he needed to ride to the embarkation point. But the galley was clearly in trouble. He reached the edge of the short pier, dismounted and dashed across the wood planking. The vessel had not gained a yard against the surf; on the contrary, it seemed to him that it had drifted back, as if the helmsman were uncertain whether to sail into the coming storm or return to the safety of dry land.

In the early dawn the glinting of the stern light on the black sea stood out clearly, bobbing with the ebb and swell of the waves. All at once the light grew blindingly intense, as if a hundred lanterns had been lit. Then a flash enveloped the hull and the ship began to glow along its entire length, radiant as a star.

Dante had heard stories told by Pisan seamen of phantom ships incandescent on the high seas. And he had always taken them for idle tales, told by tipplers to while away those nights when the wine was in short supply. Now he had one of those apparitions before his very eyes. The galley seemed enveloped in flame. He could clearly make out its rigging and sail blazing as if the sun's full light were focused on them alone, and the row of oars, raised as if to precipitate the flight of a mad bird.

For a moment it seemed the galley would disappear in a blinding globe of fire, as the tower of Santa Croce had done in the lightning that had destroyed it, years before. Then a brilliant shaft of flame rose toward the sky, clearing the top of the mast before plunging into the water with a savage hiss. On deck he could see the silhouettes of human bodies, dancing in the dazzling whiteness like priests in a temple celebrating rites to the ancient fire gods.

Engulfed in flames and out of control, the ship began to lurch violently. Its sail, transformed to a sheet of fire, flapped wildly against the darkening sky, like a funerary standard. It was then that he remembered.

He had seen that dazzling whiteness once before, while studying alchemy in preparation for admission to the apothecaries guild. A substance that burst into flame and burned with a white flash, generating a terrible heat, like the heat of the mouth of hell.

Horrified, he watched as the ship, its hull consumed in an instant, began to sink. Flickers of light glittered along the remains of the mast and quarterdeck.

Phosphorous.

Faced with that diabolical spectacle, this was the explanation his mind suggested. Not divine judgment, not the devil come to claim his due. There must have been phosphorous in the galley's hold, ignited accidentally or deliberately.

He fell to his knees on the pier as the first downpour of rain washed over him. He recognized the figure of Antilia on the burning deck. He thought he saw her turn toward him, one arm raised. It might have been her death throes, but to him it seemed like the gesture of someone saying goodbye.

He imagined her face melting like wax in that dazzling whiteness, her hair lighting up in a candid stream. Why do they say that black is the color of death? Death comes on swiftly, dressed in light and purple.

A second shadow appeared, engulfed in flame. It drew close

to the woman and pressed her tenderly to itself, as if to protect her. And then . . . only two tongues of fire, stirred by the wind.

THE SHIP had vanished in the waves. In the indistinct light between sea and storm only the top of the charred mast could still be glimpsed above the cresting of the waves: a rolling gravestone, to mark the site of a burial at sea.

Only then did Dante become aware of two figures on horseback, halted before the doorway of a fisherman's hut. Draped in heavy traveling cloaks, their faces concealed by the hoods; they must have viewed the entire tragedy. Suddenly he leaped to his feet, shaken by an intuition: those men were the two Comacine masters.

He ran down the pier, reaching the hut just in time to see them take off at a gallop. As they sped by, one of the two, a young blond man, turned his blue eyes on the poet for a moment. Dante thought of following him but saw his own mount standing dazed and motionless without even the strength to graze among the sparse weeds. The animal was so exhausted, another few thrusts of the spurs would kill it.

DANTE TURNED his gaze toward the west. The horizon stretched before his eyes, a gray line separating two realms, each obscure in different ways. Was there really a fifth body of land beyond that point, a land of gold and splendor? And did the fearful rocky promontory that Veniero had spoken of really exist, rising up from the waters like a giant, barring the way of seafarers with its retinue of monsters?

A mountain at the ends of the earth, at the center of a boiling sea. Who knew for whom God had reserved that sight? Antilia's image seemed to materialize before his eyes.

Perhaps our progenitors were like her, he thought. Perhaps her land was the terrestrial paradise.

He ran his fingers lightly over the necklace of green stones hidden beneath his robe.

Immortality.

Yes, he would attain it.

NOTE

DANTE ALIGHIERI (1265–1321) was born in Florence into a reasonably influential Guelph family. At the time of his birth, war between the Guelph partisans and their rivals, the Ghibellines, raged fiercely throughout Tuscany, but by 1267 the Ghibelline party, aristocrats and wealthy men who upheld the authority of the empire, had been driven out. Afterward, the Guelphs, middle-class supporters of the papacy, governed the area for about twenty years.

Dante cherished many of the principles of his family's party and was a devout Catholic, but he greatly distrusted the reigning pope, Boniface VIII, in whose rule he saw avarice, corruption, and political maneuvering. However, when the Ghibelline threat surfaced again in the late 1280s, and a number of Tuscan cities, led by Arezzo, went to war, Dante fought on the Guelph side. His division was broken by the initial charge but managed to rally and stand firm, and the Guelphs, led by Florence, again gained victory.

The resulting peace did not last long. By 1300, two factions within the Guelph ranks, the moderate Whites, who shared Dante's misgivings about Boniface and his court, and the extremist Blacks, had split Florence into two armed camps. That year Dante became a prior, an elected member of the Council of Florence, and used his authority as a public official to oppose a papal power grab and uphold the council's independence. In 1302, the Blacks triumphed, and Dante, along with four other prominent Whites, was tried on undoubtedly trumped-up charges of fraud and corruption and condemned to lifelong exile.

Dante had begun to write in the early 1280s and was quickly recognized as one of the most promising of the many young poets in Florence. In 1294 he published *La Vita Nuova* (The New Life), a collection of poems recalling and celebrating his youthful love for Beatrice Portinari, who died in 1290. His friendship with Guido Cavalcanti was of great importance, and his association with Brunetto Latini led him toward philosophically and politically influenced poetry.

Once Dante left Florence, the tone of his writing began to change. He was now a wanderer, penniless and bitter. When after fifteen years he was offered the chance to return to his native city on condition that he pay a heavy fine and perform humiliating penance, he refused, steadfastly maintaining his innocence. Loathing the corruption he saw in the world and in individual men, he applied himself to political debate, maintaining that the Roman Empire must reestablish its power as a stabilizing force in Europe and that the papacy should limit its rule to the moral realm.

During his exile he wrote the unfinished Latin treatise *De Vulgari Eloquentia* (1304); *Il Convivio* (The Banquet, c. 1304); *De Monarchia* (Of Monarchy, 1313); and, finally, the *Commedia*, later known as the *Divina Commedia*. Composed in the vernacular, it is an extraordinary synthesis of Dante's literary and political experience and philosophical and religious convictions. In the first book, *Inferno*, Dante describes himself setting out on a journey through the realms of the afterlife: his adventure begins during Easter, in 1300, when, at the height of his worldly power and influence, he finds himself in a dark and fearsome wood. He is guided through it by the great Roman poet Virgil, and invited by his mentor to make a living descent into Hell. In *Purgatorio*, he continues his journey up Mount Purgatory, and in *Paradiso*, he ascends through the celestial spheres and comes to gaze at last upon God, thereby recapturing his faith.

No one is certain when this masterpiece was begun. *Inferno* first appeared around 1314 and *Purgatario* around 1319, but the complete *Commedia* was not released until after the poet's death. Dante spent his last years at peace, still in poverty, but given shelter and respect in the town of Ravenna, where he settled in 1317. He died there, of fever, in 1321, following a diplomatic mission to Venice.

GLOSSARY

Almagest

Almagest (*The Masterwork*) was the popular name for the *Megale Syntaxis tes Astronomias* (Great Compilation of Astronomy) of the second century A.D. Alexandrian astronomer, mathematician, and geographer Claudius Ptolemaeus, or Ptolemy. Ptolemy's geocentric model of the universe was used to calculate the motions of the planets up to the time of Copernicus. His work might have been known to Dante through the textbook *De Sphaera* of Johannes de Sacrobosco, or John of Holywood (d. 1244 or 1256), an Englishman and a professor at the University of Paris, who was one of the first Europeans to make use of the mathematical writings of the Arabs.

Angiolieri, Cecco

Cecco Angiolieri (c. 1260–c. 1312) was known for his realistic, satirical verse, which included several bantering sonnets addressed to Dante. Born in Siena into a fairly rich Guelph banking family, he led a restless and turbulent life, performed less than heroically in the Sienese army, and was burdened by immense debts incurred by gambling. His poetry deals with changing fortunes, tavern life, family and societal conflicts, and women. The poets of the *dolce stil nuovo* regarded women as angelic, if not divine; Cecco placed them on a much lower plane.

bargello, bargellini

The Republic of Florence had a police force of sorts, the *bargellini,* armed guards charged with maintaining public order.

brigata d'Amore (Love's Brigade, Cupid's Brigade)

In 1283 the Florentine chronicler Giovanni Villani called an assembly of merrymakers a *brigata d'Amore,* describing them as "a brigade of a thousand men or more," all dressed in white robes, who played music, danced, and dined together, led by a Lord of Love. According to Villani, they exemplified the peace and joy that Guelph rule had brought to Florence.

Campaldino

This Tuscan village on the upper banks of the Arno was the site of the decisive battle in 1289 in which the Guelphs, led by Florence, defeated the Ghibellines, led by the rival commune of Arezzo. Dante fought at Campaldino on the Florentine side. (see Guelphs and Ghibellines)

Cerchi and Donati

(see Guelphs and Ghibellines)

ciompi

(see Guilds)

Comacine

This old and powerful body of medieval stoneworkers included architects, sculptors, painters, and other decorators. Their name derives either from Isola Comacina, the island in Lake Como where they supposedly had their headquarters, or from the Latin expression *cum machinis,* referring to their tools. Comacine masters (*magistri comacini*) were cathedral builders, and the development of architecture during Europe's great Gothic period is attributed to them.

Il Convivio (The Banquet)

Dante began this work around 1306–08, writing in the vernacular. He completed only four of his fifteen projected treatises: an introduction and three commentaries. These books relate in allegorical fashion how Dante became the lover of that mystical lady, Philosophy.

De Vulgari Eloquentia (On Writing in the Vulgar Tongue or On Vernacular Eloquence)

In this Latin treatise, written earlier than Il Convivio, Dante attempted to discover the ideal Italian language, the noblest form of the vernacular, and show how it should be employed in the composition of lyrical poetry.

Il Fiore

A parody of the "Roman de la Rose," "Il Fiore" is an anonymous cycle of 232 sonnets tracing the adventures, misfortunes, and triumph of a lover in his pursuit of the rose, a woman. Some attribute the work to Dante; others question his authorship. In Leoni's novel, Cardinal Acquasparta has no doubts: enraged by the poem's mockery of the clergy, in his interview with Dante he pointedly calls it a worthless book.

grimorio

A grimorio, or Book of Shadows, was a witch's journal, a personal book created by the witch over time, reflecting his personal experiences, and describing secret rites and magic spells and the herbs, stones, formulas, and chants used to perform them.

Guelphs and Ghibellines

Thirteenth-century Italy was riven by the struggle between these two powerful parties. The Guelphs, made up of an emerging, cultured middle class of merchants, traders, and shopkeepers, supported the papacy. The Ghibellines, an alliance of the feudal nobility with the most influential merchants, upheld the authority of the emperors. In 1300, the Florentine Guelphs, who had triumphed at Campaldino in 1289, split into two rival factions. The reactionary Blacks, the extreme papal party, followed the nobleman Corso Donati, a hero of the battle of Campaldino who aspired to become Lord of Florence. The moderate Whites, who favored the papacy but opposed the reigning pope, Boniface VIII, were led by the plebeian Vieri dè Cerchi. In 1301, tensions between the parties erupted into civil war, which ended in victory for the Blacks and lifelong exile for prominent Whites, among them the newly elected prior of the Republic of Florence, Dante Alighieri.

guilds

The guilds, or corporations, were professional and trade associations and were widespread throughout medieval Europe. The Italian guilds, or *arti*, developed at the beginning of the twelfth century and were prevalent in the communes of central and northern Italy, especially Florence. The seven "great guilds" were the Calimala (wool workers), Lana (wool merchants), Giudici e Notai (judges and notaries), Cambio (bankers), Seta (silk weavers), Medici e Speziali (physicians and pharmacists) and Vaiai e Pellicciai (furriers). In addition there were fourteen "lesser guilds," usually called the craft guilds, and seven liberal arts guilds. A guild afforded its members protection and political clout, and eventually even the lowest members of working society—in Dante's day, the *ciompi*, or wool carders and dyers—demanded the right to form one and to have elected representatives in the government. In Leoni's novel, even the beggars established their own "guild," outside the law.

Lagia

Lady Lagia, mistress of the brothel Paradise in the novel, is apparently named for Monna Lagia, who had an amorous relationship with the poet Lapo Gianni and is mentioned in poems by Gianni, Cavalcanti, and Dante.

natural philosophy

Natural philosophy was a medieval term for the study of observable natural phenomena.

Philosopher's Stone

This mythical substance, also known as *materia prima* or primal matter, the grail of the alchemists, was supposed to be capable of transmuting base metals into silver and gold, creating an elixir that would banish disease and greatly prolong human life, and bringing mystical enlightenment to its creator or discoverer. No alchemist ever found it, but the efforts of those who tried built a body of knowledge that eventually became the legitimate science of chemistry.

Pietra

In 1296, Dante addressed a series of canzoni and sestinas, the *rime petrose*, to a lady he calls Pietra, for her stony insensibility. "Pietra" is the Italian word for "stone." Some have associated Dante's Pietra with Pietra degli Scrovigni, daughter of the Paduan moneylender Rinaldo Scrovigni, who was assigned by Dante to the circle of usurers in *Inferno* (XVII, 64–75).

portolano

A medieval ship captain's book or descriptive atlas, giving sailing directions and charts that show the location of ports and various coastal features.

prior

Dante's Florence was a republic, ruled by the College of Priors, an elected body of six members that had evolved from the earlier Priors of the Guilds. The city's constitution, adopted in the 1290s, prohibited noble families from holding power and established the post of Gonfalonier of Justice, a magistrate elected to direct the College, also known as the Council of Florence.

sensitive soul

There were said to be three phases or levels of spiritual development. The vegetative soul, present in plants, is the most elementary; its functions include growth and reproduction. The sensitive soul, present in animals, is capable of sensitive knowledge and appetition. Superior to both is the rational or intellective soul, unique to humans, capable of understanding and volition. The theme is taken up in *Purgatorio* (XXV, 52 ff.). In the novel's discussion of Cavalcanti's canzone "Donna me prega" ("A Lady asks me"), love is located in the sensitive soul, while the lady in her visible form, as its agent, takes possession of the intellective soul.

spiriti amanti

The *spiriti amanti,* or spirits of love, are souls that move the Third Heaven, or Heaven of Venus. In *Paradiso* (VIII), they glow and dance like the flame of a torch, at varying speeds, some faster than lightning, each according to its eternal vision. These spirits are the third of nine orders of angelic intelligences (*intelligenze motrici*) that control the celestial spheres in Dante's cosmology.

They correspond to the nine orders of angels and are instruments of the First Mover.

studium generale

A *studium generale* was a faculty of arts, or university, that had a widespread reputation and attracted an international body of professors and students. The University of Florence evolved from the *studium generale* established by the Florentine Republic in 1321.

Templars, Templar commendam

The Templars were a miltary and religious order originally established to protect Christian pilgrims and settlers in the Holy Land; they took extensive part in the Crusades and also played a crucial role in their financial administrations, in the development of banking. A commendam was a benefice (lands or other holdings) granted to a layman or a cleric for a period of time; such possessions were said to be given and held *in commendam,* from the Latin "to give in trust." A benefice under the control of the Templars or other order of knights was called a commandery or preceptory. The Templar commendams referred to in the novel are examples of this type of benefice.

Third Heaven

The Third Heaven, the name assumed by the assembly of scholars in the novel, has both astrological and religious connotations. The phrase often appears in references to the realms of the hereafter. Saint Paul (2 Cor. 12) describes being "caught up by an angel, and ascending as far as the . . . third heaven into paradise itself." In *Paradiso,* Dante the pilgrim travels through a hierarchy of heavenly spheres, reaching the third heaven, that of the planet Venus, in Paradiso VIII. (see *spiriti amanti,* Venus)

vegetative soul

(see sensitive soul)

Venus

References to Venus, goddess and planet, abound in the novel. The goddess represented, among other things, vegetation, love, beauty, fertility, and the feminine virtues, and has been equated with Lilith and Ishtar, who are both mentioned in the book in connection with Antilia. The planet, equally rich in symbolism, is the herald of dawn and sometimes of evening, and is linked with the number five, the pentagram or pentacle, and with Lucifer.

The name Lucifer, or Light-bearer, was used by the ancient Romans to refer to Venus the morning star, on days when the planet rose before the sun. A similar Hebrew epithet, found in Isaiah (14:12), was translated as Phosphorus in the Greek Septuagint and later as Lucifer in the Latin Vulgate.

In the novel, Venus, the most brilliant planet in the solar system, is called "the jewel that fell from Lucifer's forehead," a reference to the Gnostic belief that a jewel or stone fell from the crown of Lucifer during his war on heaven and became the Philosopher's Stone. This fabled jewel symbolized Venus, the morning star, and contained the forbidden knowledge that Lucifer's angels shared with man, for which they were cast out from heaven.

The Venus pentagram is the diagram on the zodiac that the quintuple star makes in eight years: plotting the recurrence of Venus' westward elongation from the Sun over five consecutive synodic periods will create the points of a pentagram.

"Whatever is below is like that which is above"

"VERBA SECRETORUM HERMETIS. It is true, certain, and without falsehood, that whatever is below is like that which is above; and that which is above is like that which is below: to accomplish the one wonderful work."

This phrase is from the Emerald Tablet, one of the ancient Hermetic texts attributed to Hermes Trismegistus (Thrice-great Hermes), a legendary figure combining the personae of the Greek god of learning and science and the Egyptian scribe-god Thoth, both also deities connected with the underworld. Hermes Trismegistus is the supposed originator of the science of alchemy.

Whites and Blacks

(see Guelphs and Ghibellines)

SOURCES AND REFERENCES

CITATIONS, DIRECT and indirect, of verses found in the *Divine Comedy* are from Longfellow's translation. Citations of verses from Dante's lyric poems—*Voi che savete ragionar d'Amore...* (You, who know well how to converse of Love) and *Ché si po' ben canoscere d'un omo, ragionando, se ha senno...* (For it is possible to recognize, simply by talking, if a man is wise...) are from Joseph Tusiani's translations (Dante, "Lyric Poems," found at http://www.italianstudies.org/poetry/index.htm). Other Dante verses cited include: *Tre donne intorno al cor mi son venute...* (Three women have come round my heart...), from an unattributed translation found in L. Pertile, "Dante," in *The Cambridge History of Italian Literature* (Cambridge, Cambridge University Press, 1996); and *Amor che nella mente mi ragiona* (Love, that within my mind discourses with me) from a translation by Longfellow. Guido Cavalcanti's canzone *Donna me prega* (A Lady Asks Me) and verse 21 from it—*Vien da veduta forma che s'intende...* (Cometh from a seen form which being understood...) are from a translation by Ezra Pound. The translation of Dante's *Chi guarderà già mai sanza paura...* (Who dares to meet without dismay...) and that of the quatrain by Francesco Stabili, known as Cecco d'Ascoli, *D'amor la stella ne la terza rota...* (In the third orbit, Love's radiant star...) are my own.

Indirect citations and paraphrasing are common throughout the book. For example, when a fortune-teller demands a coin, telling Dante that he will meet his ruin, he asks her, "Why are you telling me this?" Her response, "So that it may give thee pain," echoes the words spoken by Vanni Fucci to Dante the pilgrim in the *Inferno* XXIV, 151: "*Perché dolore ti colga.*" And when Teofilo, one of the group of learned men who call themselves the Third Heaven, tells Dante, "We try to share amongst ourselves that angelic bread that each of us has attained through his own studies," his words ("*pane degli angeli*") recall the "*pan de li angeli*" of *Paradiso* II, 11 as well as the opening of the *Convivio*, that philosophical "banquet," where Dante promises: "Happy are those who sit at the table where the bread of angels is eaten." And the paraphrasis is repeated when Bruno Ammannati invites Dante to join his congregation: "Come, share the bread of angels with us."

In addition to direct and indirect citations, the novel is filled with references to Dante's works and those of his contemporaries. For example, when Francesco Stabili, the great astrologer, greets Dante as "the *dolcissimo* poet" ("And I salute in you the *dolcissimo* poet, indeed the greatest among the greats"), the reference is to the *dolce stil nuovo*, the sweet new lyrical style introduced by Dante. Then there is the *Convito* that the irreverent Cecco Angiolieri mockingly refers to: "Well then, did you ever begin that *Convito*, that Banquet of yours? That epitome of wisdom you spoke to us about?" It is of course the *Convivio* that Dante will subsequently compose in the Italian vernacular.

Indeed Dante the Prior refers frequently to works he plans to write in the future. For example, watching a group of street players perform a drama of heaven and hell, he strains to see "what the strolling players had drawn in the center of the circles' vanishing point. It appeared to be a flower, a kind of whitish rose." Clearly an allusion to the "*candida rosa*" of *Paradiso* XXXI, 1–3. As he watches the drama unfold, "in his mind the fragments of a work were forming a pattern." When he says, "I will write about a city. A city of suffering," he is clearly thinking of what will later become the "*città dolente*" of the *Inferno*, peopled with characters drawn from the life and times of the city of Florence. There is even an allusion to a work of uncertain attribution: "He was thinking about the flower, *Fiore*, that he had written: anything but a place of God." Finally, Dante's understanding of Veniero's anguish ("The pain of a soul torn from his own land and cast out into the cold, in exile. That is perhaps the greatest pain, for which there is no remedy") is an indirect reference to Cacciaguida's words to him in *Paradiso* XVII, 55–60:

> "... *You shall leave everything you love most:*
> *this is the arrow that the bow of exile*
> *shoots first. You are to know the bitter taste*
> *of others' bread, how salt it is, and know*
> *how hard a path it is for one who goes*
> *ascending and descending others' stairs* ..."
>
> (MANDELBAUM'S TRANSLATION)

—Anne Milano Appel
Note, Glossary, Sources and References

AUTHOR'S ACKNOWLEDGMENTS

MANY PEOPLE contributed to the writing and publication of this novel. When all is said and done, like all fictional works it is a distillation of the voices, images, and dreams found all around us. The majority of those who contributed did so unwittingly, perhaps while talking about something else, unaware that their words, their stories, or their own books provided material for my writing. Friends such as Diego Gabutti, with his pyrotechnical imagination, truly the last of the great Futurists. Or Igor Longo, an extraordinary connoisseur of mystery fiction from all over the world. Then, too, there were Leonardo Gori, Daniele Cambiaso, and Renée Vink, authors and enthusiasts of historical whodunits with whom I exchanged ideas and impressions many times.

Others contributed directly to the text, starting with Mondadori's editorial staff, who intelligently saw to the editing and printing of the manuscript, reviewing it a number of times and being patient past the point of exasperation with all my wavering. And, finally, there was Piergiorgio Nicolazzini, the literary agent who tracked the endeavor through every phase, helping to carry it to its successful completion with the energy that only a true friend can bring to bear.

To all of them, my gratitude. And my affection.

DANTE ALIGHIERI

Inferno

Translated, introduced and annotated by
Steve Ellis

'Energetic, racy, rude and lyrical . . . buy this translation
and spend a damn good season in hell'
Independent

Welcome to hell.

On Good Friday evening in the year 1300, Dante finds
himself lost in a dark and menacing wood. The ghost of
Virgil offers to lead him to safety but the path lies through
the terrifying kingdom of Satan. On his journey deep into
the underworld, Dante crosses paths with both old
acquaintances and famous characters from history as he
witnesses the strange and gruesome sufferings of the
damned.

Written while Dante was in exile and under threat of being
burned at the stake, this dramatic, frightening and, at times,
sardonically humorous vision of hell still has the power to
shock and horrify.

'A tour de force, alive, immediate, energetic and very
moving'
A.S Byatt

VINTAGE BOOKS
London